DAY AND NIGHT

Book Six of the Kelsey's Burden Series

KAYLIE HUNTER

This book is a work of fiction. All names, characters, places, businesses, incidents, etc., are the imagination of the author, and any resemblance to actual persons or otherwise is coincidental.

Copyright 2019 by Kaylie Hunter

Cover design by SelfPubBookCovers.com/Fantasia

All rights reserved. No part of this book may be used or reproduced in any manner without the written permission of the author except when utilized in the case of brief quotations embodied in articles or reviews.

BOOKS BY KAYLIE

KELSEY'S BURDEN SERIES
Layered Lies
Past Haunts
Friends and Foes
Blood and Tears
Love and Rage
Day and Night

STANDALONE NOVELS
Slightly Off-Balance
Diamond's Edge

Dedication

For Maggie... It's not the same without you by my side.
Happy Birthday.

To My Readers:

Do as you please, but if you are new to this series, I recommend starting with book one, Layered Lies. The cast of characters is lengthy, and it's easy to get turned around remembering who's who unless you met everyone along the way. For those who already know the gang but would appreciate a refresher, here it is in a nutshell:

At the end of book five, Hattie and Pops were tying the knot in Texas, and then everyone would head home to Michigan. Kelsey was at a crossroads of what to do with her life in the aftermath of rescuing her son and saving herself from a madman. Grady and Donovan offered her a partnership, running an investigation team for their security company, Silver Aces Security. Kelsey seemed unsure of her path but willing to put one foot in front of the other. Her cousin Charlie, on the other hand, left in a cloud of rage after learning that their grandparents' deaths weren't an accident and that Kelsey was raped as a child. Charlie has most likely returned to their hometown to punish those responsible: the local sheriff, Charlie's parents Cecil and Mark Harrison, and Kelsey's parents Audrey and Thomas Harrison.

Skipping forward, we restart our adventures back in Michigan where it all began.

Badass-cowboy Grady still stands firmly by Kelsey's side and has taken up the reins of helping to raise her son, Nicholas. Kelsey, Grady, and Nicholas live in the main house with Anne, Whiskey, and Anne's computer-genius daughter, Sara, AKA little bug. Hattie, now married to Pops, splits her time between Michigan and Texas. Sassy Katie lives above the garage with Tech, both a member of the Devil's Players and Kelsey's investigative sidekick. Lisa, Donovan, and their new baby girl Abigail live in the house next door. Alex still colors everyone's world with mixed fashions and lives in the third and last house on the dead-end street. Crazy Carl still resides with all of them as well, keeping them busy babysitting him so he doesn't order thirty gallons of blue moon ice cream or nuclear missiles online.

The girls and Alex work at the Changing Room, the resale store Kelsey owns, along with Goat, a Devil's Player and the boy-toy to Kelsey's party-girl friend Dallas. Bones, the sergeant of arms for the Devil's Players, works at Silver Aces Security when he's not chasing after Bridget. Wayne and Ryan, both guards that had protected the family back in Texas, work for Silver Aces and pop in and out of Michigan between cases.

In addition to Bones, Whiskey, Goat, and Tech, most of the Devil's Players are close by. Tyler is still a prospect but learning the ropes fast as he works personal security jobs for Kelsey. They report up to the club president, James, who isn't much of a leader, but he looks hot with his surfer-biker style as he pretends to be in charge.

Beyond that, you never know who you might bump into. Could be the local cops: long-time friends Dave and Steve. Dave is also Dallas' son, though he doesn't always admit to it in public. And he and his wife Tammy are new parents to their baby girl Juliette. Or you could run into some friendly Feds: The sexy profiler Maggie, the tightly wound Agent Kierson, or investigative guru Genie who with her pixie looks seems too innocent despite tracking down sex crime organizations for a living.

Then there's everyone else, like crime boss Mickey McNabe, Nightcrawler and Renato from the MC in the next town over, or Doc who runs the local clinic and does house calls when needed. Kelsey's network has grown diverse and deep, and her friends and family continue to be loyal and dedicated to her cause—even when she's facing darkness from her past.

Chapter One

This is a bad idea, I told myself as I picked the lock on the sliding door.

Feeling the intricate springs release on the lock, I nudged the handle, sliding the door open a few inches. I removed my tools, tucking them into the back pocket of my jeans before stepping just inside the door to listen. *Nothing*. I couldn't hear any movement in the basement or the first floor above.

Leaving the door open, I walked through the basement gym and down the hall to the furnace room. Once inside, I pulled the handle to the newly installed drop-down ladder that led into my master bedroom upstairs.

Just a few minutes, I thought. *That's all I need. In and out. No one will know I was here.*

Climbing the ladder, I pushed the panel upward until I could step aside onto the plush cream-colored carpet. I lowered the trapdoor, careful to manage its weight so gravity didn't pull it closed. Once the door was closed, I turned to step out of the closet.

"You're in so much trouble," Sara said from only a few feet away.

"Shit!" I screeched, throwing myself backward into the wall.

"Major trouble," my son, Nicholas, agreed.

"Damn it! What are you two doing home?"

"We live here," Sara grinned.

Sara was eight, going on thirty, and as smart as most college professors, if not smarter. Nicholas, her partner in crime, would turn nine next month. And while not as intellectual as Sara, he was perceptive in ways that no child should've been by his age.

"Aren't you supposed to be on a business trip until Sunday?" Nicholas asked, cocking an eyebrow in a way that reminded me of Grady, my sort-of live-in boyfriend. At least, I thought Grady was still my boyfriend. Finding out our relationship status would require some form of communication.

Nicholas adored Grady and vice versa. I was grateful they shared such a tight bond. It made running easier.

"She lied," Sara said. "She was hoping to sneak in without anyone noticing."

"Answer my question." I pushed past them toward my dresser. "What are you two doing here?"

"Mom hired a nanny so we could do our schoolwork from home," Sara answered as she led Nicholas over to the bed and climbed on top of the comforter.

"Again?" I asked, rolling my eyes as I pulled out piles of clean clothes. "And where is your new nanny? I didn't hear anyone when I came in."

"You mean when you picked the lock in the basement and snuck into your bedroom through the trapdoor?" Nicholas asked, cocking that damn eyebrow.

"I forgot my house keys," I lied.

Both Sara and Nicholas giggled.

"The nanny is out in the garage," Sara said. "She doesn't think we know, but she's on the phone with her boyfriend."

"He's in a band," Nicholas added.

"And she's going to have sex with him tonight to prove to her friend Ashley that it's true love."

"But it's not," Nicholas sighed. "He's still going on tour without her."

"It's for the best," Sara said. "The band is really bad. They don't even know how to read music. I don't know what she sees in him."

Watching the kids, I shook my head. I didn't want to know how they'd unmasked so much information about their new nanny.

"Her soap opera starts in five minutes," Sara said, checking her watch.

I looked toward the bedroom door, contemplating giving the nanny an earful. But Anne should've consulted with someone less trusting than herself when hiring. While Sara and Nicholas were capable of doing their schoolwork unsupervised, they tended to dare each other to do things they shouldn't. Sometimes dangerous stunts. Sometimes illegal stunts, like hacking into the DMV and creating fake IDs.

"Didn't Grady have a say in who watched the two of you?"

"Sure," Nicholas said. "But he told me not to set the house on fire and to call him if anything major happened."

"He's hoping Mom will stop trying to hire someone," Sara said. "He's told her a crazy number of times that we can do our schoolwork at Headquarters."

"Makes more sense than leaving you alone with a stranger."

Sara was referring to the new building for Silver Aces Security, the company Donovan and Grady owned and had relocated from Chicago. The new office, often referred to as simply Headquarters, was located across the street from the resale store that my friends and I owned. The main building held the offices, the new war room, several conference rooms, and a large training gym. Two more outbuildings were located on the back of the property. The northwest building contained a dozen apartments for full-time employees who needed a place to call home between assignments. The northeast building had dorm-style rooms and a common area kitchen for the trainees.

"What's Grady's plan to get rid of the nanny?"

"I'm not sure he has one yet," Nicholas said. "He's not as good at scheming as you are."

I looked at the kids, then back at the bedroom door. "Sneak out and get your shoes and laptops before the nanny comes back inside. Be quiet about it."

Both kids grinned as they raced to the door and down the hall. I finished packing a week's worth of clothes into a duffle bag. I felt a pinch of guilt, but only for a moment. The thought of fresh socks and clean underwear outweighed the guilt.

For three months, I'd tried staying at home. I had worked eight-to-five shifts so I could cook dinner, clean house, and be a dutiful mother and girlfriend. Then one night I stared up at the bedroom ceiling, my heart pounding as Grady slept peacefully beside me. For hours I listened to everything around me: Grady's deep steady breaths, the wall clock in the atrium ticking the seconds by, and the heavy thump-thump-thump of my heart slamming against my rib cage. By three in the morning I was sneaking out of the room, down the hall, and into the garage. I started my SUV and drove away, wearing nothing more than underwear and a T-shirt.

The more miles I traveled, the more my heartbeat settled into a steady rhythm. I kept driving. I left everyone I loved. The man who stood by my side when I was at my lowest. The son who I'd adopted only to have kidnapped and rescued years later. The people who had become like family: Hattie, Pops, Anne, Whiskey, Katie, Alex, Lisa, Donovan, and Carl. And the people who had become my friends and protected my family: Bones, James, Goat, Tyler, and Tech.

I left them all. But they were better off without me turning their lives upside down. I wasn't capable of being a girlfriend, mother, or friend. After the years of warring monsters to protect everyone, I'd become a damaged shell of the person I used to be. Pretending otherwise felt like a prison sentence.

I had thought running the new investigations department at the security company would help, but sitting behind a desk, talking on conference calls, wasn't the same as chasing bad guys. And the longer I sat, the bouncier my knees became as my anxiety levels climbed.

I tried exercise, but running three miles every morning left me feeling uninspired. I tried tossing the prospects around in training matches, but it soon bored me. I tried reading, then writing, but my frustrations only grew.

I was burning on the inside—the flames flickering just under my skin. So I ran. I ran before I set fire to everything and everyone I loved.

And, though I knew they worried about me, no one seemed surprised when I left. Hattie called me every morning to ask whether I was eating. Katie called with make-believe business questions. Anne called to complain about Whiskey. Lisa called to give me updates on the kids, including her beautiful daughter, Abigail. Donovan called to ask me to check on various security jobs. And Nicholas and Sara called several times a day, mostly to either tattle on each other or to share the latest family gossip.

Grady was the only one who didn't call. I knew he was hurt, angry. He wanted us to build a life together, to get married, and to raise a family. But I couldn't. We were the equivalent of oil and water, whether he saw it or not, and as much as I tried, we'd never fully blend together.

I wanted to explain it to him, but I didn't know how. When we were alone, usually at night curled up in bed, everything seemed so natural, so perfect. But I couldn't sustain that feeling. I couldn't carry it into the other parts of my life. I couldn't even dream peaceful dreams, often waking covered in sweat and throwing punches into the air.

He'd hold me and tell me it would get better, but we both knew on some level it was a lie. Because even though I couldn't say the words, no one, not even my cousin Charlie, knew me like Grady. He could read every facial expression, every twitch and turn, and know my thoughts. He knew, deep down, that I couldn't be the mother to his children. He knew I couldn't bring myself to marry him, committing to a life of happily-ever-after. He knew I was going to run, and he let me.

An hour after I left, Grady had sent me a text: "Be safe, my love."

That was the one and only time he contacted me.

The kids, returning to the bedroom, startled me out of my memories. I opened the closet trapdoor before taking their backpacks so they could climb down. Carrying the bags, I followed after them and then led them out the basement sliding door, past Lisa and Alex's houses, and into the woods.

"I parked about a mile to the east."

Sara stopped and looked around. Nicholas laughed at her and started jogging east. She giggled and ran after him. I double-layered their backpacks onto my back and held my duffle in my arms at my chest as I started a slow jog after them. Even with the extra weight I could easily outrun them, but I hung back so I could watch them playfully push each other about as they raced up a small hill.

I missed them. I missed everyone. I just wasn't strong enough to stay.

Chapter Two

"Aunt Kelsey?" Sara asked as we were loading the bags into my SUV.

"Hmm?"

"How scared will Mom be when she finds out we're missing?"

"Hopefully scared enough not to hire another stranger to watch you guys," I answered as I closed the SUV's back hatch. I waited for them to throw themselves into the back seat before closing their door and sliding into the driver's seat. "No worries, though. I texted Uncle Alex and Aunt Katie. They'll let your mom know that you're with me when she starts freaking out."

"I texted Grady, too," Nicholas said as he latched his seatbelt.

My brain flashed through a hundred different thoughts. My heart started beating heavily against my chest, resonating in my ears. Keeping my voice level, I started up the truck and asked, "What exactly did you tell Grady?"

"That my mom was kidnapping us, and we might be late for dinner."

I glanced to the rearview mirror and saw both kids grinning at me. "And did he text you back?" I pulled ahead, down the narrow two-track lane that ran alongside the back of the woods. I followed the tracks as they curved to the left.

"He said he already knew. Tech saw you on the security feed when you entered the basement."

"What security feed in the basement?"

"The one that Carl installed," Sara answered. "The whole house is wired and monitored."

"The whole house?"

"Well, Grady and Tech disconnected the ones in the bathrooms and bedrooms. They told Carl that if he tried that again, they'd move him over to Headquarters to live."

"That's good, I guess. Where is Carl, anyway?"

"He has to work with Alex now," Nicholas laughed. "The nannies couldn't keep up with him, and Sara and I can't get our schoolwork done and watch him at the same time. The last time we weren't paying attention, he blew up Hattie's oven."

"The *gas* oven?" I asked, hitting the brakes and looking back at them.

"It was a minor explosion," Sara said, rolling her eyes. "Everyone made way too big a deal about it."

"Grady said it was a good thing that Hattie and Pops had flown back to Texas the day before so she didn't see the damage to her kitchen," Nicholas said.

"And you two were home when Carl blew the oven up?"

"It was cool," Nicholas laughed.

"He was testing a new product to see how it reacted to heat," Sara added. "He said he'd have to start from scratch because you'd be mad if he blew up your SUV."

"What is this new product supposed to do?"

"It looks like blue putty, but it leaves a chemical trace that can be tracked on a computer," Sara said. "An invisible chemical lingers, and you can see it on live satellite images days later. Also, the residue changes colors as it ages; so you can tell how long ago the putty was at each point."

"Shit. Really?"

"Language, Mom," Nicholas said, raising that damned eyebrow.

Sara giggled. "Carl had Donovan carrying the putty around to test it for a few days. But that was before the explosion. Donovan told Carl that he won't be his guinea pig anymore."

"I don't blame him." Turning back in my seat, I followed the two-track lane again until I reached the end. Parked roadside, Tech was sitting on his motorcycle with two bags on his lap.

He jogged over and opened the front passenger door. "Grady keeps go bags in his truck for the kids. He asked me to bring these to you. He also said the brats—" he threw a wink at the kids in the back, "—are all yours for at least two days. He needs a break and is heading to the bar."

"Has it been that bad?" I asked, feeling genuinely guilty.

"No," Tech laughed. "Just busy. Between the kids and the new trainees, he's been running until he drops most days. But he's good. Promise. We'd tell you if he wasn't."

"How are the trainees doing?"

"Don't know. You've kept me jumping from case to case, so I haven't been able to check in on the other parts of the business. Which reminds me," he said as he pulled the strap of an attaché over his head and dropped the bag into the SUV, "Donovan wants a full profile on each trainee. He also wants you to look at the Stevenson stalker case."

"Homework." I sighed, looking down at the overstuffed attaché. "Lovely."

"Suck it up, buttercup." Tech stepped back, away from the SUV. "I gotta go. I'm meeting Grady for a cold one."

Before I could argue, Tech closed the door and jogged back to his bike.

Sara giggled in the backseat. "You're stuck with us now."

"I'm hungry," Nicholas said.

"Cheeseburgers and chocolate milkshakes, coming up," I said, turning left onto the paved road.

~*~*~

A half an hour later we sat in a small diner, the kids shoveling their food like they were starving and me reading the files Tech had left for me.

"Mohhhmm?" Nicholas asked with a mouthful of his burger.

I grinned over the top of one of the trainee's folders. "Chew your food first."

Nicholas dramatically chewed his food as Sara giggled. When he was done, his face transformed into his serious expression. I set the folder I had been reading down and waited.

"Do you still love me?" he asked.

"Of course. With all my heart. Even when you have ketchup smeared across your face." I reached over the table to wipe his cheek. "I didn't leave because I didn't love you, either of you."

"Grady said you left because you have the fidgets," Sara said.

"The fidgets?"

Nicholas nodded. "You can't sit still yet. He said he was like that after the war for a long time, and he felt better if he kept moving around from job to job."

"I suppose there's some truth to that. But it's hard to explain."

"Will you try?" Sara asked, not looking up from the french fry she was swirling in her ketchup. "Will you try to explain it?"

I tucked the folder into the attaché and folded my arms on the table. They deserved for me to try. "I'm not sure it will make sense. I watch all of you laughing, enjoying life, and I can't figure out how you do it. I've tried. But I've seen too many bad things. I've *done* too many bad things. I don't know how to make peace with it. Working the cases, moving around, helps somehow. I can focus on just one thing at a time."

"But it's dangerous," Nicholas said, pouting.

"I know," I said, reaching across the table to push his bangs out of his eyes. "You get scared for me, and I love you for that. But you want me to play *Mom*, Sara wants me to play *Aunt*, Grady wants me to play *Girlfriend*, and I just can't figure out how to be any of those people right now. I had to be a different kind of person to get you back and to protect everyone afterward, and I don't know how to stop being *that* person."

"I'm okay with you being a badass," Sara said.

"*Language*," Nicholas and I both said to her.

She giggled and ate her ketchup-soaked french fry.

"Will you ever come home?" Nicholas asked, pushing his plate away.

"Yes." I leaned closer, waiting to make eye contact again with him. "Maybe I won't be able to stay for long periods, but I'll always come home. You kids mean everything to me. Never doubt that."

Nicholas nodded but ducked his head and excused himself, heading for the bathroom. I knew he was trying to hide the tears in his eyes, and it about broke my heart.

"He's okay most of the time," Sara whispered, watching him walk away. "Grady keeps telling him that when you find a good balance, you'll come home more."

"That's awful nice of Grady. Especially since he's probably just as upset with me."

"He's not mad. For real, he's not," Sara said, shaking her head. "He said that if you didn't love us, you wouldn't have left."

"What do you mean?"

"That if you would've stayed, you would've lashed out at the people around you. But you couldn't allow that to happen. At least, that's what Grady thinks."

I didn't have a response, but Nicholas returned so it was best to change the subject, anyway. "Well, we have two days together. What should we do?"

"Can we go to Cedar Point?" Sara asked, her eyes lighting up.

"They're closed, dummy," Nicholas said, rolling his eyes.

"I'm not *dumb*!" Sara glared.

"*Are too*!" Nicholas said.

"*Stop*!" I said, closing my eyes and counting to five. "We are not going to Cedar Point or any other amusement park. Try again."

"Can we go to Miami? Visit Aunt Charlie?" Nicholas asked.

"Aunt Charlie's not in Miami," Sara said. "She's in jail."

I threw my head back in surprise, looking at Sara.

"No, she's not!" Nicholas yelled.

"Is too!" Sara yelled back.

I raised my hand for them to silence their bickering, which they immediately did. Last I knew, Kierson had dragged Charlie back to Miami. But I hadn't seen or talked with her in several months. She'd been angry with me because I hadn't shared secrets from our childhood. Secrets regarding both our parents and the town's sheriff where we grew up. Knowing she'd likely get herself in trouble, I had sent Kierson, both an FBI agent and a friend, to check on her. He had called a week later saying he had convinced her to go back to work. I figured she'd reach out when her anger faded, but it had been radio silence.

"Sara, what do you know?" I asked.

"You'll be mad at me if I tell you."

"You were eavesdropping on an adult conversation again, which no, I don't approve of. But regardless, tell me what you heard."

"Someone called Aunt Katie last night and told her that Aunt Charlie was in jail for assault. Aunt Katie told Uncle Grady, and Uncle Grady said he'd handle it."

"In Miami?"

"No. In Michigan. Saddle Creek, maybe?"

"Sadler Creek?"

"Yeah. That one."

The last place I wanted to go was Sadler Creek, my childhood hometown, but I didn't have a choice. Charlie was trying to right the wrongs of both our pasts. "Gather your stuff," I said as I collected my shoulder bag and the attaché case. "Let's get your aunt out of jail."

Chapter Three

After all the years I'd been away, Sadler Creek appeared unchanged. The courthouse sat in the center of town with its rich green lawn welcoming visitors to the eerily vacant park benches. The police station sat across the street next to the one-screen theatre that advertised a movie that hadn't been popular since the eighties. Only a handful of vehicles were parked along main street's curbs, but their owners were nowhere in sight. Small towns typically either thrived and grew, or they slowly withered into decay. Not Sadler Creek. It remained as it always was, perfectly maintained and frozen in time.

I drove through town, watching the speedometer, forcing myself to keep pace with the posted speed limit. Everything inside me screamed to floor the gas and get the hell out of there, but I kept going, through town and another block past, before I turned right. At the next block, I made another right turn into the parking lot of the one-story community hospital. I parked and stared at the motion activated glass doors of the building. The last time I had passed through those doors was to visit Charlie after her father had broken her arm.

The sound of the kids unbuckling their seatbelts pulled my attention away from the building in front of me. I glanced back as they shuffled forward, watching me. Their grins of anticipation had me thinking of how disturbing their own upbringing was turning out to be. I shook my head, scattering the thoughts as I reached into my shoulder bag for my tablet. I had called Tech, asking him to send me the details of the arrest. The information he'd sent was exactly what I'd expected. Charlie had attacked her father in a local bar, breaking several bones which required him to stay in the hospital. The email also said Charlie's bail was denied, despite the expensive lawyer Grady had hired.

"Charlie, you're such a dumbass," I mumbled, tucking the tablet back into my bag.

"Why are we at the hospital instead of the prison?" Sara asked.

"Charlie's not in prison. She's in jail. And we're at the hospital because I need to have a word with her father." I turned in my seat to look at the kids. "I can't leave you two in the car, but we're going to be around some very bad people, so stay close."

"Got it." Nicholas pushed his door open and jumped out of the SUV.

Sara scurried to follow him as I sighed one last time, already regretting bringing them with me. I should've found someone to watch them.

The icy air slapped my skin as the motion-activated glass doors parted and we walked past. I reached out, resting a hand on the kids' shoulders to pull them closer to my sides as I maneuvered us around the familiar hallways, past the E.R., past the radiology unit, and toward the patient section of the hospital.

"Well, I'll be damned," a familiar voice said from the nursing station.

"Marilyn." I smiled, waiting for the nurse to walk around the counter for a hug.

Whenever Charlie had been hurt enough to require a stay in the hospital, Marilyn always made sure to be assigned to her room. She was the only bright spot during those troubling times.

"I figured you'd make a trip to town when I heard Charlie was arrested, but I didn't expect you to visit your uncle."

"Believe me, he's not going to appreciate the visit. Which room is he in?"

"Room eight." She glanced at her watch. "It's time for my break. Do you want me to take these two beautiful kids of yours out to the pavilion?"

"That would be an excellent idea. Thank you."

"Ah, man," Nicholas whined.

"No fair." Sara pouted.

"No arguing," I said. "Be good for my friend Marilyn."

Sara crossed her arms over her chest, scowling. Nicholas dragged his feet as Marilyn nudged them both down the hall and around the corner. The pavilion was surrounded by glass windows and monitored not only by security, but visible from the small dining room, two waiting rooms, and some offices. The kids would be safe, and I had no doubt Marilyn could keep them out of trouble.

Turning down another hallway, I walked through the open door of room eight, closing it behind me. Aunt Cecil lowered the Redbook magazine she was reading when she heard me enter.

"Well, look what the cat dragged in, Mark," she said, tossing her magazine on the window sill as she stood to face me.

I glanced at my uncle. An arm and a leg were in heavy plaster casts, but it was the metal plate bracing the bridge of his nose with strips of tape holding it to his bruised and battered face that made me snort. Charlie had let out a shitload of rage on her old man.

"Fuck you," my uncle said, reading my thoughts.

I glanced behind me when I heard the door open. My nana, my grandmother on my mother's side, walked in, followed by Grady.

"Nana," I said before turning my eyes back to my aunt. "You shouldn't be here."

"Nonsense, girl. One of my granddaughters is sitting in a cell, and I'll be damned if she's gonna stay there."

"I'm calling the police," Aunt Cecil huffed, reaching for her purse.

I crossed the room before she had the phone's screen unlocked, snatching it from her and tossing it to the floor behind me. My aunt shrieked, moving between the bed and the window.

I glanced behind me as Nana raised her thick orthopedic black shoe over the phone and stomped with enough force that plastic pieces ricocheted against the wall.

"Grady? Would you be a dear and encourage my uncle to keep quiet?"

I heard Grady move closer to the bed. I took my aunt's purse, still clutched in her hands, and tossed it to the floor behind me. I wrapped a hand around her neck as I snaked a foot behind her ankle. In one quick pivot, I rotated her so she lost her balance and fell backward over my uncle's legs. Her eyes widened as her upper body hung upside down over one end of the bed, unable to change positions because of my tightened grip around her neck. Her legs whipped back and forth trying to find leverage from the other end of the bed. Her eyes were bright with fear, but the lack of oxygen kept her from screaming.

Grady growled from a few feet away, "You bite me, fucker, and I'll break your neck." I glanced over, noting he held a hand over my uncle's mouth. Uncle Mark thrashed in pain from my aunt's weight on his broken leg, but he managed to nod that he understood.

"*Hear me*," I hissed, leaning over to glare at my aunt. "Get my mother and your husband in line. I want the charges against Charlie dropped. If you don't, I'm coming after you. Never forget, I'm my mother's daughter. You *do not* want to find out how ruthless I can be."

My aunt's eyes widened again as she attempted to nod. I relaxed my grip enough for her to suck a minute amount of air into her lungs.

"Don't think of trying to double-cross me, either. You can't win in a war against me. Others have tried. They found themselves six feet under. You get Charlie out by the time I get to the police station—or I'll be back."

She nodded frantically again as tears washed her black mascara in streaks across her face.

If I was dealing with my mother, a different tactic would've been necessary. But my aunt was simple, vain, and shallow, only caring for her own welfare. She enjoyed watching pain inflicted on others, but a threat against her own body was unimaginable.

I released her neck, stepping back as she rolled to her side to gain her balance. My uncle's muffled screams were contained by Grady's tight grip.

Nana walked to the opposite side of my uncle's bed. "The girls won't tell me how bad things got when they were kids, but I'm glad Charlie got a chance to give some back. And this is from me," she said before she punched him in the nose.

Blood gushed across his face as the bridge of his nose flattened under the flimsy metal support. Both Nana and Grady stepped back as Uncle Mark covered his nose with his hand. Blood ran between his fingers as he sobbed.

"Nice jab." I pulled Nana by her elbow around the bed and toward the door.

"Next time warn me," Grady said from behind us. "I got blood on my shirt."

"Sorry." Nana snickered. "Didn't know it was gonna just pop like that. I hardly touched the thing."

My brother Jeff was walking toward my uncle's door as we walked out. He stopped, looked at me, then Nana, then at the hospital door. A slow grin tipped the corners of his mouth before he turned on a heel and walked away.

"I don't like your brothers," Grady said.

"They're good boys, as far as pansies go," Nana said, shaking her head. "It's the women in our family who run the show, though."

"I wonder where that tradition started," I said as I led us toward the pavilion.

"According to my great-great grandmother, we're descendants of Queen Mary."

"Which one?" Grady asked. "The one who burned people at the stake, or the one who was beheaded?"

"I don't know," Nana said, turning to loop her arm through Grady's. "My great-great grandmother drank heavily and bent the tales enough that I could never get an answer from her."

"What about Mary II?" I asked as we exited into the pavilion. "It could've been her?"

"Not likely," Nana said, shaking her head. "History books say she was a nice queen."

"I'm nice!" I said, raising an eyebrow at Nana.

"You can't fool me, dear," Nana said as she walked toward the kids.

Grady's arm wrapped around my shoulders as he pulled me against his warm body. His chest shook as he laughed.

"Nana!" Nicholas called as he raced over to embrace her.

"There's that handsome devil of mine," Nana bellowed. "My, you've grown so big. Breaks my heart that you were away so long."

"Who are you?" Sara asked.

"I'm Nicholas' grandmother. And, you, little lady, must be Sara. I've heard you're a treat to hang out with."

Upon hearing that Nana was a relative, Sara took a step back and looked at me.

Nana chuckled. "Ah, she's smart, too! She knows being family isn't necessarily a good thing."

"Depends on the definition of family," Sara said, narrowing her eyes at Nana.

"I agree." Nana patted her head. "Now, shall I call you Sara? Or I hear the nickname little-bug is more common."

"Only Aunt Kelsey calls me little bug, and I'm getting too big for nicknames."

"Too big for nicknames?" Nana barked out a laugh. "Oh, little one. Give it twenty years. The nicknames change, but they get a lot racier, so—"

"Ahem," Grady interrupted by loudly clearing his throat.

"What do you mean?" Sara asked, stepping closer.

"Ask her twenty years from now," Grady said. "We need to go."

I walked over to Marilyn, hugging her goodbye. The kids surprised me by hugging her as well, thanking her for watching them. Both Nicholas and Sara tended to distrust adults. But Marilyn was a straight shooter, even with children. If asked a question, or fifty, she'd answer honestly every time. It was that trait which drew me to her when I was their age.

"Did you guys have fun?" I asked as we walked back to the parking lot.

"Marilyn said that Charlie's dad is a shithead," Sara said.

"Language, Sara," Grady growled.

"It's a direct quote," Nicholas said. "It doesn't count."

"Nick's right." Nana smirked. "Doesn't count if it's a quote."

Sara slid her small hand in mine. "And she said that your mom is a demon. Said she's as smart as you, but pure evil."

"A demon possession would explain a lot," Nana said, walking beside us. "But no way is she smarter than Kelsey."

"You kids don't need to worry about my mother," I told them.

Nicholas reached up and wrapped his hand through my other one. "Promise?"

"I swear it."

"Are we heading to the police station?" Grady asked.

His silver truck was parked next to my SUV. On the other side was a red two-seater convertible that I knew had to be Nana's.

"Yes," I answered before turning to Nana. "It's best if you leave town before Mother finds out you're here."

"Fine. But I'm not ready to go home yet. Are you going to put me up at your house for a few days? I want to spend some time with my grandson and get to know this bewitching sidekick of his."

Sara tucked closer to my leg, but she was smiling up at Nana.

"We'll find a room for you." I leaned over and kissed Nana's cheek.

"See you back at the bunker then." Nana waved as she climbed into her convertible. She barely turned the ignition key before she floored the gas and squealed the tires out of the parking lot.

"She reminds me of Dallas," Sara said, giggling before running over and climbing in the back of my SUV.

Nicholas raced in after her.

"She's not as crazy as Dallas, is she?" Grady asked.

"Just help me keep her drinks watered down during her visit."

Grady sighed before kissing my forehead and climbing into his truck.

Pulling into the police station, I smirked as I parked beside a familiar black SUV. Katie, Anne, Whiskey, and Tyler climbed out.

"Kids, stay in the car."

"I want to go inside," Sara whined.

I looked at the small gathering just outside the police station. "With any luck, none of us are going inside. Just stay here." I climbed out and motioned to Tyler to stay with the SUV. He moved over to my vehicle and opened the back door to talk to the kids. Though he was only a prospect for the Devil's Players, we'd all had a hand in his training. I had personally taught him how to shoot the pistol he was carrying concealed. He'd keep the kids safe.

"I won't be long," I said, waving off Katie and Anne from following. As I crossed the lot, Grady exited his truck and moved toward my SUV to lean against the front, arms crossed over his broad chest.

I turned my attention to the gathering in front of me. Just outside the building doors, my mother stood arguing with the sheriff and another man in a suit. I was guessing the man was from the prosecuting attorney's office. As I got closer, I heard enough of the argument to confirm my theory. Ten feet away, my mother noticed me and walked a few paces away from the sheriff toward me. I closed the distance, not stopping until I stood firmly within her air space, mere inches from each other.

Her eyes flashed with hatred, as I was sure mine did too. We stood silent, glaring with such intensity that the temperature seemed to jump at least ten degrees around us. My mother was used to commanding her household with a flash of anger in her eyes, but I'd rather chew off my arm than cower to her ever again. Her reign over me had ended when I was a teenager, and it was time she learned I was in charge now. My muscles clenched, hopeful she would strike out against me. I stepped another inch forward, each of us close enough to feel the other's breath.

Her eyes narrowed slightly, almost hesitantly, until the sheriff's hand wrapped around my forearm.

The corner of her mouth tipped up in arrogance.

A slow grin spread across my face. I didn't have to hear Grady cross the lot to know he was the one who twisted the sheriff's hand off my arm and shoved him away from me. Grady was always there for me. Beside me. Protecting me.

My smile widened as my mother glanced nervously behind me. Anne, Katie, and Whiskey were not as stealthy in their approach. I knew they'd formed a wall of protection behind me.

"Sheriff? You need assistance?" I heard another officer ask as my mother took a step back.

"Release Charlie Harrison," the sheriff called out.

I glanced over at the sheriff, a shrunken old man standing in the shadow of an enraged Grady. Whiskey walked over and placed a casual arm on Grady's shoulder. To a stranger, it would appear that the gesture was jovial. To anyone who knew the men, Whiskey was reminding Grady to keep his shit together.

"Wasn't bail denied?" the officer asked.

"It was," the attorney said.

"Young man," my mother snapped toward the officer. "Do as you were told and release Charlotte Harrison. The charges have been dropped."

The attorney turned to argue, but my mother's icy blue eyes speared him, chocking his words off.

My mother turned back to me, but kept her distance. "Take your cousin and get the hell out of *my* town."

"Or—*What*?" I snapped, stepping toward her. Anne and Katie grabbed my arms, keeping me in place. We all knew I could break their hold if I wanted, but I didn't. "I will *not* follow your orders, *Mother*!"

"You're forgetting where you are," my mother said, laughing coldly. "Either you leave on your own, or I'll have you dragged out of town by your hair."

Anne and Katie both stepped around me and squared off with my mother, continuing to advance as my mother retreated until her back was flat against the brick wall.

"She's mine," I said, approaching as they stepped away. I leaned in to whisper, "How dare you threaten me. I can snap your neck in one move. I can sneak into the house in the middle of the night, and you'd never open your eyes again. I can have you ruined. I can have you killed. I can do whatever the hell I want—so don't give me a reason to come back to this shit-hole of a town."

A spark of fear appeared in her eyes before they turned cold again. She held my glare, fighting to keep her composure, until I snorted and walked away.

Sensing Charlie walking up beside me, I stopped briefly to turn to face her. Her happy smile instantly fell as she saw the level of my anger. She stepped back, bumping into Grady.

"You best ride with me," Grady said, placing an arm in front of her, protecting her from me.

"I'll drive your SUV," Anne said, taking my keys. "You need to decompress before you get behind the wheel." Whiskey joined Anne in my SUV.

Knowing she was right, and also knowing I wasn't in the best mental frame to be around the kids, I climbed into the passenger seat of Katie's SUV.

Tyler slid into the backseat. "Well, that was interesting."

"The kids okay?" Katie asked.

"They're disappointed that nobody threw a punch," Tyler answered.

"I'm not," Katie said, pulling out of the parking lot. "I thought my mother was bad. But her drunk ass never made my toes curl like that hateful woman. I wouldn't have gotten any closer if Anne wasn't beside me."

"Mama bear was mad," Tyler chuckled. "And don't fool yourself, Katie. That sheriff is lucky Grady got to him before you did. I saw you reaching for your knife."

I glared over at Katie, and she smirked. "Instinct."

"Why are you mad at Charlie?" Tyler asked me.

"Because she's stirring up shit that's best left buried," I said as I glanced back at him.

My facial expression must have been intense, because Tyler cringed into the back seat.

Chapter Four

"You look like an enraged dragon ready to scorch the Earth," Dallas said from a stool at our breakfast bar. She had helped herself to my liquor cabinet and had what appeared to be a Hurricane sitting in front of her. Most likely she'd used the top-shelf liquor to make it.

"Don't be giving me the evil eye. I made a pitcher and left a glass out for you." She pointed at the glass sitting next to the refrigerator.

I pulled the pitcher and filled the glass. "Where's Nana?"

"The crazy old lady? I sent her over to Lisa's house. I told her I wasn't allowed to let strangers inside."

"She's my *grandmother*!"

Dallas shrugged, inspecting her manicure. "She scared the hell out of me. She's four feet tall and as tenacious as a pit bull. I thought she was actually going to bite me when I wouldn't let her inside."

I shook my head and looked back toward the door where the kids stood grinning. They ran back out the door laughing, likely heading to Lisa's. Tyler turned and followed them, ever the bodyguard.

Grady stepped through the garage door, and I looked over his shoulder for Charlie. "Figured you could use some time to either cool off or get drunk," he answered my unasked question. "She's at the store with Anne and Katie." Grady wrapped one arm around me and used the other to steal my drink. Taking a sip, his face puckered, and he handed it back. "I'll stick to beer."

I took a long sip of my drink before turning back to Dallas. "What brings you by?"

She leaned over and lifted a tote bag onto the counter. She pulled a box from the bag—sapphire blue hair dye. "Just a few streaks." She winked.

"What the hell." I pulled the pitcher from the refrigerator and moved it and my glass to the dining room table. "I need new black tips and a cut, too."

"That's obvious," Dallas said, emptying the rest of her supplies beside me. "Your hair is downright boring these days. If I crossed paths with you as a stranger on the street, I'd imagine you to be a housewife."

Grady snorted, grabbed three beers and left the house through the garage door.

"What are you really doing here?" I asked Dallas.

"Tyler sent a text to Goat, who called me. Word is you're in a particularly evil mood. Alex found a few new outfits for you. Lisa's cooking enough food to feed the security firm, the store employees, and the bikers. And everyone promised to hide until I got you good and drunk."

"And Nana?"

"She was the first to ask where to hide when we got word you were feeling extra bitchy. Lisa's house seemed the safest place to stash her for the time being." She nudged the back of my head, forcing my chin to my chest as she pinned most of my hair up with a clip. She pulled out the lower layer, snipped a good inch off the bottom, and began coating it with a jet-black dye.

"Hurry up. I can't drink with my head this way."

She leaned over, reached into her bag, and tossed a straw onto my lap. Dallas planned like a girl scout—an older, more devious girl scout in a push-up bra. I peeled the wrapper off before sucking half my glass down.

"Now we're talking," Dallas said, lifting her own glass to take a drink.

"You can't get drunk and do my hair."

"Please. I dropped acid before doing your hair last time, and it turned out great."

I laughed, because the last haircut was the best yet. Even Katie was jealous. I knew Dallas had been high, but I'd figured it was a mix of marijuana and alcohol.

"You know, you could make a lot of money styling hair as a career. You're good at it."

"I'm good at sex, too. Doesn't mean I want some fat, hairy, lard-ass sticking it to me doggy style to make a buck."

I choked on my drink, coughing as it went down the wrong pipe. Dallas beat on my back a few times and then yelled at me to hold still as she wrapped more of my hair in foil.

~*~*~

Dallas was finishing the foil wrap on the top highlights when Grady returned. "Is it safe to be inside yet?"

"Depends on who enters."

"Should I send word that Charlie needs to find somewhere else to sleep tonight?" Grady asked as he sat next to me.

"Sounds tempting." Despite Dallas' protests, I raised my head to look at him. "Where did you run off to?"

"Headquarters. Bones took over working with the trainees today so I caught up on my paperwork."

"Did Donovan tell you he wants me to write profiles on all the trainees?"

"No, but I support Donovan's decisions. And I trust your profiles. It actually takes the pressure off." He leaned back, relaxing into his chair. "I can't get a read on a couple of the trainees. I know their skill level, but I can't figure out what makes them tick."

"I've barely made a dent in the files, but one stood out already. I texted Tech to run a deeper background."

"Which I did," Tech said as he entered through the front door. "Nice catch." He dropped a folder next to me before going to the refrigerator.

I opened the file and scanned the information before sliding it toward Grady.

Grady glanced at the closed file before looking back at me. "Do I even want to know?"

"I noticed in Scott Bailey's file that he was a high school dropout from East Garfield Park in Chicago. Then the file was blank for the next six years. Tech found gang affiliations."

"Damn. I liked him."

"Just because he was in a gang, don't cross him off the list. He was sixteen and living in a crap neighborhood. Dig in. If he tells you his story, you might find that his history gives him the experience to do this job."

"Or I might just hear more lies."

"Tech can fact check anything he tells you." I shrugged. "Or I can interview him. Get a personal read on him."

Grady tapped his fingers on the file, thinking. "No. I'll talk to him tomorrow. If he passes a sit down with me, then I'll have you grill him next. You're right. Sometimes shitty choices when we're young build moral character later."

"And sometimes you're just left with a stinking pile of shit," Dallas slurred from behind me.

Grady grinned and looked at me. "I'm afraid of what your hair looks like under all that foil. She's loaded."

"It's time to find out. Luckily, I was timing the dye myself."

I got up and went to my private bathroom. I started the shower before pulling the individual foils from my hair. Looking in the mirror, the sapphire blue streaks were brighter than I anticipated, but it looked cool with the maroon streaks and black tips. I stepped into the shower, rinsing my hair before I added a healthy dose of expensive conditioner. A half an hour later, still wrapped in my towel, I had just finished blow drying my hair when Grady entered.

"Damn." His eyes sparkled with mischief as he looked back at me in the mirror. Stepping forward, he proceeded to show me with his hands and other body parts just how much he liked the new look.

~*~*~

Forty-five minutes later, I finished dressing and walked back into the dining room. The house was full as usual, but it was familiar, homey. The only face I wasn't ready to see was Charlie's, but she kept her distance, leaning on the wall next to the basement staircase. Likely, she was prepared to run down the stairs and out the door if needed.

Grady's arm wrapped around my waist as he steered me toward the table. My usual chair was left vacant and waiting for me. As soon as I sat, Lisa started serving bowls of soup to everyone and placed one in front of me. I could feel Charlie's eyes on me, but I shook it off as I grabbed my spoon, determined to ignore her. But my plan to ignore her was short lived as I watched my spoon, filled with soup, knocked out of my hand and into the credenza.

"What the fuck, Charlie?" I stood and glared at her, fists clenched. "You really want to do this? You really want to hash our shit out in front of everyone?"

Grady wrapped both his arms around me, pinning my arms to my side and pulling me back as Donovan and Bones moved between Charlie and me.

"You don't get to call me *Charlie*!" she yelled. "Not *you*! I tried for years to get you to call me by my name and to quit calling me Kid. You don't get to change the rules now just because you're pissed. To you—I'm *Kid*. I'm still family!"

"Fine. *Kid*," I snapped. "It's a better fit, anyway."

"Are you sure about that?" she snapped back, leaning as far forward toward me as Bones and Donovan would allow her. "Or are you so hell-bent on thinking the worst of me that you missed the fact that you were about to eat *clam chowder*?"

Her words doused my anger. I looked at the bowl and then back at Charlie. "You sure?"

"No." She rubbed the back of her neck and paced a few steps away. "But it looks and smells like it."

I looked at Lisa who stood frozen mid-way to the table with two full bowls in her hands. "Do we not like clam chowder?"

"I'm allergic," I answered, grinning.

Lisa dropped both bowls, shattering them across the floor as she raised her hands to her cheeks in full-out Lisa freak mode. "*EpiPen! We need an EpiPen!* Someone call an ambulance!"

"Stop, babe." Donovan chuckled, moving to stop her before she tore the house apart looking for an EpiPen. "Kelsey didn't eat any of the chowder. Charlie stopped her."

Big alligator tears poured out of Lisa as she clung to Donovan.

"What the hell?" I asked, looking over at Katie.

"This is nothing," Katie said, rolling her eyes. "She's been a basket case for a month now, but when Hattie left, she got worse."

Donovan moved Lisa into the kitchen and was whispering in her ear as he rubbed her back.

Grady leaned closer to me so Lisa wouldn't hear. "Donovan found her up at three a.m., sterilizing their kitchen floor. She said she didn't want Abigail to get sick from anything they tracked inside."

Carl, having heard, nodded from the end of the table. "She sorted and cleaned all the closets yesterday. All of my shirts are arranged by type of material and color, though I found a few that had higher polyester blends that were categorized out of order, but I fixed it." He turned to look at me and cocked his head, thinking. Sometimes it was hard to remember how intelligent Carl was when he wore his adult-sized bib that said Party Boy on the front of it. "Or maybe it was a test. Most clothing has a percentage of synthetic material these days, but regardless, the arrangement by color I've found to be beneficial."

I glanced at Carl's outfit which consisted of a neon green T-shirt, orange corduroy pants, and purple running shoes.

"She made us a three-course meal for lunch Monday," Nicholas said.

"Served on Hattie's good china," Sara added.

"I was trying to be nice!" Lisa wailed from the kitchen, having overheard. "I should've known you kids would make fun of me."

"They're not picking on you. But why are you cleaning everyone's closets and scrubbing floors in the middle of the night? And why are you making extravagant lunches for the kids when they'd be perfectly happy with soup or a sandwich—both of which they're capable of making themselves."

"I just want everything to be perfect!"

"For who? Nobody here is looking for perfect."

"It's good to have goals!" she yelled.

"Donovan? Why isn't she making any sense to me?" I asked as I threw my hands up into the air.

"Because she isn't sleeping," Donovan said.

"*Tattletale!*" Lisa snapped at Donovan.

"Enough!" I said, before walking to the other side of the breakfast bar and pressing my hands against the counter as I faced her. "Lisa, go home. Get some sleep. *Please*. I promise, we'll handle everything here."

"You just want me to go away!" she squawked before she started bawling again.

I had to turn my back to her to keep her from seeing the smirk on my face.

"Donovan!" Katie yelled. "Get her out of here!"

"Abigail's in the living room," Donovan said, somewhat panicked.

Anne rolled her eyes. "We can handle a *real* baby. We can't handle Lisa when she's acting like a baby on crack! Go!"

Donovan nodded, pulling Lisa toward the door as Tyler held it open for him. When the door closed, everyone turned back to me for some odd reason.

"Is there anything for dinner other than clam chowder?" I asked. "I'm starving."

"Only bread and salad," Nana answered from the kitchen. "Don't worry, though. Give me a few minutes. I'll scavenge something up for you."

"She likes grilled cheese sandwiches," Grady said, pushing me into my chair and sliding my bowl down the table to Tech.

"Nana, your cooking is worse than Katie's," I said. "I'll just eat some bread and salad."

"I'm tempted to see how bad she can screw up a grilled cheese sandwich," Anne said. "But instead I'll heat the chili that Hattie has in the freezer."

"And a grilled cheese sandwich?" I asked, batting my eyelashes.

"I'll make the sandwich," Sara said, sliding out of her chair and following her mom into the kitchen.

"I want to help," Nicholas insisted, chasing after them.

I smiled as Nana stepped back to watch with curiosity as Sara and Nicholas got out the supplies.

"Doesn't Nana live alone? What does she eat?" Grady asked.

"Cereal and takeout," Charlie said, taking Sara's place at the table.

I turned and looked at Grady, willing him to help me escape another confrontation. He shook his head, sighed, and kissed my forehead before stepping back and leaning against the wall.

"Ah," Charlie said. "The mighty boyfriend is leaving this mess for you and me to sort."

"It's not his mess."

"You're right. It's *yours*."

"That's pretty funny, Kid," I said, pressing my palms against the table and leaning toward her. "If it wasn't for me, your ass would still be sitting in jail."

"Because I was cleaning up the shit your cowardly ass ran from years ago."

I didn't think. I just acted. My hand moved from the table and across her face with enough speed and force that she flew sideways into Whiskey's lap. He caught her but his eyes, and everyone else's, were on me.

Their combined looks of shock stabbed me with such intensity that I forced myself to stand and step back. "Oh my God," I gasped as I looked down at my own hand. I took another step back.

"I've got you," Grady whispered in my ear from behind me. "Just listen to my voice. It's going to be all right." His hands flexed on my hips, pulling me against him.

I shook my head, unable to talk. My vision blurred and my hands shook.

"Get out," I heard Anne say louder than normal.

I looked up, surprised to find that she wasn't yelling at me, but at Charlie.

"*She's* the one who hit *me!*" Charlie glared, pushing herself away from Whiskey and standing.

Abigail started to cry from the living room and Alex, bless his heart, moved around Anne and raced in that direction.

"You deserved it." Anne stepped into Charlie's space. "I don't know what happened between the two of you, but my best friend faced something today that sickened her. And she did it for *you*! She did it to get *you* out of jail. She loved you enough to wade into that cesspool of a town and drag your ungrateful ass out." Anne pulled a dining room chair out of the way and moved closer to Charlie. "Not all of us were lucky enough to have someone like Kelsey in our younger years. But you were. And what did you do to repay her? You forced her to return to a place she vowed she'd never go again. You forced her to face her mother and declare war. You forced what you wanted on her, without considering what she needed. I've watched my best friend go through some of the most terrifying things imaginable. She's barely been able to keep afloat these past few months as she's tried to rebuild her life. You disappeared—angry about some bullshit that happened a decade ago. But we've been here. We've watched her struggle to keep one foot moving in front of the other. And then you call—and once again—Charlie needs to be saved. Charlie needs to be protected. And, *that's her job, right?*"

My friends and family shifted closer to Anne. I wasn't sure if their movements represented unity or if they were moving in to prevent bloodshed.

"*Well, not anymore!*" Anne closed the distance, standing nose to nose with Charlie. "*GET OUT!*"

Charlie kicked her chair back to gain space and moved out of striking distance. She looked to her left, then her right, finding nothing but scowling faces. She looked at me, surprise and shock etched on her face. As she turned to leave, she came face to face with Katie.

"I get it," Katie said in a low calm voice that warred with her angry eyes. "It felt good to beat the shit out of your old man. That makes sense to all of us." Katie shrugged, but didn't break her eye contact with Charlie. "But you chose to get your revenge in a bar filled with witnesses, because you *knew* Kelsey would save your ass." Katie shook her head. "That was cruel and selfish."

Charlie's head dropped. With her back toward me, I couldn't see her face. She stepped around Katie, walked past Nana who had tears in her eyes, and slipped out the garage door. I stepped forward, reaching toward the door as it closed, still unable to speak.

"No," Grady said, stopping me. "Let her go. She's not a little girl anymore."

"He's right," Nana said, wiping her tears. "I love her too, but she can't tie herself to you and then jump into the ocean. Let her figure it out."

"I had to get her out of jail. I didn't have a choice."

"Of course," Anne agreed. "But now she needs to feel the consequences."

"You'd make us suffer," Katie said. "It's how you taught us to be strong for ourselves."

I turned, feeling eyes on me. Bones was watching me, gauging my emotions. He must have decided the danger was over, because he pulled his chair out and sat. "Any more of that chowder left?"

Anne seemed relieved with a task to do, taking Bones' bowl with her into the kitchen.

Katie slid into an open chair at the table and looked back at Bones. "Where's Bridget?"

Bones snorted. "Said it wouldn't be right to mingle with the bosses while she was a trainee."

Alex returned, bouncing Abigail in his arms as she gurgled happy noises up at him. Everyone settled into regular conversations as if nothing had happened. But something had. Something inside me had cracked open. The feeling of boiling lava filled my chest. Sara and Nicholas returned with a bowl of chili and a grilled cheese sandwich, setting both in my spot at the table—at the head of the table. Where I always sat. A place meant for the person in charge of the family. Responsible for all of them.

My hands shook violently. I tried to pull air into my lungs. My vision swirled at high speed, everything spinning around me. I felt myself pulled and turned before being pushed forward. I knew I was being led down the hall, but I wasn't able to control my own movements. I wasn't able to breathe.

Chapter Five

I wasn't sure how much time had passed before I realized I was naked, leaning against Grady's chest, with steamy water nearly to my shoulders. I closed my eyes as I listened to the low whirl of the bathroom fan and Grady's deep voice vibrating against my back as he sang a slow country tune. The melody lulled me as my muscles relaxed and my breathing slowed. I could feel one of his arms bracing me up and his other hand slowly stroking the side of my ribs. The steam dampened my face and neck above the water line.

"I love you," I whispered, keeping my eyes closed.

"I know," he whispered back, kissing the back of my head.

"You shouldn't have to take care of me."

"It's no chore. You were there for me when I needed your help. Like during the flashback I had after the bomb went off. And when I was arrested for murder."

"But I'm not getting better. Hell, I'm getting worse. I slapped Charlie."

"I'm glad you hit her." Grady chuckled. "It was a shock, yes. And I know it scared you. But maybe she'll pull her head out of her ass and start thinking about you for a change."

"That's not fair, Grady."

"Isn't it? She's so angry that she can't see the truth. She has no idea about the guilt you carry over the decisions you made as a kid. You sacrificed everything to get her out of that town." He wrapped both arms around me, snuggling me tighter against him. "I'm proud of you. And you'll get better at the day-to-day stuff. It takes time."

"How much time?"

He chuckled, making the water ripple around us. "Always so impatient."

I leaned my head back and to the side, looking up at him. He grinned down and kissed me before he stood, dragging me upward with him. "You need to eat."

I released a long sigh. "I don't want to go back out there."

"Good." He handed me a towel. "I don't feel like sharing your attention."

He dried himself before walking into the bedroom. I heard him rummage in the dresser, followed by the bedroom door opening and closing. After drying myself off, I hung both towels on the rack and slipped into my bathrobe.

I strolled into the atrium, hitting the button on the wall for the blinds to close. Light still reflected from the glass ceiling, but none of our friends and family would be able to see into the room. I turned on the corner lamp, the one with the low-wattage bulb that cast barely a glow within the room. Walking to the stereo, I turned it on and smiled when jazz music streamed out of the speakers. Grady must have sat in the atrium listening to music while I was away.

Grady entered a few minutes later, carrying a tray of food and setting it on the coffee table. I settled myself on the floor and we moved the bowls and plates around.

"This reminds me of the time we spent at the cabin," he said as he placed a glass of milk in my hand.

I accepted the not-so-subtle hint and took a drink of the milk before setting it down. "Thirty people, including kids, weren't in the other room when we were at the cabin."

"Yeah. It's definitely crowded."

"Do you regret moving here?"

"No," he answered before leaning over to kiss my cheek. "But we should talk."

I dragged my spoon through my chili, unsure I was ready for another serious conversation.

"We need your signature giving us permission to build two more houses at the end of the road."

"You don't want to live in the main house?"

"It's not for us. Tech and Katie will move into one of the houses, which frees up the apartment above the garage for guests. Then Lisa and Donovan will move into the other new house. Anne, Sara, and Whiskey will move into their house next door."

"This is what everybody wants?"

Grady nodded. "Hattie and Pops went back to Texas because Pops needed a break. I'm sure when it was just you girls it was cozy, but now that Carl, Pops, Whiskey, Nicholas, and I have moved in, it's become tight quarters."

"But why would Lisa and Donovan move into one of the new houses?"

"Sara panicked when we talked to her about moving down the road. Katie suggested that if Sara was next door, she could use the tunnels connecting the houses. Everyone, including Sara, was okay with that."

"What about Pops and Hattie?"

"We'll open up the spare room upstairs and build a kitchenette for them. That way they can have some quiet time away from everyone when they want, but I'm worried that eventually they'll need to swap rooms with us downstairs so Hattie doesn't have to go up and down the kitchen stairway."

"Did you ever notice that stairway next to the kitchen is an odd layout?"

Grady raised an eyebrow but didn't say anything.

"It's the exact dimensions needed to install a personal elevator."

He shook his head, grinning. "Only you would have planned so far in advance."

"They're my family," I said, shrugging.

"I know. And we all agreed that the common areas would still be a public space for everyone to come and go as they please. But if we can break up the sleeping quarters a little, we won't feel like we're living in a boarding house."

I scrunched my nose, thinking about it. How many times had I escaped to my atrium to have some peace? Whiskey and Anne didn't have that option. Sara didn't have that option. Hattie had a small sitting nook in her room overlooking the field, but that was it. The changes made sense.

Grady grinned. "The paperwork is in the top drawer of your desk. The contractors start next week." He scooped a large spoonful of chili into his mouth.

"I don't want Sara using the basement tunnel every time she comes over. Can you build a walkway from their living room to our family room?"

"Maybe. I'll take some measurements tomorrow and talk to Whiskey."

"What about you? Do you need more space? A kitchenette? A man cave?"

"No. I like the atrium."

"No fifty-two-inch TV?"

Grady's grin widened. "We have a sixty-inch TV in the lounge at Headquarters. I can run over there if I'm having a testosterone crisis. Now quit playing with your food and eat."

I looked down and noticed I had torn my grilled cheese sandwich into small pieces. I took one of the pieces and dipped it into my chili. "Why aren't you eating the chowder?"

"Because I plan on doing things to you later tonight with my mouth and didn't want to worry about you having an allergic reaction."

"*Oh my.*" I smiled at him as I ate the piece of sandwich, thinking of all the things I liked him doing with his mouth.

"Eat faster." Grady chuckled, scooping another bite of chili.

I followed orders.

~*~*~

I woke at dawn, snuggled into Grady's side. I looked up and saw he was awake. "Why are you watching me?"

"Because you're beautiful."

I leaned over and kissed his nipple.

"Careful. I'm ready for round three." He stroked a hand up my ribs and over my breast.

"Not happening. You wore me out last night."

"The best way to build your stamina is by practice." Grady leaned over and kissed down my neck.

"Later, cowboy." I laughed, sitting up and wrapping the sheet around me.

"Fine. I'll let your body rest, but I'm not promising for how long." He leaned back against the headboard. "What time is it?"

"Seven-ish."

Grady rolled over to the nightstand for his phone and texted someone. I tilted my head, watching him. He answered my silent question. "I told Donovan to send the trainees out for a five-mile run."

"A run sounds good. I've spent too much time in my SUV lately."

"And after your run?" Grady asked as he extracted himself from the tangled sheets to stand. His back and shoulders muscles tensed as he waited for me to answer.

"Shower, check on the kids, and then I'll finish going through the trainee files."

Grady nodded, not turning to face me. He wanted to know when I was going to disappear again, but he didn't ask. I was acting like a spooked horse these days, always ready to bolt.

"You? What's on your agenda?"

"I'll be working with the trainees the rest of the morning, then I'll turn them over to Bones for the afternoon." He sighed as he walked around the bed and sat next to me. "As much as I hate it, I know you'll leave again. Just promise you'll stay in touch."

"I'll try," I said, lifting a hand to run it along his arm.

"You're doing better than you think," he said, taking my hand. "Don't be so hard on yourself."

"Maggie called." It was all I said, but his hand tightened on mine as his shoulders tensed again. Maggie was a friend despite being an FBI agent. The last time we saw her, she was being treated for the injuries that Jonathan Vaughn had inflicted during her captivity.

"How's she doing?"

I shrugged. "She went back to work, but the FBI reassigned her to a drug trafficking unit. She says her reporting supervisor is an asshole."

"Damn. Couldn't Kierson stop the transfer? Keep her in sex crimes?"

"Kierson benched her to a desk because she was a bit of a loose cannon. Then she went over his head to complain and found herself assigned elsewhere."

"So—she lost her temper, and now they're punishing her."

"That was my interpretation."

"That doesn't sound like Maggie," Grady said, shaking his head.

"Being tortured changes a person," I whispered, squeezing his hand.

"It makes an impression, but it doesn't have to define you." He lifted my hand and kissed it before he got up and went into the bathroom.

I heard the shower start up and decided it was best if I was escaped quickly. If I was still in the bedroom when he returned covered in wet rippling naked muscles, I'd likely find myself tangled in the sheets again. I snuck into the bathroom long enough to use a wash cloth for a quick wipe down and brush my teeth before I slipped back into the bedroom. I dressed in cotton shorts, a sports bra, and a loose-fitting T-shirt before lacing a well-worn pair of running shoes. Ready to go, I turned toward the atrium before I remembered the contracts that Grady had told me about for the new houses. I pulled the file out and scanned the documents before signing all the marked signature lines. I was pleased to see that Whiskey was hired as the general contractor. I moved the folder to the dresser before exiting the atrium side door. Crossing the street to the woodlands, I started down the outer running trail.

Chapter Six

Two miles into my run, I heard voices up ahead. I slowed to a walk, careful of where I stepped so I wouldn't be heard. At the top of a small hill, I crept toward the edge until I could see two men below, talking. Neither of them noticed me.

"We need to break this case soon," the tall man with black hair said to the other. "I'm not sure how much more physical training I can take."

"Tell me about it," the stouter blond said. "Grady's worse than my basic training sergeant. And Bones scares the shit out of me."

"If you tell anyone back at the office that Bridget took me down during practice yesterday, I'll kick your ass."

"She's crazy," the blond said. "I can't decide whether I want to hit her or fuck her."

"Better not let your wife hear you say that," the other said, laughing as he lit a cigarette.

The blond took the cigarette, grinding it into the dirt with his shoe. "I ain't getting my ass kicked off this op because you needed a nicotine fix. And we need to get back, anyway, before someone comes looking for us."

"Fine. But the first one of us with an opportunity to look around Donovan's office, needs to take it. We need to get that intel."

"Agreed."

They jogged off in the direction of the road. The woodlands were off limits to everyone except Grady, Donovan, and me. I didn't even allow the kids to play in the woods unless Grady or I were with them. Those two men definitely didn't have permission to be on my land.

After waiting until they were out of hearing distance, I jogged the next mile, exiting at the end of our dead-end street. I walked the rest of the way, waving at Lisa who was washing her kitchen window. She smiled briefly before continuing to attack invisible smudges. I shook my head and continued on. I wasn't equipped to know what to do with a woman obsessed with cleaning.

Not having my keys on me, I went to the front door and rang the bell. Sara opened it a minute later, leaping into my arms for a hug.

"What's this all about?" I laughed, carrying her with me through the door into the dining room.

"The glass walkway to connect the houses," Whiskey answered, saluting his cup of coffee at me. "She's already added it to the blueprints."

"I'll be able to run back and forth any time I want. It will be like a hallway." Sara's smile beamed back at me.

"I like that thought too," I said, rubbing my nose against hers before I set her down in the chair by her laptop.

I walked into the kitchen for a cup of coffee. Grady was already there, sliding a cup my way. "You have a good run?"

"Let's say it was interesting," I answered, glancing toward the dining room table. "I'll fill you in later, but tell Donovan to keep all the offices locked and supervised."

Grady raised his left eyebrow. "That doesn't sound good."

"Could be worse. I don't think we have anything to worry about, but I'll make some phone calls."

"I trust you." Grady planted a hard kiss on my forehead before he poured his coffee into a travel mug and left through the garage door.

~*~*~

After showering and throwing on a clean set of clothes, I grabbed my shoulder bag and moved into the dining room to work at the other end of the table from the kids. I reviewed the trainee files of the two men who were in the woods. Both files were thin—and completely fabricated. I was surprised Tech didn't notice the lack of details as a red flag. I grabbed my cell phone and called Agent Kierson.

"I'm busy," he answered. "Unless you're calling to accept the offer to be our profiler, I don't have time to talk."

"Are you sure you can't convince Maggie to come back? I hear she hates her new boss."

"He's already gone. She's stuck between assignments right now, bored."

"What happened to her boss?"

"He got demoted to no-man's-land. Maggie insists she didn't have anything to do with it, but she's definitely laughing about it. I worked with the guy once and have to admit I enjoyed hearing his career crashed and burned."

"Damn. You FBI agents are brutal."

"He's a class A dickhead. You'd have dropped him."

"Well then, I'm glad he's out of the picture, but that's not why I called. I need a favor."

Kierson sighed dramatically but didn't say anything.

"I'm looking at two fake trainee files and overheard them say they were undercover investigating Silver Aces Security."

"Feds?"

"They're not local cops. And their backgrounds have holes, but the basic details passed preliminary vetting."

"Is this about you? Aren't you part owner now?"

"I bought in recently, but Grady and I are silent partners. We let Donovan stamp his name on everything."

"This has to be about you, then. I can't see any of the agencies looking into Donovan or Grady. What did you do this time?"

"If I knew that, why the hell would I be calling you?"

"Smartass. I'll make some calls and ask Genie to do her computer thing. Give me a couple hours." Kierson disconnected.

I looked up to find both kids watching and listening to me. "Shh," I said, putting my finger near my lips.

"Your work looks like a lot more fun than mine," Sara said, coming over to look at one of the files.

"Shouldn't you be listening to some online professor or something?"

"We've already watched all of our lesson plans and have most of our homework done," Nicholas said, moving over to look at the other file. "Are these bad guys?"

"I don't think they're bad. I just think they're sneaky," I answered, reaching out to tickle his ribs. "It's not even nine o'clock yet. How can the two of you be almost done with your work?"

"We worked ahead last week. We were bored."

"You both need someone to manage your schedules. And you need physical education and some arts-based studies."

"Another nanny?" Sara sighed.

"No. But a teacher would be a good idea. Get online and post an ad. Put down that a teaching degree is required. Set up interviews for Wednesday."

"Will you still be here?" Nicholas asked as Sara moved to her laptop to start writing the ad.

"I don't know, but if I'm not here, I'll ask Lisa or Grady to do the interviews. Will that work?"

"Nicholas and I should get to pick the teacher," Sara said.

"Not happening. But you can give us your opinion."

"Deal," Sara said.

"You're not supposed to agree right away," Nicholas said, glaring at her.

Sara's eyes sparkled with mischief. "We can force someone to quit if we don't like them."

"You two are monsters," I said, rolling my eyes to the ceiling.

I looked over when Nicholas' laugh cut off abruptly. His face was whiter than the sheet of paper he was holding. I took the paper from him and looked at it. I didn't recognize the picture of the trainee stapled in the upper corner. It was a file I hadn't reviewed yet. I skimmed the profile before looking back at Nicholas. "Do you know this man?"

He looked up at me and nodded slowly. His eyes were wide, and he was breathing in quick shallow breaths.

I reached out and held his hand. "You're safe, Nick. You're at home with Sara and me. Did this man hurt you?"

He shook his head no as his breathing started to even out.

"Did he work for Nola?"

He looked back at the picture and nodded. "He dropped off kids to her," he whispered.

"What the hell?" Whiskey gasped, standing at the bottom of the stairs.

"Watch the kids and go through the rest of the trainee files with them. See if they recognize anyone else," I ordered as I tucked my phone in my pocket and grabbed my keys off the hook. "I have some ass kicking to do."

~*~*~

It took me less than thirty seconds to drive over to Silver Aces. As I was getting out of my SUV, my phone rang.

"Give me the quick version," I said to Kierson as I jogged toward the door.

"Not FBI, but possibly DEA."

"What the hell would the DEA want with Silver Aces?"

"No clue. Still trying to get someone on the phone with enough clearance to answer that question."

"Screw it. I'll ask them myself. I just need to take out the trash first."

"Literally?" Kierson asked.

"No!" I snapped, hanging up on him. He probably didn't deserve my anger, especially when he was doing me a favor. But my ire was spiking and my heart slammed against my chest with each beat. My ears made whooshing noises as I stormed past the front receptionist and into the gym.

The gym was in the center of the building with a conference room and several offices on the far-left of the oversized space. Also on the left was an open stairway that led to the second floor. The south side of the second floor housed a glass-walled office that Tech and I shared for a war room. The north side was Grady's office and a few empty offices.

Grady sensed my presence and watched me with a raised eyebrow as I barreled between the trainees to the center of the room. I spotted my target and when I was close enough, I swept his legs out from under him and placed a booted heel at his throat.

"*Who the fuck are you?*" I screamed down at him as I pressed more of my weight against him. "*And what the hell are you doing here?*" One wrong move on his part, and my heel would puncture a life-ending hole through his neck.

I sensed Bones, Grady, Bridget, and Donovan close in around me.

"Who is he?" Grady asked, reaching a hand out and lightly touching my shoulder.

"One of Nola's delivery boys," I said, spitting in the man's face.

"I don't work for her no more," the man wheezed.

"Since I *killed* her—I already *know* that!"

"Oh, shit," he whimpered. "You're her!" His face paled, and he moved his hands off my boot and held them up in surrender. "Please, don't kill me!"

"You kidnapped children *and sold them*!"

"I'm sorry!" he whimpered. "I needed the money!"

"Piece of shit," I said, kicking him in the face before stepping away.

"Can we kill him now?" Bones growled.

"I wish. But the DEA agents planted as trainees would be required to arrest us," I said, motioning to the agents. "In fact, they witnessed the confession of a federal crime which I believe they're required now to report."

Both men sighed, one ducking his head and placing his hands on his hips. The other moved over to the man on the floor and pulled him up, rattling off his Miranda rights. I looked over my shoulder as Donovan scrubbed a hand over his face, Grady raised his left eyebrow, and Bones laughed. Bridget looked mad.

"What am I missing?" I asked her.

She moved over to the shorter blond and stomped her heel on his toes.

"Shit!" he screeched, jumping up and down on his good foot to keep the weight off his smashed one. "What the hell was that for?"

"You were flirting with me to get info on the company!" she fumed. "Like I'm some airhead tart who would betray her friends just to get a little attention?"

"Well it didn't work," he grumbled. "Damn. You broke my toe."

"Good!"

Bridget stormed out of the gym.

I reached inside my boot for flex cuffs, passing them to the agent holding Nola's goon.

"Thanks," the agent grumbled.

"You can thank me by telling me what the hell the DEA is doing investigating Silver Aces Security."

"How did you figure out who we were?" the shorter, blond agent asked.

"I caught you talking in the woods. For future reference, never meet up in a low valley. It makes it easier for people to spy on you."

"Our boss is going to be pissed."

"If you or your boss want to know something—*ask*!"

Grady placed a gentle hand on my shoulder, reminding me to calm down.

"Take him out to the car. I'll talk to them," the shorter agent said to his partner before he started limping toward Donovan's office.

"I don't think so," I said, walking toward the main conference room. "This way."

As I entered the room and turned on the lights, the green light for the concealed video camera turned on. Tech must have heard the chaos and was recording the meeting. Unless you knew the camera was there, you'd never notice it. It blended with a security panel on the wall that had various green and red lights in a strip. Only Tech, Grady, Donovan, and I knew that the top right light was for the video recorder.

"Let's start with your name," I said, pulling out a chair and sitting at one end of the table.

"Agent Leighton. My partner is Agent Thomas."

"What's the basis of your case and how does it tie into Silver Aces Security?" Grady asked, leaning against the glass wall with his arms crossed over his chest.

Bones wandered over and stretched out in a chair near me. Donovan paced near the exterior windows.

"We've been monitoring shipments of drugs along the east and west coast that tie back to Kalamazoo. We can trace deliveries on three different dates that correspond to private jet rentals this company made."

Bones snorted. Grady rolled his eyes. Donovan continued to pace.

"What are the dates?"

"February 16th of last year. January 1st of this year. And April 23rd of this year."

On the screen behind the agent, Tech typed in the details of each flight including passengers, plane staff, dates, times, and terminals.

"Well, it seems that the only thing those three flights have in common is the pilot," I said.

The agent smirked. "That's it? You drop a different suspect and expect us to move on to someone else?"

"The flight last year in February was me," Bones said. "I was flying out to my family's estate."

"January 1st was a whole crew of people, everyone in this room except Donovan, plus about a dozen more men and women," Grady said. "But we flew south, not east or west."

"April 23rd was just me," Donovan said. "But I was working with the FBI on a case. Unless I was carrying dope for your fellow Feds, I'm covered for that flight."

"And you expect me to believe you remember all those dates?" the agent asked.

"Turn around, Agent Leighton," I said, pointing to the screen behind him. "The information you've been looking for is on the screen behind you. I suggest you track down the pilot and ask him a few questions." I stood and moved toward the door. "And next time you need information from our company, save the taxpayers some money and ask."

I walked into the gym and scanned the room. Bridget had returned and was running laps with a few other trainees. The rest of them stood around talking.

"Trainees! Line up!" I yelled, calling their attention and pointing to the red line in the center of the room.

Most of the trainees immediately went to the red line and stood anxiously waiting. A few more dragged themselves over, looking annoyed. Two of the men glanced my way, but continued to talk and joke around.

"I'm Kelsey Harrison," I called out to them. "Lead investigator for Silver Aces Security. Line up, or get out." One of the men looked surprised and quickly joined the line. The other snorted and meandered to the line looking bored. "Do we have a problem?" I asked him.

He scanned my body slowly before raising his eyes to meet mine. "The only problem I see is that we're not in my bed."

"Interesting," I said as I maintained eye contact. "I thought the problem was that you were still on the premises." I turned toward the offices where several off-shift employees were watching. "Could one of you gentlemen escort this asshole to the dorms to collect his shit?"

Everyone laughed, and two of them jogged over and motioned for him to leave.

"Who the hell do you think you are?" the trainee yelled as he stalked over and leaned over me.

"A partner of this company," Donovan answered from somewhere behind me.

Grady walked over to stand in front of me, nose to nose with the trainee. "And my future wife, motherfucker."

"Calm down, cowboy." I pulled him back by his elbow. "You've had the trainees for a few weeks now. It's my turn to play."

The off-duty guards shoved the asshole toward the door. I walked down the line, stepping into each trainee's personal space to see how they'd react. Most stood military straight, appearing to be made of stone. When I stepped into Bridget's space, her body stayed frozen but the corners of her lips turned up. She was struggling not to laugh. The next two men and a woman passed first inspection. The next man looked me in the eyes with contempt. I finished moving down the line, reading the last two as bored.

"Donovan, Grady, if the two of you are ready for my feedback, I'm ready to give it."

"Do you want to go into my office?" Donovan asked.

"She wants it to be public." Grady said, answering for me.

"Whatever," Donovan said, shaking his head as he sighed.

"Bridget," I called out. "I'm starting with you because I know you."

"I'm ready," she called out in excitement, stepping forward with a bounce. "Hit me with your best shot."

Bones and Grady chuckled from behind me.

"Grady?" I called over my shoulder.

"Yeah, babe?"

"You're in charge of Bones."

"Shit," he mumbled, but I heard him moving.

"Why do I need a babysitter?" Bones growled.

"We don't need a lawsuit because you beat the crap out of someone."

I heard Donovan sigh and assumed he was moving closer to Bones as well.

"Bridget, you have a bruise circling your neck. Nice job with the make-up, but as you know, I have my own experience covering bruises. Who did it?"

Her grin fell, and she looked at me with a determined look in her eyes. She wasn't going to tell me.

"I'll only ask you one more time, and only because we're friends. Who put that bruise on your neck?"

Her eyes flashed with anger, burning brightly with unshed tears before she turned her head away defiantly.

"Anyone else care to answer the question for me?"

Trainee Drake stepped forward. "I have no proof, ma'am. But two days ago, Bridget was running down the dorm hall toward her room. She'd been crying. I tried to talk to her to find out what was wrong, but she refused to answer. I've noticed she's been purposely steering clear of trainee Henderson ever since. I've heard him make a few inappropriate comments about her since that day."

"Thank you, Drake," I said, nodding. "Did anyone else see or hear anything?"

Another man in line squirmed for a minute before stepping forward. "I witnessed the incident. Trainee Henderson pinned trainee Delany to the wall, holding her by the throat as he fondled her breast. I yelled at him, and he let her go."

"Fucker," Bones growled from behind me. I could hear Grady and Donovan grunt as they restrained him.

"Thank you, trainee Kemp. But why didn't you report the incident?"

"I didn't feel it was my place, ma'am."

"Hmm. Trainee, what is the most common security assignment that this firm takes?"

"Protection duty, ma'am."

"Who are we hired to protect?"

Dropping his shoulders in defeat as he answered, "Mostly single women."

"Yes. And by not coming forward, future clients—female clients—could've been targets of sexual assault by one of our own employees."

He slowly nodded, dropping his head to look at the floor.

"You and trainee Delany are dismissed. Go pack your bags."

Bridget walked toward me, head held high. "I didn't do anything wrong."

"You failed to report a dangerous man. This is a life and death business, Bridget. Loyalty to your team doesn't count if it puts our own clients in danger. You of all people should understand that."

Her chin trembled. "I thought I was doing the right thing by keeping quiet. Proving I could handle him on my own."

"And the next woman? What do you think her chances of fighting him off were?"

She held my stare for a good minute as the tears slipped past her guard.

"Donovan?" I called out.

"Yeah," he answered in a strained voice, still helping to hold Bones back.

"I'd like to recommend that both trainee Delany and trainee Kemp be considered for the next recruiting cycle if they wish to reapply. Both of them are learning a lesson that I don't think they'll ever forget."

"We'll consider their applications if they wish to reapply," Grady answered for him. "They've both been excellent candidates."

"Thank you," Kemp said, before throwing an arm over Bridget's shoulder and leading her out of the gym.

"Trainee Henderson." I smiled, stepping closer to him. "I suggest you forgo packing and run like hell. I'm not sure how much longer Donovan and Grady are going to be able to hold Bones. Bridget is *his* woman, whether she knows it or not."

Henderson's glare turned into a look of surprise. He glanced briefly at Bones before running toward the front doors. Hopefully, he had a spare set of keys hidden in his vehicle because as the doors to the gym closed behind him, Donovan and Grady lost their hold on Bones and he went running after him.

"As for the rest of you, your next assignment is to restrain Bones, so he doesn't kill Henderson. Good luck."

They stood stunned for a brief moment, eyes wide in shock, before they ran toward the exit.

"Work together as a team!" I called after them.

Grady laughed, throwing an arm around my shoulders. "That was mean."

"On-the-job training," Donovan said before turning to me. "Did the rest of the trainees pass?"

"You've got three more that lack initiative, but I'm sure Grady will eventually deal with them. And Grady's having a sit down with another one of the trainees to dig around his background. But after one child abductor, two DEA agents, and a sexual predator—maybe we should do the profiling during the initial interviews next time?" I turned to grin at Donovan and Grady who were both scowling. "Nice job, boys."

My cell phone rang, and I moved away to answer it. "Hey, Kierson. Sorry about earlier."

"I've become accustomed to your bitchiness," he said, snorting. "I got a call from your DEA agents. Seems they had your help in apprehending one of Nola's henchmen. Any clue what kids he kidnapped?"

"Off the record?"

"If we have to."

"Nicholas recognized him. I'd focus on where the guy lived around the time Nick was kept with Nola in New Orleans. I can't ask Nick to relive it by going through a pile of photos, though."

"I don't blame you. Poor kid has been through enough. I'll fly out and pressure the guy until he squeals."

"Thanks, Kierson. I owe you."

"You owe me a dozen at least," he said before hanging up on me.

"Is Nicholas okay?" Grady asked.

"I think so. I left him with Whiskey, but I need to get back."

"I'll be home in about an hour."

I nodded as I walked away, but before I got to the exit the war room door slammed open and Tech came charging out. *"Security alarm at the main house!"*

Chapter Seven

"What do you mean I can't kill him?" Whiskey argued, standing over Henderson's crumbled body, holding a gun to his head. "The law says that if someone breaks into your home intending to harm you, you have the right to shoot him."

"Not after you kicked his ass," Sara argued back.

"Language," Nicholas corrected her.

"Sara's right," Nana said. "You broke his leg, a few ribs, and maybe his collar bone. And he's unarmed, so I don't think you can shoot him."

"But that's not fair," Whiskey said, looking over his shoulder toward where we stood staring. He threw us a quick wink before he continued his argument. "What about the fact that he got blood all over the carpet? That's damage to personal property."

Sara giggled. "He wouldn't have bled all over if you wouldn't have beaten the snot out of him. Look at him. He's a mess."

"His cheekbone looks broken too," Nicholas said, leaning over to push a finger against Henderson's face.

"How can you tell under all that blood?" Sara asked, squatting down for a better look.

"This sucks." Whiskey fake pouted, holstering his gun and pulling the kids away from Henderson. "Get him out of here, boys! The kids say I'm not allowed to shoot him."

Donovan and Tech gathered Henderson from the floor, both grinning as they roughly pushed, pulled, and kicked him out of the house. He screamed in pain which made their grins widen.

"I'm not cleaning this mess," Nana told me before she strolled into the kitchen.

"My poor carpet," I said, looking at the once cream-colored carpeting now smeared with blood from the dining room into the living room.

Grady laughed. "I'll call Lisa. She can finally put her cleaning obsession to good use."

I turned to look at the kids. "You both okay?"

"It was *awesome!*" Nick said, jumping up and down in excitement. "That guy came running in and before he even saw us, Whiskey flipped him over—" Nicholas acted out the movements as he narrated "—and body slammed him into the floor! Then he kicked him before twisting his arm back and—"

"We heard it pop!" Sara yelled over Nicholas, just as excited.

"I was going to say that!" Nicholas complained.

"You were taking too long!"

"Don't fight!" I interrupted them before things escalated. "I don't want to hear you squabbling at each other right now."

"She started it—"

"Did not—"

"Run," Grady said, pushing me toward the back deck. "I've got the brats."

Grady interrupted them, asking for an update on their homework as I hurried out the sliding door. I spotted Whiskey at the far end, leaning against the rail, smoking a cigarette.

"Rewarding yourself?" I laughed, walking over to lean against the railing next to him.

"Trying to calm myself before I say something I shouldn't."

"You looked pretty calm after beating the crap out of that guy."

"Until I realized what would've happened if the kids were at home, alone, with a nanny."

I fell silent, thinking out that scenario. Whiskey was right. We had too many run-ins with bad men to leave the kids unprotected. "I'll talk to Anne and Grady. We can use one of the upstairs offices at Silver Aces Security as a classroom for the kids. They'll have ample protection."

"They need you." Whiskey slowly exhaled a stream of smoke. "Starting next week, I'll be working full-time again. They need you around to watch out for them."

"I can't," I said, shaking my head.

"You'll get past the panic attacks. You've gotten past worse."

"The panic attacks aren't the problem." I turned toward the field, leaning my head back to feel the sun on my face. "I've boxed myself into a life I don't even recognize."

"You have a great life," Whiskey said, looking confused.

"Does she?" Grady asked.

I stiffened at the sound of his voice, but I didn't turn around.

"Sure, we envy everything she has: a nice home, a big happy family, a smart healthy kid, great friends. But did Kelsey ever choose this life?"

"She created this life," Whiskey insisted. "Built it from the ground up. Hand-picked this family."

"Out of necessity," Grady said, placing a hand on my shoulder and rubbing the tense muscle between my shoulder and my neck. "She had to hide from Nola and keep busy. She built a life that she never planned on living." He moved a palm to my cheek and turned my face toward him. He saw the tears I was trying to hide. "And now she feels trapped."

I wanted to say something, anything, to yell and scream that it wasn't true, but I couldn't. I just stood there, seeing the pain in his eyes before he leaned in, kissed my forehead, and walked away.

He reentered the house, closing the sliding door behind him. I felt myself slowly sink to the deck floor.

"Shit." Whiskey sighed, sitting beside me. "I didn't know."

"I'm a horrible person."

His chuckle vibrated against my shoulder. "Not even close. You're just feeling lost at the moment. We've all been there, just for way simpler reasons."

"I don't know what to do." I heaved several deep breaths, trying to get control of my breathing.

"Maybe we can help," Anne said.

Anne, Alex, Katie, and Lisa walked toward us and squatted down beside me.

"We've packed your bags and called Kierson," Alex said. "He's short a profiler until he can convince Maggie to come back."

"You can meet him at the Detroit FBI office. He'd like your help with the scumbag trainee who used to work for Nola," Katie said.

"I'll take care of the kids," Anne added. "Even if I have to quit working at the store."

"Not necessary," Whiskey said, nudging my shoulder. "Kelsey had Sara place an employment ad for a full-time teacher to work with the kids. Within the first hour, twenty applicants applied. I'll do the interviews next week. And we're setting up a classroom at Headquarters, so they'll be safe."

"I'm so relieved." Anne exhaled a long breath. "I really didn't want to give up the store."

"Tech and I will take care of Carl," Alex said, still focused on me.

"And I'll get the blood out of the carpet." Lisa smiled, but it didn't reach her eyes. "I've already sprayed it to presoak."

"Then it's settled," Grady said, carrying out my suitcase. "I'll load the SUV, but you need to say goodbye to the kids."

He didn't look at me as he carried the bags around the corner of the deck and through the back door of the garage.

"He's so angry," I cried, holding my fingers against my lips to stop the air that whooshed out of my lungs.

"No, he's not," Alex said, leaning in to tilt my chin upward. "He's just trying to shield himself, luv. He knows he might lose you."

"We'll take care of him," Lisa said.

Katie smirked. "And kick his ass if he gets too down."

The sliding door opened again, and Nicholas stepped out. His eyes were swollen and red from crying. As everyone stepped back, I opened my arms, and he ran into them. We both cried as I rocked him, and everyone drifted away to give us some privacy.

"I love you," I whispered, stroking his hair. "More than you will ever know."

"Then stay," he cried. "Don't leave me."

My breath rattled in my lungs as the tears filled them. "I'm so sorry, Nick. I wish I could be the mother you need right now."

"You can. You are. Don't leave me."

"Look at me," I said, pulling him away from my chest and leaning my forehead against his. "I wouldn't leave if I didn't know that you were safe and loved here. You have Grady, Sara, and your aunts."

"It's not the same," he whined, wiping his cheek.

"I know it's not. But you'll be okay. I'll come back as soon as I can. And we'll talk on the phone every day, just like we have been. And you'll keep an eye on Sara and Carl for me. I trust you to watch out for them."

"You promise you'll come back?" he asked as he sniffled.

"Nuclear bombs couldn't keep me away." I kissed his forehead before lifting him in my arms and carrying him with me around the side of the house to the driveway.

Covering his face with kisses until a smile appeared, I told him I loved him again before passing him to Anne. I squatted in front of Sara and held my arms out. She grinned and wrapped her little arms around my neck.

"I'll miss you, little bug," I whispered.

"You'll be back. You always come back."

"You keep reminding Nicholas of that, okay?"

"Deal." She kissed my cheek and then ran over to Whiskey who lifted her into his arms.

I waved to everyone else, unable to say individual goodbyes, and walked around the SUV to where Grady was waiting. "I love you," I whispered.

"I know," he whispered back with a gravelly voice. "Be safe." He pulled me into his arms for a deep kiss that had me questioning whether I was doing the right thing by leaving. When the kiss ended, he opened the driver's door and gently pushed me toward the SUV, before he turned and walked toward the house.

My heart tore open as I slid behind the steering wheel and drove away.

Chapter Eight

"The blue streaks in your hair don't really scream FBI," Kierson muttered, signing me into the FBI satellite office in Detroit.

I grinned. "I don't plan on turning into one of you tight-ass suits any time soon."

The security guard working at the reception desk snorted.

"Classy," Kierson said, steering me through the metal detectors.

When the red lights and a siren went off, Kierson rolled his eyes and handed me a plastic tub.

"Seriously?" I asked, with a raised eyebrow. "Can't you just turn that thing off and let me pass?"

"You'll get everything back when we leave."

I unloaded my gun, placing it in the tub, followed by two switch blades and a taser. Kierson raised an eyebrow, and I sighed, pulling another knife from the underside of my bra and dropping it loudly in the tub.

"That can't be comfortable," Kierson laughed.

"Christmas present from Hattie. Katie helped her find a slim switchblade, and Hattie sewed in a sleeve for it into the base of my bras. I can get through most airports with security thinking that it's an under-wire bra."

Kierson scowled. "That's a federal offense."

"Good thing I have a few federal connections." I people watched as we waited for the elevator. "Genie here?"

"No. I asked her to stay in the Atlanta office. I'm not sure how much information we're going to get out of this guy. So far, he's not talking."

"Oh, he'll talk," I said, checking my hair in the reflection of the elevator as we rose to the eighteenth floor.

"You can't torture him," Kierson said, looking at me sideways.

"I don't need to." I stepped off the elevator and waited for Kierson to take the lead down multiple hallways, through several security doors, and finally into an interview surveillance room. The double-sided mirror provided a view of the six-by-nine room with Nola's goon cuffed to the table. "What do we know?"

"Not much," Kierson said, handing me a file from the nearby table. As I flipped through the file, Kierson provided me with the highlights. "Name is Axle Sorato. He's had a few arrests for assault, mostly domestic. He lived in the Midwest and might've been associated with the motorcycle club you obliterated a year ago."

"The Hell Hounds?" The Hell Hounds were a violent motorcycle club who at one point went to war with my family, trying to get to Anne and Sara. It ended with a shootout that left several members of their club in the morgue and two dozen more in prison.

Kierson nodded. "He wasn't part of the group arrested in Michigan, but he was affiliated with them at some point. He has the tats," he said, flipping to the pictures of Sorato's tattoos.

I easily recognized the Hell Hounds tats, but he had others that I flipped through. "What's this one?" I asked, pointing to an odd shaped cross with a key hole in the middle.

"No clue. Could mean anything," Kierson said, shrugging.

"What was his upbringing?" I asked, flipping to the back of the folder.

"Single mother, two sisters, father was in prison before Axle was out of diapers. They lived in Jacksonville, Florida most of his childhood, before relocating to Birmingham, Alabama when he was fifteen. His father was released a year later, but he killed a man within the first two weeks of freedom and landed right back in prison. Didn't even try to hide the murder."

"Who did he kill?"

"A priest." Kierson shook his head in disbelief.

"Got it." I read a few more paragraphs before closing the file. "I'm ready." I walked out of the room and through the next door. I held Sorato's stare as I moved to the chair on the other side of the table. "You've had a tricky life, Mr. Sorato," I said, shaking my head as I sat. "A priest, huh? Kind of a cliché if you ask me. The priest diddled you as a child, your mother moves the family away, your father kills the priest, and you follow your father's path into a life of violent crime. I'm unimpressed."

His glare hardened as his eyes narrowed.

"Here's the part I do care about," I said, taking the pile of photos I had carried in and spreading them on the table. "I want to know which of these children you were responsible for kidnapping and selling."

"Fuck you."

"Pause, Mr. Sorato," I whispered, leaning toward him. "Think this out for a moment. You know *who* I am. You know *what* I'm capable of. I killed Nola. I killed so many Hell Hounds that I never bothered to tally the numbers. I know people who can get to you whether you're locked up or running free. And most of them owe me personal favors." I leaned back, away from the table, and relaxed in my chair. "You don't want to make me drag my son into a police station to look at the photos of the children you sold—because it will cost you. Whether by my hands or the hands of my family, you'll pay a very high price."

"Ms. Harrison," Kierson said over the intercom. "May I have a moment?"

"No," I answered without my eyes leaving Sorato's.

I sat watching him in silence for a long time. Beads of sweat formed on his brow. He knew my reputation. He knew I was well connected. He finally leaned back in his chair. "I never wanted to hurt the kids."

"But you did," I said, pushing the photos closer to him. "Now you'll burn for it."

Sorato pulled several photos out of the pile, and Kierson came into the room with a notepad and pen. I stood to leave the room.

"They call you *demonio de muerte*, a death demon," Sorato said.

"I've been called worse." I shrugged a shoulder before walking out.

~*~*~

Following the hallway to the end, I waved my visitor badge in front of a security panel. The light turned green, and I opened the glass door into a large room filled with desks and people. I stole a chair at an unoccupied desk and pulled my cell phone out of my handbag. I almost called Tech out of habit but caught myself, calling Genie instead.

"Please tell me Kierson wasn't pulling my leg, and you're filling in while Maggie's away," she answered.

"Demonio de muerte at your service. At least temporarily while Maggie's figuring shit out."

"The demon of death?"

"It's not important," I said as I grinned to myself. "Axle Sorato caved, but it was way too easy. What am I missing?"

"I sent Kierson everything I had. The information available on him is pretty light. The only good quality in his otherwise miserable life, was that he sends his mother money."

"How much money?"

"Wires her a couple thousand every few months. The last wire was three weeks ago to the tune of three-thousand five-hundred dollars."

"Nola and the Hell Hounds are out of business. Where's he getting the cash?"

"No legitimate income that I found. He visited his father two months ago, though. Daryl Sorato is serving twenty-five years in Jacksonville for the murder of a local priest. Want me to pull the visiting room security video?"

"Not necessary. They would've talked in riddles. I'll call you back."

I hung up and called Mickey McNabe, a Miami crime boss and former convict. We had an odd friendship of sorts, held together by a web of violent history. Mickey was far from being one of the good guys, but there were lines he'd never cross and after the murder of his only daughter, his vengeful streak against child molesters was larger than my own.

As I listened to the phone ring, a skinny, pale man in a navy suit walked over and stared down at me. "That's my desk."

"So?" I raised an eyebrow, looking up at him.

He looked confused for a moment before sighing and walking away. I smiled, propping my boots up on the corner of the desk as I leaned back in the swivel chair.

"What now?" Mickey answered.

"Long time, no talk. Did you miss me?"

Mickey chuckled. "That's a trick question. How's my *only* cop friend?"

"Ex-cop. And I find myself a bit turned around at the moment. I'm sitting in an FBI office trying to decipher a child predator. He's being too cooperative, and I've got a bad vibe."

"And I was your first call?"

"Honestly, you were my second call, but you have a unique set of skills that could assist me."

"I'm listening."

"Seems the goon I'm talking with was recently in contact with his father, Daryl Sorato, who rents a room at Jacksonville. After their visit, the son drifted into another business arrangement of some kind. I'm trying to find the root of that business arrangement."

Mickey chuckled, but it sounded a little sinister. "I'll make some inquiries."

"Appreciate it. Tell Daryl that demonio de muerte says hello."

"Death demon," Mickey said as he laughed. "I like it." He disconnected.

I set my cell phone on the desk and looked at the ring on my right hand. The gems sparkled under the harsh fluorescent lighting. I lifted my hand, turning the ring in circles with my other hand. I looked up, finding the agent whose desk I had confiscated glaring at me from across the room. He was working from a table next to the coffee pot. I offered him a finger wave before I picked my phone up again and called Maggie.

"Agent O'Donnell," she answered on the first ring.

"You sound like all the other drones."

"I feel like a drone. I'm surrounded by stuck-up suits."

"I'm temping as a profiler for Kierson in your absence. I'm surrounded by the same ilk. What I wouldn't give to see the looks on their faces if Alex strolled in wearing one of his more colorful outfits."

"That would be a sight. Why are you temping? What happened with Silver Aces Security?"

"Nothing. I needed a change of scenery."

"Let me guess. The constant glee of others was making you want to punch something?"

"Pretty damn close," I admitted. "What are you working on?"

"Nothing. I'm stuck at a desk while I wait for another reassignment."

"Heard you got your boss demoted."

"I had nothing to do with it! Why doesn't anyone believe me?"

"Because it sounds like a lie."

"Well, I didn't. But someday you and I have to have drinks at a particular bar with a wicked-ass bartender. She's a criminal through and through, but she's got style. She's the one who tanked the agent's career."

"I'll check my social calendar. It sounds interesting. Meanwhile, can you spare the time to do some research for me?"

"As long as Kierson doesn't find out, no problem. What do you need?"

"I need more information on a man we have in custody, Axle Sorato. Start with his sisters. Genie can get you their addresses. I need a history on this asshole: friends, business associates, behavior, trade skills. The list of associates I have are already dead."

"Who do we already know about?"

"Hell Hounds and Nola."

"Cheerful start," she said. "I'll run with it and let you know where I land. Do you need me to check into his parents?"

"His mother profiles as the type to stick her head in the sand and hide from reality. I already have someone digging into his father. He's a guest of Jacksonville prison."

"Mickey." I visualized her nodding her approval. "All right. I'll root out the rest of the intel you need."

She disconnected the call, and I swiveled in the chair as I replayed the meager paper trail in my head. Kierson returned with four names and pictures of the victims. I checked the disappearance dates, rolled my eyes, and made my way back to the holding cell.

~*~*~

"*Who do you think you're dealing with, ass-wipe?*" I asked, bracing my hands on the table and leering over him. "These cases are too old and too few. We can trace back every wire transfer you've made to your mother over the years and four victims don't account for that much green. Either confess your shit, right now, or face the consequences."

"I got nothing else to say," Sorato said, trying to cross his arms over his chest, but the long cuffs attached to the table prevented him.

"Kierson," I said, knowing he was standing somewhere behind me.

"Yes, Harrison?"

"This beautiful boy—the second victim—was from Miami. Transfer Mr. Sorato to the Miami correctional facility. I have some friends who'll take special care of him there."

"You can't do that!" Sorato said, trying to stand. "You arrested me in Michigan!"

I shrugged, turning to leave. "You didn't commit a crime in Michigan that we're aware of."

As I opened the door, I heard Kierson offer Axle another chance to save himself. I walked down the hall and back into the main room. The desk I had borrowed earlier was occupied by its owner. I could've scared him off, but I decided to grab a cup of coffee instead. I poured the sludge into a cup, but after seeing the thick oily mixture floating on top, I tossed it into the nearby trashcan.

"I have a fresh pot in my office," an older man in a suit said as he walked by.

I followed him between the desks and around the corner into a glass-walled office.

He pointed to the pot. "Help yourself."

"You look familiar," I said, pouring coffee into one of the available ceramic cups.

"We met in Florida. I'm Special Agent in Charge, Jack Tebbs."

"Ah, yes. I remember now. You backed me when I was arguing with a lazy Fed."

"He's still lazy. But he's the nephew of a Senator, so the FBI's stuck with him."

I snorted. "Figures. What brings you to Detroit?" I confiscated a guest chair as he sat behind his desk.

"I'm on loan until they hire someone to run this office. The previous agent in charge retired. Hopefully, they'll find a replacement soon. I'm not interested in spending a winter season in Michigan."

"Some people say it's beautiful here in the winter."

"And yet you carefully exclude yourself from that population."

"I'm not a fan of the cold, but as long as you don't have to go outside, it is pretty." I turned my attention to a bookcase on the far wall, scanning the pictures on display.

"I hear Kierson hired you to consult with a detainee. How's that going?"

I looked back at Jack as I answered. "Axle Sorato is talking. We'll get his past crimes, but he's holding something more recent back that he doesn't want us to know about."

"At least some of the victim's families will have closure."

"The lies of a cop," I whispered more to myself than him.

"Come again?" he asked, sitting up straighter and turning hard eyes on me.

"It's the lie we tell ourselves." I shrugged, leaning back into the leather chair. "As if finding the truth somehow lessens the pain. It doesn't. It can't. Maybe finding the buried bodies helps in some small way, but when your life is ripped to pieces, nothing is ever the same. It hardens you. It breaks part of your soul. It crushes your belief that good outweighs evil."

The room was silent as I stared into my coffee.

"Who did you lose, Harrison?" Tebbs whispered.

"Myself," I whispered back, getting up and walking out of the office.

I spotted Kierson standing in the middle of the room looking around.

"Done already?" I asked as I walked over.

"Where were you?"

"Jack's office."

Kierson's eyes widened as he looked toward the hallway. "Please tell me I still have a job."

"As far as I know," I said, shrugging and drinking my coffee. "What did you get out of Axle?"

"I assigned two other agents to get the rest of this joker's confession. We need to hop on a plane and head to North Dakota."

"Can I take my coffee?"

He released a frustrated growl and walked out of the room. I carefully hid my smile as I followed, deciding to keep the borrowed coffee mug.

Chapter Nine

"What are we walking into this time?" I asked as I fastened my seatbelt. I was relieved to find that we weren't flying commercial and instead occupied a cozy six-seater jet. I wiggled back and forth into the soft leather seats.

Kierson had stopped speaking to me shortly after leaving the FBI office. It seemed the gun I had checked in with security was from my *unregistered-and-missing-serial-numbers* stash. According to the other agents, carrying such a gun was a no-no. After an extensive argument, I took my knives and told them they could keep the gun. Kierson was less than impressed by my generosity.

"Kie-rr-son..." I teased. "You'll have to talk to me, eventually. You might as well give in now. What's the case?"

He sighed dramatically but handed me a tablet. "A possible kidnapping. Laurie Simmons, mother to Caleb Simmons, went missing sometime early this afternoon. But when the police started investigating, they discovered Laurie Simmons doesn't exist. Her driver's license and birth certificate are fake. The local cops have no idea what's going on. The only things they know for sure are that when Caleb got out of school, his mother was gone, and there were signs of forced entry at the house."

"Definitely forced entry," I said, scrolling through the pictures. "And, they're on the run."

"What?"

"Laurie has go bags stacked in the corner of the bedroom. They don't have more than a handful of personal items lying around. How long had she been living there? I'm guessing not more than a year."

"Nine months," Kierson answered. "You think she was a criminal?"

I shrugged. "Not everyone on the run committed a crime. Parental kidnapping is a possibility, though."

Kierson called Genie and asked her to look into a match to any open parental kidnapping cases.

"Tell her to focus on domestic abuse situations." I zoomed in on the blood splatters near an overturned chair. Laurie didn't leave without a fight. I had no doubt the blood was hers, but it wasn't enough to kill her.

Kierson repeated my request to Genie before hanging up.

"The kid can tell us more if the locals haven't scared the bejeebers out of him before we get there."

Kierson snorted as he reclined his chair and closed his eyes. "You better sleep while you can. It's going to be a long day."

There was no way I'd chance sleeping on a plane across the aisle from Kierson with my habit of having violent nightmares. He'd likely handcuff me and have me transferred to a mental ward and fitted for a straitjacket.

I waited until the plane leveled off before going back to the beginning of the electronic file and reviewing every detail. Several hours later, as the plane dropped elevation, Kierson woke and straightened his already straight tie.

"It's like an alarm clock, isn't it?" I asked. "The plane's descent."

"I sleep more on planes than I do in a bed. Welcome to my life."

"I don't get it," I said, passing him the tablet. "Why were you called in on this case? Why isn't the nearby FBI satellite office taking it?"

"Donovan called," Kierson admitted while cringing slightly. "Laurie's boyfriend is one of his employees. He wanted you on the case. I'm just along for the ride."

"Which employee?"

"Casey Roberts."

I nodded, remembering Casey. "He was assigned to the ranches in Texas for a few weeks. I don't know him well, but Grady does."

"That's the other part I left out," Kierson said as the plane smacked hard onto the runway.

"Son of a bitch," I cursed as the tires locked up and screeched against the tarmac.

Kierson's shoulders sagged. "Yeah. I was afraid you'd be pissed."

I shot him a glare as I unbuckled my seatbelt and pulled my carry-on bag out of the upper cabinet.

"Welcome to North Dakota," the flight attendant announced, opening the plane's door.

I ignored her as I stomped down the portable metal stairs. I heard Kierson apologize for my rudeness and follow after me.

"Wait a minute!" Kierson yelled as I continued across the asphalt. "Fine. Storm off. But our rental is this way!"

As much as I wanted to continue stomping my anger against the tarmac, I had no clue where we were other than the state of North Dakota. I grimaced and turned to follow Kerson to the SUV waiting in the other direction. He didn't look to see whether I was still behind him as he took the keys and loaded his bags in the back, leaving the hatch open for my bag. As I slid into the passenger seat, he pulled away from the curb, following the instructions on the GPS unit.

"Look, I get it. You needed some space. *Whatever*. But now a woman's life is on the line, and everyone is counting on you to help. Grady's not here to stalk you."

"Every time I turn around, I'm pushed or pulled in another direction."

"And you thought working with the FBI would be different?"

"I just needed a distraction."

"Then find the missing woman, and we'll jump on the next plane out."

"I knew that plane was too nice for the Feds."

"I'm no fool. Someone offers me a ride on a private jet, I'm taking it."

I rolled my eyes, looking out the window. "Where are we going first?"

"Crime scene, then police station. Caleb Simmons is under police protection until they can find his mother or next of kin."

~*~*~

It was a twenty-minute drive to reach the small town, and another five minutes before we parked in front of a cottage-style house at the end of a residential street. Grady, Casey, and two cops were standing in the driveway yelling at each other.

"Distract them for me," I told Kierson as I pulled a pair of latex gloves out of my shoulder bag and slipped them on.

"I'm going to regret this," Kierson mumbled as he slipped out of the SUV and joined the circus.

As Kierson got the officers to turn their backs to the house to talk to him, I slipped under the crime scene tape and inside. The front door opened to the kitchen. The sun was starting to set, casting shadows, but I didn't dare turn on any of the lights. I carefully stepped over the fallen chair and glanced at the blood smear on the refrigerator. At the end of the short hallway was a bathroom. A bedroom door was on each side of the hall. I opened the door to the right and discovered the boy's room. Other than a twin-size bed, the room was empty. No posters or pictures. No toys scattered about. I opened the closet, and as expected, I found two duffle bags with the zippers open showing stacks of boys' clothes. Next to them was a trash bag filled with two days' worth of dirty laundry.

I stepped out of the room and crossed over to the mother's room, finding it much the same. The only difference was the gun with the scratched out serial number in the drawer of the nightstand. I stuffed the snub-nose revolver into the back of my jeans and pulled my jacket down to cover it. It was unlikely that the police had done a thorough inventory yet.

I moved over to the closet, opening the door and searching the duffle bags. At the bottom of one of the bags, I found an envelope with Casey's name printed on the outside. I paused, considering my options. The right thing to do would be to give him the envelope, but I didn't think she intended for him to see it until the next time she had to run. I shook off my guilt and opened the envelope, pulling out the letter.

I'm sorry. I can't explain, but we had to leave. It was too dangerous for us to stay. Know that I care deeply for you and wish things were different. But I have to do what is right for my son—no matter the cost. Don't look for us. Please.

Love, Laurie

"Shit," I said to myself, stuffing the letter back into the envelope and sliding it into my pocket.

Walking back through the small house, I pulled the curtain back to see if the deputies were facing the house. Grady saw the movement and gave me a small nod before he shoved Kierson into one of the cops. The cops scurried to keep the two men separated as I slipped out of the house and back into the SUV. Once seated, I leaned out the door and whistled, gaining everyone's attention.

"This is getting us nowhere. Agent Kierson, take me to the police station."

"Fine," Kierson said, glaring at Grady and storming over to the rental.

When we were turning on main street, Kierson smiled. "That was fun. Did you find anything?"

"Go bags. She was definitely on the run. She had a Dear John letter ready to leave behind for Casey when the time came to split."

"Shit. He's not very stable at the moment. I'm not sure how well he'll handle that."

"No worries. I pocketed the letter."

"That's evidence tampering."

"Good thing you're an accomplice. Saves me worrying about you turning me in."

Kierson's smile was long gone, and he punched the steering wheel. He squealed the tires as he pulled into the lot behind the police station and parked. I exited the vehicle, leaving him to deal with his hissy fit in his own way, and walked over to the truck Grady was getting out of.

"I need you to hide something for me." I pulled the gun from the back of my jeans, handing it to him. "Didn't figure the police or Kierson needed to know she had an unregistered gun."

Grady palmed the gun and slid it under the rental truck's seat as Casey got out of another truck and stormed our way.

"He's going to lose it," Grady whispered.

"Hey, Casey," I said, greeting him.

Casey nodded, but his eyes were on fire with a whirlwind of emotions. "Thanks for coming, Kelsey. I'm not getting through to the local cops that Laurie's not the type to run off and leave Caleb."

"I believe you. But I need you to reel it in, because this next step is really going to suck. If you want my help to find Laurie, you'll need to take a step back from the case and let me handle it."

"You expect me to sit on my ass while the woman I love is missing?" His anger had every muscle in his body knotted and ready for a fight.

"If you go in there with me, Caleb is going to latch on to you, and I'm not going to be able to get a read on him. I need to see him first, away from you."

"But he trusts me. He *needs* me!"

"I'm sure he does." I placed a hand on his forearm, hoping to steady his emotions as I explained. "But Laurie and Caleb have been living on the run. And he knows his mom didn't want you to know. That makes him *less likely* to tell you the truth. I'm a stranger, a woman, not a cop, but someone of authority. He might confide in me if you're not around."

"Shit," Casey said, running a hand through his hair. "I knew something was off, but hiding? On the run? What the hell?"

"Give Kelsey a chance to go in first," Grady said to him, lying a hand on his shoulder.

Casey gave a brief nod as he started to pace back and forth. I led Kierson into the police station, knowing I wouldn't have long with the boy before Casey would charge inside. "Get me access to that kid," I whispered, stepping aside for Kierson to flash his badge at the desk officer.

The scream of a child had me walking through the open doorway into a large room. The boy was huddled on the floor in the corner and screamed again when one of the officers went to hand him a cup of cocoa. The officer stepped back, and the boy quit screaming. I took the cup and nodded for the officer to step away. He gladly did so but kept his eyes on us.

When I approached, the boy leaned to the side to watch everyone behind me. I sat on the floor next to him and handed him the cocoa. I sat there, not saying anything as he scanned each cop, jumping anytime someone entered the room.

"Hi, Caleb. I was at your house today," I said, leaning against the wall to watch the room.

Caleb glanced at me before turning his attention back to the room.

"It reminded me of when my cousin was younger and lived with me. We had to be ready to leave if something happened. Our bags were always packed." He turned to watch me, his eyes narrowing. "And we *always* had a plan. If something happened to me, there was someplace she was supposed to go or someone specific she was supposed to call."

The boy nodded before quickly turning away.

"I'm going to find your mom, Caleb. But until I do, I need to know what the emergency plan is."

He glanced up at me again, tears filling his big eyes. He set the cup of cocoa on the floor beside him before opening the zipper on his backpack. I took the piece of paper he handed me and read the note.

If anything happens to me, I give Casey Roberts full rights and guardianship over my son, Caleb Simmons. Signed: Laurie Simmons.

The note was notarized.

"Is there anything else? Are you supposed to tell Casey anything special?"

Caleb scanned the room again. "We need to run," Caleb whispered.

"I'll let Casey know. We'll get you out of here. But first, I need your help. Is it your father? Is he the one your mom is scared of?"

His eyes widened, but he nodded yes.

"And is he like them? A cop?"

"Like him—" Caleb pointed.

I followed the direction that Caleb was pointing. Agent Kierson was standing at the end of the row of desks with a hand cocked up on his hip, exposing his gun and badge.

"Like him, how?" I asked Caleb. "The suit? Or the badge?"

"Both," Caleb whispered back.

"Do you know where your father works?"

He shook his head no. I wasn't sure if he was telling the truth, but he was shutting down.

I pulled myself up and grabbed Caleb's backpack before holding out a hand for him. He looked up at me for a long moment before standing and taking my hand. I led him across the room toward Kierson and the Chief of Police.

"Do you know Eleanor Vannet?" I asked the Chief.

"Sure," he answered. "She's our court clerk."

"She notarized the note from Caleb's mother giving Casey Roberts guardianship," I said, holding the short note out for him to review.

"Kurt! Call Elly down at the courthouse and confirm she remembers witnessing this," he said, passing the letter to another officer.

Caleb released my hand and wrapped both arms around my leg, cowering away from the officers as they moved past. I reached down and stroked his soft blond curls.

"It's legit, Chief," the deputy said, returning with the note.

I took the note before the Chief could. "Casey's going to need this for his lawyer and the school. You understand, I'm sure." I started leading Caleb out of the station with me.

"Where are you heading with him?"

"Casey's in the parking lot," I answered, not turning around.

As soon as Caleb saw Casey, he took off running and jumped into his arms. I motioned for Kierson and Grady to follow me over to the other side of the parking lot while the Chief talked to Casey.

"We've got a huge problem," I said in a low voice.

"What else is new," Grady said, rubbing the back of his neck.

"They were running from Caleb's father."

Kierson shrugged. "You already suspected parental kidnapping."

"Yeah. But I never guessed the guy wears a gun, a badge, and a suit."

"Shit," Grady swore, turning to look toward Casey and Caleb.

"This piece of paper gives Casey temporary custody," I said, handing him the notarized note. "They need to run. It's what she told Caleb to tell Casey."

A black SUV pulled into the lot and Grady waved an arm for them to stop. I recognized them as employees of Silver Aces Security. Donovan must have sent reinforcements. Grady said a few brief words to them. They nodded, staying in the vehicle. Grady walked over to Casey and pulled him by the arm away from the Chief. He talked to him in a low voice as he guided him over to the SUV, opened the door, and gently pushed them inside. When the door closed, the tinted windows rose, and the SUV left as quickly as it had arrived.

The Chief sputtered in shock as he watched it drive away before he started ranting at Grady. Kierson walked over to smooth the ruffled feathers. I called Genie and updated her to search for law enforcement officers. Then I called Tech and had him do the same.

The sun had set, and I was running out of energy. I didn't have a choice but to keep going though. None of us did. Laurie was still out there. I didn't want to think about what would happen to her if we didn't find her in time.

Chapter Ten

Thirty minutes later, Kierson and Grady were still talking to the Chief. I walked over and pulled the keys Grady had hanging from his front pocket. He nodded and turned back to the Chief as I slid into the truck and left.

I followed the street lights back into town and found the diner where Laurie worked. I jumped out of the truck and walked inside, nodding at a few friendly faces as I approached the customer counter and took a seat.

"What can I get ya, hon?" the waitress asked as she walked by.

"Coffee, black, and whatever information you can provide on Laurie Simmons."

She glanced at me for a second before she finished filling her tray with the waiting food, walking off to deliver it.

"You a cop?" one of the other customers asked.

"No. I used to be. I work as an investigator for Silver Aces Security in Michigan."

"Ain't that the company that Casey Roberts works for?" another customer asked.

"Yes, sir. Same one. Casey asked for my help to find Laurie."

"Damn," the waitress said, returning to pour a cup of coffee for me. "She's really missing, then? Where's Caleb?"

"He's with Casey, but Laurie's definitely missing. When was her last shift?"

"This mornin'. She opens for breakfast and only takes a break to walk Caleb down to the school."

"What time did she leave today?"

"Near two o'clock, I'd say," she answered, placing a fist on her hip.

"Not today," one of the customers from a booth said. "She must have left early today. I was in town around one o'clock picking up supplies and saw her crossing the street to walk down her block. She seemed jumpy. I waved, but she didn't wave back. She kept looking over her shoulder."

"Did anyone else see her this afternoon?" I asked the other customers.

Everyone shook their head no.

"I need everyone to send text messages to everyone you know. Ask them if they were in the diner when Laurie left today. If they were, I need them to come in and talk to me or one of my coworkers."

Everyone hurried to grab their phones and help. The waitress called the other employees who had worked the earlier shift and asked them to come in. As people started to arrive, Grady and Kierson showed up and helped interview everyone.

~*~*~

Two dozen interviews later, we had no new leads. The bells on the front door jingled and a middle-aged woman held the door open for a petite elderly woman with a cane.

"I knew he was no good!" the little old lady yelled, waving her cane in the air. "He had that look in his eyes!"

"Mom, what are you going on about?" the middle-aged woman asked. "And why are we at the diner near nine at night?"

I jumped up, pulling out a chair for the elderly woman. "Is this about Laurie, ma'am? You saw a man with her?"

"He looked shifty!" she barked, sliding into the chair. "I told Laurie to stay put, and I'd call the cops. *But, nooo*... She said she knew him and not to worry 'bout it."

"Where was he when you saw him?" I asked as I slid back into my own chair across from her.

"Standing right on the other side of that-there winda'," she said, pointing to the side window. "Just staring at her with that mean looking grin on his face. I've known me a few of those mean ones in my days. Best-ta steer clear of 'em. But Laurie wouldn't listen. No, sirree. She took off her apron and headed out da back door."

"What did the man look like?" Kierson asked, holding out a pen and a pad of paper.

"Real slick type," she answered, driving the end of her cane against the floor a few times. "Like a used car salesman." She turned to look over at the diner's counter. "No offense, Fred."

"Not the first time you've insulted me, Mable," the customer at the counter said, shaking his head.

"Pardon me, ma'am," Grady said, sliding smoothly into the chair next to Mable and pulling out his country-boy charm. He stretched an arm across the back of her chair as he winked at me. "By chance could you tell us what color his hair was? What he was wearing? How tall or old he was?"

"Well, aren't you somethin'." She smiled sweetly, turning to face him. "Well, let me think on it some. I'm not as quick as I used to be." She leaned closer to him. "But I'm betting he was late thirties or early forties, not much older than that on account of he still had a full head of dark hair. Didn't see a speck of grey in it. I couldn't tell what he was wearing on account of the sign in the winda was blocking most of him exceptin' his head."

"So only his head was visible above the sign?" I asked.

"About right," she said to Grady as if he'd asked the question. "Maybe an inch or two of his neck."

Kierson walked outside and stood in front of the window. His chin was level with the top edge of the sign. He walked back in. "I'm five foot eleven, so he's six foot to six foot two?"

"I reckon," Mable agreed.

"Did you see him leave? See which direction he went?" Grady purred, grabbing her attention again.

"Wish'n I did, but Laurie dropped a glass when she saw him. Spilt water on my new shoes. By the time I looked again, he was gone. That's when I warned her that he seemed like one of those mean ones, and we should ring the cops."

"Anything else you can remember? Anything at all?" I asked.

"His eyes," she answered, leaning onto the table and lowering her voice. "His hair was dark, blackish-brown like, but his eyes were an eerie light blue. Seemed a strange mix. Like he was a mutt or something."

I was taking a drink of my coffee when she called the man a mutt. The coffee went down the wrong way, and I started to cough.

Mable's daughter stepped over to me and beat on my back a few times. "You get used to her inappropriateness. Nothing she says fazes me anymore."

"Your teenage years were a nightmare, weren't they?" I asked, looking up at her.

"It was a living horror show." She turned back to her mother. "Come on, Mom. Time to get home."

"I'll leave when I'm ready," she snapped.

"Fine. But you're going to miss the late-night news. And I didn't set the recorder."

"I guess I've bothered these good folks long enough for one night. You best drive me home. But don't dawdle like you did coming here. You drive slower than an old lady."

Mable continued to bitch as she pulled herself up and moved with the use of her cane out the door. The daughter held the door open and waved goodbye to everyone before following her out. I looked down at my coffee which was half empty, contemplating a refill. Instead, I grinned and reached into my handbag, pulling out a pint of whiskey. Grady slid his cup next to mine. I poured a shot in each our glasses. Kierson disconnected a call he had taken and set his own cup down for a top off.

"You never cease to surprise me, Kierson," I said as I added a shot and slipped the bottle back into my shoulder bag.

"You might want to drink straight from the bottle when you hear what happened," Kierson said before he took a big drink.

"Rip the Band-Aid off," I said, bracing myself for bad news.

"Axle Sorato committed suicide in holding."

I sat back in my chair, looking up at Kierson to see if he was joking. He wasn't.

Suicide didn't fit with the man I'd spoken with earlier in the day. Axle Sorato was afraid, but I didn't see any signs of desperation or depression. When we left Detroit, Axle was still looking for an angle to get himself out of the situation he'd landed in. He hadn't even asked for a lawyer.

"*Bull-shit*," I said.

"Hung himself. It happens."

"I'm not saying he's not dead. I'm saying that if he's dead—*it wasn't a suicide*. I'd bet my best pair of black boots on it."

Kierson stared at me and then looked at his phone. "Damn."

Grady reached over the table and freed the pint of whiskey from my handbag, uncapping it and handing it to Kierson. Kierson took a swig before passing it back and making another call. "Special Agent Tebbs, I need a favor, sir," he said as he walked out the front door.

"Who's Axle Sorato?" Grady asked, taking a drink from the bottle before passing it to me.

"Nola's former goon who was pretending to be a trainee this morning," I answered before taking a drink.

"You interviewed him?"

"I got him to start spilling and then left him with Kierson. Something was off though."

"What do mean?" he asked, taking the bottle back for another drink.

"I'm not sure. He was giving us a boatload of historical crimes but kept us at arm's length from anything more recent. I have Genie and Maggie tracking down friends and relatives. And I called Mickey McNabe to reach out to Axle's father who's in prison in Florida."

Grady was passing the pint back, but upon hearing Mickey's name he changed his mind and downed a good inch of the bottle. I snagged the bottle, capped it, and dropped it back into my bag.

"Does Kierson know any of this?"

"No," I said, shaking my head. "I didn't want to overwhelm him."

Grady snorted, pulling himself up from his chair. "Drop some cards and then let's go find a place to crash for the night."

I pulled a pile of business cards out of my shoulder bag and passed them around, asking everyone to call me if they had any more details. Fred the car salesman told us where to find a bed-and-breakfast and said he'd give them a ring to let them know we were on the way since it was getting late.

We paid our bill, left a generous tip, and waved goodbye to the last remaining customers before we slipped outside.

"Thank you, sir," Kierson said into his phone as he paced the sidewalk outside the restaurant. He slid the phone into his jacket pocket and shook his head. "That was not the most pleasant conversation I've had today."

"I'm driving Grady's rental to a B&B. Follow us out," I said as I walked to the driver's side of the truck.

"I could've driven," Grady said, yawning as he slid inside and pulled his seatbelt on.

"You're exhausted, and you just chugged a half pint of whiskey."

"You have a point." He leaned his head back and closed his eyes.

Chapter Eleven

"Three rooms, please," Grady said to the innkeeper.

"We're not sharing a room?"

"Hell, no." Grady passed his credit card to the woman behind the reception counter. "At least six mysteries are roaming around in that head of yours right now. You won't sleep until you fall over. If we share a room, I'll feel obligated to distract you with sex—and I'm too damn tired."

"I don't think she wanted to know all of that," I said, nodding toward the innkeeper.

Kierson snorted. "She gets paid to hear inappropriate crap. I don't."

"I'm Mrs. Androsky, but everyone calls me Mrs. A." The innkeeper smiled politely, placing two keyrings with room numbers on the counter but keeping the third in her hand. "I don't usually have more than one or two rooms booked at a time. I'll have to clean the third room."

I took the third set of keys from her. "Find me a dust rag, a vacuum, and glass cleaner. I can clean while I think. No reason for you to stay up."

"I couldn't," she said, shaking her head.

"You can," Grady said through a yawn. "It will help wear her down. You'll be doing us all a favor."

She still seemed unsure but pulled the cleaning bucket and vacuum out of the closet. Grady carried the vacuum and both our overnight bags up the stairs. I followed him with the cleaning bucket, stopping at the door with the number two painted on the front.

"You've got until I'm undressed to get the vacuuming done," Grady said before unlocking the next door down.

Kierson chuckled, walking past us to the last door at the end of the hall. "Mrs. A said we could help ourselves to the kitchen. I'm going to drop my bags off then make some coffee if you want to meet me downstairs."

"We'll see how the cleaning goes," I replied, dragging everything through the door into my room. "Oh my!"

"What's wrong?" Grady called out.

"My room. It's ah—pink."

Grady and Kierson walked over to stand behind me. A large bed with a pink canopy sat center of the room. The other furniture was bright white, but the walls were covered with human-size pink flowers. The men laughed before walking away and entering their own rooms.

"This room doesn't need to be cleaned; it needs to be doused in battery acid," I mumbled to myself.

~*~*~

Even though it was against my cleaning code, I vacuumed first, then dusted. The bed had a dust cover that I carefully rolled back before laying it in the hallway to take downstairs later. Entering the small bathroom, I spent another five minutes doing a quick wipe down before I washed my face and dragged my hair into a messy bun. Back in the bedroom, I walked over to the far wall, pulled back the thick, room-darkening curtains and opened the window. The temperature had dropped, but it was still warm enough to allow some fresh air to move around the room. I grabbed my phone and laptop and curled up in the Queen Anne chair to check my email and voicemail messages.

Tech had left me a voicemail saying to check my email. Genie had left me the same message. I opened the laptop and checked my email. The email from Genie was a list of over a hundred parental abduction cases involving a father who was in law enforcement and a boy of the approximate age as Caleb.

"Insane," I said to myself, shaking my head.

Before diving into the list, I switched over to read Tech's email. He had Donovan reach out to Casey for a picture of Caleb. The employees at Silver Aces Security split up Genie's list and found two possible matches. Tech included only the two names and said Genie was working backgrounds.

My laptop dinged, alerting me to another email. I moved back to my inbox and read the new message. Tech confirmed with Casey that the woman he knew as Laurie Simmons was McKenzie Griffith. Caleb's real name was Shawn. And his father, Brian Griffith, was a U.S. freaking Marshal.

I replied to make sure Casey was deep underground and to tell him to contact Katie if needed. They'd know I meant regarding fake IDs, though I hoped it wouldn't come to that. Katie was good with the IDs, but the U.S. Marshals hid witnesses for a living. They knew all the tricks, because they invented most of them. "Shit, shit, shit," I cursed, thinking of all the ways our involvement could backfire.

A light knock on my door pulled my attention from my laptop.

"Come in."

"I'm hoping you have more booze in your bag," Kierson said after he opened the door.

"You heard?"

"That we're dealing with a U.S. Marshal? Yeah, I heard."

"Carry the vacuum downstairs. I'll bring the booze." After tucking my laptop under my arm, my phone in the top of my bra, and the cleaning bucket in the hand with the laptop, I pulled a bottle of vodka from my duffle bag and followed Kierson downstairs.

At the bottom of the stairs he tucked the cleaning supplies behind the check-in desk and led me into the kitchen. I slid the vodka bottle to Kierson, and he pulled glasses from a cupboard. Finding orange juice in the refrigerator, I slid that to him as well.

"If the father was a cop or FBI, it would've been bad, but—" I started to say.

"A U.S. Marshal means we're screwed. If I request his files—"

"We'll be required to turn Caleb over."

"But if I don't request the files—"

"We're walking in blind."

Kierson handed me my glass. "As I said, we're screwed. It's near impossible to hide from these guys."

"Do we know what office he works out of?" I asked as I followed him to the kitchen table.

"Arlington, Virginia. Why?"

I opened my laptop and scanned through the missing person report. According to the report, Caleb was last seen at his school. The file also included Laurie's last employment information at an insurance agency. I picked up my phone and called Charlie.

"Kelsey? I'm so glad you called. I—"

"Stop. I'm not calling to discuss the situation between the two of us. I have a job for you. A little boy's life is on the line."

"What do you need?" she asked cautiously.

"I'll text you the name of the kid and his mother. They disappeared three years ago and have been living on the run. The kid's father is a U.S. Marshal. I need you to go to Arlington, Virginia and dig for intel at the school, the wife's former employment, and medical facilities. I need as much dirt on this guy as you can gather before we're forced to turn his son over to him."

"Shit."

"Yes or no, Kid."

"Of course. Send me the info. And Kel?"

I didn't say anything. I let the silence hang between us.

"I'm sorry."

"I have to go. Get the information we need. And try not to get yourself arrested."

I disconnected, tossing the phone on the kitchen counter. I shouldn't have called her. I should've called Maggie or one of the regular guards from Silver Aces Security.

"I heard there was bad blood between the two of you, but damn."

"Don't start, Kierson."

I took a drink of the cocktail, cringing when I realized how strong it was. I walked over and poured a third of the drink into Kierson's already half-empty glass before retrieving more juice from the refrigerator.

"Anything on Axle Sorato's death?" I asked.

"They tried to fingerprint the holding cell, but apparently there were too many samples to run. Tebbs said it was a dead end, but he's put a rush on the autopsy."

I was tempted to call Mickey, but he'd call me when he had information. Pressuring him sooner could piss him off. "All right. Our hands are tied regarding Sorato and Brian Griffith, but Laurie is still missing. What do we know?"

"She worked the morning shift, taking a break to walk her son to school, then returned to the diner. She spotted a man we believe to be Brian Griffith outside the diner around one o'clock. She snuck out the back door and was last seen a block away from her home."

I bit my lower lip, thinking. "Where's her car?"

"Maybe she doesn't have one. She lives close enough to town to walk everywhere."

"No," I said, shaking my head. "She owns a car. You don't have go bags and boxes ready to load into a car, if you don't *have* a car. Transportation would be crucial in a small town like this if they needed to get away quick."

"There wasn't a car at her house."

I turned, hearing a noise behind me. Mrs. A. walked into the kitchen.

"Pardon me. I just need a glass of water. I didn't mean to interrupt."

"Mrs. A., do you know Laurie Simmons?"

"Yes, I know Laurie. Works down at the diner. Sweet woman," she said, smiling sadly. "Fred told me when he called earlier that you folks were trying to find her."

"Do you know if she owns a car?"

"I'm not real sure, dear. I saw her walking a lot in town, but then again, most of us walk from place to place when the weather's nice. But Fred will know. If you're unfortunate enough to need your car towed, Fred's guaranteed to call you and ask if you're ready to trade it in for a newer model."

"I imagine most people would be annoyed, but I'd find that to be a convenient service." I grinned, turning to look at Kierson but he just rolled his eyes. I looked back at Mrs. A. "Do you have Fred's number? I know it's late, but we need that information."

"Of course. Anything to help Laurie. I'll get my phone and be right back."

When she returned, she was already on the phone with Fred. "Quit cussing. This is important business. That nice lady from Silver Aces Security needs to ask you a question or two. Are you going to be nice?" She nodded at the phone before handing it over.

Fred not only knew the make, model, and color of Laurie's car, but he kept records of everyone's license plate numbers as well. As I wrote down the information, Kierson was entering it into a text message. I thanked Fred and ended the call before turning back to Mrs. A. "Thank you. That was very helpful."

"If you need anything else, just come wake me. I don't mind."

"That should be all for tonight, thank you," Kierson assured her with a warm smile.

"I'll see you in a few hours for breakfast then," she said before waddling back down the hallway.

I walked back to the foyer and looked at the oversized, framed, and encased map displayed on the wall. I carefully lifted the picture off the nail and carried it back to the kitchen.

"I'm not sure Mrs. A. would appreciate you taking down her wall art."

"I need a map."

"Ever heard of Google?"

"I work better with large visuals."

Kierson rolled his eyes but moved our glasses aside so I could lay the picture down on the table. "What are you thinking?"

"Find something I can use to mark places on the map."

"You can't destroy her map."

"It's behind glass. I just need something to stick to the glass."

"Like what?"

"Cheese." Grady yawned, coming into the kitchen. "Last time we used cheese." He stopped at the refrigerator and got a slice of cheese out, passing it to me. Picking up my drink, he choked on the cocktail and set the glass back down. He shook his head and went to the sink for a glass of water.

"Did we wake you?" I asked as I tore the slice of cheese into small bits. I placed one piece at Laurie's cottage, another at the diner, and a third at Caleb's school.

"No. I couldn't sleep. Casey would kick my ass if I didn't do everything humanly possible to find his girl."

"You *were* doing something. You were sleeping so when I figure this asshole out, you can go beat the crap out of him for us."

"And spend the rest of your life in prison," Kierson grumbled.

"Kierson, if you don't have the balls for this case, fly back to Detroit. We don't need you," I snapped.

"I could lose my badge for just knowing what I know and not reporting it."

"Fine. Report it. But report it to Jack. He's our best shot at keeping it quiet. Tell him to give us forty-eight hours."

"Report what?" Grady asked.

"The boy's father is a U.S. Marshal," Kierson answered.

Grady froze mid step. Only his eyes moved, landing on me. He set his glass of water down and gave another glance at my drink. I moved my glass out of range.

"I should call Casey," Grady said, rubbing his forehead.

"I sent a message for him to go underground."

Grady nodded. "Kierson, you can't report this. It's one thing to hide Casey and Caleb from *one* marshal. It's a whole lot harder to hide them from both the FBI and the U.S. Marshal's office. Hell, they'd probably expand the alert to every unit under the DOJ. We'd have thousands of Feds crashing down on us."

"And even if we managed to keep Casey and Caleb hidden, Laurie would be killed as soon as the alert was issued," I admitted aloud.

"You think she's still alive?" Kierson asked.

"At the moment, yes, she's alive. Brian Griffith isn't doing this to get his son back. It's about Laurie."

"Explain," Grady said.

"He found them. He could've gone to the school and had Caleb held until he could prove that he was his father. But he didn't. Instead, he went to the diner to spook Laurie. Then when she ran home to grab her go bags, he was waiting for her."

"He wants to hurt her. Make her suffer," Grady said.

"Exactly. And he had a plan. He studied the area. He knew how to get in and out of Laurie's neighborhood without being spotted. Where did he park his car? Where's Laurie's car?"

"The police talked to her neighbors," Kierson said. "The ones who were home didn't see or hear anything."

"This is a small town. The neighbors would've noticed an unfamiliar car on a dead-end road."

"You think he walked there?" Grady asked. "Then how did he get her out?"

"He either knocked her out, thus the blood that was found in the kitchen, or he drugged her. Maybe both. Then he loaded her into her own car and drove away."

"I'll get a BOLO out," Kierson said, pulling his phone out.

"Wait," Grady said, shaking his head and moving over to the map. "I don't think you need to."

Grady leaned over my shoulder, studying the map.

"This is her house?" Grady asked.

"Yup. Acres of woods border the property."

"He must've parked somewhere on the outskirts of the woods and walked to Laurie's from there," Grady said.

"But the river cuts through a good chunk of the woods. He would've avoided that," I said, pointing to the map.

"Right, so that leaves only two areas. Here and here." He pointed to the map.

"Has to be the first one. The second area would force him to drive Laurie's car back through town to get back to his car. He wouldn't risk it."

"Who's sober enough to drive?" Grady asked.

"I am," I answered before running to my room to grab my shoulder bag.

Chapter Twelve

"Turn right," Kierson said as he monitored his Google map from his phone. "We're in the right area. We'll need to search the next dozen or so dead-end roads for the next half mile."

"Or flag down some help," I said, flashing my headlights at the approaching cop car and pulling to the side of the road. "Well?" I looked at Kierson. "Get out your badge and do your part."

The cop car did a U-turn and parked behind us as Kierson got out, flashing his badge in clear view with his hands visible.

"Fed?" one of the officers said, climbing out of the patrol car. "You lost?"

"We're looking for a 2012 blue Honda. You see a car like that abandoned around here?"

The other officer nodded. "Down on Dung Trail. We tagged it to be towed in the morning if it's still there."

"We need you to take us to that car. It's evidence in an abduction case."

"Sure. Follow us."

Kierson slid back into the passenger seat and looked at me. "Well? Do *your* thing. Follow the cops."

"Did they really say Dung Trail?" Grady chuckled.

I pulled out behind the cops. We passed four gravel roads before turning right. A blue Honda sat at the end of a cul-de-sac. I flashed my lights for the cops to stop as I pulled off to the side. They had most likely already disturbed the ground near the car, but we didn't need to add more tire tracks to the mess.

Kierson got out to talk to the cops as I handed latex gloves over my shoulder to Grady and put on a pair for myself.

"Flashlight?" Grady asked.

I handed him one of four mini-mag lights I kept in my shoulder bag.

"You sure you want to walk up there? You could be wrong. She could be dead already."

"She's not," I answered as I got out of the SUV.

Kierson kept the local cops back as Grady and I searched the ground in a slow grid starting twenty feet from the car. He worked his way toward the passenger side as I worked toward the driver's side.

"Cigarette butt!" Grady called out.

Kierson approached from behind Grady and bagged the cigarette, asking the officers if it could be theirs. Both officers insisted they didn't smoke.

"Three more," Grady called out. "Looks like someone stood here waiting for something."

"If he got here early, he may have waited until late morning for any local hunters to clear out," I said, without looking up from the ground I was searching.

"I don't understand," Kierson said.

"A lot of hunters will hunt early morning until late morning, then hunt again mid afternoon until dark, like a split shift."

"She's right," one of the officers said. "It's not typically an all-day event around here."

"Would our guy have known that?" Kierson asked.

"I don't know. I did."

Grady chuckled, and Kierson bagged the other cigarettes.

My side of the car was so covered with layers upon layers of tire tracks, trying to decipher any of it was a waste of time. I turned and shined my light inside the car. A section of the back seat was darker, most likely a blood stain. The driver's seat was set as far back as it would go. I tested the driver's door and found it unlocked. Reaching in, I popped the trunk. Four sets of eyes turned and waited for me.

"How many times do I have to repeat myself? *She's not dead*," I said, lifting the trunk lid.

The trunk, as expected, was filled with boxes, garbage bags of clothes, and non-perishable groceries. Laurie had kept it loaded and ready to leave at a moment's notice. Nothing appeared to have been disturbed.

I turned my attention to the police officers. "Is there a local tow guy who can store this car for us? I need it to be locked down and everything kept just as it is until we find the victim. It's evidence, but it's useless to us at the moment."

"We could impound it."

"No. I don't want local cops getting curious. No offense. I'm thinking more like someone's pole barn."

"Sure. Marty could tow and store it."

"Call him. I'll pay two hundred now and two hundred when we pick it up later, but he has to make sure no one goes near this car."

"Well, shit. Now I wish I had a pole barn." The other officer pouted as he scratched his head.

"Shut it, Nelson. Can't you tell these folks are professionals," the first officer said.

I wasn't sure how many professionals had evidence stored in someone's pole barn, but I was glad they weren't putting that together. I walked back to the SUV and pulled a business card and two-hundred dollars. On the way back, I asked for one of Kierson's business cards. I handed both cards and the money to one of the officers. "Only Kierson or I have clearance to retrieve this vehicle. No one else. I don't care who they are or how shiny their badge is."

"Yes, ma'am. Marty will do right by you. He likes getting paid cash."

"Just make sure he knows that if anyone else claims the car, he doesn't get the other two hundred."

"For two hundred, Marty would hide a body for you," the officer said. "Don't you worry none. He'll lock it up good and tight."

I smirked "Nice to know."

Grady had one eyebrow cocked as he looked around. "You boys got a local map handy?"

Officer Nelson got the requested map as Officer Kern called tow truck driver Marty. I helped Grady spread the map out on the hood of the police cruiser while Nelson and Kierson held flashlights for us. It was nearly three in the morning. We were way behind our kidnapper.

"You're the profiler," Grady said.

"This is the main road. He wouldn't take it back the way he came. His natural instinct would tell him to go the other direction. He also wouldn't want to hit any of these small towns. He'd still be worried someone could later identify him as being in the area."

"He's not driving his own vehicle, right?"

"No. He's more likely to rent a vehicle under fake ID. His job definitely gives him the ability to set up fake credentials."

"So he went north? To the interstate?"

"Probably not," Kierson said. "There are cameras all along the interstate that could prove he was in the area when Laurie was abducted."

I followed the lines. "He cut around the city, and then would've taken Highway 83 south."

"But then where? If he heads back to Arlington, there are a hundred different highways he can use to turn east."

"No clue," I said, stepping away from the map. "He could be anywhere." I dragged my hands up into my hair and pulled the hair scrunchy out. Grady reached out and rubbed my shoulders. "We need more information. Even if we confirm which way this guy is heading, we have no way of tracking him at this point. Kierson, it's time to call Tebbs."

"It's the middle of the night."

I glanced over at him. "She's still alive, but she's running out of time. Make the call."

Kierson muttered a few cuss words but stepped away to make the call. A few minutes later he walked back, handing me the phone.

"Good morning, sir," I said as I glared at Kierson.

"Harrison, what the hell is going on?"

"What did Kierson tell you?"

"That you ordered him to call me."

"Well, sir, you're not going to like what I have to say."

"Out with it."

I flipped Kierson the bird before walking toward the road to speak freely away from the local officers. "We have reason to believe that a deputy U.S. Marshal kidnapped his estranged wife and is taking her to an unknown location to kill her. But if an alert goes out, he'll execute her quickly and scurry back to safety."

"Shit."

"It gets worse. His wife ran away with their son. We relocated the boy, and he's protected. But at this point we're obstructing justice by not reporting it. And before you ask, Kierson doesn't know where the boy is, we made sure of that."

"And you called me? Why?"

"We need the marshal's employee file to help us build our profile. But the U.S. Marshal's office can't be aware that we requested it."

"*Is that all*? Just a classified file from another federal agency?" Jack sputtered.

"Come on, Jack. Don't tell me you don't have the cajones to go after that file."

"Shit," he mumbled.

"It's not great news, but it could be worse."

"How?"

"Oh, I don't know. Like having a prisoner in an FBI holding cell murdered?"

"Not funny," he snapped.

"It's a little funny," I said, holding back my laughter.

He was silent for a few moments before he sighed. "I know a director at the Marshal's office, but he'd turn the request over to an analyst to pull the file."

"That doesn't work, sir. But what if he met with one of our FBI analysts and allowed her to use his password while she pulled the records?"

"Sharing passwords isn't allowed."

"It's unconventional, but if he watched her while she ran the search, then changed his password afterward, I'd think in a life and death situation it would be ruled acceptable."

"Who's the analyst?"

"Genie. You met her in Miami," I answered as I walked back to the vehicles to stand with the others.

"The soft-spoken girl who looks like a high school student?"

"She's a wiz, sir. And she can be in Arlington in three hours."

"Have her call me when she lands. I'll call Richard."

"Thank—" I heard the bleep on the phone telling me the call had ended. I looked up at Kierson. "You suck."

Kierson grinned at me. "Special Agent Tebbs likes you for some reason. He would've screeched at me for thirty minutes."

"Wake Genie and get her on a plane. She's to call Jack when she lands."

Kierson continued grinning as he took his phone back and made the call. I pulled my own phone from my back pocket and called Maggie.

"Do you know what time it is?" She laughed, sounding wide awake.

"Obviously, I'm not dragging you out of dreamland. What are you doing up this late?"

"I've been getting a biker drunk enough to talk. It took a while, but it was worth it. He had a lot to say about your boy Axle Sorato."

"That will have to wait. I need you to man up and fly to Virginia. When you get there, meet up with Genie and stay by her side. Consider your little pissing match with Kierson on hold until this case is closed."

"If this is a formal case, I have to get approved."

"Use the credit card I gave you and get your ass there. I'm not asking." I hung up, stuffing the phone back into my pocket.

"You think she'll show?" Grady asked.

"She'll show. Maggie and Charlie are two peas from the same fricken pod. They'll throw their tizzy fits, but when someone's ass is on the line, they step up to the plate."

"You're tired. You need some sleep." He rested a hand on my shoulder and pulled me into his chest.

"Laurie doesn't have much time, Grady," I whispered.

"There's not much we can do right now. Let's head back to the B&B until we know which direction to move next."

I nodded. It wasn't much of a plan, but we'd hit a dead end. At least back at the inn, we'd be only twenty minutes from the private airport.

Chapter Thirteen

It took just under an hour to get back to the B&B. We found Mrs. A in the kitchen, picking dried cheese off the map that I'd left on the table.

"Sorry." I grimaced, tucking my bag into a chair and helping to scrape the dried chunks off.

"No worries. I actually thought it quite creative," she said, not looking up from her task. "Visitors arrived while you were out. One of them is sleeping on the couch in the parlor. A man and woman went upstairs to drop their luggage off in your room. They said you wouldn't mind."

"Really? It's near four in the morning. Did you get their names?"

"Bridget and I stole your room," Bones said, entering the kitchen with an arm wrapped around Bridget's shoulder. "Pink, huh?"

"Yeah. Makes me feel like a princess." They both knew that I abhorred Sara's obsession with pastels.

Bridget giggled, and Bones' grin widened.

"Why is Donovan sleeping on the couch?" Grady asked, entering the kitchen.

"Unfortunately, the inn's fourth room is out of commission at the moment," Mrs. A. said. "I never assembled the new bed. I sent a text to Fred, though. He'll likely arrive near dawn. Car sales aren't a booming business around here, so he sidelines as a husband for hire."

We all grinned at Mrs. A., not saying anything.

"*Not like that!*" she sputtered. "Single women hire him to do their honey-do lists."

Bridget and I looked at each other and giggled. Grady wrapped an arm around my waist and pulled me against him. I could feel the vibrations of him silently laughing as he tucked his face into my shoulder.

"I hired him to set up the *bed*! *That's all*!" Mrs. A. muttered before spraying some glass cleaner on the map and polishing it. "You youngins' have dirty minds!"

"I'll rehang the map," Grady offered after she had cleaned it.

"You don't have to do that. You're a guest."

"I'm sure most of your guests don't take your wall hangings down and keep you up all night."

"You're trying to find Laurie. What's a little lost sleep compared to that. Any luck?"

"We found her car," I answered. "But the man who took her is long gone."

"You know who it is then?"

"We have a name, but we're waiting on the rest of the details." I looked up at the clock. "Looks like we have time for a two-hour nap."

"All of us?" Bridget asked. "Or do you have something you want us to do?"

"There's nothing on the task list at the moment that hasn't already been assigned out. I'll need everyone ready at dawn, though."

"You got it boss," Bridget said as she pulled Bones by the hand out of the room.

"Are you going to let me bunk with you since I lost my room?" I asked at Grady.

He rolled his eyes, throwing an arm over my shoulder as he led me upstairs.

~*~*~

My phone alarm went off at a quarter after six. I hurried to shut it off so it wouldn't wake Grady. Two hours of sleep wasn't close to being enough. Other than running a brush through my hair and pulling my jeans back on, I didn't bother sprucing up. I needed coffee before I collapsed.

In the kitchen, Bones, Bridget, and Mrs. A. sat at the table drinking coffee. I retrieved a cup for myself, but before I made it to the table Donovan walked in and stole it from me. I returned to the pot, filling my cup with what was left. Before I had a chance to start another pot, Mrs. A. shooed me to do it herself.

"Fill us in," Bridget said as I sat across from her. "Do you know who took Laurie?"

"We know who he is, but so far, we don't have the evidence to have him arrested."

"What about Mable? Can't she ID him?" Mrs. A. asked.

"It's not enough. This guy's a U.S. Marshal."

Bones let out a slow whistle. Donovan thumped his forehead against the table.

"No wonder poor Laurie was on the run," Mrs. A. said, shaking her head.

"Is there anything we can do to help?" Fred asked, appearing out of nowhere at the kitchen entrance.

"I wish there was." I opened my laptop but no new emails had come in. "Right now, we're waiting for intel. We should start getting information any time now."

"Then I best get some breakfast cooking, while you have time to eat," Mrs. A. said as she walked around the table and refilled our cups.

"That sounds great," Grady said as he walked into the room.

As he walked over to retrieve a coffee cup, I noticed his hair was wet and he was wearing fresh clothes. He must have taken a shower. I lifted the collar of my shirt and sniffed it. I wasn't sure how long it had been since I'd hosed myself down.

"You're fine." Grady laughed, sitting beside me. "You showered yesterday after your run."

"The days are starting to blur together."

"What's the plan?" Bridget asked.

"I'm expecting a photo of our suspect any minute. When daylight hits, you guys can walk around town and ask the locals if they recognize him. Maybe we'll get lucky."

Donovan sighed. "That's it? That's the plan?"

"It's all I've got until I get this guy's personnel file and other background information. He could be anywhere by now."

"Still nothing on the laptop?" Grady asked, nodding toward my laptop.

I sighed. "Not yet."

"I'll help cook breakfast," Bridget said as she bounced to the other side of the kitchen to help Mrs. A.

I shook my head and grinned at her excess energy. Bones was doing the same as he watched her bop around, helping Mrs. A. "I didn't get a chance to ask yesterday," I said to Bones. "How did trainee Henderson go from you chasing him out of the building to ending up at the main house?"

"That's your fault." He pointed at me, but he was grinning. "I'm good, but a dozen trainees tackling me was more than even I could handle. By the time they let me go, you and Grady were running past me on your way to the house."

"Tech recorded the trainees taking him down," Donovan said, laughing. "It was a giant pile of arms and legs. We even have a great still shot of Bones' face just before they pounced. We're going to frame it and hang it in the gym."

I smiled, sipping my coffee and imagining it.

"I'm just glad Whiskey was at the house," Grady said.

Bones nodded at him before turning back to me. "The new classroom for the kids is the room between Grady's office and your war room. Some of the off-duty guys are helping get it ready."

"We're also turning one of the downstairs offices into a nursery," Donovan said. "Lisa wants to go back to work, but neither of us like the thought of leaving Abigail with a stranger at home. I figured it made more sense to hire someone to watch her at Headquarters since there are always trained guards around."

"Especially since Lisa is an overbearing, over protective mother who's in the middle of some type of neurotic crisis about germs?"

"It was the only idea I could come up with that didn't involve Lisa strapping Abigail to her body and dragging her into the store," Donovan said. "The doctor told Lisa to start spending time away from Abby. He's hoping it will help her relax."

I couldn't relate to whatever Lisa was going through. "Where's Kierson?" I asked Grady.

"He was on the phone talking to someone in the front room."

"And now he's not," Kierson said, joining us in the kitchen and pulling out a chair. "That was Special Agent in Charge, Jack Tebbs."

I snorted. "Why can't you call him Jack or even Tebbs? You sound so pompous when you pile on the rest of it."

"It's professionalism. You should try it. Besides, he's not a happy camper right now so fair warning. The preliminary autopsy came back on Sorato." Kierson leaned back in his chair, giving me his annoyed look.

"I already told you he was murdered," I said, shrugging. "You might as well say I was right—get it over with."

"Profilers will be the death of me. You're all impossible," Kierson said, shaking his head.

"I'm not actually a profiler, remember? I've never taken classes to become one."

"No. You're just the person my top-level profiler calls when she needs someone to read a case for her. That's even worse. And, yes, you were right. The ME said there were definitive signs of a struggle and the damage to the windpipe is not consistent with suicide."

"Told you," I teased, sticking my tongue out at him.

"So, what does this mean?" Kierson asked.

"That someone wanted him dead."

"He was in FBI *custody*!"

"Yeah. Sucks bad for you and Jack, doesn't it?" I hid my smirk behind my cup of coffee. "Did Genie get access to Brian Griffith's file yet?"

"Maggie and Genie are at the US Marshal's office now. We should have it any minute."

My phone rang, and when I looked, I saw it was Maggie. I answered as I got up and walked out the French doors into a private garden. "Tell me you have something."

"Genie and I are on our way back to the hotel. You're on speaker phone."

"Hello, Kelsey," Genie giggled.

"Hi, Genie. Thank you for traveling to Arlington for me."

"All part of the job. We couldn't copy and send the information to you while still at the Marshal's office. Their internet servers could've traced and tracked it. But we'll send it as soon as we're back at the hotel."

"Okay. Maggie, did you get a chance to look at Griffith's file?"

"Yeah, but I can't get a read on this guy. He's good, too good. He has a score of accomplishments, but then there's a crap load of complaints against him too. None of the complaints have turned into formal reprimands though. There's always either lack of evidence or the people speaking against him pull their complaint before there's a formal investigation. He tends to work alone, and because he's *that good*, they let him. The few partners he has had, never lasted long."

"What about around the time when Laurie and Caleb disappeared? Did Griffith have a partner back then? It would've been a little over three years ago."

"Not when she ran, but six months earlier, he had a partner request reassignment to another unit. It stuck out in the file because the new job was a step down. Basically, career suicide."

"We need to interview him. He's not going to talk to a Fed, though. Get his details to Charlie. She's somewhere in town digging into Laurie's background. If he'll talk to anyone, it will be her."

"We ran into her earlier. She was checking in as we were leaving the hotel. We scheduled to meet up later to compare notes. What's happening there? Any luck tracking Griffith down?"

"No. We found Laurie's car, but he was long gone. Where does the Marshall's office think he is?"

"His schedule says he was in the office three days ago, but left to check on someone in witness protection and would be back on Thursday."

I tried to see the timeline in my head, but I couldn't figure it out. "What day is it?"

"Tuesday."

"If he left Friday and drove straight through, he would've arrived Saturday night. He waited another day to take her, narrowing his time to get back home. It's a tight timeline. Everything points to him heading your way, but where? It doesn't leave him much time to spend with Laurie at a third site."

"You don't think he can inflict enough damage in twenty-four hours to make her suffer?" Maggie snapped.

"We both know that's not what I meant. Get out of your own head." Maggie and I both had been in torture situations, hers not that long ago. "If we're going to catch this guy, we need to look at everything from his perspective. He's meticulous. He wants to punish Laurie. He wouldn't take her anywhere that could tie back to him, but he'd also want a location where he'd feel confident that he wouldn't be interrupted."

"If he's as smart as I think he is, he may have already killed her," Maggie said.

"No. I don't think so. He's got a plan. This was premeditated. He knew where she worked. He knew where she lived. He knew the terrain. If he was going to kill her quickly, he would've done it at her house. No," I said, shaking my head. "This isn't a crime of passion. He owned her, and she betrayed him. He's going to take his time to teach her a lesson." I let out a slow breath, trying to clear my thoughts. "Did you get any other insight from his file?"

"He's highly intelligent, but he's a show-off, always needing to prove he's better than his coworkers. His lack of keeping a partner could be that he's a control nut. You could be on to something there."

"All right. Send me the file when you can and make sure Charlie talks to his old partner."

"What are you going to do?"

"If he left Virginia three days ago, then he was here, watching Laurie. This is a small town. Someone had to have seen him. I'm going to talk to as many people as I can until I have a better lead to follow."

"Good luck. We're just pulling into the parking lot at the hotel. Give Genie five minutes to send the file, and I'll go wake Charlie."

"Later." I hung up and looked around. The sky was starting to move from black to blue and soon would be light enough to see more than a few feet. I heard the patio door behind me open and close, but I knew it was Grady even before he folded his arms around me.

"You're cold," he whispered, leaning in to kiss my neck.

"I just need a few minutes," I said, leaning my head back to rest against him. "It's nice out here. Calming."

"Take a moment then." His arms held me snugly as he hummed a peaceful tune and swayed us back and forth as I looked at the slowly brightening sky.

~*~*~

Ten minutes later, I was about to tell Grady it was time to go back inside when my cell phone rang again. "I guess break time is over," I said as I looked at the screen and saw it was Charlie.

"Duty calls." Grady kissed my cheek before releasing me and stepping back inside.

"Kelsey," I answered.

"McKenzie's coworkers were a bust."

It took me a minute to remember that McKenzie and Laurie were the same person. Lack of sleep was slowing my brain. "It was a long shot. Did they say anything?"

"Everyone was eager to help, even though I was calling them in the middle of the night. They suspected she was being abused, but no one could get her to admit it. They also said it was unlikely she had any friends outside of work. Her husband had a tendency of showing up at the office to check on her. No one had a good vibe about their relationship."

"I'm reading him as the controlling type, so that fits."

"And jealous. I called Griffith's ex-partner Lincoln, too, instead of driving all over to track his ass down. He was quite chatty once I convinced him that we were talking off the record. Just before he requested a transfer, he had stopped by Griffith's house. Griffith wasn't home yet, but his wife said he could wait on the patio. She was bringing him a glass of lemonade when Griffith got home and freaked out. He called her a whore and ordered her back inside the house. Then Griffith turned on Lincoln when he tried to defend McKenzie. Things got heated, and Griffith told him that if he ever went near his wife again, he'd kill him. Lincoln told me that based on the way Griffith was acting, he didn't doubt him for a minute."

"Why didn't he report Griffith?"

"He was worried he'd make the situation worse for McKenzie. He wasn't sure what Griffith would do to her if he reported the threat. I did get the impression that Lincoln might've helped her and her son flee though. It explains how she was able to hide for so long."

"Shit."

"Yeah. I'm not sure how helpful any of this is, but it's all I've got."

"It's more than what I had. I need to go. I'll call if I can think of another lead to follow."

My thoughts jumbled as my brain tried to put all the pieces together. A cool breeze drifted by and I shivered, deciding to head inside.

"I was about to fetch you," Grady said, turning his head to grin at me. "What's wrong?" he asked, reaching out for my hand as his smile faded.

I sat next to him and shook my head. I was still in processing mode. Mrs. A. set a plate of french toast, fried potatoes, and a bowl of cut fruit in front of me. I looked around, seeing that everyone else had already eaten. "Thank you," I said, picking up my fork.

I watched the fork shake in my hand before setting it back down.

"Talk to me, babe," Grady whispered, wrapping his arm around me. "You're trembling."

"He's not just going to kill her. He's going to torture her. He's prone to violent rages, and not only did she leave him, but she's been with another man. He's going to—"

I gasped, trying to catch my breath, but couldn't get my lungs to inflate. I looked up at Grady as my nails dug into his hand. In a blink, he had me sitting on his lap on the floor and both of his arms wrapped around me as he rocked me back and forth. I knew he was talking to me, but I couldn't make out the words. Someone turned off the light above the table, and while the light on the other side of the room was still enough to illuminate where I was, it didn't seem as glaring. As Grady's voice penetrated my ears, I closed my eyes and concentrated on pulling a slow breath in. Then another.

"Damn," I heard Kierson say. "I heard about her panic attacks, but that was the first one I've witnessed."

I leaned my head against Grady's chest as he continued to sing a slow country tune and rub my back.

Bones was sitting on the other side of the table and leaned over the side to look at me. "You going to eat that french toast or can I have it?"

Grady and I both laughed.

"It's yours. Leave the fruit, though." I took a few more purposeful breaths before I nodded to Grady. I climbed off him, then offered a hand to pull him up.

"If you get the french toast, I get the potatoes," Donovan said, taking the plate away from Bones and winking at me.

Bridget set a glass of milk in front of me and took my coffee cup away. I didn't complain because I knew I'd had too much already. The panic attacks were worse when I was hyped on caffeine. I looked over to see Fred holding Mrs. A. as tears streaked her cheeks.

"I'm sorry. I didn't mean to scare you."

"Is the man who took Laurie really going to kill her?" she asked.

I nodded. "If she's still alive, she doesn't have much time."

Bones and Donovan both set their silverware down and pushed their plates away.

"What do you know?" Donovan asked.

"He's prone to jealous rages if she even talks to another man. He threatened to kill his old partner after his wife did nothing more than get him a glass of lemonade. Griffith abused her regularly. And he's been in the area at least a few days before he took her. He would've seen her with Casey."

"Son of a bitch," Fred swore. "What's this guy look like?"

"I have the file from Genie," Kierson said, clicking on his laptop. He turned the laptop to show us the picture of Brian Griffith. It was a profile picture, most likely from his ID badge. His pale blue eyes stood out eerily against his tanned complexion and brown, almost black, hair. The smile on his face wasn't fooling me. Those eyes were cold, heartless eyes.

"Oh, my God!" Mrs. A. screeched before she fainted.

Bones dove toward her, and with Fred's help, they caught her before she hit the floor. Bridget ran to the sink to wet a towel.

"He was here!" Fred said, still staring at the picture as he held Mrs. A's head on his thigh. "I sold him a car two months ago!"

"Two months? Are you sure?" I asked, moving closer to Fred.

"I'm sure." He nodded. "My dealership is between here and Brighton, so I get a lot of customers from out that way that I don't know personally, but I remember him. He paid cash for a used 1996 Ford Bronco. It was blue and the rear quarter panel was smashed in. The engine still had some good miles to burn, though. I gave him a good deal."

"Can you remember anything else? Anything he might've said?"

"Said he was going fishing," Fred said. "Strange though, because he didn't look like a fisherman. He was wearing jeans and a T-shirt, but they looked brand new. His shoes were those fancy leather loafers, not boots."

"And you're sure this was two months ago? Not this week?"

"I'm sure," Fred said. "I keep records on my phone. Never know when it will lead to another sale."

Bridget and Bones were helping Mrs. A. off the floor and into a chair. I squatted down in front of her as Kierson got the date from Fred and called Genie.

"Are you okay?" I asked.

"Just a shock, I suppose," she said, glancing briefly back at the laptop. "He stayed here."

"At the inn? When?"

"A couple months ago. The dates will be in my ledger at the guest station. I remember he seemed nice, but not real chatty. He kept to himself for the most part."

"How long did he stay?"

"Not more than two or three days as I recall."

"What name was he using?" Bridget asked as she walked back into the room carrying the ledger.

Mrs. A. turned a few pages and then pointed to the entry. "Bradley Whit. Stayed August 27th and 28th."

"That's the name he gave me, too," Fred said, looking up from his phone.

I looked over at Kierson. He nodded that he'd heard before he moved into the foyer to continue talking to Genie.

"Where's the best place to talk to as many people as possible? I need to find out who else saw him and what he was up to."

"Fred can handle that," Mrs. A said, turning and nodding at Fred. "Have them meet at the school gym."

"I'm on it," Fred said, nodding to his phone.

"What's he doing?"

"Fred has everyone's numbers set on his phone for emergency alerts. We used to arrange call trees, but Fred's more effective. It's voluntary to be put on the list, but everyone signs up. He'll send a text alert notifying everyone to get to the school for an emergency meeting."

Mrs. A. stood and walked over to the closet, pulling out her coat.

I turned back to the guys. "Gear up. Be ready for anything."

They nodded, hurrying out of the room. I walked over and using my fingers, picked up a piece of cantaloupe. "How does him being here two months ago change his plans?" I asked myself, before biting into the cantaloupe.

~*~*~

I was still lost in thought when I reached for another piece of fruit and realized I had eaten it all. I turned as Grady was pulling a bullet-proof vest over my head and securing the straps.

"You know my arm is working just fine these days, right?"

"You're in thinking mode. I didn't want to interrupt you."

"We better get going," Mrs. A. said as she passed me another bowl of fruit. "Take that with you."

"Can we take your map, too?" I asked, pointing to the wall hanging.

"Of course, dear. Whatever you need."

Grady grabbed the framed map, and we all loaded into various vehicle to follow Fred to the school. When we got there, a hundred or more cars already filled the parking lot.

Chapter Fourteen

Following Mrs. A. into the gym, I was surprised by the crowd that had gathered. Fred offered to go to the office and get a projector while Kierson went to the front of the gym and set up his laptop on a table. Dragging a chair over, I stood on it and raised my hand to get everyone's attention. At least two hundred people, in various states of dress, quieted to listen.

"Thank you for coming. I'm Kelsey Harrison with Silver Aces Security. Many of you know Casey Roberts. He works with us and asked us to help find his girlfriend, Laurie Simmons, who was kidnapped yesterday from her home."

Several gasps escaped.

"That case is a police matter," the chief of police hollered.

"By my estimate, Laurie has a matter of hours before she will be killed if she's not dead already. The man who took her is her husband who is employed as a U.S. Marshal. He beat her regularly before she managed to escape with her son. As an investigator of violent crimes, I can promise you—he *will* kill her."

The chief gasped, turning white.

"Behind me, Agent Kierson with the FBI is setting up his laptop to a projector."

"Why is a Fed working with a civilian company?" one of the deputies asked.

"She's not your average civilian," Kierson answered, standing on another chair. "I've worked with Kelsey on several cases. She's a profiler, and I hire her on occasion to consult on our cases. She's *that* good. And the team she works with is military trained for hostage situations." Kierson nodded for me to continue.

"We have a picture of Brian Griffith, but we just discovered he was in town late August and using the alias of Bradley Whit. We need anyone who talked with him to come forward and tell us as much as you can remember. We know he bought a blue 1996 Ford Bronco from Fred. We also know he stayed at the B&B. I'm guessing more of you will remember him. He has distinctive eyes."

"Mean eyes," Mable called out, pounding her cane into the gym floor.

"Yes, thank you, Mable. He has *mean* eyes." I turned to glance at Kierson.

He finished adjusting the projector, pointing it at the white wall. After clicking something on his laptop, Griffith's picture appeared. Someone turned the main light off so only the perimeter lights were on. Griffith's eyes seemed to spear me, sending a shiver down my back. I stepped off the chair, onto the gym floor.

"I remember him, but not from two months back," an older man called out, moving forward through the crowd. "I work part-time at a hardware store in Brighton. He was in three days ago."

"Do you remember what he purchased?"

The man seemed to turn a bit green and raised his hand to his stomach. He shuffled closer to me so he didn't need to shout. "He bought sheets of plastic, a small hatchet, and rope."

The old man, and probably everyone else who heard the answer, was imagining what Griffith planned on doing with that hatchet. I, however, was stumped by the list. It didn't make sense. Why would he want rope if he had cuffs? And if he was moving her to a remote location to dump her body, why did he need plastic? And despite not having a full profile on him, the hatchet didn't seem his style. And why would he buy supplies in Brighton? He drove across half the country. He could have stopped anywhere. I was missing something.

"How did he pay?" I asked, looking at the old man.

"Plastic. Same as everybody else these days."

"You're sure? He didn't pay with cash?"

"Only us old timers use cash. I would've remembered."

That also didn't fit. Did he create a fake credit card account just to buy the supplies? Seemed too risky.

"Can you call and have someone pull the charge card information?" Kierson asked.

"Of course," the old man said. "The manager lives near the store. Give me five minutes."

A young guy had moved forward and was staring at the picture.

"Do you recognize him?"

"Yup, sure do," he said. "I'll be damned if I can remember the where, why, and when, though."

Two women stepped forward, pulling my attention away. "He showed up the day we took the kids on a field trip to the town library. We stopped for ice cream cones on the walk back."

"I saw him too," the woman next to her said. "He was watching the boys. When he noticed us look at him, he turned and left."

"Was Caleb Simmons one of the boys?" Grady asked.

Both women nodded.

"Do you remember the date?" Bridget asked.

"August 28th," the second woman said. "It was the second day of school, and it would've been around two in the afternoon."

Bridget moved them off to the side to write down their information. I turned and saw the young man was still looking at the photo. He was rubbing the back of his neck, getting frustrated. I started toward him, when the old man shuffled back and grabbed my arm.

"This makes no sense," the old man said, shaking his head.

"What?" I asked as the hairs on my arms rose.

"Manager says the name on the card was Casey Roberts. But I know Casey. It wasn't him that bought that stuff. I swear it."

"That's it!" The young man turned to face us. "That guy was parked a few months ago on the side of the road near Casey's ranch. I stopped to see if he needed some help, but he told me he was all good. He said he stopped to check his tires. When I started to drive away, I saw he was still standing there, looking at Casey's place. I stopped again, staying in my truck, while I watched him. Something seemed off. He glanced up though, waved at me, then got in his SUV and drove away. He was definitely driving a blue Bronco for sure, but I don't know about the year."

I stepped back and grabbed Grady's arm. "The map. I need the map."

"Show me where Casey lives," Grady ordered the young man as he lifted the framed map onto the table.

We all stepped around the map as the young man pointed out the quickest way to Casey's house.

"We have to move," I said before I ran toward the doors and the rest of the team followed. "He's trying to frame Casey for her murder."

~*~*~

It didn't take us long to get to Casey's ranch. The roads were straight, and between half the town being at the school and it being so early in the morning, there were no other cars on the road. Grady led the charge, driving ninety miles an hour.

"The ranch should be up ahead," I warned Grady. "Cut the lights and pull to the side. We don't want to spook him."

Grady tapped the brakes twice to warn Kierson in the SUV behind us before cutting the lights and drifting the truck to the side of the road. When we stopped, we slid out, closing the doors quietly.

"Bridget, lock yourself in one of the SUVs and wait for us to call. We may need to get Laurie to the hospital as fast as possible, so look up the directions and be ready to drive. Her life may depend on it."

Bridget grabbed Bones' keys and walked away.

"Bones and Donovan, take the back entrance. Grady, take the garage. Kierson and I will enter through the front."

"This is likely to turn into a hostage situation," Donovan whispered. "Who's going to order the kill shot?"

"Kelsey will make the call," Kierson answered. "But because she's a civilian, when we file the report, I'm going to take the credit."

"You're assuming I'll make the right call."

"I'm betting my career on it," he said as we all moved down the drive toward the small ranch house.

The blinds on the house were closed, but the lights were on in the center and right side of the house. I moved up the front porch, careful to stay on the outward edge where the planks would be less likely to creak. Kierson mirrored my approach.

Glancing at the door, I noted it was steel with a steel frame. It wouldn't be easy to kick in, which I was sure was Casey's intention when he'd built the house. It was also likely that the other doors would be the same, and everyone would have to adjust how they entered. I moved to the left, toward the window that wasn't illuminated. Checking the lock, I grinned, seeing it was the same style locks we had on our houses in Michigan. Pulling a jimmy tool off my vest, I slid the metal in the frame, popped the end up, and jerked the slide to the right. The latch snapped open, and I stilled to see if anyone moved into the room on the other side of the glass. Not hearing anything, I moved aside as Kierson raised the window and climbed through. I followed him into an empty bedroom. The door was closed, but we could hear Griffith on the other side.

"Your new boyfriend will go to prison for the rest of his life," I heard Griffith say as I moved closer to the door and turned the door knob while holding the door tight in the frame. "You'll be dead. He'll be in prison. And my son will be with me, where he belongs."

Feeling the latch fully retracted, I held the knob as I pulled the door open and looked in. Griffith's back was turned to us. Laurie was sitting in a chair in front of him, sobbing and shaking. I motioned to Kierson to move as I stepped back and opened the door. I pulled my gun, aiming it at Griffith's back as I followed Kierson. I stayed near the bedroom while he moved toward the front door.

Griffith sensed our movements and pulled Laurie from the chair by her hair as he moved the hatchet to her neck. Grady moved into the living room from the kitchen. Bones and Donovan moved in from the back hallway.

"*Who the fuck are all of you?*" Griffith yelled.

"They call me *demonio de muerte*, or so I hear," I answered, holding my gun sight trained on him as I focused my attention on his eyes. "You have only two options here. Drop your weapon or die."

His eyes shifted from me to the men surrounding him before turning back to me. I could see he was calculating his odds.

"Holster your weapon, Kierson," I called out.

Griffith looked frantically between me and Kierson, jerking Laurie's head back in the process.

"Donovan!" I called out.

Donovan fired. As the bullet exited Griffith's forehead, his body was thrown forward. Kierson leapt toward Laurie, catching her and pulling her away from Griffith before she fell on the hatchet. She crumbled in his arms, sobbing.

Bones called Bridget while Donovan found a sheet to wrap around Laurie's naked and damaged body. Grady carefully lifted her and carried her out to the SUV as it pulled up. The white sheet was blotched with large red patches of blood that had already seeped through. Bones climbed into the backseat of the SUV from the other side and took Laurie from Grady. As soon as the doors closed, Bridget took off like a bat out of hell down the drive.

Kierson placed his hands on his hips and turned to face me. "I'll need to call this in and stay on scene until FBI forensics gets here."

"I'm going to head back to the school and tell everyone it's over. Then I'll be at the inn, sleeping."

Kierson nodded. "I'll send agents your way when they need your statement."

"Best if I stay," Donovan said. "I'm sure they'll want to take my gun and confirm gunshot residue."

Kierson raised the back of his hand to wipe the sweat off his forehead before turning back to me. "Nice job. I wasn't sure why you were ordering me to holster my weapon until you called out for Donovan to take the shot. Good thing I'm quick or that hatchet would've ended her."

"I had faith in you, Kierson," I said, slugging him in the arm before walking out to join Grady.

As we walked down the driveway, Grady intertwined our fingers. "The sun's finally coming up."

Orange and yellow beams split through the trees and danced off the dewy grass. "It's going to be a nice day."

Grady chuckled. "Too bad we're likely to sleep through most of it."

Chapter Fifteen

As Grady drove us back to town, I called Tech.

"What do you need?" Tech yawned into the phone.

"I need you to let Casey know it's over. We found them. Griffith is dead."

"And Laurie?" Tech asked.

"She was in bad shape, but she should pull through. Bones and Bridget took her to the hospital."

"Casey's still in North Dakota. He didn't want to go too far in case he was needed. I'll reach out and tell him to head to the hospital."

"It wasn't smart of him to stay so close, but I get it. I'd probably have done the same."

"Anything else?"

"No, we're set. We'll update the locals, and then I have a date with a pillow."

"I'm going back to bed then. Later."

Tech ended the call, and I looked up to see we'd arrived back at the school. I sighed. The parking lot was still full of vehicles. "You can stay in the truck. This shouldn't take long," I told Grady.

"Where you go, I go. We're a team, remember?"

We climbed out of the truck and made our way into the school, down the hall, and into the gym. As everyone started to notice us, a hush fell over the crowd.

"She's alive," Grady called out.

Cheers echoed throughout the gym until it quieted again to hear more.

"She's injured and was taken to the hospital," I called out. "Casey is on his way and should be there soon. Griffith died during a hostage situation."

Grady and I knew better than to stick around for the million questions, so we quickly turned and left the gym while everyone was loudly celebrating the news. On our way across the parking lot, Grady's phone rang. I heard him purring his country charm over the phone and put enough together to know that he was trying to calm Nicholas down. I climbed in the truck and leaned my head back, closing my eyes as I listened.

"Yes, I know that usually one of us is there. But buddy, you have a whole house full of people with you, and I've only been gone one day. You need to learn that sometimes our work requires both of us to take off for a few days, but we'll always come back."

There was a long pause and another sigh from Grady. "I'll be home as quick as I can, but until then, I want you to clean your room like I told you to do three days ago. And today is Tuesday, so you know what that means, don't you?

"Yes, that's right. Dusting day. You and Sara better be doing your chores because I'll be checking when I get there."

I grinned, listening to the conversation. I could hear Nicholas' whine over the phone, not happy about the reminder. They talked for a few more minutes before Grady hung up and started the truck.

"Dusting day?"

"I know," Grady said, chuckling. "We could afford a housekeeper, but those kids are so damn bored most of the time, it was a two birds one stone, kind of thing. And it's good for them. They're old enough to pull their own weight."

"I'm all for it. I'm hoping we find a good teacher who can break up their days a bit. It'd do both those kids wonders to spend part of their time away from their laptops."

"Just don't let Anne hire someone," he grumbled. "That damn woman sees the good in *everyone*."

I snorted, my eyes still closed, as I leaned my forehead against the passenger window and fell asleep.

I woke, hours later, as the tires of the plane smacked and bounced twice on the tarmac before screeching to stop the forward momentum. "What the—"

"It's fine," Grady said from beside me, pulling my hand into his. "We're back in Michigan."

"How the hell did we get here?" I asked as I sat up and looked around. I dragged a hand through my hair until it got stuck on several snarls.

Grady chuckled beside me. "You were dead to the world when we got to back to the inn so I called the pilot and loaded up our bags. Decided it didn't matter whether I slept on the plane or at the inn, and you were already out, so what the hell." He shrugged as he stood and pulled our bags out of the overhead cabinet. "Come on, gorgeous. Let's get you home."

I shuffled along after him, trying to clear my foggy brain. When we exited the airport, one of the security guys from Silver Aces was waiting to pick us up.

"Shit. I left my SUV in Detroit."

"Kierson said he'd drive it over when the dust settled in North Dakota. Bridget is returning my truck rental, then she'll drive back with Donovan. Bones has another job starting Friday in Nebraska, so he was going to drive South."

"Laurie's car? I told Marty the tow truck driver to only release it to Kierson or me."

"Kierson said he'd take care of it and deduct the money from your consulting fee."

"I'm not sure how you're keeping track of everything." I yawned. "I can barely put one foot in front of another."

Grady opened the back door of the SUV, and I crawled in, stretching out on the seat. I heard him chuckle before I fell back asleep.

~*~*~

"*Give that back!*" Sara screeched just before the sound of breaking glass.

I jumped out of bed and ran down the hall before I'd thought to see if I was wearing clothes. Glancing down, I wasn't sure whether I was relieved or disgusted to find I was still wearing the same outfit I'd put on Monday morning.

In the dining room, I found Anne and Grady glaring at Nicholas and Sara who both stood pouting, looking at the floor.

"What's up?" I asked, noticing the glass of orange juice shattered across the table.

Both kids opened their mouths to speak but Anne raised a hand into the air to silence them. They both looked back to the floor.

"Seems we had territorial issues over a glass of orange juice," Grady said.

"I heard," I said, taking a seat next to him. "And which one of them is in the most trouble?"

"Pretty even-steven right now," Anne said. "They've been at each other's throats for nearly twenty-four hours."

I looked back at the kids who hadn't moved. "If it weren't for the broken glass, you'd be cleaning this mess up yourselves. Instead, though, both of you go shower, dress, and brush your teeth. Then meet back here for your punishments."

"Ah, man," Nicholas whined, moving toward the hallway.

"It's all your fault," Sara said, glaring at Nicholas as she walked toward the stairs.

"*Enough!*" was all I said to have them hurrying to their rooms in silence.

Grady turned to me and smiled. "I'm afraid you'll have to handle this one without me. I need to go to work."

I grinned back. "I'm sure you do."

"Me too!" Anne said, laughing. "They haven't eaten yet. We didn't get that far."

"It's all good. I'm contemplating starving them to death, anyway."

Anne snorted as she picked up chunks of glass. I retrieved the trashcan and a towel from the kitchen to finish cleaning up the mess.

"The applicants for the teaching position will start arriving in the next hour. Will you be able to watch the kids today, or should I make other arrangements?" Grady asked.

"They can help me do the interviews."

"I'm heading into the office," Grady said, kissing me on the forehead before moving toward the garage door with a to-go coffee cup. "I typed up our statements for Kierson this morning and signed my copy. They're on the credenza. Sara said she'd scan them to Kierson after you sign."

"Do I need to read it or can I just sign it?"

"Up to you," he said as he walked out.

After cleaning up the mess on the table, I skimmed through the statement before signing. I looked longingly toward the coffee pot but I didn't have much time before the kids would be back and I didn't dare leave them unsupervised. I turned down the hall toward the shower while I still had time.

~*~*~

Three hours later, Nicholas elbowed me in the ribs when I started nodding off. The fifth applicant was reading her credentials from what looked like a novel-size stack of paper.

"Thank you," I interrupted her. "I appreciate your time, but I don't think you're the candidate for the position." I stood and motioned her through the side door of the atrium. "This isn't going well," I said when the door closed.

"I'll go get the next one," Sara said, walking toward the bedroom door.

Whiskey was manning the front door and having the applicants wait in the dining room for their turn. Nicholas and I leaned back on the couch and sighed.

"Well, this is downright depressing," a female voice said from the atrium entrance. The woman standing next to Sara had bright red hair, rosy cheeks, and a big smile.

"How many interviews have you dragged yourself through?"

"You're the sixth," Nicholas said.

"And you kids have been cooped up in here all day?"

"We're used to it." Sara shrugged. "We go to school online."

"Sounds exciting. What grade are you in?" she asked as she joined Sara on the opposite couch.

"It depends on the class," Sara answered. "I'm not so good with my English classes, but I'm taking college courses in mathematics and computer science."

"I'm not as smart as Sara," Nicholas said, pouting. "I'm only in fifth grade classes."

"I'm not a computer and math whiz either, but there are lots of things I am good at," the woman said.

"Like what?" Sara asked.

"Well, I was a cross-country runner in college. And I like to swim and ride my bike. And I like to go to museums and the zoo. I also paint, but I'm not very good at it. And I like to sing, but I'm horrible. And I love to read. All kinds of books. You can travel all over the world in a book."

Nicholas was leaning forward now, grinning. Sara came over beside me and pulled the woman's application from the pile and handed it to me.

"You're Beth Michaelson?" I asked.

"Yes. If it's okay with you, since this is a home environment, I'd like to forgo the formality of the Ms. Michaelson and stick to Beth, if that's all right. Your ad appealed to me because this gig lacks the institutional brick and mortar feel."

I glanced through her resume. "Why did your employment end mid-term last year?"

"After six fulfilling years, I was fired," she admitted, looking directly at me.

I raised an eyebrow, waiting for further details. She looked from me to the kids and then back to me again.

I looked at the kids, then back at Beth. "You can speak freely in front of the kids. They've had an odd upbringing."

Sara giggled.

A slight smirk overtook the corner of Beth's mouth. "One of the parents, a father of one of my students, decided to get handsy with me. We were in my classroom, alone, and the situation escalated. The school decided that I'd acted too aggressively when I sprained his wrist and broke his nose."

Both kids giggled.

I cleared my throat to get them to settle down. "Was there an investigation for assault?"

"There was. No charges were brought against me. The police told the DA it was self-defense."

I picked up my phone and called Dave, friend and local cop.

He answered on the first ring. "You in town?"

"At the moment. I'm sitting with a Beth Michaelson, a former teacher over at the academy school. She was involved in an assault case last year. I was hoping you could get a confirmation for me on the details."

"I remember that case. I wasn't assigned to it, but Nate Coulder was the detective. He said it was bullshit she was fired. He deserved his injuries and more. We've had a couple complaints about him. He's also on our domestic abuse watch list."

"Anything I can do to help with that?"

"Not at the moment. One of the female officers has been trying to encourage the wife to leave, but until she wants out, everyone's hands are tied."

"Got it. How's Tammy?"

"A mess. But don't tell her I said that." Dave said, laughing. "She's fretting over Juliette morning and night. But the doctor said she and the baby are healthy and that Tammy will stop being so anxious as the newness wears off."

I snorted. "Good luck. Lisa's getting worse."

"I can't even imagine. I gotta run, though. We just got a call for a disturbance at The Changing Room." Dave was laughing as he hung up. I was tempted to call the store, but figured I'd hear about it at dinner tonight.

"Your story checks out," I said to Beth. "What do you envision your daily agenda to be if I were to hire you?"

She hesitated, contemplating her words.

"Aunt Kelsey's a straight shooter," Sara said. "Whatever you're thinking, just spit it out."

Beth grinned over at Sara before answering. "The kids are smart, obviously, and it would make sense to continue the online classes since their education levels are so varied. But I wonder how much time they spend outdoors, playing in team sports, or going on field trips? I'd like to make sure that half of their schedule is outside of their core classes so they can explore other things."

"That could be arranged, but with some limitations. We are preparing a school room across the highway for the kids at Silver Aces Security. I work as an investigator and travel a lot. Sara's mother works at the store, The Changing Room. When she's working, it's busy, and she doesn't have the time to keep a close eye on the kids. We all felt Silver Aces was a safer environment for the kids to spend their days. When activities are scheduled off site, I'd require one of the security guards to accompany them."

"Are the kids in danger?"

"Not normally."

"Aunt Kelsey has a tendency to piss people off." Sara giggled.

"*Language*," Nicholas and I both scolded Sara.

"Sara, what are the consequences when you swear?" Beth asked her.

I sighed, leaning back into the couch. "I'm afraid we're pretty lax about punishing her."

Beth nodded her understanding. "Maybe we need a swear jar?"

"Sara's rich," Nicholas said, shaking his head. "She's got three piggy banks full of money."

"He's right. Both the kids work the adults over for money all the time. I'd hate to think how much money they have squirreled away. But a punishment is needed." I raised an eyebrow at Sara. "Ten pushups, young lady."

"Ten?" Sara whined.

"Get to it, or I'll make it twenty."

Sara got down on the floor and struggled to push herself up.

Beth laughed, watching Sara as Nicholas counted out the push-ups. "Maybe we need to focus on physical education right away."

"Mom hasn't offered you the job yet," Nicholas said.

"No, she hasn't. You're right. I'm getting ahead of myself."

Whiskey stepped into the room. "We have two more applicants waiting." Whiskey grinned down at Sara as she pushed up for number seven.

"Send them away," I said. "We've found our teacher. Meet Beth Michaelson."

"Ma'am," Whiskey said, nodding to Beth but he was still watching Sara. "What's this all about?"

"Get ready. We're installing a rule of ten pushups for every swear word."

Whiskey's face fell. "For just the kids, right?"

"The adults don't have to participate," Beth said, seeming nervous that she had instigated drama.

"Yes, they do," Sara insisted.

"She's right. We need to break the habit, at least while we're around the kids. And Sara has picked up quite the potty mouth."

Whiskey sighed. "I'll call and cancel the other appointments," he said before turning out of the room.

Nicholas laughed. "Sara and Whiskey are going to be sore tomorrow."

"I was thinking Aunt Katie," I said, laughing.

"Well, it's certainly different." Beth smirked as Sara dragged herself up from the floor.

"Kids, go play. We have adult stuff to talk about." I grabbed a folder off my desk as the kids raced out of the room. "I have the specifics of salary, time off, and benefits ready for you, and the employment forms that will need to be filled out. Let me know if you feel there are any issues."

"Oh," Beth said, when she looked in the folder. "This is very generous."

"You'll earn it. Those kids will challenge you."

Beth winked, filling out the forms. "I'm sure I can keep up."

Chapter Sixteen

"*Kelsey! Kelsey! Kelsey!*" Carl yelled, running into my bedroom and then into the atrium.

"Hey, Carl," I said, stepping around the coffee table to greet him.

Carl plowed into me.

"Are you home for good now?" Carl asked.

"I'll be home for a few days," I said as I pulled him along with me to sit on the couch. "I'm sorry I didn't get a chance to talk with you earlier this week. But I did hear about you blowing up Hattie's oven."

"I didn't mean to." Carl pouted. "Everyone but Alex and Grady yelled at me."

"What did Grady say?"

"That the kids could've been hurt."

"And what did Alex say?"

"He said I was grounded. And I had to move in with him and go to work with him for a while."

I grinned at Carl who was trying to look sad, but I could see the mischief in his eyes. "And does Alex know where you are right now?"

"Yes, luv," Alex said, entering the room wearing a white silk blouse, black dress pants, and black heeled boots. "I decided to turn him over to you for a couple hours. He keeps running around yelling at the customers to hurry up and leave so he can visit you."

Carl raised a hand to cover his grin.

I shoulder nudged him before looking back at Alex. "It's fine. I have to work for a couple hours, but Tech and I can keep him busy."

Alex blew air kisses at me before turning on a heel and leaving again.

"Why don't you check on the kids for me, Carl. And if you catch the kids swearing, they have to do ten pushups."

"Sara's going to look like Popeye," Carl said before running out of the room.

"How did he blow up an oven?" Beth asked as she stacked the completed forms and passed them back to me.

"He invents things. He was working on some type of traceable chemical, and when he tested it for heat tolerance—kaboom. Test failed."

"He should've used a smaller sample in a controlled environment. I don't mind working with him when the kids are doing their online classes."

"I was hoping he could go on some field trips too. I can send two guys on days that he goes, to help keep track of him."

"Won't be a problem. He seems to have a busy mind, but he has good listening skills. I worked with a woman who had a head injury and had similar behaviors. As long as I kept her busy, she stayed out of trouble."

"He won't always be around. Tech, our computer investigator, takes him for a couple of shifts a week, and when I'm home, I pick up a few shifts too."

"Offer stands. I'm used to juggling thirty or more kids, so it won't be a problem." She shrugged. "Now I better check on them. Wouldn't want anything to explode on my first day."

I laughed. "I didn't even ask, when can you start?"

"I'm already here. I'll stick around for a couple hours and work out a lesson plan with Carl and the kids before I leave. I'll need to know what my budget will be for our field trips, though."

"No worries over a budget. Kelsey's loaded," Katie said, standing at the entrance of the atrium.

"Nice, Katie," I said, rolling my eyes. "Very professional."

"You know you love me," she said, turning back to Beth. "I'll arrange a charge card and a petty cash box. Hi, I'm Katie."

"Beth," she said, shaking Katie's hand.

I handed Katie the stack of forms, and she turned to leave. "The kids are playing on the back deck, if you want to follow me."

Katie led Beth out of the room as my phone rang.

"Kelsey."

"It's Maggie. You got a minute?"

"Actually, I do. I just hired a teacher for the kids, and she's offered to keep Carl busy too."

"That's good, because we have a problem. Get the kids and yourself over to Silver Aces, and go on red alert. Call me back when you're in your war room."

"Give me five minutes," I said as I hung up and ran down the hall.

Once in the dining room, I hit the alarm on the wall. Sara dragged Carl by the hand into the living room followed by Nicholas pulling Beth into the house. Whiskey ran over and locked the sliding door.

"What's wrong?" Katie asked.

"I don't know yet. Maggie called and said for me to move the kids to Headquarters and go on lockdown."

"I'll get the backpacks," Sara said, running over to the dining room table and loading up their laptops and school work.

"I'll get the go bags," Nicholas said, pulling duffle bags out of the coat closet.

"I'll man the front door," Whiskey said. "We'll leave when the SUV pulls up."

I turned to Beth.

"Umm," she said, grinning nervously at me.

Katie laughed. "I'll make sure the house is locked down after everyone's been moved."

"Just watch your back until we know what's going on," I said to Katie. "And then get to the store and keep an eye on everyone."

"I know the drill," she said. "We'll be fine. Maggie said for you and the kids to go on lockdown. If it was a bigger threat, she would've told you to put everyone on lockdown."

"Aunt Kelsey pissed off another bad guy," Sara said.

"Pushups!" Nicholas and I told Sara.

She sighed, dropping to the floor. "This is going to get old real fast."

I did a full three-second eye roll before turning back to Beth. "You might as well learn as we go. When I was made aware of a threat, I activated the alarm. There's a panel in the upstairs hall, Sara's room, Nicholas' room, the basement gym, and here in the dining room. The alarm sends text messages to the family and to the war room, where Tech and I work. If Tech doesn't respond to the alarm within thirty seconds, the building alarm at Silver Aces goes off. As long as it's safe to do so, you wait wherever you're at for backup."

The doorbell rang, and Grady entered.

I turned to Beth to explain. "The guys will ring the doorbell before they enter, so you'll know it's them. Bad guys don't ring doorbells. Everyone who's allowed inside the house during a red alert, has a key."

"Where's the threat?" Grady asked.

"Maggie called. We need to move the kids to Headquarters."

Grady picked up Nicholas with one arm, keeping his other arm free for his gun. Whiskey took both backpacks and go-bags and picked up Sara while she was still struggling to complete her last pushup. Bones looked at me, waiting for the nod. Pulling my gun, I threw an arm over Beth's shoulders and pulled her close to me as we moved into the garage and inside the awaiting SUVs. Bones reversed our SUV out of the garage as the last door closed.

A minute and a half later, both SUVs were parked perpendicular to the front entrance of Headquarters with security guards bordering the path to the doors. I pulled Beth along with me into the building and didn't stop until we were in the gym.

"Holy shit," Beth said, looking around. "I feel like I'm in a movie. How'd we get here so quick?"

"Practice," Nicholas said as he smiled up at her. "And you owe ten pushups."

"She's a newbie, so we'll give her a pass on the swear word," I said to Nicholas before turning to Beth. "And I said the kids weren't usually in danger. That doesn't mean we don't take threats seriously."

"All right, then." She handed her purse to Nicholas and dropped to the floor to do ten pushups. "But I'm willing to take the same punishment as the kids. Nobody's allowed to laugh at me, though."

"What on earth?" Grady said, raising an eyebrow at Beth on the floor.

The kids counted out Beth's pushups and cheered when she got to ten in record time.

"New rule for swearing," I answered Grady. "Kids, can you take Beth up to the classroom and show her around while I figure out what the lockdown is about?"

The kids giggled as they offered Beth their hands and pulled her up from the floor. "This way," Sara said as she dragged her toward the stairs.

Grady braced a hand behind my neck and pulled me tight against him. His lips found mine and demanded attention. I released an involuntary moan as my nipples rubbed against his hard chest.

I was panting when he finally ended the kiss. "What was that for?"

"I needed to release some stress," he said, leaning his forehead against mine. "I hate it when the house alarm goes off. Every time Tech yells red alert and to get to the kids, I swear my blood turns cold."

"Well, starting today, they'll be in their new classroom. Maybe then you won't feel so anxious," I said as I wrapped my hands around his neck. "And maybe later tonight, we'll work on releasing some more stress."

Grady grinned as he lifted me by the ass and my legs wrapped around his hips. He kissed me again as he walked us back and pressed me against the wall.

"Mom! Gross!" Nicholas yelled from the open walkway on the second floor.

Both Grady and I laughed, breaking the moment.

"I better go find out why Maggie sounded the alarm."

He smirked as he lowered me to my feet. "Fine. But I'm holding you to tonight."

"Head back to your trainees. I'll loop you in later."

"You sure?"

I laughed. "Yeah. You still have a couple of slackers. Better go teach them what real men are made of."

Grady looked over his shoulder to see two of the guys looking bored, leaning against a wall as the others ran laps. *Did I say it was break time?* Grady yelled as he turned and moved their way. "What? Did you both stay up past your bedtime last night?"

I laughed as I jogged up the stairs and entered the war room.

"What's all the yelling?" Maggie asked from the TV screen mounted on the wall.

"Grady's got a couple lazy trainees. They're going to flunk out, but he's having a little fun with them before he cuts them loose."

"Hey, we all need to direct our frustrations somewhere," Maggie said, grinning.

"Talk to me. Why are we on lockdown?"

"You better sit and get comfy while I patch Genie in. She ran into the Atlanta office to work today."

"Where are you?"

"I'm in Atlanta too. I drove her back yesterday. But I'm waiting on approval to get my old job back. You're fired, by the way."

"I'm sure Kierson will be relieved."

"I talked to him yesterday. I can't believe you took an unregistered gun into FBI headquarters. Nice."

Genie's smiling face popped up on the other screen, and Tech used the remote to turn up the volume. "Hello, my sweet friends."

"Hey, Genie."

"Has Maggie filled you in?"

"She was waiting for you."

"You should sit," Maggie said.

"Shit," Tech grumbled, pushing one of the rolling chairs toward me.

Donovan walked into the office as I was sitting down. I kicked another chair over to him. "You just get back?"

"Yeah," he said, throwing himself into the chair. "I was pulling up to the house as Lisa and Abigail were being loaded into an SUV and moved here. I'm wiped out though. What the hell is going on?"

"Not sure yet. Maggie's stalling."

"You're going to be pissed," she said.

"How pissed?"

Genie snickered. "Lethal pissed."

"With a dollop of acid on top," Maggie added.

"I'm already getting pissed that you two are wasting my time. Now spill."

"Remember Axle Sorato?" Maggie asked. "And how you sent me to dig up dirt on him?"

"It was only a few days ago, so yes, I do. What of it? You said you found a biker and got some intel, but we didn't have time to talk."

"Well, the biker I talked to had left the Hell Hounds when they started getting into human trafficking. Now he's with another club, but he still keeps a close eye on the Hell Hounds."

"Don't tell me the Hell Hounds are back in business."

"No, not really. The club has been dismantled, all six chapters, but some members started to gather and reopen for business. They don't wear a cut, but their link is the former club."

"So Sorato banded together with some of his former brothers in leather. Okay. What's their play? Reopening their drug market? Or worse, human trafficking?"

"The guy I talked to didn't know what they were into, only that they started regrouping."

"None of this is equaling a red alert for my family. What am I missing?"

"No, it was merely interesting at that point. But when we got back to Atlanta, I had some extra time on my hands and started digging up the records for the other known members of the Hell Hounds—at least the ones still breathing and not residing in a six-by-eight cell. I dug into the club's previous arrest records too and kept digging deeper. Then I remembered that the Hell Hounds did jobs for Ernesto Chaves."

I was watching Maggie on the screen and noticed her release a slow breath. *"No..."* I said, shaking my head and standing.

Maggie nodded. "Charges were dropped. Ernesto Chaves is a free man. After Penny died, his lawyer made the claim that Penny was running the show without his knowledge."

Donovan stood abruptly, his chair rolling back. "He ran a sex slave operation from his home estate!"

"He claimed his estate was large enough that he never noticed what was happening."

"What about the bank accounts?" Tech asked. "They showed the money trail started years before he met Penny."

"We couldn't directly tie those accounts to him. The funds were wired to a third-party account in the Cayman Islands."

"*So that's it? He's out?*" I asked.

"He was released four and half weeks ago," Genie said. "His estate in Texas was seized and will be retained by the federal government, but he reclaimed the rest of his assets."

"Unbelievable!" I turned and kicked my chair into the wall. "So Chaves was the one who hired Axle Sorato to spy on me?"

Maggie shook her head. "For once, I don't think you're the target. You were still searching for Nicholas back then, so we kept your name out of the reports."

"Who's he after then?"

"Bones, Donovan, and Grady's names were part of the arrest report. Along with Reggie, Wild Card, and a couple of the other guys from Texas."

"Grady was on that job? I didn't even know him back then."

"He was one of the guys Wild Card called to meet us," Donovan said, nodding.

"Call Texas and get everyone's asses locked down," I said to Donovan as I stormed out of the room.

I stomped down the stairs as my temper rose. Ernesto Chaves was an insult to humanity, a waste of space, slicker than dog shit, the worst kind of predator. I was thoroughly pissed that an operation I had turned over to the FBI was threatening so many of our lives.

I looked across the gym and made eye contact with Grady as I stepped off the last stair.

"Clear the mats!" Grady yelled as I crossed the gym floor and kicked off my boots and socks. Grady grinned down at me. "Do you want to change first?"

"Hell, no," I snapped as I walked onto the mat. "Give me your best."

Grady ordered everyone to put on safety gear and then ordered three of them to attack me. When the first three crawled off the mat, I motioned to Grady and he sent four more at me. One guy almost landed a strike, *almost*. When Grady ordered the next batch of men to the mat, they didn't move.

"Chicken?" Grady asked them.

"Do you blame us? She's a raging bull with a black belt!" one of the guys answered. "You're the one who told us to know when we're outmanned."

Grady smirked as he pulled off his shoes and socks and joined me on the mat. We circled each other, watching the other's body for the slightest twitch.

"I take it the news from Maggie wasn't pleasant," Grady said before he attempted a kick that I easily side stepped.

I charged with a punch that I knew he'd easily block, but I turned and swept his right leg, taking him to one knee. He spun and used the force of his arm to sweep my legs out from under me. I rolled back, then up and over my shoulders to a standing position before he was able to pin me.

"Nice move." He rolled to the side out of my range before standing. "Talk."

"Ernesto Chaves was released." As Grady's face reflected a moment of shock, I swept both his legs and threw an arm across his chest with enough force that he landed flat on his back. His body curled slightly as he pulled air into his lungs.

"Shit. You all right?" I asked, leaning over to check on him.

He grabbed one of my legs, pulling me off balance as he twisted it behind me. I hit the mat, and he rolled his weight on top of me to pin me down. "Trainees! Thirty laps!" Grady hollered without looking away from me. "What the fuck? We caught him red handed!"

"His lawyers blamed it all on Penny. And seeing she's dead, she can't defend herself and testify against him."

Grady growled, punching the mat beside my head.

"Well, don't you two look cozy," Nana said, standing at the edge of the mat.

"Nana, didn't you go home?"

"No, dear. I've been around. You slept all day yesterday so Dallas and I went out for drinks. We overdid it a smidge, so I slept in this morning. Boy, was I surprised when a bulky security guy stormed into my bedroom at Lisa's house and declared that I needed to leave. Man, he was smokin'."

"Why are you staying at Lisa's?"

"It was less crowded over there. Besides, that woman is unraveling and someone needs to keep an eye on her. Now, are you going to get up, or are you two going to make out with everyone watching?"

"I don't mind a crowd," Grady said, nipping at my chin.

"The kids and my Nana?" I slugged him in the arm. "I don't think so."

"Well when you put it that way." He sighed as he rolled off me and stood up. "So where do we stand with Chaves?"

"Maggie's guessing he's coming after you guys because your names were in the arrest report. He could be coming after the whole company, though."

"This is our mess then, not yours. You take the trainees, and I'll catch up with Donovan and Maggie to gather more intel on Chaves."

"Really?" I asked surprised.

"I got this one, babe," he said, leaning down to kiss me before he jogged away toward the stairs.

"He makes me all tingly," Nana said, watching Grady jog up the stairs. "If I was ten years younger…"

"He'd still be mine," I said.

She snickered and then amused herself by watching the trainees run their laps. I pulled my phone from my back pocket and cursed when I realized the lens was cracked.

Chapter Seventeen

"Trainees, line up!" I called out to the room. "Can I also get a couple off-duty guards?"

Several of the off-duty guys jogged over.

"You and you." I pointed to two of the trainees. "Grady has other priorities, and I'm not as entertained by your laziness. Go pack your bags. You're both out of the program."

"We have more experience than any of the other trainees," one of the guys said.

"I don't give a shit. We don't hire sloths," I said, nodding to the off-duty guards who escorted the trainees from the gym. "And now we're down to nine. How many did we start with?"

"Twenty-two," Bones answered, walking over with Bridget.

"I was told you were on your way to Nebraska."

Bones shrugged. "They arrested the stalker before I left, so I didn't have to go. Where's Grady?"

"He's in the war room. You, Donovan, and Grady are officially on lockdown. Chaves was cut loose, and he's looking for payback."

"What the fuck?"

"And we initiated a swear rule. Ten pushups if you swear in front of the kids. But I'm thinking dropping the f-bomb might require more."

He glared at me a moment before heading for the stairs. Bridget bounced next to me.

I handed her my cell phone. "Can you take this to Tech?"

She looked at the phone and giggled before skipping off toward the stairs.

"Darling..." Dallas called out, swaying all hundred and thirty pounds of herself, which was mostly boobs and ass, into the room. "You missed a bitch'n night last night. Your nana is a hoot."

She blew air kisses at me and then at Nana. Nana made awkward kissy noises back at her. Dallas shook her head. "That's not how you do it, dear. I'll teach you later. You have so much to learn."

"Trainee Scott Bailey," I called out to the group, ignoring Dallas.

Scott Bailey stepped forward. "Ma'am."

"Did Grady get a chance to talk to you about your background?"

His shoulders deflated before he answered. "No, ma'am."

"Enough of that ma'am crap. My name is Kelsey. How did you get out of the gang in Chicago?"

"Walked away. My momma was shot by someone gunning for me. After the funeral, I left Chicago and never went back."

"No contact at all?"

"No, ma—, uhh, Kelsey."

"Why did you lie on your application?"

"I'm not that person anymore," he said. "I even had the tats re-inked."

"Anything else in your history that you failed to disclose?"

"No."

"Fine. We'll keep you on—*for now*. But if you're hired in, we'll have to restrict your assignments away from inner cities."

He released a breath and stepped back in line.

"All right boys and—girl." I grinned at the one female trainee still remaining. "This afternoon we are going to try some on-the-job training. Hope you're ready for this. I need two volunteers to step forward."

Everyone stepped forward.

I laughed. "If you think you're the best candidate for the job, step forward."

Everyone stepped forward again.

"Pretty arrogant bunch," Nana snickered.

"We'll see," I said before turning back to the trainees. "If you're willing to go up against me on the mats again, step forward."

No one stepped forward.

"Smart too," Dallas said to Nana from behind me.

"Okay, fine!" I laughed. "Bailey and Alverez."

Bailey and Alverez stepped forward.

"Go shower and change for plain clothes security. Meet back here in ten minutes."

Bailey and Alverez jogged toward the gym's doors.

"Drake, step forward."

Trainee Drake took one military step forward, his back ramrod straight.

"Drake, you are tasked with shadowing Donovan's wife and child. They are currently upstairs in the classroom. If Lisa tries to leave, you stop her. Whenever she's not with Donovan, you are to be close by."

I swear he almost saluted me before he stopped himself and merely nodded.

I turned to the other trainees. "The rest of you will be split between the resale store across the street and the private residences and woodlands surrounding them. Go shower, change, and report back in ten minutes to start your assignments."

Bridget returned with a new phone, handing it to me. I called Whiskey, knowing he and some of the other club members from Devil's Players would be at the store. I updated him on the threat and let him know I was sending rookies over to help with security. He promised to get them set up with stations.

Next, I texted Tech and told him I'd need seven linked earpieces, plus a couple for the Devil's Players. Then I called Tyler and asked him to come over to retrieve the guys who would be assigned to patrol the houses and woods. As one of the club's prospects, Tyler knew the drill.

~*~*~

Alverez and Bailey both jogged back into the gym with three minutes to spare. Both were wearing black suits with white shirts, but Alverez's fit horribly.

"Bridget?"

"Yeah," she said from beside me as we looked at Alverez. "I can fix it, but not today. I'll go talk to Alex."

"Fix what?" Alverez said, looking down at her outfit.

"It was a nice try, but that outfit is all wrong for you," Dallas said.

"How tall are those shoulder pads," Nana asked, walking over to smoosh down the pads. "Nearly three inches thick, I'd say."

"Don't forget shoes, Bridget," Dallas called out.

Bridget waved a hand, indicating she'd heard. I looked down at Alverez's shoes and chuckled. She had on black Nikes with white stripes. I checked Bailey's shoes and noticed he had on regulation security shoes which looked like dress shoes but were flexible like running shoes.

"Have you done security detail work before?" I asked him.

"I worked for a smaller company in Oregon before they folded," he said. "There wasn't enough work to go around, so I didn't get much field experience, but some. And, I took a course in Executive Protection."

"Good. Then you can share your knowledge with Alverez. Today, the two of you are a team. And you'll need to rely on each other to succeed. Your assignment is to keep track of these two," I said, pointing to Nana and Dallas. "I'll warn you—the last pair of security guards assigned to Dallas failed miserably. I was lucky we weren't arrested." Bailey and Alverez both appeared dubious. "Your task will be to keep them safe, from outsiders and themselves. You are to deliver them to my house by no later than eight o'clock tonight. Understood?"

"What's the threat?" Alverez asked.

"It's doubtful anyone would go after either one of them. But Nana is related to me, and a nasty scumbag was set loose who is a credible threat to Silver Aces staff and my family. More importantly, though, this assignment will give you both a chance to learn how to handle difficult clients without the worry of Silver Aces being sued."

Both of them raised an eyebrow but remained silent.

"Best of luck."

Dallas looped her arm through Nana's and towed her toward the door. "Tootles," Dallas called over her shoulder.

Bailey and Alverez hurried after them.

The remaining trainees returned, and after I updated them on an unknown threat against the security firm and their families, I handed out the earpieces that Tech had brought down to me. Dispersing in different directions, Drake went upstairs to guard Lisa and Abigail, three guys followed Tyler to the houses, and three guys left to meet with Whiskey at the store.

Alone again, I walked across the gym and entered Jerry's office. Jerry was one of the site managers and helped with case assignments.

"Hey, Kelsey," he said after he ended the call he was on. "What can I do for you?"

"What's the expectation of privacy for the bunkhouse?"

"You sound like Grady." He snorted. "None. Grady had the lawyers add into their contracts that we can search their rooms and belongings during their training period. We don't need to provide notice, nor tell them that we even looked. I assume you'll want the master keys and a list of room assignments?"

"That would save time, yes," I said, grinning. "Was Axle Sorato's room searched?"

"Nope. Feds never came back. And his truck is still here, too." Jerry handed me a clipboard and a set of master keys. "I don't have the keys to his truck, but they're probably in his room. Happy hunting."

"Jerry, what the hell is going on?" Wayne asked as he stepped into the office. "I was ready to board a plane when you called me back."

Wayne was one of the full-time guards who took high target cases. He'd once gone with me to visit a voodoo witch in New Orleans. It didn't go well. We ended the night with him singing karaoke at a biker bar.

"Hey, Wayne," I said. "Were you part of the team who took down Chaves in southern Texas?"

"Yeah, I was there." Wayne cocked his head, his scowl deepening.

"Chaves was released. He's coming after someone or everyone. We don't have enough details to know who his targets are yet. Want to help me dig up dirt?" I asked, holding up the clipboard and keys.

"Whatever you're up to, does Grady know?" Wayne asked as he shook his head in disbelief.

"What fun would that be?" I asked, walking out of the office.

Wayne followed me and took the clipboard. "We're searching the bunkhouse?"

"Room to room, including the room of the guy Chaves hired to spy on us. And his truck."

Wayne whistled at the off-duty guys who were sitting around playing cards. "Need some more hands. We got trouble brewing and need to search the bunkhouse."

All the guys stood and followed us out.

On the way over, I updated everyone on what little intel I knew. Then I explained that I wanted to know about anything odd in any of the rooms. Wayne and I would take Sorato's room and truck. I unlocked Sorato's door and then handed the keys off to one of the other guys. They took the clipboard and divided up.

"What are we hoping to find?" Wayne asked as he opened the closet and I walked over to the small desk below the dinky window.

"Anything: a phone, pictures, letters. I need to build a profile on this guy."

"What about explosives?" Wayne asked.

I walked over to where Wayne was squatting in front of a duffle bag in the closet. "Is that—"

"A shitload of C-4? Yup." Wayne stood and took a step back. "Luckily it doesn't seem to be hooked to anything, so we should be safe. I wouldn't light a cigarette right now, but other than that..."

I stepped into the hallway and called Grady.

"Yeah?" His short, clipped response told me he was already on edge.

"I need you to stay calm."

"How calm?"

"Calm enough to keep everyone else from panicking as you evacuate Headquarters and move everyone off site."

"What happened?"

"Wayne just found a duffle of C-4 in Sorato's room."

"*Fuck*. He was here for weeks!"

"Grady, get the kids out of the building. I'm pretty sure he didn't have a chance to act on anything, but until we know for sure, I don't want them on the property."

"Sounding the alarm now. I'll have a team take the kids for ice cream while the off-duty guys sweep the houses."

"They're already over here. I'll send them back your way. I'll also have them sound the alarm in the apartments."

"Stay safe," Grady said as he hung up.

"He pissed?" Wayne asked.

"He's not happy, that's for sure." Several of the guys had stepped into the hall and had listened to the call. "Lisa and the kids are being relocated until we can do a full sweep. We'll also need security rotations setup."

Wayne split the guys into teams to protect the main house and search all the buildings from the roofs to the basements.

"Ryan?" Wayne called. "The bag I found appears safe to relocate, but I'm not as comfortable with that shit as you are."

"Show me," Ryan said, following Wayne into the room.

A moment later, Ryan walked out with the duffle bag thrown over his shoulder, heading for the exit. Wayne came out shaking his head.

"Where's he taking it?"

"Don't know. Don't care," Wayne said. "He wants us to stay clear of the room and Sorato's truck until he does a full search. He's going to go grab some of his gear."

"Didn't he get married recently?"

"He did. And his woman would freak if she knew he liked to play with things that go boom, so don't slip up and mention this to her should you ever meet her."

"She knows he works for a national security company though, right?"

"She knows he's a badass. She just doesn't know he's a crazy fucking badass."

Chapter Eighteen

It took five hours to search all the buildings from top to bottom. By the time Wayne and I returned to Sorato's room, we tossed his keys, phone, pictures, and any scrap of paper we could find into a gym bag and carried it out to his truck to repeat the process. Then we took the bag to the main house where we could sort it while enjoying a cold beverage.

"What took you so long?" Grady asked, greeting me at the door and taking the bag I was carrying. "I was told the buildings were cleared half an hour ago."

"We went back for Sorato's personal effects," I answered, stepping up on my toes to kiss his scowl away.

"We closed the store down early," Katie said, walking over and taking the bag from Grady. "There's a pitcher of Margaritas in the fridge."

"Yum," I said, getting a glass out.

Wayne pulled the pitcher, filled my glass, and returned it to the refrigerator before grabbing himself a beer.

"You both need to eat first," Lisa scolded, filling plates and passing us each one. "I had food sent out to the guards too."

I was about to ask where the kids were when my phone rang. I set my dinner plate on the counter and carried my drink with me to the back deck to answer the call. Grady followed me out.

"Kelsey."

"It's Mickey."

"Hey, I was—" I stopped mid-sentence, my blood turning cold as I dropped the phone and drink and barreled into Grady. "Sniper!" I yelled, pushing us both to the deck floor as I heard the bullet hit the side of the house where Grady had been standing.

Grady rolled us toward the door before getting his feet under him and dragging me with him inside the house, through the living room, and around the corner into the kitchen.

"Aunt Kelsey?!" Sara yelled from somewhere upstairs.

"Stay upstairs! Is Nicholas with you?"

"Yes! Carl's here too!" she called back from somewhere out of sight.

"Safe room! *Now*!" Grady yelled back.

"Kelsey?" Anne called from the hallway on the other side of the dining room.

Whiskey had her pinned to the floor with his body draped over her. Drake was also crouched in the hallway, his arms wrapped around baby Abigail.

I nodded at Whiskey. "Drake, give Abigail to Anne. Whiskey, get them through the access in my room to the safe room upstairs. Stay locked in until it's clear."

Anne took Abigail, and Whiskey shielded both of them as he moved Anne down the hall, disappearing into my bedroom.

"Kelsey," Lisa cried, clutching my arm from beside me in the kitchen.

"Lisa, I know you're scared, but that room has three-inch steel walls. Nobody's getting in or out unless Sara knows them."

"Okay, okay," Lisa mumbled. "What do I do?"

Just then, Drake dove from the hallway, past the open area of the living and dining rooms, and pulled himself up between Lisa and me.

"I've got her," Drake said, holding Lisa away from the living room and shielding her with his body.

"Dumbass," I said, grinning. "There's five trained guards on this side of the room."

"You told me to protect them," he said, grinning back.

I rolled my eyes and felt Grady's body beside me vibrate from his laughter.

"Donovan?" I yelled out.

"Basement!" he answered back. "A second shot was fired through the glass door down here. We're trapped on the far side."

"How many guys are with you?"

"I've got six."

"Take the tunnel to Alex's house and follow the trail back to the east property. Grady and I will split up and take the woods from the north and east while your team comes in from the south. Let's trap this asshole!"

"Furnace room!" Donovan ordered the men with him.

Grady, Wayne, and I ran into the garage and got into one of my SUVs. Tyler and two of the trainees who were guarding the front of the house squeezed in as well.

"Drop me, Tyler, and one of the trainees off at the road, then you, Wayne, and the other trainee can come in from the center of the woods on the east side."

Grady nodded but he let out a growl, looking in the rearview mirror. I jumped out of the SUV and yelled at the guy who had pulled in behind us. "Move your car!"

"Are you Kelsey Harrison?" the guy asked, stepping out of his car. "I was asked to give this to you." He handed me a manila envelope that had *Summons to Appear* stamped on the front.

"Job well done, now move your *fucking* car!" I yelled, raising my gun at him.

He jumped in his car, putting it in gear to back up, as I climbed back into the SUV. Grady reversed onto the street, cutting off the guy and pulling out ahead of him. I tossed the summons on the floor of the SUV and yelled at Tyler to pull the flak jackets. His tall skinny frame was able to turn around in the crowded seat and stretch far enough to open the back compartment and pass jackets forward. I strapped one on before dropping another one over Grady's head and securing the Velcro straps while he drove.

"First stop," Grady called out, pulling to the side of the road.

I swung out of the car, shutting the door behind me as Tyler pushed one of the trainees out of the back and jumped out as well.

"If you're not up to this, you can hang back," I told the trainee.

"I'm game, but unarmed. I'm not licensed to carry a gun in Michigan yet."

Tyler handed him a Glock. "It's from your stash in the SUV," Tyler told me as he pulled his own Glock. "So be sure to collect it later."

"Okay, we go in quiet but quick. V-formation. I'll take point. Fist up in the air means hold and freeze. If I drop to the ground, you better follow suit and take cover. Are you guys ready? This isn't a drill."

The trainee shrugged as he checked the clip in the Glock. I glanced at Tyler, and he grinned.

"Let's root this fucker out," I said, starting into the woods.

Tyler and the guy nicknamed Trigger flanked both my sides, about two dozen feet away. We were moving at a good clip but quiet enough that we'd hear anyone trying to move past us.

Fifty yards into the woods, I raised my fist into the air. I sensed someone nearby, but I couldn't pinpoint the location. I glanced back at Tyler. He was scanning the woods. I glanced over my other shoulder at Trigger, and he was crouched down, aimed up ahead at the trees. I followed his line of sight and saw the shooter in camo, rifle still aimed to the west, toward the main house. I didn't have a clear shot from my position. I glanced back at Trigger and gave him the nod, hoping his nickname was related to his shooting capabilities.

Trigger fired. The sniper screeched and was flung away from the tree. We watched him bounce off two large limbs, yelping each time, before he landed on the hard-packed ground with a loud *whoof*.

"We have a sniper down," Tech called over his earpiece as we moved in.

The sniper was trying to reach for his rifle when I crushed his hand under my boot. He yelped again. I aimed my gun between his eyes, and he stopped moving.

"Search him. Check for an earpiece. There might be more than one shooter."

"Found one," Tyler said, pulling it out of his ear and cringing. "It's all yours."

"No, thanks." I took a step back, away from the earpiece.

"Hand it over," Trigger said, reaching for it.

A moment later Trigger jumped back at the same time we heard a gunshot in the distance. Trigger pulled the earpiece out and threw it to the ground. "Second sniper down. Now I know what it sounds like when a guy's head pops."

I reached into my boot and pulled flex cuffs out, handing them to Tyler. He rolled the guy and zipped his hands tightly together. We heard movement ahead of us and simultaneously crouched down and raised our weapons.

"Hold your fire, babe," Grady called out before coming into view.

"Donovan's team?"

"Pissed that they didn't get to shoot anyone. I told Donovan it was unlikely your guy was dead so he could have first dibs."

"I wasn't sure if you wanted him dead or disabled." Trigger shrugged. "I took out his kneecap."

"Kelsey let you take the shot?" Grady grinned with a raised eyebrow. "Usually she gets pretty territorial when it comes to threats against the family."

"Damn tree was blocking my view," I grumbled. "But I broke a few bones in his hand with my boot, so I feel better now."

"That's my girl," Grady said, leaning in to kiss me. "Head home. Wayne and I will take care of this."

"I'll stay," Tyler said. "Trigger, stay close to Kelsey until she's back inside."

I grinned at Tyler's take-charge manner and shoulder nudged him. He'd likely go from prospect to challenging James for the president's seat at the rate he was learning. Tyler holstered his gun, giving me a push in the direction of the house, before he leaned down to help Grady drag the guy off the ground and through the woods.

"Come on, Trigger. I'm not really sure what they have planned for that guy, but it might not be legal, so the fewer witnesses the better."

"Fucker shot at a house full of women and children. He doesn't deserve to live," Trigger said as he walked with me through the woods.

I decided it was best to change the subject. "What's up with the nickname?"

I looked over when he didn't answer and saw him blushing.

"I was told never to lie to you, so I'll tell you the truth. I was fifteen when I got the nickname. Let's just say I'd get a little too excited on the few occasions that I ended up naked with a girl, and the rumor started that I had a quick trigger. By the time I was eighteen, I couldn't shake the nickname, so I decided my best option was to learn to shoot guns really well." He smirked over at me. "I also got better at sex."

I laughed. "Who told you never to lie to me?"

"Everyone. They said you were a walking lie detector. They also said to never play poker with you."

"Appreciate your honesty, but from this moment forward, you have my permission to lie your ass off if anyone asks about your nickname."

"Thanks," he said, before stopping and turning a scary shade of white.

I froze and looked around. "What is it?" I whispered.

"Fuck!" he yelled, pulling out the earpiece that was linked to the other security teams. "I must've left the mic on."

"Everyone heard you?" I laughed, doubling over and grasping my knees. "You are so screwed. By tomorrow, every guard with Silver Aces is going to know."

"Shit. I'll have to quit," he said, starting through the woods again.

"No, you won't. They'll tease you, but they won't hold it against you. You weren't the only teenage boy who was quick on the draw. And look at it this way, at least they'll know who you are. Most of the time, these guys ignore the new guys."

Trigger snorted and shook his head. "You're one odd lady."

"I've been called worse."

I rang the doorbell before entering the house through the basement sliding door. Trigger followed me up the stairs and into the open kitchen.

"All clear!" I called out and heard a collective sigh throughout the house.

"I'll get Anne and the kids," Katie said as she ran up the stairs.

Lisa ran after her, with Drake following.

"I'll call someone to replace the glass in the basement," Goat said.

I walked out to the balcony and retrieved my phone, carrying it back inside before tossing it to Tech.

"This phone was brand new," Tech said as he looked at the cracked plastic. He was laughing as he walked down the stairs where we kept a stash of replacement phones.

Sara, Nicholas, Anne, Whiskey, Lisa carrying Abigail, and Drake came down the stairs.

"Where's Carl?"

"He won't come down," Sara said, running over to me to pull at my arm so I'd lean forward. "He peed his pants, and he's embarrassed," she whispered.

"Got it." I started for the stairs. I found Carl pacing with tears in his eyes in Sara's room.

"I got scared."

"Everybody gets scared. Come on. We'll take the secret passageway to Alex's house so you can change."

"Nobody will see me?"

"Nope. Nobody will know."

I led the way down the ladder from the safe room, into my bedroom, then down the hidden ladder from inside my bedroom closet into the furnace room below. From there, I opened the hidden door behind the furnace and followed the tunnel first through Lisa and Donovan's basement, then the next tunnel over to Alex's house. Carl happily skipped past me to run upstairs and change his clothes. When he was ready, we followed the tunnels back to the main house, stopping in the basement gym.

"Thank you, Kelsey."

"You're welcome. Now go find Sara and Nicholas and make sure they're behaving while I clean up down here."

"Okay," he said, running up the stairs.

I pulled the trash can out and grabbed the broom and dustpan, carrying both over to the sliding door and sweeping up the glass. When I was done, I turned to see the trajectory of the bullet and cringed. The bullet hole was dead center on the back rest of the leg press.

"Bones was on it," Katie said, handing me a drink. "They heard you call out, and he rolled off the chair onto the floor right before the bullet came through."

"Shit."

"Yeah. Nicholas and Goat are searching for a contractor to install bullet-proof glass. The windows on the back of the house need to be upgraded."

"I'm good with that," I said before taking a drink. "But maybe we should level the woods. Clear all of it. This isn't the first time we've been in danger because of them."

"Let's wait. Carl and Sara are going through ideas to combine her heat sensor program to the new cameras Carl built. We might be able to have the woods covered electronically to alert us of a threat."

"Shit," I said again, walking over to sit on one of the barstools. "What am I doing? These kids aren't safe with all this chaos around us."

Katie shrugged, following me over to sit beside me. "Even with all the precautions we take, yes, sometimes the shit is going to float back up to the surface. It's inevitable."

"Not if I quit. Not if I move the kids away from all of this."

We both sat there in silence, drinking our drinks.

"Katie without a snarky retort?" Lisa said from the stairs. "You must be tired."

Katie shrugged. "I don't have kids. I don't know how I'd feel if I did."

"Well, I have a kid," Lisa said, gliding down the rest of the stairs, followed by Alex and Anne. "And while days like today scare the shit out of me, I'm proud of my husband for going after the bad guys. I'm proud of Kelsey for tracking their asses down. I'm proud to be part of a family that's fierce, loyal, strong, and has saved so many victims, including myself. I want my daughter to grow up learning to be brave, and to fight back, even if it's only in some small way. And like today, we'll continue to protect them until they're old enough to protect themselves."

"Kelsey," Anne said, walking over and grabbing my hand. "Sara and the rest of the kids were safe today because you made sure of it. You not only built a safe room, installed alarm systems, and designed secret tunnels, but you taught them what to do when an emergency does happen. My kid feels safer here than she ever did in our old life. Neither one of us has any interest in leaving."

"You are who you are," Alex said from behind me, wrapping his arms around me. "And we love you for it. How many lives have you saved in the last year alone? Thirty? Forty? More? And that's not including the people who would've become victims if you wouldn't have taken the bad guys down." He smacked his lips against my cheek and gave me a loud raspberry kiss.

I giggled and pushed him away.

"You making a move on my woman, Alex?" Grady grinned, stepping off the stairs and walking over.

"I knew her first," Alex said, pulling me away from Grady.

"And now she's mine." Grady said, pulling me off the stool and down the hall toward the old war room. I laughed as he somehow managed to manhandle me while being gentle at the same time.

Lifting me onto the table before the door had closed, Grady started pulling at our clothes until we were skin to skin. He entered me slowly, filling me as I leaned back and arched to take him deeper.

"Fuck," he growled as he pulled back and slammed into me again.

I moaned, gripping the edge of the table and holding on for the ride.

Chapter Nineteen

I stretched my arms above my head, breathing heavily as Grady laid his upper body across the table beside me, breathing just as hard.

"Your pep talks are way better than Lisa's," I said, reaching over to stroke my hand across his panther tattoo.

"You didn't need a pep talk," Grady said, raising enough off the table to lean over and smack his lips against mine. "You needed to release some of that inner frustration, and so did I."

There was a loud knock on the door.

"Go away," Grady growled.

"Wish I could, man. This is totally awkward," Tech yelled back. "But Mickey's on the phone, insisting on talking to Kelsey—*right the fuck now*. The dude scares the hell out of me."

Grady growled again. He picked up his shirt and tossed it to me. He waited for me to pull it over my head before he threw the door open, grabbed my cell phone, and slammed the door closed again. Seeing as Grady wasn't wearing a stitch of clothing, Tech likely saw more than he expected.

"Mickey," Grady said into the phone. "You have really bad timing." There was a pause before Grady replied. "Yeah, she's still alive. Hang on."

He handed me the phone and then picked up our clothes, tossing them on the table.

"Hey, Mickey. Sorry I hung up on you earlier."

"It's to be expected. But so is a call back next time!"

"I've been busy. *Geesh*."

"Ducking bullets or screwing Grady?"

"A bit of both," I answered, holding in a laugh. "Do you have intel?"

"Yes and no. My boys inside confirmed that Daryl Sorato played the middle man to connect his son with a guy by the name of Ernesto Chaves. I don't know who Chaves is, but it took one hell of a beating to get information out of the old man. Interestingly enough, Daryl was found shanked this morning, and I swear, my guys didn't do it. They roughed him up enough for a twenty-four-hour stint in medical, minus a few fingernails, but he was returned to his cell last night cleared for gen pop."

"His son died two days ago while in FBI custody. No surprise the father was next on the list. You better separate yourself from this one. I appreciate the intel, but we've got it from here."

"Who's Chaves? And why is he coming after you?"

"He's not really coming after me, at least we don't think so. Grady and some other guys were part of a raid last year that took Chaves down. Unfortunately, the case fell apart. Now he's running loose and looking for people to punish."

"Thus, you yelling sniper and dropping the phone earlier?"

"Yeah. But we're whole. Nothing more than a broken window."

Grady looked up with an evil grin.

"Well, at least on our side," I said, thinking of the snipers.

"Put Grady back on the phone."

I rolled my eyes, handing the phone to Grady.

"Yeah," he answered while pulling on his socks. He already had his jeans on, but was bare chested. "That's the plan." He noticed me watching him and tossed my bra at me with a chuckle. "I'll call when it's over. I still owe you a beer." There was another pause, and then Grady laughed. "I would, but she's being stubborn. Later, man."

I hooked my bra and pulled my V-neck sweater over my head. "What were you two discussing?"

"He asked me whether I was going to make an honest woman out of you and marry your ass."

"I was referring to the earlier part of the conversation. The 'call when it's over' part."

"Guy stuff." Grady smirked, smacking a kiss on my cheek and turning toward the door. "Hurry up. I'm starving."

I jumped off the table and pulled my jeans up, nodding to him that he could head out. He opened the door but waited patiently for me to put my socks and boots on. When I walked past him, he grabbed a handful of my butt in a squeeze that made me squeal. "Behave."

"No." He chuckled from behind me.

He was in an awfully good mood for a man who had a target on his back. I glanced over my shoulder at him, but he gave me a playful shove to get me moving. Using my hands to protect my backside, I ran up the stairs two at a time ahead of him and was greeted at the top by Lisa, who shoved a loaded dinner plate into my hands.

"Eat. Both of you." She handed Grady a similar plate.

In the dining room, our usual seats remained vacant. I chose to take Grady's chair, not the end chair where I usually sat. Several people paused around the table, noticing. Grady shrugged and sat at the head of the table.

He stretched his legs out, hooking a foot behind one of my ankles. I grinned to myself as I dug into the beef stroganoff and buttered French bread on my plate. Bridget walked over and placed a beer in front of Grady and a glass of milk in front of me. I happily accepted the milk.

"Hey, Tech? Do you like our new war room?" I asked.

"It's got everything I could think of," he said, nodding. "I handpicked the equipment myself."

"She means the room itself. The *ambience*," Bridget said. "The walls. The furniture. The décor."

Tech rolled his eyes. "It's a war room. It doesn't need ambience. Besides, I seldom look up from my computer monitors, so I don't care about the rest of the room. Though, the glass wall makes it awkward when I need to, umm... adjust the family jewels."

I grinned over at Tech, shaking my head. Working with mostly men these days, I'd become accustomed to the awkward fidgets and movement when they needed to adjust their boy parts. "Bridget, can you fix the room up for me?"

"Sure. I have credit cards for both Silver Aces and your personal account. Which card do you want me to use?"

"Personal. And get some of that tinted film to cover the windows so we can see down into the gym, but they can't see us. Then Tech can do whatever he wants when I'm not in there with him."

Bridget giggled. "I'll get started in the morning. Haley and I are going dancing tonight."

"The hell you are," Bones said from the other end of the table.

"Nobody's trying to kill *us*. As long as you're not with me, we'll be safe."

The front door opening paused their argument as everyone turned to see who it was. Alverez escorted Nana inside with a firm grip on her elbow. Bailey followed her through the door holding Dallas in a similar position.

"Permission to clock out," Alverez said, looking my way.

"Not until you report what happened. Were they arrested?"

"We got them out of the store before the police showed up," Bailey said, sighing. His shirt was torn with several buttons missing. He also had a bruise forming on his jaw.

"Got them out of where?"

Dallas and Nana stared down at the carpet, looking quite embarrassed. Bailey tugged on Dallas' arm, pulling her forward.

"Oh, for Pete's sake," Dallas said to Bailey before turning back to me. "It wasn't that big of a deal. We were at a sex toy store, and we decided to sneak into one of the back rooms to watch."

I looked around for the kids and noticed that they were standing off to the side with a pad of paper and a pencil. "What are you two up to?"

"Logging swear words," Nicholas said.

"Give me the sheet," I said, holding out my hand.

Sara skipped over and handed me the sheet. I rolled my eyes after scanning through it. "I'll handle it. Why don't you both head upstairs to play, though."

They both giggled and ran up the stairs. I set the pad down and motioned for Dallas to continue.

"We were perfectly fine."

"I was punched!" Bailey glared.

"You shouldn't have interfered," Nana said. "What happens in back rooms, stays in back rooms."

Grady was looking down at his plate, shaking with laughter.

"Tell them what you did next," Alverez said, pushing Nana in front of her.

"We were having a perfectly lovely time at a local bar. We weren't doing anything more than having a beer and dancing."

Nana's shirt was buttoned wrong, and no longer tucked in. Her hair was also standing up at odd angles.

"You were strip dancing in a biker bar!" Alverez yelled, throwing her hands up in the air.

"I only took off my shirt!" Nana yelled back at Alverez.

"Very true. She only took off her shirt," Dallas said, grinning.

"And you?" I asked.

"I might've taken off more than just my shirt." Dallas looked down and raised her breasts in her hands. "The girls looked especially good today."

"What bar?" I asked, gritting my teeth.

"The Last Season, just outside of Bangor," Bailey answered.

"I know it."

Grady pulled my phone from his back pocket and handed it to me. I called Renato.

"I was expecting a call." Renato laughed lightly. "They get home safe?"

"They're here. I'm not sure if they're safe, though. I'm still mad. Any damages?"

"No. And I encouraged the locals and ordered my guys to delete the videos from their phones. I recognized Dallas from your house. Who's the little old lady, though?"

"My *nana*."

Renato laughed and hung up.

I looked back at Dallas and Nana, pointing a finger at them. "From now on, you two are not allowed to be together outside this house. I mean it! If I catch you sneaking off, I'll put Nana on a plane back to North Carolina. And, Dallas, I'll rat your ass out to Dave and tell him what you did in Miami!"

They both inhaled sharply.

"Dallas, go home. Nana, go to Lisa's and clean yourself up."

Both of them scurried for the door, and as soon as it closed, we all started laughing.

"All right, everyone," I said, reviewing the list of logged swear words. "Every curse word said in front of the kids is ten pushups. Katie, you're at a hundred and twenty. Tech, you're in second place with forty."

I only logged twenty pushups because most of the swearing I had done hadn't been in front of the kids. I passed the list to Grady who called out everyone else's numbers.

"Shit," Tech grumbled as we all moved to the floor to pay up.

"We heard that!" Nicholas called down.

"Fifty!" I said, laughing at Tech as he struggled to push himself up. "By the looks of things, you'll need to do yours in batches."

Katie was already up to fifty by the time I was settling back at the table. Everyone else was getting up as well, including Tech who took a break at ten and promised to finish the rest later.

I was a little dismayed at how many swear words the kids had overheard.

"No wonder Sara has such a bad habit," Grady said. He was the only one not on the list. "Let's all see if we can curb our language in front of the kids. It's not just Sara and Nick. We have to remember that it won't be long before Abigail starts talking too."

"Yeah," Donovan said. "I really don't want my daughter's first word to be fuck or shit."

"Twenty pushups, Uncle Donovan!" Sara called down.

Donovan let out a frustrated groan, but got back down on the floor, grumbling to himself.

Bridget got up and started clearing the dirty dishes, and I got up to help her take them into the kitchen. Anne followed me in with another load and stayed to help me wash, dry, and put away, while Katie and Grady sorted the leftovers.

"Hey," Grady said, turning to me. "Was that a process server in the driveway earlier? When we were heading over to search the property?"

"I forgot," I said, drying my hands. "He served me with a summons."

I walked into the garage to the SUV, pulling out the envelope which was still lying on the floorboard. Grady, Anne, and Katie had followed me into the garage. Lisa and Alex must have seen us walk out and followed as well.

I tore the end off the envelope, pulled the papers, and hissed between my teeth.

"What is it?" Katie asked.

Grady took the one-page document from me and his whole body stilled. "It's a custody hearing for Nicholas. Kelsey's mother is suing for visitation rights."

"No judge in his right mind would grant that," Alex said. "She's on crack."

"It's Judge Wynhart. He's been in her pockets for years," I whispered. "He signed the emancipation documents. It was too easy. We never even had to speak to him. We filed the documents, and they were returned to us signed."

"Your mother's pocket or the sheriff's?" Grady asked.

"I don't know. I never bothered to look into it. I just steered clear as much as possible."

"We need to get the venue changed," Katie said, taking the summons from Grady. "I'll call Cameron Brackins and have him get started on this." Cameron was the attorney we'd hired to get Grady out of prison in Miami, and later to get me cleared of charges as well.

"Can he practice law in Michigan?" Anne asked.

"Probably not. But he can find out who the best attorney around here is for custody cases and get in touch with them," Katie said.

My brain was spinning. Grady wrapped an arm around my shoulders and tugged me into his chest. "It's time to finish this, Kelsey. She won't get visitation of Nicholas, but she's got you on her radar now and will keep coming at you until you stop her."

"I know. I'm just not ready to deal with it."

"Want her dead?" Lisa asked, cocking her head to one side and placing her hands on her hips. "I know a guy."

We all looked up at Lisa. She was perfectly serious and seemed so much the mafia princess that we all smiled.

"Let's hold off on whacking anyone," Katie said, laughing at Lisa.

"I agree with Katie. I have other options," I said.

"By the look on your face, those other options don't seem all that pleasant," Alex said, rubbing a hand up and down my arm.

"Kelsey has only walked away from the bad guys once in her life," Grady said. "And the bad guys were her mother, aunt, uncle, and the local sheriff. She doesn't like to talk about what happened, but Charlie recently found out and that's why she went back there to go after them."

"We don't need the details," Anne said. "But you're not a little girl anymore. You're stronger now. It's time you showed them that."

I nodded, giving her a brief hug, before I walked back inside and down the hall to my bedroom. I entered the atrium and curled up on one of the sofas. Grady came in a few minutes later, stretching out on the sofa behind me and tucking me into his strong frame. I drifted off to sleep in his arms.

Chapter Twenty

I woke early, well before the sun broke through the night sky. I slid away from Grady and made my way to the bathroom, closing the door before turning on the light. My reflection in the mirror somehow seemed unfamiliar. My skin paler than normal. Dark circles shadowed my eyes.

I shook my head, disappointed with the person I saw. Over the years, I had faced down the cream of the crop of the criminal world, so why did I feel the need to hide from my childhood?

I moved away from the mirror, not wanting to see the person staring back. I started the shower, undressing quickly before stepping inside. I had set the temperature higher than normal, but it felt good as it scalded my skin. I turned to let it burn against my back.

I heard the door open, and the fan turned on. "I have a job out of town. It should only take a few days," Grady said from within the bathroom. "Are you going to stick around to keep an eye on the kids until I get back?"

I could hear tension in his voice, and I knew what he was really asking. He wanted to know whether I was getting ready to bolt again.

"Anne wants me here this weekend to help with the kids and Lisa. So yes, I'll be here until at least Sunday night."

"That'll work. I'm heading over to Headquarters to square up a few things, but I'll check in with you before I leave."

I heard the bathroom door close, but I didn't call out to stop him. I couldn't. After all the times I'd run away, I couldn't tell him that I needed him to stay. I couldn't share with him that something inside felt like it was going to break, that I wanted him by my side. I couldn't say any of it, because telling him would force me to face my biggest fears.

I sat down in the tub, feeling hollow, letting the scalding water pound against my skin.

~*~*~

When I was sufficiently waterlogged I reached behind me and turned the water off. The bathroom, despite the fan, was thick with steam. I dragged myself up and stepped out, wrapping my hair in one towel before wrapping another around me.

I entered the bedroom, pulling clothes out to wear. Even the simple task of getting dressed seemed to zap what little energy I had. I decided to wear slip on pumps so I wouldn't have to hassle with socks or laces.

On the way down the hall, I opened Nicholas' door and peeked inside. He was stretched out with an arm thrown over his head, and one leg tangled in the blankets. I closed the door and went to the kitchen, finding Bridget there. She was dressed to the nines in a slinky black dress and to-die-for heels.

"Damn, girl," I said as I appreciated her outfit. "You just getting in?"

"The security guards Bones assigned made us come back here last night after we closed down the club. They wouldn't let us go home, and I couldn't fall asleep on the couch, so I borrowed one of the computers and started working on your war room. Are you looking for more of an oasis vibe? Or urban street?"

"I have no idea what urban street looks like, but definitely not an oasis. The war room is boring, plain and simple. I'm bored just walking through the door."

"Good. We're on the same page." She giggled as she poured me a cup of coffee. "I already placed an order. Most of the décor should arrive by tomorrow. Can I get a couple guys to help me on Saturday?"

"Steal some guys from the club, and the trainees can take their place for security at the store. It'll be good crowd-control experience."

"That'll work." She bit her lip and looked toward the garage door. "Is Grady okay? He didn't seem like himself this morning."

I got the eggs and bread out and pulled a pan from the rack to start breakfast. "I'm not sure. He's upset with me, but I didn't ask why."

"Why didn't you ask?"

"I don't know. Why haven't you asked Bones how he feels about you?"

Bridget sighed and nodded. "Because I'm afraid of what his answer will be."

"Does it bother you? That he and I used to... yah-know."

"Screw like monkeys?" Bridget giggled. "No. I was around back then, remember? You both cared for each other, but you never looked at him the way you look at Grady."

"Bones never looked at me the way he looks at you, either." I smiled. "That man would notice a tick landed on you from a half mile away."

"And yet in all the years I've known him, he's never made a move to have sex with me."

"You used to sleep with the other club guys," I said, shrugging. "If he had a thing for you, I'm sure that wasn't easy for him."

"I only slept with Tyler and Sam. When I first arrived at the club, it was obvious I'd been through some shit. Most of the guys were there for me as a friend, but they didn't seek out sex with me. By the time Tyler, then Sam, prospected, I felt safe enough to explore sex. I almost hooked up with Goat once, but he stopped it." Bridget laughed. "I think he stopped because of Bones, even though Bones was seeing you at the time."

"Wouldn't surprise me. Last year when Sleazy Tony groped you, Bones' reaction gave me chills. I could feel the rage rolling off him. He doesn't hide his emotions well."

"Not like Grady?" Bridget asked with a raised eyebrow.

"Are you going to help cook, or what?" I asked, changing the subject and handing her packets of bacon.

"Sure," she said but put away the bacon. "But I bought crescent rolls and sausage to go with the eggs this morning." She pulled pre-made crescent roll dough out and rolled the sausage up in the dough, placing them in neat rows on cookie sheets. I started a big batch of scrambled eggs, and despite it being early still, everyone started to drift from various corners of the house toward the kitchen.

~*~*~

I was out of practice preparing the kids for school. It took an hour to push them through showers, dress, eat, brush their teeth, and gather their bags. Sara had decided it was a special occasion, wearing one of her party dresses. Nicholas had the opposite inclination, wearing a T-shirt and grass stained jeans. I made him at least lace his running shoes.

"All right, you monsters, let's go!" Bridget called from the door to the garage. "Hurry up! You don't want to keep your new teacher waiting."

The kids ran squealing out of the house. I looked back at Anne as she thumped her forehead on the table. I gathered my shoulder bag and the breakfast leftovers, and walked into the garage, closing the door behind me. Bridget slid into the driver's seat, and I handed her the keys as I settled into the passenger seat.

"Everyone buckled in?" Bridget asked. We listened for both seatbelts to click before Bridget reversed from the garage.

Two security guards met as at the entrance of Headquarters, escorting the kids into the building as Bridget and I gathered everything before following. Everyone had stopped near the entrance of the gym, and I could hear Grady and Bones yelling. I walked around the group and stood next to Beth. Donovan, Wayne, and a couple other guys were on the opposite side of the gym, trying to separate Bones and Grady who looked ready to tear each other's heads off.

"Get to your classroom," I told the kids before I walked toward them.

Crossing the gym, I stepped in front of Grady, shoving the casserole dish into his chest, forcing him to take it. "Breakfast."

"I'm not hungry," he said, glaring down at me.

"I didn't ask if you were. But you can take it to the break room."

He glared at Bones again before stomping toward the break room. I looked back and noticed that Bridget was gone.

"I know that whatever is going on, it has nothing to do with you and I, but Bridget might've misinterpreted the situation. You should track her down before she gets too far."

Bones was still being held back by Wayne and Donovan, but he nodded for them to release him. When they did, he turned toward the gym exit and strode out.

"Can either of you tell me anything?"

"Sorry," Donovan said, shaking his head.

Wayne looked at the floor, unable to face me.

"Fine." I looked around the room. "Are the kids safe here today?"

"We had shifts running all night. The property is secure," Wayne said.

I started toward the stairs. "Until one of you is ready to fess up, I'll be in the war room. Make sure Grady eats something."

"Yes, Mom," Wayne said.

I held my middle finger up over my shoulder, without bothering to look back at Wayne.

"Beth says giving someone the bird counts as a swear word!" Nicholas called down from the upper walkway.

"Put it on my tab," I said, giving him my serious face. "Shouldn't you be in class?"

He scurried into the classroom, laughing as he ran.

~*~*~

Tech was already in the war room when I arrived. I threw my bag in the corner chair, pulling out my laptop. "Do you know why Grady's so wound up?"

"Yup."

"You going to tell me?"

"Nope."

"Fine. Get out."

Tech turned away from his computer monitor and looked at me.

"Not kidding." I slammed my laptop on the table and turned my back toward him.

He sighed as he gathered his stuff and left. I sent Maggie a text to video call me in the war room when she had a second. While I waited, I looked out the glass wall and saw Bones below, carrying totes into the gym. Bridget must have called the trainees over, because they all joined her. A few minutes later, Alex walked in carrying an arm full of suits. I heard the computer chime and turned back to the table to answer the call. Maggie's face appeared on the center TV screen mounted to the wall.

"What's up?" she asked, watching me pace in the war room.

"Are you officially back on Kierson's team?"

"Not until Monday. Until then, I'm bouncing between the hotel bar and pool."

I looked out the glass wall again and watched Grady stomp past the trainees toward Donovan's office.

"Hey!" Maggie called to me. "What's going on?"

"I don't know." I sighed, throwing myself into a swivel chair. "Something has Grady walking the edge of a cliff.

Everybody at Aces seems to know what it is, but they won't tell me."

"Loyal bastards," Maggie said, sarcastically. "What do you think is bothering him?"

"I think he's going to leave me," I admitted, looking up at Maggie. "I think he's had enough of my shit, and he's planning on setting himself free."

"What the hell are you talking about? Grady loves you."

"I know! I think that's why he's so angry."

Maggie shook her head and rolled her eyes. "Why now? Why would he leave *now*, after everything the two of you have been through?"

"I don't know. He seemed fine yesterday when we learned Chaves was set free. He was pissed when we found the explosives, but he shook it off. And after we took care of the snipers, he was in a great mood. But when he saw the summons, something changed."

"I'm going to skip the sniper and explosive comments for the moment and ask—what summons?"

I grit my teeth as I answered. "My *mother*." I dragged a hand through my hair. "Charlie stirred up some shit from the past, and I challenged my mother in the process of getting Charlie released from jail. Now my mother is messing with me, filing for visitation rights for Nicholas."

"And a judge signed the summons?"

"A dirty judge, yeah," I answered. "Katie's working with Cameron to hire a lawyer. Then they'll file for a change in venue to have the hearing in Kalamazoo. The case should be thrown out at that point. But Grady warned me last night that if I don't deal with my mother, she'll continue to come after me."

"What's stopping you?"

"I'd have to tell them." I nodded toward the gym. "I'd have to tell all of them the things I did. How I freed Charlie and myself. How we lived."

"And what? Are you worried they'll think less of you?"

"No."

"Then what?" Maggie leaned closer to her laptop. "Kelsey, this isn't making any sense."

"I'm worried they'll realize I've always been broken. That I can't be fixed." I swiveled my chair away from Maggie, facing the windows. "They'll see that I've been running for so long, I don't know how to stop. That I've never been able to depend on anyone else, and probably never will. They'll give up on me."

"You're wrong," Charlie said from behind me, just inside the war room.

I stared at her, surprised to see her. The tears I was holding back slipped past my eyelids.

She walked over, pulled me up from my chair and wrapped her arms around me. "You are the strongest person I know, but even if you weren't, you're not alone. I'm sorry you had to fight the battles by yourself when we were kids, but I'm here—right here. We're in this together."

"This is my mess. It's the choices *I made* that started it all."

"You didn't *have* a choice. You had to cross a lot of lines when you were barely a teenager to save me. That's on me, not you."

I turned away from Charlie toward the windows overlooking the field.

"Maggie, we'll call you back," Charlie said before I heard the beep that ended the call.

The room was silent as I stared out the window. I took a moment to gather my thoughts and inhaled a deep breath. Charlie waited for me to collect myself, always the patient one. When I finally turned around, I found her sitting at the table, studying me.

"I didn't have to make the choices I made, Kid. I had other options. I could've called the state police. I could've called Nana. I didn't have to seduce the sheriff and blackmail everyone."

"You were young and scared. You probably weren't thinking that clearly."

"I knew all those options," I said, shaking my head. "I chose to do what I did."

Her eyes narrowed as she studied my face. "Then why? Why did you do it?" I didn't sense accusation in her voice, only curiosity.

"Because all the other options would've taken you away from me," I admitted, walking over to kneel in front of her. "If I'd let someone else step in to help, they would've taken you far away. And my fourteen-year-old self couldn't bear the thought of not having you around to lean on. You were all I had. I didn't have any friends. My mother was hateful. My father was indifferent. My brothers were in college or married. But I had you. And you loved me. I didn't want to lose that connection." I leaned my head on her knee. "But it was selfish. You could've had an easier life if I would've made a different choice."

Charlie chuckled, placing a hand on my head and tousling my hair. "You think growing up without you in my life would've been better for me? You, idiot." She pulled my face up with her hands. "Without you, I'm not sure I'd have recovered from the shit my father put me through. You dragged me through the muck, hosed me off, and pushed me into making something of my life. Nana would've coddled me. Children's Services would've stuck me in a group home and labeled me with a troubled past. You gave me a life—a future. And I needed you just as much, if not more, than you needed me."

"Without you, I had no reason to live. You were everything to me. You were my whole world."

Charlie stroked my hair out of my face. "You're going to be okay. I'm here. I'm not leaving. You didn't abandon me, and I won't abandon you. I've got you, Kelsey. I'm right here."

"Even if everybody else leaves?"

"Who's leaving? I know you're going through your running phase again, but I'm pretty sure your new family would track your ass down if you stayed away too long."

I shook my head, but there was a brief knock on the door before it started to open. I stood and turned toward the windows to wipe my face dry with the back of my hand.

"Hey," Grady's voice called out. "What the hell is going on?"

"Are you leaving Kelsey?" Charlie asked.

"What? I'm heading out of town for a few days on business. I'll be back Sunday."

"Then why does she think you're leaving her?"

"*What the hell are you talking about?*"

I sensed Grady cross the room before his hands turned me to face him. My heart broke as I looked at him, scared that he'd run away. "Ah, Kel," he whispered, pulling me into his arms. "Charlie, we need a minute."

I sobbed as he held me tight with one arm and rubbed my back with the other. I clung to him, hoping he wouldn't slip away.

"Shh, babe," he whispered. "I'm not sure what's happening, but I'll cancel my trip. I'm not going anywhere." He sat down on the floor, pulling me down onto his lap. "Shh," he whispered again, kissing the top of my head. "Settle, hon. I need you to tell me what's going on."

I pulled several raspy breaths into my lungs, trying to stop the waterworks. It took a few minutes, but I finally gained control again.

"What am I missing? What don't I know?" Grady whispered as he continued to rub my back and hold me.

I shook my head.

"Are you scared of Chaves? Because I have a plan to take care of him. I'll handle it. Is that why you're upset?"

I shook my head again.

"Your mother? Is that it?"

I looked up at Grady. "I can't do it. I can't face the past."

"Why? I don't understand." He stared down at me, waiting for me to explain, but I bit my lower lip, unable to answer. He sighed in frustration. "I'll admit, the petition for custody made me furious. I feel like Nicholas is my kid too. But at the same time, he's not. He's yours. And that's probably never going to change. I have to accept that. I don't like it, but for whatever reason, you don't want to marry me."

"I want to. I just can't."

"Why?"

I shook my head.

"There's more to the story, isn't there? There's something else you haven't told me. Something from when you were a kid."

My body trembled, and I looked away. The tears were a steady river down my face.

"Whatever this is, Kelsey, it's eating you up. You have to face it. Just tell me, so I can help you."

I didn't want to say the words. It would change how he looked at me. How he felt about me.

"What don't I know? How could anything be worse than the hell Nola put you through?"

I looked up at the ceiling, shaking my head. "It's different. I had to survive Nola torturing me. It wasn't something I chose, though."

"So you *did* do something—in addition to blackmailing them. Whatever it was, Kelsey, I'll understand."

"No, you won't," I whispered, closing my eyes.

"Why can't you trust me? *Damn it!*" Grady placed his hands on the side of my face and forced me to look at him. "I love you, but I need you to tell me what is going on. I need you to say the words."

I trembled, feeling the anger rolling off him, directed at me.

"*Tell me!*" he yelled.

"*I needed money!*"

Grady seemed to stop breathing as he stared down at me, still holding my face in his hands.

"Charlie was hungry! *I was hungry!*"

Grady's body stiffened, his hands dropping their hold on me and clenching into fists. "But you had the money from the books." His eyes were wild, sensing what I was trying to explain.

"I lied. It took me two years to start making any money on the books."

"*Finish it*," he growled in a low whisper, closing his eyes.

I remained frozen, unable to answer.

"No more lies, Kelsey," he said as he opened his eyes and glared down at me. "No more *secrets*! Tell me!"

A deep streak of coldness started in the center of my body and worked its way outward. I could've sworn my heart stopped beating all together as I shut my emotions off—shoving them back into their bottle. I held Grady's stare as I answered him. "I was a *thief*. I was a *whore*." I lifted my chin, ready for a fight, accepting that I would lose him. "I was *anything I had to be* to get us enough money to survive and get the hell out of that town."

I pushed myself off Grady's lap, crawling a few feet away before standing and moving over to the table. I heard Grady stand and start pacing. I could feel his rage heating the air in the room.

I heard the door to the war room open, and Tech stepped in, looking between Grady and me.

"Tech, send the kids outside to play."

Tech nodded before quickly leaving.

Grady continued to pace, like the panther tattoo on his back, ready to strike out at anyone or anything that moved wrong. "*Why didn't you tell me? Why did you keep this from me?*"

"I've never told anyone. I didn't want anyone to know."

"But *she* knows, *doesn't she? Your mother!* And she did nothing to help you?"

"It's a small town. It's *her* town. Of course, she knows. She's always known," I answered before I turned and walked out of the war room.

I heard a window in the war room shatter as I walked down the stairs. Tech and Charlie stood at the bottom of the staircase and when Charlie reached out, I shook her off.

"Tech, I'm sorry I was short with you earlier."

Another window broke and Bones and Donovan raced past us up the stairs.

"I'll be working from home today. I'd appreciate it if you guys can keep an eye on the kids."

"Kel?" Charlie asked with concern etched in her voice. "Were you right? Is he leaving?"

A desperate laugh escaped my lips. "He wasn't, but he will now."

I walked out of the gym.

Chapter Twenty-One

I meant to turn right, toward home. But while I sat waiting for traffic to clear, I made the decision that I wasn't ready to go home yet. I needed to hide. Not for long but at least for a few hours. I needed to not feel the pain. I needed to just exist in the world, without the weight of my troubles.

So, I turned left, heading to the one person who always let me do just that.

~*~*~

Dallas opened the door and looked at me from head to toe. "You're a mess. Get in here before one of the neighbors sees you." She pulled me through the door, closing it behind me. "I'm assuming you came here for a reason," she said as she led me by the elbow down the hall into the spare bedroom and shoved me toward the bathroom. "Shower. It'll be easier to start over than fixing whatever you've got going on with your hair and makeup."

After showering, I dried off and put on the semi-slutty outfit that Dallas had laid out on the bed for me. Then I followed the hall to the kitchen where I knew she'd be waiting with a variety of makeup and hair styling supplies. I sat in a chair, and we remained peacefully silent while she worked me back into a human likeness.

An hour later she stepped away and moved over to the coffee pot. "You want coffee or something stronger. I usually don't drink this early," she winked, "but I can make an exception."

"Stronger."

"Margaritas?"

"Stronger."

"I see," she said. "Only one cure for that." She got the tequila and shot glasses out. "Do we need to call Goat and have him shoot someone? I might have to repay him by letting him do this special *something or other* he's wanted to try, but for you, I'd do it."

I snorted and downed the first shot, tapping the glass on the table for a refill.

"You are aware that it's barely ten in the morning, right?"

I tapped the glass on the table again as I glared up at her.

"Looks like even a bullet wouldn't turn this day around for you. So be it," she said, filling the shot glass to the rim. "Not today." She held her glass up before downing her shot.

"Not today," I said before downing my second shot.

~*~*~

After four or five shots we had switched to margaritas, but those were going down rather quickly too. When Grady and Goat walked into the house mid-afternoon, I was half falling out of my chair, laughing. Dallas was standing in the middle of the kitchen imitating Nana's horrific attempt at strip dancing. The way Dallas was rubbing a hand up through her hair like Marilyn Monroe explained why Nana's hair had been sticking up oddly on the sides.

When she started squatting and doing weird forward thrusts while undoing her shirt, I had to yell for her to stop. "No more! I don't want to know. She's my *nana*."

"I'm telling you, we need to get that poor woman to a pole dancing class, or she'll never get laid."

I laughed, wiping the tears from my face. "I have no interest in helping my grandmother get laid."

"I don't even want to know," Grady said. "Are you ready to go home?"

"No," I said, shaking my head. "I'm not even close to being ready."

Dallas poured two shots and slid one to me. We clanked our glasses and yelled, "Not today!" before downing the tequila.

"Fine." Grady pulled out a chair. "Goat? Tequila?" he asked, stealing the bottle from Dallas and reusing our shot glasses.

"Sure. Bridget took the kids to the movies. I've got the night off."

"All the kids?" I asked, looking at Grady.

"Relax. I sent four guys with them. I'll have to pay them hazard rates for sitting through a PG movie, but it's also keeping Carl and Nana out of everyone's hair, so it's worth it. And Charlie went too."

I sighed, relaxing once I knew Charlie was with them.

Grady downed his shot before refilling his glass. "Not today," he said, looking up at me. "*But tomorrow*—you and I need to talk." He downed his second shot, not bothering to wait for Goat.

~*~*~

Hours later...

"And then... Kelsey tells this dancer named Rocket that she's better than him..." Dallas said as we both laughed, remembering the night we went to the strip club. "He, of course, balked, so she wagged her ass cheeks right up on stage. The DJ started a song, and she had every woman in the joint screaming for her."

"I even got a few lap dance requests," I said, half falling out of my chair as Grady caught me and pulled me upright.

Bones, Donovan, Lisa, Tech, and Katie had arrived at some point and laughed with us. Everyone except Lisa was well past the buzzed phase.

"They didn't kick you out?" Lisa asked.

"Hell, no. They asked her if she'd consider becoming a regular dancer!" Dallas laughed. "I was so disappointed when she turned them down."

"Remember the time we stole that dingy in South Haven?" I laughed. "I can't believe we did that."

"I can't believe you convinced the police that we mistook it for our own. That was the best straight-faced string of bullshit I'd ever heard a person spin."

"Then we slept on someone's yacht, and they found us the next morning."

"And made us breakfast!" Dallas barked out a laugh.

"That does it," Grady said, laughing. "You two are now banned from hanging out without supervision. I can't believe neither of you ended up getting arrested."

"They did." Dave said, walking into the kitchen, followed by Steve. "They got arrested at Cedar Point. Steve and I had to go bail them out."

"What did you do?" Katie asked.

Dallas and I both made zip-the-lip signs and then snagged each other's pinky fingers.

"All we know is it had something to do with one of the water rides," Steve said. "And when we picked them up, they were both wearing jailhouse orange tops."

"And we were told to get their asses out of Ohio," Dave said, grinning.

"It wasn't as bad as it sounds," Dallas said, rolling her eyes.

"No. We were doing the community a service," I agreed.

"Oh, fuck me," Grady groaned.

"Why are you guys here?" I asked Dave and Steve, seeing they were still in uniform.

"We stopped by the house, and they asked us to check on you guys. I feel better knowing that Donovan and Grady are here babysitting."

"Hey? Don't I count?" Goat asked.

Dave glared over at Goat, making us all laugh. Dallas wasn't quiet about her sexual adventures with Goat, and as her son, Dave struggled to even acknowledge Goat most days.

"Kelsey? How trashed are you?" Steve asked.

I could only laugh.

"All right then," he said. "I'll call you in the morning."

"Better make it late morning," Lisa said as they were turning to leave. "I've never seen her this drunk."

"Oh, we've seen her worse," Dave said as he followed Steve toward the door. He glanced over his shoulder and winked at me. "Remember getting caught skinny dipping at the YMCA pool?"

Dallas and I laughed, and this time I did fall and when Grady tried to grab me, he ended up beside me on the floor. He wrapped an arm around me as I laughed into his shoulder. Bones and Donovan came over and helped us back into chairs.

"How many times have you been arrested?" Donovan asked

"We weren't arrested for the YMCA thing," Dallas said, shaking her head.

"Okay, how many times did you two get caught doing something illegal?" Donovan asked before downing another shot.

"When we were together? Or individually?" I asked, trying to be serious.

"Together," Bones said.

Dallas and I both started counting on our fingers, but lost track and laughed.

"We got caught a lot," Dallas admitted.

"I've been arrested nine times," Lisa announced, proud of herself.

We all turned, big-eyed, toward Lisa.

"What could the little princess possibly have done to get arrested?" Katie snorted.

"The first eight were all part of my rebellious teenage years. My last arrest was for trespassing. Only Papa knew the whole story. The Feds had been watching Papa and his men, and he couldn't get a shipment moved. I stepped in without permission and had it transported from point A to point B. But after the shipment departed, I spotted a police car and ran. I was caught in a neighboring warehouse and pretended I was drunk when the cops found me."

"I don't want to know," Donovan said. "We could all be murdered in our sleep for knowing."

"Don't be silly," Lisa said. "It was a simple transaction."

"I have to know," Dallas said, leaning forward. "What was it? Drugs? Weapons?"

Lisa leaned forward, first looking at Dallas, and then at each of us as we leaned closer, wanting to know as well. "Counterfeit lingerie," Lisa whispered.

"Like G-strings?" Grady laughed.

"It's a serious market," Lisa said, holding in a smirk. "But Papa has rules. He won't work with any sweat shops, and he's careful that the employees are all willing participants."

"That's why you can pick out the high fashion items so easily!" I laughed, pointing at Lisa. "It's part of the family business!"

"Believe me, my father has been pestering me to see if we'd expand our sales base for some of his goods. But I've told him—no way in hell."

"And I'm sure you said it just like that," Grady said, laughing and clinking beer bottles with Donovan.

"Okay, so maybe I told him that Kelsey would figure it out and have us arrested," Lisa said, snickering.

"Here, here," Katie said as we clinked our drinks.

"Does he have counterfeit Armani?" Dallas asked.

"*No!*" we all yelled at once.

~*~*~

I woke on the couch, discovering Grady was half lying on top of me and half wedged in the back crevice between the cushions. I heard Dallas counting off numbers along with a voice on the TV. I turned my head in the direction of the noise and regretted it immediately as Dallas bent at the waist to touch her toes, her backside spread in front of me in a form-fitting purple leotard, complete with pink stockings.

"I did not need to see that," Grady grumbled, rolling over me so he could get up.

Following after him into the kitchen, Goat greeted us with cups of coffee. "Damn, I love that woman." Goat grinned as he watched Dallas through the cutout in the wall. "She's so damn flexible."

"Don't," I said, holding up a hand to stop him.

Grady chuckled as he sat at the table. "It's too early to hear about Dallas being naked."

"Never too early for her," Goat said, winking my way. He didn't say any more when I glared back at him.

"What time is it?" Grady asked.

"Almost nine," Goat answered. "I texted Katie that I'd be late this morning, but if I don't leave soon, she'll fire my ass."

"Doubtful, since they were here until one in the morning." I looked around for Goat's daughter. "Did you get Amanda to school on time?"

"Bridget took her to school. Haley and Bridget babysit twice a week so I can spend time with Dallas."

"Amanda doesn't like Dallas?"

"That's not an issue," Goat said, shaking his head. "The last time Amanda spent time with Dallas, Dallas dyed her hair purple and pierced her ears. I'd only run to the store to pick up bread."

I snorted into my coffee. Amanda was only eleven, and Dallas had no understanding of age appropriateness.

Grady pulled out his phone and as he read his messages his grin vanished. "I need to go handle a few things." He got up and rinsed his coffee cup. "I'll see *you*—" he said to me as he tugged on my chin "—in about an hour. Meet me at the house, so we can talk."

I sighed, and he shook his head at me before walking out.

Goat leaned against the kitchen counter and turned to face me. "I'm not sure what's going on with you two, but I've never seen a man more crazed than when he came to the store yesterday looking for you. He was scared to death that he'd never see you again."

I looked back at the door. Grady had been by my side through hell and back. He didn't deserve for me to keep shutting him out. It was time to face him. Time to face my past. "I'm so tired of running," I said, walking over to the sink to rinse my cup. I grabbed my shoulder bag and waved to Dallas before walking out.

Chapter Twenty-Two

Returning home, I showered, ate some dry toast, vacuumed the living room, and emptied the dishwasher. Then I sat, watching the clock. Two hours crawled by before Grady walked through the garage door into the house.

"You waited," he said, coming over to sit at the dining room table.

"Were you hoping I wouldn't?" I asked, honestly.

Grady sighed again, standing and pulling me up. "First, I am not leaving. Get that through that thick skull of yours." He leaned down and kissed me, tugging on my lower lip until I opened for him. My body melted into his. When the kiss broke, he looked down at me until I nodded that I understood. I didn't, not really. I couldn't. But I knew that at least he thought he meant it.

"Let's go to the atrium. Carl wired the main rooms for surveillance." He tugged at my hand, pulling me with him down the hall and into the atrium.

I'm not sure why, but I chose to sit on the floor, leaning against the couch with my knees up, tucked against my chest. Grady chuckled and sat beside me.

"I'm sorry about yesterday," he said, placing a hand on my knee.

"You have nothing to be sorry for."

"Let me finish," he said, turning my chin to face him. "I was angry. First, I was angry because once again you wouldn't tell me what was happening inside that brain of yours. Then I was angry because your mother had watched her only daughter, the woman I love, suffer, and did nothing to stop it." Grady's hands tightened into fists, and I felt the anger cascading from him. "I wanted to hurt her. I wanted to hurt your father. I wanted to do something so I wouldn't feel so damn helpless."

"I should've told you a long time ago. It would've been easier for you if I had."

"You should've, but because I've earned the truth, not because it would've changed anything between you and me. That's what you're not getting. It doesn't change how I feel about you. It doesn't change who you were a year ago or who you are today. It's your past—not your future."

"How can you say that? I was a prostitute at the age of fourteen! I'd wait until Charlie was asleep and walk down to the local bar and wait for johns. I'd pick up extra cash giving handjobs behind the laundromat to the high school boys after school. I was *that* girl. And everyone knew it."

Grady sighed, shaking his head. "You were a fourteen-year-old girl, not old enough to get a job at the local grocery store, yet responsible for not only yourself, but for Charlie too. I should've put it together long before you told me. Hell, now that I know, I'm amazed at how far you pulled yourself and Charlie out of that mess. You not only survived it, you fought your way out of that life and became a cop."

"I had to find a way." I rubbed my hand against my constricting chest. "Charlie was getting older. She started questioning where our money came from. I remember the day that my sixth book sold twenty copies in one day. It wasn't much, but it was hope. Finally, there was a spark at the end of the tunnel. The next day I had twenty-two book sales, and the day after that, twenty-six. I planned another break-in and got lucky that I cashed out enough to keep us afloat for a long while. Then I spent sixteen-hour days, every day, writing. I don't know what would've happened to us if the sales would've stopped, but they didn't. And the light at the end of the damn tunnel was finally bright enough to walk through."

Grady wrapped an arm around me and pulled me into the crook of his shoulder. "Explain the stealing," he said as he leaned in and kissed the side of my head.

"Not much to tell," I said as I relaxed against him. "I robbed houses. I didn't have the skills back then, but I was smart. I knew to wear gloves, secure my hair, and leave everything exactly how it was when I arrived, minus anything that left with me. And because I was my mother's daughter, I knew something else: knowledge was power. I picked targets who not only had excess funds but also met the horrible-human-being requirements. The gym coach who beat his wife if dinner wasn't on the table when he was ready to eat. The soccer mom who would leave her toddler at home while she ran out to score pills from her dealer. The farmer who hired illegal immigrants to harvest his fields and paid them a fraction of minimum wage.

"I watched them, learning where they went, when they were home, what windows they left unlocked. And when I was confident that all the dots lined up, I'd steal whatever cash I could find, or things that were easily turned into cash. I'd take a few grocery items or household goods too, like soap or shampoo, but never enough to be obvious. And then I'd take whatever I could find that would incriminate them. That was the key. That was the part my mother taught me. If I could find something they didn't want anyone to know, then they wouldn't report the break-in. And most of the time, I'd find their secrets."

"Who was the last person you robbed?"

"My mother." I waited a moment before I glanced up at Grady to see if he was grinning too. He was.

"Please tell me you made it hurt."

"My parents had a safe, and I knew the combination. I knew they kept cash in there, though not a lot. But the kicker was, I knew where my mother hid money from my father, and vice versa. Both of them had healthy nest eggs tucked away."

"But they would've known it was you who broke in."

"Sure. But I also took a revolver, the box of love letters my dad had hidden away, and the blackmail files my mother had. Neither of them dared to call the police."

Grady chuckled. "What did you do with the letters and the files?"

"I read a few of the letters, then tucked everything into a plastic tote and buried the mess behind Nana's shed. I knew they'd come looking for them, and as long as they didn't find them, I was protected."

"And did they come looking?"

I nodded. "I spotted them sitting in a car down the street two days later. It was a nice day, so I took Charlie to the park. I put the cash and our laptop in a backpack and took the backpack with us. When we came home, it was obvious everything had been searched."

"How much cash did you get?"

I laughed. "Nine thousand, two hundred, and fifty-three dollars. My parents' lack of trust in each other paid off nicely. Between that money and the book sales, we managed to keep our heads above water until Charlie turned sixteen."

"You never had a regular job? Bagging groceries? Waitressing?"

"Couldn't. Not in that town at least," I said, shaking my head. "Between my mother ordering everyone not to help me and half the town knowing how I'd paid the bills for the first two years, no one would hire me."

Grady growled. "I *hate* your mother."

"Yeah." I sighed. "I'm not her biggest fan either."

"You know I still want to kill her."

"She's not worth the jail time."

"If you helped me plan it, I wouldn't get caught."

"Or you could send someone for the files," I said, looking up at him. "I never looked. I have no idea what's in there."

"Are you sure?" Grady asked, raising an eyebrow.

"No," I laughed without humor. "I don't want to face it. I don't want everyone knowing what happened. But if you're right, and she keeps coming after me, I have to protect Nicholas and Charlie."

Grady pulled his phone out of his shirt pocket. I wasn't sure who he was calling, but I trusted him. A minute later, he was talking to someone on the phone. "I need you and Bridget to go dig up buried treasure. Come over to the house, and we'll give you the details."

Grady disconnected the call and tossed the phone on the coffee table.

"Hello? Anyone home?" a voice called down the hallway.

"Coming!" I called out as I stood.

Grady grabbed my hand, preventing me from walking away as he stood. "One more thing," he said before he kissed me again.

When he pulled back, I looked up at him and smiled. "Oh, we're not done talking yet. You haven't told me what the hell was going on with *you* yesterday." I walked to the doorway and looked down the hall to see Steve waiting at the end. "Come on back. Carl has the front rooms wired for sound and video, so we're hanging out in the atrium."

"Am I intruding? I can come back later," Steve said.

"It's fine," Grady said, walking out to shake his hand. "Hey, Steve. Were you looking for Kelsey or both of us?"

"My go-to is to talk to Kelsey, but I know she'll tell you anyway, so you might as well stick around."

"Sounds intriguing," I said, leading us back into the atrium. "What's up? You have your serious face on. You usually only sport that face when you're on the job."

"Best if I'm not wearing my uniform when I break the rules and repeat what the police chief said yesterday." Steve sat down on one of the couches, leaning forward and resting his forearms on his knees.

"This can't be good," Grady said, sitting on the other couch and pulling me down next to him.

"Spill," I said.

"The sheriff in Sadler Creek is stirring up trouble. He called my chief and asked us to keep extra eyes on you and report anything suspicious. Says you're a person of interest in some crimes up his way."

Grady snorted. "Person of interest."

"Well, I am an interesting person," I said, smirking.

Steve rolled his eyes. "The chief took the request seriously. He knows Dave and I are friends of yours, so he asked us to keep our distance. He plans on having officers patrol, photograph, and document the happenings around here."

"But nobody was watching two days ago, right?" I asked.

"You mean Wednesday, when a call came in saying a woman with multi-colored hair and two guys ran into the woods with guns? Nope. No one was watching with a camera that day, thank goodness. But the chief questioned the call. I told him that you nutjobs were having a paintball war."

"Actually, that sounds like fun," Grady said, turning to grin at me.

"Right? I'd be game," I agreed. "You and me against Bones and Donovan?"

"Katie would want in. I'm sure she could find a partner."

"Maybe Whiskey? Or Wayne?"

"We could set the trainees to go against each other too. The acreage in the east woods would be big enough."

"Focus—" Steve said, snapping his fingers out in front of us. "This is a problem."

I shrugged, throwing my hands up in frustration. "The sheriff from Sadler Creek is an asshole. He and I have a long, disturbing history. We'll warn everyone to be careful, but other than that, what do you want me to do?"

"Why's he coming after you?"

"He's digging," Grady said. "Her mother filed a custody visitation suit. They're looking for any dirt they can find to make Kelsey's life miserable. We're working on a plan to get rid of them."

"Get rid of who?" Bones asked, walking into the room with Bridget.

"I'll explain later," Grady said.

"You two finish this fun little chat," I said, nodding between Steve and Grady. "I'll get Bridget and Bones the shovel and address they need."

"And why do they need a shovel?" Steve sighed.

I laughed and led Bones and Bridget back to the dining room.

"Are we burying a body?" Bones asked.

I wrote down Nana's address and handed it over. "There's a plastic tote buried behind Nana's shed. I need it brought back, but it's not a good idea if I go myself. If Nana's neighbor, Mr. Webster, comes out and asks what you're doing, tell him I sent you."

"Henry Webster died years ago," Nana said from the living room couch where she sat knitting. "Heart attack. Died while getting the mail. The political junk mail probably pushed him over the edge."

"Shit," I said, biting my lip. "A new neighbor might call the cops if they see someone digging in your backyard."

"No worries. I'm not sure what you buried behind my shed, but there's not a damn thing anyone can say about me having it dug up. I'll go with them and check on the house."

"I don't know," I said, hesitantly. "If you're caught by Mother or the sheriff, they'll want to know what's in that tote."

"We'll pretend we're moving some of Nana's stuff," Bridget said. "No way they'll be able to get a warrant to search the truck. Nana, get a shovel from the garage.

Kelsey, get Grady's truck keys. I'll grab some empty boxes from the basement."

"That's a good plan," Nana agreed. "And if anyone asks, we'll say we dug up some of my daylilies to plant at Kelsey's."

I retrieved Grady's keys and handed them to Bones, giving him the *look*, letting him know that I was holding him responsible. He snorted and walked out. Grady and Steve walked into the dining room, laughing. Grady shook Steve's hand again before Steve waved at me and left.

"Alone again," Grady said, wrapping his arms around my waist.

"Time for part two of our serious talk," I said, taking his hand and pulling him down the hallway.

"Okay, let's hear it."

"I need you to explain what happened yesterday. You were avoiding me. And you were fighting with Bones. And nobody would tell me what was going on, though it was obvious they knew."

"Is that why you got it in your head that I was breaking up with you?" he asked with his eyebrow cocked.

I shrugged, sitting at the end of the couch. "You've never avoided me before. I figured you'd finally hit your breaking point."

Grady laughed, sitting on the couch and pulling me over next to him. "Woman, sometimes you can be so blind it baffles me. Yes, I was avoiding you. But only because I didn't want you to know what I was up to."

"Why?"

"Because you would've stopped me."

I was confused, but mentally retraced the conversations and events over the last few days. The summons had upset Grady, but he was acting off before that. He had been keeping me away from whatever he was working on. "We're not talking about my mother, are we?"

"No."

"Chaves?"

"Yes. I have a plan to deal with him, but Wayne, Bones, and Donovan don't like it. They wanted me to talk to you, and I told them off."

I looked at Grady and studied his face. "You've got to be kidding me! *Kill him*? That was your master plan?"

Grady shrugged, the corner of his mouth tipping up.

"And what about me? And Nicholas? You said you think of Nicholas as your son, and I know damn well he thinks of you as a father figure. Neither one of us would've been okay if you were arrested or killed."

"I know. But with Chaves dead, the threats would end. We can't wait around for the next sniper to show up."

"Even if I agreed that killing him was the best option—which I don't—if the guys were against your plan, then your plan sucked."

Grady's grin widened.

"You were going to *wing* it?"

He laced his fingers behind his head and leaned back into the couch.

"Dumbass." I laughed, slapping his leg. "Come on. Let's go."

"Where?"

"To the war room. We need intel. I also haven't sorted through Sorato's personal effects yet. We can pick through everything over there."

"Sure. They should be done replacing the windows by now."

"How many did you break?"

"All of them." Grady barked a laugh. "I *really* hate your mother."

CHAPTER TWENTY-THREE

When we arrived at Headquarters, we were told that Bridget had started the redesign on the war room early and had painters upstairs, so we joined Tech in the first-floor conference room. I sat next to Tech and waited for him to look up from his monitor.

"What?" he asked, grinning over at me.

"Sorry again for behaving like an ass yesterday and kicking you out of your office."

"It's *our* office. And Katie has a habit of kicking me out of our apartment, so I'm used to it."

"And yet you two are building a house together?"

"I figure if I build a man cave in the basement, I can put a bed in there for when she's having her meltdowns," he said with a smirk.

"I'll buy you one of those Murphy beds that looks like a cabinet."

"Sweet. That'll piss her off."

Grady chuckled. "I really don't get you and Katie as a couple."

"Fire and ice, man," Tech said, laughing. "That's my Katie."

Tech pointed to the gym bag Grady had tossed onto the table. "What've we got cooking?"

"Personal effects of Axle Sorato, the goon who was pretending to be a trainee," Grady answered. "Wayne and Kelsey collected everything, but nobody has filtered through the crap yet."

"Does this mean we're going to come up with a real plan?" Tech asked Grady.

"Yeah. Avoiding Kelsey backfired on my ass. I had to confess. Best if I get her stamp of approval before I use my plan."

"There wasn't enough *planning* involved to call it a plan," I said, getting up and dumping the contents of the gym bag onto the table. "Tech, can you get me a background on Chaves? I only have the arrest reports."

"Maggie sent me some information, but I'll dig deeper."

"Speaking of Maggie, I'd better call her back."

Tech slid an extra laptop my way, and I clicked the video-call icon, calling Maggie.

Maggie's face appeared on the screen after the first ring. "You good?" she asked.

"Yup. Thanks for letting me vent yesterday."

"You're not pissed at me for sending Grady your way?"

I looked at Maggie and then glanced over at Grady, who was chuckling.

"You just ratted yourself out," Grady hollered across the table. "I didn't tell her you texted me and sent me to the war room."

"Oh, oops. Oh well," Maggie said, grinning. "What are we working on? I'm bored. Kierson won't let me near any live cases yet."

"Can you come to Michigan for the weekend?" I asked.

"Sure. Genie was only going to work a few hours today, so I'll drag her with me. I take it you need help with the Chaves mess?"

"We'll handle Chaves and loop you in if we need the FBI. But I'd like your help with my mother. Yesterday, I spilled the rest of my childhood secrets to Grady, and he smashed out all the windows in the war room. I don't know how everyone else is going to react when they find out."

"Sounds like you need someone who can help you work it as a case instead of polishing their sniper rifle."

"Something like that."

"Got it. We'll be there in time for dinner."

"Thanks," I said before disconnecting.

"Do you remember that you're in charge of dinner tonight?" Tech asked, not looking up from his laptop.

"Crap." I sighed. "I'll have to order something. Who's available to pick it up later?"

"If I get a free dinner out of it, I'll pick it up," Wayne said, walking into the conference room and grabbing a chair.

Grady slid a pile of Sorato's junk toward Wayne. "Until then, you can make yourself useful and help me sort."

"No problem. And Ryan wanted me to share that he thought it was odd we didn't find charges, caps, and wires in Sorato's room or truck."

I thought about the C-4 and the other components that would be needed. I wasn't trained in explosives, but I had taken a course that the bomb squad offered in Miami. I mentally retraced searching Sorato's room. "He also didn't have any tools like pliers or wire cutters."

"What are you thinking?" Grady asked.

"That he had a partner."

"Another spy?" Tech asked.

I nodded. "I read the report the FBI had on Sorato. There was nothing indicating he had any training in explosives. I've also read several reports on the Hell Hounds. I don't recall anything exploding in their long list of crimes."

"You can learn a lot on the internet," Wayne said.

"Sorato didn't have a moral bone in his body, but he wasn't stupid. And you have to be pretty dumb to teach yourself online how to build things that can blow your face off."

Tech stood and turned toward the door. "I'll grab the trainee files."

"Shit," Grady cursed.

"I'm going to go warn the other guys," Wayne said. "Be back in a minute."

"The C-4 wasn't left on the property, was it?" I asked.

"No. Ryan took it home with him," Grady said. "Don't tell his wife."

I shook my head. "If we ever get married, I expect you to tell me shit like that."

Grady looked up from the pile of Sorato's crap he was sorting. "Does that mean you're considering marrying me?"

"No," I laughed. "Maybe. No—I don't think I'm ready."

Grady chuckled and went back to reading. Flustered with myself, I exhaled a long breath and printed the list of the original twenty-two trainees. I crossed off Bridget's name and sighed. Twenty-one to go.

~*~*~

Two hours later, I had the list narrowed down to five trainees: Ross, Scallon, Bailey, Alverez, and St. Clair.

"Why do you have Bailey on the list?" Grady asked.

"We fact checked everything we could find, but during the time he was in the gang, there's a lot we don't know. I can't eliminate him as a suspect yet."

The door opened and Bridget entered, followed by Bones, who carried an old plastic tote. I nodded toward the corner of the room and Bones walked over, setting it on the floor.

Grady tapped a pencil against my notepad to capture my attention. "But do you think Bailey's our guy? I'm not a profiler, but I can't see him coming after us."

"Can you see any of them as the bad guy?"

"No," he admitted. "But I didn't think Sorato would turn out to be dirty, either."

"Well, it can't be Alverez," Wayne said. "She's too damn cute to be the bad guy."

"What are you guys talking about?" Bridget asked, a puzzled look on her face.

"We think Sorato had a partner."

Bridget turned toward the gym and then looked back to me.

"What is it, Bridget?"

"Alverez was pretending she knew nothing about fashion." Bridget moved over to the files and dug through them, pulling out Alverez's file. After flipping through it, she grimaced. "She has her high school listed as Clarence High, but it's really Clarence Milborne Academy—a very expensive boarding school."

"But she's a veteran. Why would a boarding-school girl go into the Army?" Wayne asked.

"Bridget was a boarding-school girl," Bones said. "Just because you come from wealth, doesn't mean you follow the family mold."

"You're right," Wayne said, frowning. "But I've hung out with Alverez. Hell, I even asked her out on a date."

"But she turned you down," I said as a statement, not as a question.

"It's that obvious?" Wayne asked. "I must be losing my touch."

"You've still got it." Bridget winked at Wayne. "But if she's Sorato's partner, she wouldn't want you to get too close."

"Grady—" Tech said. "Can you reach out to someone in the military and find out if Alverez was trained in explosives?"

Grady nodded, pulling his phone and walking over to the corner of the room.

I turned back to Alverez's file. "We need her family history. Her file is pretty sparse."

"She doesn't have any social media accounts," Tech said. "I'm working through county records for birth and death certificates, but it takes longer. I know from her application that her mother died when she was five and her father died when she was sixteen."

"Not a single social media account? Are you sure?" Bridget asked. "Is she using an alias?"

"Her military discharge papers and photo match what we have on her application."

"What if she was married and changed her last name?" I asked. "Her social media accounts could be in her maiden name. Especially if the marriage didn't last long." I looked over at Grady.

He nodded to me that he had heard us as he continued with his phone conversation. "Thanks, Mike. One more question, is Alverez her married name?" Grady paced as he talked until he stopped mid-step and turned cold eyes back to me.

"*Shit*. Her maiden name is *Chaves*! They're related."

"Thanks again, Mike. I owe you," Grady said before disconnecting. Grady tossed the phone across the room, nearly hitting the window that overlooked the gym.

"Watch it!" Bridget snapped. "You've broken enough windows this week."

"*Arianna Nicole Chaves* married Sergeant Alverez while on leave. He died in combat two months later."

"Was she trained in explosives?" Tech asked as his fingers clacked furiously across the keyboard.

The TV screens lit up with social media accounts of Alverez, including pictures of her and Ernesto together at her high school graduation. The comments read that she was excited to see her brother at the event.

"The army trained her for ground level explosives," Grady said as he looked at the pictures on the TV screens. "This makes no sense. Just like Bailey—I can't see Alverez hurting us. It doesn't feel right."

"I agree, man," Wayne said, shaking his head. "She's not the most personable gal I've ever met, but she doesn't strike me as a cold-hearted killer."

I stood, walked to the door, and opened it. Looking across the gym, I saw several of the trainees, including Alverez, working out on the mats. "Alverez! I have a job for you!"

She jogged over. "What's up?" she asked as I held the door open and gestured for her to enter.

Bones moved toward the door and blocked the exit as Alverez stared at her face on the TV screen. "Game over." Bones glared, slamming the door closed.

She pulled out a chair at the end of the table and sat. When she looked up, she was glaring at Grady. I leaned against the wall to wait and watch.

"You destroyed my brother," she hissed, pointing at Grady. "His reputation was ruined. He wasted a year of his life sitting in a cell. He was innocent."

"Your brother is a bastard," Grady said, dropping his weight into the chair next to her. "He makes money on the lives of innocent women and children."

"You're lying! My brother is a kind, decent man. He gave me everything I have in this world. After our father died, Ernesto took me in. He paid for private schooling. He supported my choice to go into the military."

"I'm sure he did," Bridget said. "Hiding his criminal enterprise from you was easier if you weren't around to witness anything."

"You don't know what you're talking about," Alverez said.

Wayne sighed. "Ari, we know about the C-4 and your training. Were you going to hurt the kids?"

"Of course not! I wasn't going to kill anyone! I planned on blowing up the building when no one was around, but there was *always* someone around. I told Sorato to get rid of the C-4, but before I could confirm he had, she—" Alverez nodded toward me "—discovered who he was."

"How could you work with someone like Sorato?" Tech asked, shaking his head. "He kidnapped children and sold them for money."

"I'd never met him. I was told he was a little flakey, but someone I could trust. I didn't know he had a criminal past or that he'd worked with that Nola woman."

"Last summer we caught a sniper after he shot someone who's like a brother to me," I said, pushing away from the wall and sitting next to Alverez. A shiver raced up my back as I remembered Reggie lying on the plateau of the ridge while his horse danced around his unmoving body. "My friend ended up with only a minor wound, but when we questioned the sniper, we discovered he'd been manipulated into thinking he was working for the good guys. He believed the lies he was told without looking any closer."

"My brother is a *good man*."

"Your brother is a broker in human trafficking. And we can prove it," I said, tossing a pile of folders in front of her. "Are you willing to pull your head out of your ass long enough to review the evidence? Or are you going to keep blindly following whatever bullshit your brother feeds you?"

She glared at me. "It was you."

"Who figured out what your brother was up to? Yes, it was me. Others helped me put the puzzle pieces together, but I was the one who turned everything over to the FBI, which led to the raid."

"The case was thrown out. My brother was innocent."

"No," I said harsher than I intended, but holding eye contact with Alverez. "Your brother was released because he plays the legal game well. He buried the money in the Cayman Islands and has good lawyers. That doesn't mean he's innocent. It just means we couldn't prove he's guilty."

"Same thing."

"Ari," Wayne said. "It's not the same thing. Especially to the innocent women and children your brother destroyed. *Torture. Rape. Murder.* He allowed his clients to do whatever they wanted as long as he got paid."

She glanced over at Wayne, doubt showing in her eyes for the first time.

"Before you continue to judge our actions," Grady said, tapping on the stack of files, "read the files. Wanting him to be innocent won't make it true."

She glared at Grady before turning toward me. I held her stare until she nodded and opened the top file. Based on her tightly clenched jaw, she had no intention of being proven wrong.

CHAPTER TWENTY-FOUR

We all worked quietly for the next hour, passing scraps of information we'd discovered between us to share, but careful not to say anything in front of Alverez. Grady found two notes, both appearing to have been from Alverez to meet up at different times. Tech pulled Sorato's phone history, but only found calls to various burner phone numbers. Wayne found a Playboy magazine that seemed to entertain him until Bridget told him it probably had Sorato's man juice all over it. The magazine was tossed in the trash, and Wayne went to wash his hands.

Bones doled out work assignments for the trainees and managed the other security assignments for Headquarters, the store, and our houses. Bridget bounced back and forth between the conference room and the war room as deliveries for the war room arrived. Tech and I both watched as large wooden slabs were carried past the conference room windows and up the stairs.

And I sat trying to read through everything relating to Chaves: his finances, friends, enemies, and employees, but my focus kept drifting toward the tote that sat untouched in the corner.

"Go ahead," Grady said, nodding in that direction.

"No. It can wait. We're not meeting with the lawyer until Monday, so I have the weekend to go through it."

"What is it?" Tech asked.

I glance back at the tote. Truthfully, I wasn't sure what was in there. "Hopefully, the witch's spell book."

Grady laughed while trading laptops with me. Tech looked between us and shrugged.

I leaned back and stretched my arms above my head, glancing over at Alverez. She was reading the fourth file which held witness statements from the victims who were rescued, along with statements from some of Chaves' staff who had intended to testify against him. Wayne returned and moved to sit beside her, handing her another tissue.

"Wayne," I whispered. "Why don't you both take a break?"

Wayne nodded and pulled Alverez up from the table.

"Aren't you worried I'll escape?" Alverez asked.

"If you want to leave, then leave," I answered.

Alverez looked at Wayne, then back at me. "What if I go to my brother and tell him what you're doing?"

"Tell him what? That we know he's trying to kill us? That we're studying him? Go for it. I'm sure he already knows since the snipers he sent didn't succeed."

"What snipers?"

Wayne placed a gentle hand on Alverez's shoulder. "Snipers shot at Bones and Grady the other day when you were working security for Nana and Dallas."

"Did you catch them?" Her eyebrows scrunched, causing deep lines to form across her forehead.

"We haven't been able to ID them yet," Grady answered, sliding two pictures from a folder down the table to her.

She studied the photos before laying them back on the table. "That's Parker Hanner and Teddy Bear Curtis. They work security for my brother." She moved away from the table and looked out the exterior window to the field beyond. "If the witness statements are true, why wasn't it enough for a trial?"

"As you read, some of the victims are too distraught or too young to testify," Tech said. "Then the three top witnesses were executed, scaring the rest into recanting their stories. I'd be surprised if Chaves lets them live, though. They know too much."

"Video evidence?" she whispered.

"The night of the raid, the guards destroyed the servers before we could access the security room," Wayne said.

Alverez snorted. "I should've known. So that's how this ends."

"What do you mean?" I asked. "What are we missing?"

She returned to the table and looked down at the files. "I don't know that man," she said while pointing at the file. "He sounds nothing like the man who raised me." She turned to face me. "But if he's guilty of these crimes, he needs to be punished. He needs to be accountable to those women and children."

"That doesn't answer my question."

She dragged a hand through her hair. Her focus shifted from the files, to the windows, then back to me. She finally nodded. "Years ago, I was home for Christmas when his security system crashed. I helped reset it. Ernesto was upset that some of the data was lost so I built a backup system that could be accessed using a ten-key password."

"Do you have the password?" Tech asked.

"No. But I can get it."

"It's too dangerous," Wayne said, shaking his head. "If he catches you, he'll kill you."

"The brother who raised me would never harm me. This man..." she said, waving a hand to the files. "I have no idea what this man would do. But if my brother sent Teddy Bear and Parker to kill you, then he knows I don't have the C-4 anymore."

"He knows. He had Sorato killed while in FBI custody," I said, leaning back in my chair and tapping a pen on my knee. "Chaves would've expected us to search Sorato's room and find the C-4."

"Forrick," Alverez said.

"What's that?" Wayne asked.

"Agent Forrick and Ernesto grew up together. He's been around my whole life. He's an arrogant ass, but he's loyal to my brother."

"Damn," Kierson said from the doorway where he stood next to Charlie. "I had personal plans this weekend. I wish I wouldn't have heard that." He tossed my SUV keys to me before wrapping an arm around Charlie.

"You might be able to keep your plans," I told him. "If we call it in, then no offense, but the FBI will screw it up. Bones—can you pull a team of four together to do recon on this guy?"

"For what purpose?" Grady asked.

"To our knowledge, he's not a threat at the moment. But if he's arrested, Chaves will know. And if we don't watch Forrick, he could either surprise us or disappear."

"You don't think the FBI can handle a simple surveillance job?" Kierson asked.

"They'll fail," Wayne said. "Either the rumor mill will tip him off, or he'll spot them because he was trained in all the same moves."

"I have to at least update Special Agent in Charge Tebbs," Kierson said.

"For Pete's sake, call the man Jack, will you," I said, rolling my eyes. "If not to his face, at least around here." I pulled my phone from my back pocket and called Jack.

"Tebbs," he answered.

"Hey, Jack. It's your favorite consultant."

He grunted. "If you're calling me instead of Kierson, you're going to tell me something I don't like."

"Bingo. We know who killed Sorato, but I don't want to share the information just yet. He's a pawn in a bigger game. We're putting our own team together to keep an eye on him until we're ready for you to question him."

"How much time do you need?"

"A couple days. Plus or minus."

"You've got until Monday, and then I want the bastard's name." Jack disconnected the line.

"We have until Monday to nail Ernesto for his crimes." I looked over at Alverez, and she nodded.

"I can't believe you called him Jack," Kierson said, shaking his head and pulling Charlie toward the door.

"Charlie?" I called out before the door closed.

She turned back to look at me.

"Are you sticking around?"

"I heard about the custody case. No way in hell am I leaving. I booked a room at a nearby hotel."

"Family meeting tonight. I'll need you."

She watched me for a moment, trying to read my expression. "Text me the time. I'll be here."

Tech stopped clacking against his keyboard and looked over at me. "Should I text Alex and the girls?"

"Yes, please."

Grady walked over to me. I hadn't realized I was trembling until he pulled me up from the chair and held me. "It's going to be okay," he whispered.

"Come on, Alverez," Wayne said. "I have to check on security, run a couple errands, and pick up the catering order. Why don't you come with me and take a break?"

"I want to stay and help."

"It's time for everyone to take a break," Grady said as he turned me toward the door. "We can regroup tomorrow when our brains are fresh. We have a couple days before Ernesto orders another hit."

Grady stayed behind to help Tech lock the conference room while I went upstairs. The war room's windows were covered with tinted film, preventing me from seeing inside. Bridget ran out of the room and held her arms out in front of the door so I wouldn't enter. I smirked and turned toward the classroom.

I listened just outside the door as the kids and Carl summarized to Beth what they'd learned today. Nicholas' hands danced around as he described the dinosaurs that used to roam the Earth. Sara sat up straight as she described the micro-something structure of something—leaving me and my human brain in the dust. Beth seemed to understand enough of what she said to ask a few questions. When it was Carl's turn, he recited the headlines from twenty newspapers, making me laugh. When Carl finished, Beth told the kids they were done for the day. I opened the door and walked in.

"Kelsey!" Carl yelled, throwing his arms around me.

"Hi, Carl. Did you have fun today?"

"Beth has a box with my name on it. When I get bored, I pull a piece of paper from the box which tells me what my next project is. I estimate the ratio of picking something enjoyable to be one to one-point-six-eight, rounded to the hundredth decimal."

"Is that good or bad?" I laughed.

"Good. But the odds could change as I analyze the experiment over a longer period of time."

"Okay, then," I patted Carl's shoulder. "Why don't you go downstairs and wait with the kids."

"Last one there's a rotten egg!" Carl called out as he raced toward the stairs.

The kids took off after him.

"No running on the stairs!" Grady yelled from below.

Beth and I laughed.

"I'm surprised you stuck around," I said.

"I am too," she admitted. "I'm not one for living on the edge, and in the past few days, I've been exposed to bomb threats, guns being shot at people, and your boyfriend smashing windows."

"Grady's not someone you want to cross, but he's usually very much in control of his emotions. You joined us at a bad time."

"I doubt it was just bad timing," Beth said, raising an eyebrow at me as she smirked. "But the kids are very perceptive for their ages and persuaded me to stick around. They explained some of what you and the others do, and how at times, it can come back to bite all of you. They also trust that you, Grady, and the others will keep them safe. I decided that if they could handle it, then so could I."

"They've had more practice than you. Sara and Nicholas have seen firsthand what cruel people are capable of. Nicholas' biological mother was beyond psycho. Sara's biological father was a member of a dangerous biker gang. Both kids were born into chaotic and violent lives."

"And now they're safe," Grady said, walking in and wrapping one arm around my waist and raising his other hand to shake Beth's. "I'm Grady. Sorry if I scared you yesterday when I smashed the windows. I promise, it won't happen again."

"Only because Bridget threatened to box your ears," I said, laughing.

Beth grinned, shaking Grady's hand. "The kids and I tried to peek into the room today, but Bridget wouldn't let us. What's she doing?"

"We call the room the war room. It's where Tech and I run investigations. I told Bridget that the room was boring and gave her a green light to redecorate. She won't let me in either, so I have no idea what to expect."

"Whatever she's doing, it won't be boring," Grady said on a chuckle. "Beth, would you like to join us for dinner tonight? Kelsey ordered takeout Italian. We usually eat around six-thirty."

"I'm not sure." She hesitated. "It might be best for the kids to see me as only their teacher."

"Too late. As you said, the kids are perceptive. If I asked them to write a profile on you, they'd probably have 98 percent of your life detailed out."

Beth laughed. "Well then, what the hell. I have some errands to run, but I'll see you both about a quarter after six."

We followed her out of the classroom.

Chapter Twenty-Five

The kids rattled non-stop for twenty minutes about their day until they ditched me to help Nana in the kitchen. Based on the smoke that billowed from the oven when she opened it, I expected whatever she was baking to be a lost cause.

Grady and Carl had gone to the store to help shut down. Everyone had agreed to have the family meeting at Headquarters before dinner. Whiskey, Bones, and Bridget would stay behind to watch Carl, Nana, and the kids.

And as the time drew closer, my stomach rolled thinking of how they'd react. I walked outside, around the corner of the garage, and lit a cigarette. Because it bothered Nicholas, I seldom smoked anymore. But right now I needed something, anything, to calm my nerves.

"Am I early?" Maggie asked, walking around the corner.

"Yes, but I'm glad. We're having a family meeting before dinner."

"And what's on the dinner menu? I'm hoping you'll say it's your famous pot roast that I've heard so much about."

"Sorry. I ordered Italian from a local restaurant. Maybe I can throw together a pot roast later this weekend." I grinned over at her.

"Italian sounds good too," she said as her eyes scanned our surroundings.

"How have you been, Maggie?" She knew I was asking how she was coping with what she went through when Jonathan had kidnapped her.

"Better. At least, most days."

"And the nights?"

"The nights were easier in the safe house when Nightcrawler was with me. But I'll get a handle on it."

"Was your bed warmer when you were with Nightcrawler?" I asked, shoulder nudging her.

"Not the first month," she answered, her eyes sparkling as she cocked her head toward me. "But the following two weeks…"

"He's in Michigan, you know. He came home after you split."

Maggie leaned against the side of the garage and sighed. "He's a criminal. I'm an FBI agent. Our worlds don't exactly mesh."

"He's a man who makes you feel safe. With the work that we do, you need that. You should talk to him."

"I could recommend the same to you," Maggie said, lifting an eyebrow. "I stopped at the Changing Room before coming to the house. Your family's pretending they're fine, but I see the worry in their eyes."

"I called a family meeting, but they don't know why." I sighed. "It's time to tell some truths."

I started to walk toward the front of the house when Maggie grabbed my elbow to stop me. "Whatever it is you have to tell them, it won't change how they feel about you."

"You can't guarantee that."

"I'm a profiler, remember?" She threw an arm over my shoulder. "I know these things."

~*~*~

Everyone divided between multiple vehicles and regrouped at Headquarters in the first-floor conference room.

"I brought some apples," Alex said as he dumped a bag on the credenza along the far wall. "Don't think I haven't noticed you've barely eaten the past few days," he added as he pointed at me. "After you clear the air on whatever is troubling you, I expect your bitch-ass to eat."

Grady rubbed my back. "I have something I want to say before we get started," he announced. "As many of you know, I had a temper tantrum yesterday and smashed a shitload of windows."

Katie grinned. "Everyone noticed. Are you going to tell us why you did it?"

"I'm going to tell you that my reaction—my anger— damaged more than just a few windows. Kelsey was convinced, and still is, that I'll leave her because of what she told me."

"Bullshit," Donovan said. "You'd never leave."

"I know," Grady said. "And I will prove that to her, eventually. But the point is, she cares for everyone in this room, and how you respond to what she has to say, *can* hurt her."

"Is this about our parents?" Charlie asked, sitting next to Anne on the other side of the table.

"Yes and no," I answered, taking the seat across from her. "I've kept secrets from everyone, and with Mother coming after me, I need to prepare everyone for those secrets to become public."

"Will this impact the custody case?" Katie asked.

"It's the perfect opportunity for my mother to expose me, but I still don't think she'd be able to get visitation of

Nicholas. I talked to Cameron, and there are only a few exceptions the court will make to allow grandparents custody arrangements." I stared at my hands, watching them shake.

"Do you want me to tell them?" Grady asked.

Tears choked my throat, so I nodded.

Grady stood behind me, his hands braced on my shoulders as he began. "Kelsey told us that when they were kids, Charlie and she survived from the profits of her books. But the truth is, it took several years for her books to make any money."

Anne pulled a quick breath into her lungs and reached out, grasping Charlie's hand. "Stop. We don't need to know. It doesn't matter."

"What doesn't matter?" Lisa asked before Alex pulled her away from the table.

I couldn't look up. I couldn't face them. The silence in the room was the loudest thing I'd ever heard.

"I don't understand," Lisa whispered.

"There are only two ways a fourteen-year-old girl can make enough money to survive," Charlie answered, speaking slowly.

I took a deep breath and raised my head to look at her, but her eyes were focused on the table between us.

"Stealing and selling her body." Tears streamed down her face as Anne held one of her hands and Katie held the other. "I should've known," she said as she raised her eyes to mine. "You shouldn't have had to carry that secret." Charlie shook her head, and I could see the dots connecting as her mind worked out the details. "In Miami, the mentoring programs you volunteered for to help the girls get off the streets were so important to you. I saw them as lost causes, but you couldn't walk away. No matter how many times you were disappointed, you kept telling me it was worth it. That saving one girl was worth a year's worth of misery. I didn't understand."

Donovan set the box of tissue on the table in front of Charlie before walking over to join Lisa and Alex. Lisa looked from Alex to Donovan, then to me, shaking her head.

Alex held Lisa's hand as he turned to me. "Not many girls that young survive the streets. I'm proud of you for being one of them."

"I'm not proud, Alex," I said as my chin quivered. "I lied. I cheated. I stole. I sold my body for money. I'm so ashamed of the things I've done. And I never wanted any of you to know."

"But your *mother* knows," Maggie said, barely louder than a whisper. "No wonder Grady smashed the windows." Her fists clenched as she turned to face me. "That bitch *knew*—and did *nothing*?"

Grady reached over and braced a hand on Maggie's shoulder. She looked at him a long moment before she nodded and moved away, taking deep breaths.

"The witch's spell book," Tech said, nodding toward the tote. "You've got something on your mother."

"I don't know what I have. When I robbed my parents, I stole files from my mother and love letters my father had hidden away." I looked over at Maggie and smirked. "When I allegedly robbed my parents."

Maggie rolled her eyes.

"This is my fault," Charlie said. "You kept asking me not to dig around in our past, but I did it anyway."

"You wanted justice for our grandparents and for what the sheriff did to me. I understood that."

"What happened to your grandparents? And what did the sheriff do?" Anne asked. "What else don't we know?"

Grady's grip tightened on my shoulder, but he answered. "When Kelsey moved Charlie out of her house, she blackmailed their parents with the evidence that proved they were involved with her grandparents' deaths. She also has a video involving her and the sheriff. She used the video for protection and for the sheriff to rent her a house."

"What's on the video?" Tech asked.

"It shows me successfully seducing the sheriff," I whispered.

"Up to and including," Grady added, "when she cried out for him to stop once she succeeded."

"Motherfucker!" Donovan yelled at Grady. "She was *fourteen years old*! Why haven't you ended this piece of shit yet?"

"Because he knows me," I said, standing to defend Grady. "He knew I'd never be free from my past until I faced it down."

Grady grasped my hand and intertwined our fingers.

"How much more can you possibly take?" Lisa whispered. She looked up, and I saw the tears slide down her cheeks. "We all watched you struggle after the things that happened with Nola. Then you went through hell again with Jonathan. You may have superpowers compared to the rest of us, but everyone has a breaking point. What if facing your family is too much?"

"Then it breaks me," I whispered as my own tears escaped. "I don't have a choice. I can't keep running from this."

"I was just a kid." Charlie chuckled to herself. "That was what you kept reminding me when we were growing up. It was you against the world, trying to protect me—because I was just a kid." She stood and walked over to me, placing her hands on my shoulders. "God, I hated that nickname! Every time I heard it, it reminded me that you'd always be older, smarter, faster, and I'd never measure up."

"No one is comparing the two of us except for you," I said, shaking my head. "You have qualities that I'll never master. You are patient, focused, and so damn moral it makes me want to vomit. You have the ability to keep the lines between right and wrong clear in your head. I lost that a long time ago."

"Like when I beat the shit out of my father?" Charlie snorted.

"I said you had the ability. I didn't say you always used it."

"And you," she said, smiling at me through her tears, "are not alone anymore." She moved a hand to cup the side of my face. "Back then, you were right—I was just a kid. And I might be stuck with the nickname of Kid the rest of my life, but you don't need to protect me anymore. That's how you'll get through this. I'm here. Grady's here. Your new sisters and brothers are here. You've been dealing with everything that's happened to you on your own, because that's what you had to do when we were young. But that's over. Lean on us. We won't abandon you."

My chest tightened, my chin trembled, and I forced myself to look at the floor. "What if you change your mind?" I whispered. "What if your feelings change when you hear the details of the things I've done?"

"We couldn't give a rat's fart what you've done in the past." Alex snorted. "Luv, each of us has done shit we ain't proud of. You're forgetting I lived on the streets for several years."

Anne chuckled. "I seduced my husband's friend so I could steal his keys and escape with Sara. I've never felt the least bit guilty."

"I killed someone when I escaped from Tommy," Lisa said. "Fuck 'em."

Donovan laughed, leaning in to kiss Lisa's forehead.

"I couldn't convince my younger sister to leave," Katie whispered. "But I couldn't stay. I had to get out. I joined the army and never went home again. I don't even know if she's alive. Or if she turned into an abusive drunk like my mother."

"She's alive," I said, reaching across the table to grasp her hand. "She has issues, but drinking isn't one of them."

"You know about Lindsey?" she asked, her eyes widening.

"I've always known. Your mother died a few years ago, and I tracked Lindsey down to make sure she was okay." I grinned as I wiped my tears. "She's a bitch, but she's made a decent life for herself."

Katie laughed. "Bitchiness is sort of a family trait. Let me guess, you offered help, and she told you to go to hell?"

"She had a brighter vocabulary, but yeah." I looked around the room. "It's not very fair, is it? I've meddled in everyone's lives while keeping secrets from all of you."

"That's not meddling," Alex said, shaking his head. "You're the head of our family. You've carried that weight from the beginning, watching over all of us until we were strong enough to do it for ourselves. But now it's time to show your mother just how strong you made us."

"Damn straight," Anne said.

"Agreed," Grady said, walking over and picking up the tote. "This damn thing has been a distraction all day."

He set the tote in front of me, but I motioned for him to open it. I barely looked at anything when I was younger, and I was afraid now of what we would find.

"It can't hurt you," Maggie whispered over my shoulder as everyone dug into the tote and grabbed folders. "They won't let it."

I looked around the room as everyone started sorting and organizing the files. I hoped Maggie was right. I hoped that when the dust settled, they'd still be standing beside me. Grady handed me a pile of letters, held together by dried out rubber bands that fell to pieces when I took the stack from him. I pulled a handwritten letter out of the first envelope.

"Kelsey," Lisa said. "There are files in here on you and your family. Even your dad has a file." She lifted almost a dozen files out of the tote.

"Grady takes my folder and my father's. Charlie gets her file and her parents. I'll read my brothers' files when I'm done with the letters."

"Fine by us. Looks like we have the rest of the town to sort through," Donovan said. "She must have a file on everyone she ever met."

"My mother would've built a file on anyone she could use to do her dirty work or who could provide a future favor. She's a master at manipulating others to do her bidding."

Chapter Twenty-Six

I was reading the fourth sappy love letter when I sensed Grady's anger. He closed the file he was looking at, but not before I saw a photo. I reached over, opening the folder to look. The photo was of me, probably around fifteen years old, and I was sexually interacting with an older man. He was one of my regulars, the son of the local grocery store owner.

"Figures. My mother probably got a discount on groceries with that photo in her pocket."

Grady slammed the file closed before storming out of the room. I looked over at Maggie and nodded toward the door. She followed him out, closing the door behind her.

"Is he going to smash more windows?" Katie asked, not looking up from the file she was taking notes on.

"I'd say the odds are fifty-fifty. My mother has photos of me prostituting myself to older men."

"Why did you give him your file?" Donovan asked. "Especially after yesterday."

"Because Grady has to decide for himself how much he wants to know at this point. There's a fine line between knowing someone's secrets and knowing too much. But I can't keep deciding for him where that line starts and stops."

"Like when Katie thought I should know the names of all the men she'd slept with?" Tech said, rolling his eyes at Katie.

I laughed. "No. That was Katie trying to scare you off."

The door opened, and Maggie stepped back inside, returning to the files she'd been reading. Grady walked in next, sitting back in the chair beside me. I didn't ask if he was okay. I knew he wasn't. I placed my hand on top of his. He turned his hand over and intertwined our fingers.

Grady turned to look at me. His eyes were glassy with unshed tears. "I love you."

"I know you do."

"But I don't think it's a good idea for me read your file."

I kissed his cheek before turning to Maggie. "Can you take my file?"

"Yeah. Sure," she said, reaching in front of Grady for it. "That's why you asked me to come, right? To work the information like a case?"

"At least the parts concerning me, yes. You don't mind?"

"No problem. I'll work my notes in Donovan's office. Be back in a few minutes."

I turned my attention back to the thick stack of letters I was reading. I finished four more and looked resentfully at the large pile still to go. The letters were in date order so I decided to skip toward the back, picking the third from the end. The letter was much more entertaining and didn't take me long to read. I sat up straight, grabbing the next letter, then the last one. I looked over at Charlie, wondering if what I was thinking was real.

The door opened, and Maggie walked back inside.

Grady raised an eyebrow at her. "You're done already?"

"There's not a lot in here that Kelsey didn't already tell us. Just a few names and dates," Maggie said. "I have three men and one woman that I need you to identify," Maggie said, nodding for me to move away from the table.

I followed her over to the credenza and looked at the photos. I was disgusted by them, both for my involvement with the men and my mother's participation in taking and keeping the photos, but I gave Maggie the names of the men. The fourth photo was a picture of Marilyn, the nurse who helped Charlie and I when we were kids. "Why does she have a picture of Marilyn?"

"That depends. What's the woman handing you?"

"Shit. What's Michigan law on birth control prescriptions for minors?"

"Did you have a prescription?" Maggie sighed.

I dragged a hand through my hair. "No. Marilyn knew I couldn't afford a doctor."

Maggie stepped around me and toward the table. "Was there a file on a nurse by the name of Marilyn?" Maggie asked Tech.

"Yeah," Tech answered as he dug through a stack of files. "Distribution of prescription drugs. Odd stuff like antibiotics, insulin, steroid shots, birth control."

"Not odd stuff," I said, shaking my head.

"Prescriptions you can't afford if you live in a small town and there's no free clinic," Anne said. "How much trouble is this Marilyn woman in?"

I looked back at the photo and sighed. "I'll get her an attorney, but she'll probably lose her nursing license if my mother turns her in."

Katie got up and took the file from Tech. "I'll call Doc and see if he has any suggestions. We'll keep her clear of this if we can."

"What the hell?" Charlie said, standing up with the folder she was reading still in her hands. "This says my mother had a hysterectomy."

"Why is that important?" Anne asked.

"Because it was a year before I was born!"

Everyone in the room stopped what they were doing and looked first at Charlie, then at me.

"So, how would you feel if I told you we might be half-sisters?" I asked as I moved back over to my section of the table.

Charlie looked up from the file with widened eyes.

"You should sit down and read these letters. It appears my father had an affair with a woman who might be your mother." I pushed the stack of letters across the table toward Charlie.

"That's messed up," Katie whispered.

"Does it say why she gave me up?"

"No. But the last letter reveals that my mother caught him in the affair, so my father ended the relationship with the other woman."

"Did you get a name?"

"Rose Peterson."

"There's a file on someone with that name," Tech said. "We have notes on her already. She was a hairdresser. There were some racy pictures of her with a man." Tech dug out the file from the already read pile.

"She left town after the stillbirth of her daughter," Anne said, pointing to the TV screen behind me.

I turned to see a list with notes next to each person's name and near the top was Rose Peterson. Next to it was an indication that her daughter died during childbirth on April 10th, twenty-nine years ago.

"I can't look in the file," Charlie whispered, staring at the file that Tech was holding out for one of us to take.

I grabbed the file, opening it to the photos. It was indeed my dad, sticking it to a woman. I didn't know her, but she had a face I'd known my whole life. I got up and walked over to the credenza, fishing around in one of the drawers for a pair of scissors. I cut the head and neck out of one of the photos and set the smiling woman's face down on the table in front of Charlie.

"Look familiar?" I asked as I walked back to sit next to Grady.

"She's beautiful," Charlie gasped.

"So are you, luv," Alex said. "Now we need to track her down."

"This is huge," Maggie said, grinning. "Setting aside the fact that Charlie's brain is probably imploding right now, if we can prove that the records were falsified, then this becomes a federal case that we can use against your family."

"I'm not ready to decide what we'll do with any of this information yet. Let's just keep digging."

"Call Genie and have her join us," Tech said. "She can run backgrounds on Rose and anyone else who pops up while I keep categorizing the rest."

"I already called her," Maggie said, nodding toward the doorway where Genie stood.

"And I already arrived," Genie said, giggling as she walked over to set up her laptop at the end of the table. "What can I do to help?"

"Find this woman," Charlie said, holding up the photo. "We think she might be my mother."

"Is that a good thing or a bad thing?" Genie asked.

"We won't know until we track her down and ask a few questions," I answered, because I knew Charlie couldn't.

She wanted to be hopeful that she was related to someone kind and compassionate, but neither of us had had good luck where family was concerned, the only exception being the two of us.

"Where's Kierson?" I asked Genie.

"At the hotel."

Charlie looked up at me, looking as scared as she had when we were kids.

"Call him, Charlie."

"We're not like that. Just because we occasionally sleep together, doesn't mean anything. He should enjoy his time off."

"Call him," Grady said. "You're not alone, either."

Charlie stared down at her phone in front of her.

"I know how you feel. It's hard to ask for help," I said to Charlie as I squeezed Grady's hand. "But Kierson's waiting for you to let him in, not the other way around."

Charlie picked up her phone and called. "Can you come to Headquarters?" There was a pause as Charlie's lower lip quivered. "Thanks," she said before hanging up. "He was already on his way. He'll be here in a minute. I can't believe he's coming."

Genie snorted. "He grins for weeks after he spends time with you. It freaks the shit out of the rest of the suits and ties at the office. They literally jump out of the way like his smile is radioactive."

"It's probably because of this thing I do with my tongue—" Charlie grinned as she wiped a tear away.

"Stop!" I laughed.

"La, la, la, la," Lisa said, holding her hands over her ears.

"Am I the only one who wants to know what she does with her tongue?" Alex asked.

"If it wasn't Kierson on the receiving end..." Genie said, scrunching up her face in disgust. "But with Kierson? Ewe. I'm with Lisa. La, la, la, la..." she said as she covered her ears.

Kierson came running into the room, looking frantically around until his eyes locked on Charlie. When Charlie noticed him, her lower lip started to quiver again. He walked over, pulling her up from her chair and tucking her head under his chin.

"I found Rose Peterson," Genie said. "She's living in the Traverse Bay area. Single, employed hair stylist, no record of any dependents. She moved up there right after her baby was born, apparently to live closer to her brother and his family."

"Criminal record?" I asked.

"Nothing. She and her brother are clean."

"Doesn't mean anything," Charlie said, pulling away from Kierson. "Our parents don't even have a speeding ticket, but that doesn't make them good people."

"Only one way to find out, Charlie," I said. "How do you want to play this?"

"Who's Rose Peterson?" Kierson asked Charlie.

"She might be my mother," Charlie answered.

Kierson glanced over at me, and I shrugged. "Seems my father played hide the salami with this Rose woman and got her knocked up around the time that Charlie's mother had a hysterectomy. We don't know much more than that, other than if she is Charlie's mom, then someone faked a death certificate."

"And a birth certificate," Maggie added.

"Genie, text me the address," Kierson said, pulling Charlie toward the door.

"Kierson?" I asked, standing and stepping in front of him.

"I've got her, Kelsey," he said before steering Charlie around me and out of the room.

Grady pulled me back into my chair and handed me one of my brother's files. I glanced back at the door one more time before opening the file.

~*~*~

Twenty minutes later, Grady cursed from beside me. "I keep thinking this insanity has to end, and then there's another sick layer."

"My father's file?" I asked as I closed the last file I had in my stack.

Grady nodded slowly, staring at the file he held.

"It has to be something good," I said, chuckling. "He sure as hell didn't love or respect my mother. And he was distant to me and my brothers. What is it? What has she held over his head? Nothing short of murder would make sense to me."

Grady stiffened, turning to face me.

"No..." I grabbed the file, opening it to see for myself. "He killed someone? Who?"

"A homeless man was hit by a car late at night while walking along the edge of the road. Someone found the body the next morning. Police were asking for information on a suspect driving a dark blue car with chrome trim and round headlights."

"My father's Nova," I whispered, pulling a photo out of the file which showed the front-end damage to the headlight and front-quarter panel.

"He doesn't still have the car, does he?" Grady asked. "That's a 1972 Chevy Nova. It's a classic. Someone would've noticed it."

"No." I shook my head. "He doesn't, but my mother does."

Everyone was already listening, but their eyes got a little bigger.

"How do you know your mother has the car?" Anne asked.

"I was young, maybe four or five? I was in the backseat of my mother's car while she drove around doing errands. She may have forgotten I was with her. But I remember her getting out of the car at a storage facility. I was curious why we were there. I released my seatbelt and sat on my knees to watch her from the rear window. She looked around and then opened the storage unit. She walked past the dust covered car toward shelves filled with boxes on the other side. I could only see the front of the car, but it had a broken headlight and a University of Michigan vanity plate. This plate!" I pointed to the picture before turning back to Grady. "A few years later, I found a picture of my dad and my uncle standing in front of the same car. I asked my dad about it, and he said that he'd bought it when he was in high school and drove it until his sophomore year of college. He looked sad, though, and put the picture away. I was going to ask him why it was in the storage unit, but my mother called us to dinner."

"Why do you remember?" Maggie asked. "Most kids that age remember bits and pieces, but not details like being called to dinner."

"I have very few memories of speaking to my dad. He usually didn't speak to anyone except my mother, and even then, he said as little as possible. It was probably the longest interaction I ever had with him."

"Do you think your mother still has the car?" Tech asked.

"Yes. She saves everything, as you can see by the number of files here. But I don't remember where the storage facility was. I wasn't paying attention until she went into the storage unit."

"Do you remember anything? The color of the buildings? Or nearby buildings or houses?" Genie asked.

"I don't think so. Maybe if I were to drive by a bunch of them?"

"Was it during the day or at night?" Grady asked.

"Daytime. When I was younger, she'd sometimes drag me along while she did her errands, like her hair and nail appointments. I don't remember everywhere we went that day, but I remember for sure that she went to the bank. The bank was always her last errand, so it was strange that we went to the storage facility instead of home."

"She kept you in the car during all those errands, didn't she?" Maggie asked.

"You know she did. She'd usually either take me with her, leaving me in the car while she ran the errands, or she'd leave me at home by myself."

"At four years old?" Anne asked.

"Oh, since before then. My earliest memory was when she slapped me for crying to be let out of the car. I still had a car seat, not a booster seat, so I was maybe two?"

Grady stood, radiating anger, and I grabbed his arm, pulling him back into his chair.

"You need to chill, man," Tech said. "The building won't survive you exploding again."

"Or the furniture," Bridget said, walking into the office. "Tyler is helping Whiskey watch the kids. Bones and I came to help."

"We need more recon done in the morning," Grady said.

"Tomorrow's Saturday," Bones said. "I promised James I'd run security at the store while he's out of town on club business."

"Most of us will be working at the store tomorrow," Anne added.

"I'd go, but I have a few guys helping me finish the war room tomorrow," Bridget said. "I can't wait for you guys to see it."

Grady stood, handing a stack of files to Lisa to put in one of the boxes. "I'll go."

"No way in hell, cowboy," Donovan said.

"I second that," I said, smirking at Grady. "You're not going anywhere near Sadler Creek without supervision. We can send Trigger and Drake. See how well they do."

"It's a risk. They're pretty green," Grady warned.

"They are polar opposites," I said. "As a team, they should be able to bullshit their way through any situation."

"I'm not even sure if Trigger's going to make the cut," Grady said. "I can't see him doing bodyguard work, and he doesn't have the discipline for rescue work."

"I've had the same feeling," Bones agreed. "But he's got other talents. He'd make a great prospect for the club."

"Don't be marking him club property just yet," I said. "If Grady and Donovan don't have a place for him, I'd like to try him out on some ideas that I have."

"Are these ideas legal?" Maggie asked, not looking up from the file she was reading.

"Mostly." I shrugged. "Take the Reno case for example. I tagged along behind Ryan and the woman he was protecting and within two days, I spotted the stalker."

"Ryan was happy," Donovan said. "He couldn't get a bead on the guy."

"It was quick and easy. But it takes someone who can blend in and who has a sharp set of eyes."

"Do you have enough cases like that?" Bones asked.

"No. But I have plenty of investigative cases that require someone to go out and ask a few questions. I can keep him busy."

"I agree," Tech said. "We have a pile of cases we can't take because we don't have anyone to knock on doors."

"Can he read people?" Maggie asked.

"Nope." I grinned, turning to look at Bridget. "But he's not the only one I'm interested in hiring."

Bridget squealed, jumping up and down.

"No," Bones growled. "It's not safe."

"Trigger would protect her," Donovan said, nodding at me in favor of the idea. "He's a top-notch shooter and ballsy as hell in a fight."

"And Kelsey's right. He's alert," Grady agreed.

Bones stormed out of the room, growling.

"Ooh." Bridget sneered at the door. "That man is so infuriating! Who does he think he is?"

"Go tell him—not us," I insisted, pointing toward the door.

"I'm going to do just that," she said before storming after Bones.

Grady smiled down at me. "You're a wicked woman."

I stood to kiss him briefly. "You love my wicked layers."

"Damn straight." One eyebrow rose and I could read his eyes as naughty thoughts crossed his mind.

"Later," I whispered.

We all turned toward the door hearing Bridget and Bones screaming and yelling at each other. We could make out the entire argument for a good five minutes. Then it was quiet, very quiet.

I turned back to Grady, but he had his head bent, shoulders shaking as he laughed silently.

"If they have sex in my office, you're cleaning it!" Donovan said as glared at me.

"It'd be worth it. Those two need to get it out of their system."

Grady was still smiling when he tapped on the stack of files in front of me. "Anything in your brothers' files?"

"Same old motherly love. She's been interfering in their lives and holding petty crap over their heads since they were born. Worst thing I found, though, was that she pressured a young girl into getting an abortion, but kept the records to blackmail the girl with."

"Your mother is a b-i-t-c-h," Genie said before handing me a stack of papers. "Here. I printed a list of storage facilities that existed twenty-five years ago and were within a twenty-mile radius of your parents' house. Some of them have photos."

I took the stack she handed me and turned to Tech. "Can you print the summaries you guys made, and I'll read through it later tonight?"

"Sure. Do you want me to send a copy to Charlie too?" Tech asked.

"No. She has enough on her plate right now. I'll go through everything with her when she gets back."

"Are we wrapping up?" Donovan asked, looking hopeful.

"Yeah. It's almost time for dinner and the kids will be worried if we don't get back to the house. And Lisa looks ready to fall over."

"I've been exhausted all day, so I won't argue. If you're watching Carl and the kids tomorrow, can you take Abigail too? I want to work at the store for a couple of hours."

"The doctor said to take it easy, babe," Donovan said to Lisa. "Why don't you stay home and sleep in."

"I'm only planning on working for a couple of hours. Quit worrying."

Donovan looked over at me, waiting for me to say something.

"The kids can help me with Abigail, but let's wait to see how you're feeling in the morning. Spending a day lying on the couch, watching TV, doesn't sound like a bad idea to me. We can make fun of all the sorry saps who have to work."

"Hey," Anne whined. "No fair."

Tech handed me a stack of papers and I added it to the storage unit printouts. Grady pushed me toward the door as everyone followed us out.

Chapter Twenty-Seven

"Mohhmm?" Nicholas mumbled around a mouth full of food.

"Chew your food, then talk," I said before taking another bite of garlic bread.

Nicholas dramatically chewed his food while bouncing his head up and down. Grady leaned over to wipe pasta sauce from his face.

He thanked Grady before turning back to me. "Is your demon mother going to get custody of me?"

He was trying to hide his fear, but I saw it. My chest tightened. "No." I leaned past Grady and grasped Nicholas' hand. "My mother will never get custody. In fact, it's my intention that the two of you never meet. Not unless you choose to when you're an adult. But I don't recommend it."

"But she wants custody?"

"No. She wants to punish me, and she knows that you're the most important person in my life."

"More important than Grady?" he asked, seeming surprised.

Grady laughed. "It doesn't matter how much your mom loves me, buddy. You'll always be her number one guy." He reached over and tussled Nicholas' hair.

I squeezed Nicholas' hand one more time before releasing it and leaning back in my chair. "How did you hear about the custody case?"

Nicholas turned and looked at Sara who was giving him a death glare.

"Sara? How do you know about the custody case?" I asked.

Grady sighed. "Carl has the inside of the garage under surveillance. Sara has access to it."

Abigail started fussing from her pen in the living room, and Anne went to get her. When she returned, she deposited Abigail into my arms. The look on my face must've been bad, because Grady laughed and reached over to take Abigail from me.

Anne laughed. "Oh, come on. Why won't you hold her?"

"When she gets older, I will." I watched Grady make noises at Abigail and cuddle her into the crook of his arm. "Until then, you all can handle it."

"Did you hold me when I was a baby?" Nicholas asked.

"You weren't that little when I adopted you. You were just over a year old and almost walking."

"Have you ever held a baby?" Katie asked.

I shook my head. "Not an infant. I was only two when Charlie was born. So, no, not really."

Grady tried to hand Abigail back to me, but I held my hands up and leaned away. "I'm good. Thanks. Abby and I will bond when she's older."

Grady chuckled. "You're over thinking it."

"Over thinking that the only thing she does right now is poop, pee, spit up, and throw up? I'm good. Seriously."

Beth stood and took Abigail from Grady. "I think they're perfect at this age."

"I loved it when Sara was a baby," Anne said, sighing. "I was actually smarter than her back then."

"At what age did she pass you?" I asked.

"She was two and a half when she started reading her bedtime books to herself and from there it was a whirlwind trying to keep up with her. I don't know where the hell she gets it."

Nicholas smirked at Anne. "Pushups."

"*Ugh!*" Anne lowered herself to the floor. "Are you sure we can't just pay money or something?"

Katie laughed. "I hear ya. I had to take a hot bath this morning to loosen my arm muscles. Tech couldn't even lift his arms to make a pot of coffee."

"I bet if we watched the surveillance videos, we'd hear a lot more swear words," Nicholas said.

"Won't work," I said.

"How come?" Sara asked, looking suspicious.

"Because after dinner, you, Tech, Carl, and Nicholas are taking all the surveillance equipment down and deleting the electronic files. And if any of you spy on us adults again, there will be serious consequences. We're talking groundings, losing your phones, losing TV time, losing desserts."

Carl pouted from the end of the table. "*Ah, man.*"

"All of them?" Tech asked.

"Any piece of equipment that is recording video or sound within twenty feet of the house is to go. No exceptions. No arguments, Tech. This is our home. I refuse to feel like I'm a prisoner and need to write secret messages and make a shiv out of my toothbrush."

Katie pointed her fork at Tech. "And if you decide to get sneaky and leave any up, I'll take away your *favorite* dessert."

Beth choked on her food, and we all laughed.

"I'll get started now," Tech said, jumping up from the table and heading into the living room.

"Aunt Katie, are you talking about sex?" Sara asked.

"Eat your dinner, Sara," Anne said as she reached over and took Abigail from Beth who was still coughing. "You need to get the surveillance equipment down before bedtime."

"Anything special on the schedule tomorrow?" I asked Anne.

"Since you'll be home with the kids, the rest of us will be at the store. Whiskey plans on splitting his time between the store and the house."

"I can be around the house all day if you need me," Whiskey said.

"I can handle it. No worries."

Lisa grinned. "You said you'd help watch Abigail tomorrow. How are you going to do that if you won't even pick her up?"

"I don't have to pick her up to change a diaper or feed her," I said, rolling my eyes. "Besides, your ass will be parked on my couch all day. If I run into a problem, you can help me. But you've been pushing yourself too hard and need to take a break."

Abigail let out a loud happy squeal.

"See? Even Abby agrees."

Nicholas was watching me with a raised eyebrow, having noticed that I swore. I fake scowled at him while getting on the floor, counting out ten pushups.

"Can I be done?" Nicholas asked.

"Me too?" Sara asked.

As I crawled back up from the carpet, I looked at Nicholas' plate, then Sara's. "Sara can be done—scrape your plate, please. Nick, you need to eat some of your vegetables."

"Awe, man," Nicholas grumbled. "No fair."

"It's fair," Carl said, gathering his plate and a few others. "Sara ate her vegetables, and you didn't."

"Do I have to eat my veggies too?" Nana asked as she pushed her food around. "The broccoli is overcooked."

"Nana, you are not helping. Eat your vegetables."

"Overcooking vegetables causes them to lose a good portion of their minerals and vitamin content," Sara said, gathering her plate and her mom's.

"But even overcooked, broccoli is still is a good source of fiber," Beth said, challenging Sara.

"Fiber helps you poop." Carl giggled on his way into the kitchen.

"See! There you have it!" I said.

I turned to Grady to see him chewing his food as he looked down at the table, laughing silently.

"To pooping!" Whiskey said, stabbing a chunk of broccoli and eating it.

"Is this the normal dinner conversation?" Beth asked, laughing.

"We've had worse," Lisa said as she stabbed a chunk of broccoli.

The doorbell rang and I went to see who it was. As one hand wrapped around the door handle, I reached the other behind my back to my Glock. Cracking the door open, I saw Doc standing on the front stoop and opened the door to let him in.

"Hey, Doc. Were we expecting you?" I asked as I swept my arm out, inviting him in.

"Katie called and told me a nurse friend of yours was in a jam. We arranged for the nurse to meet me here, but Katie also told me that if I came early, I could mooch dinner. I hear Italian was on the menu tonight."

"You're always welcome for dinner. I've told you that before. Plates are in the kitchen, help yourself. Did Katie explain to Marilyn what was happening?"

"No. Katie gave me Marilyn's number, and I called her and asked her to meet me here. I told her that there was some type of investigation and that I'd help with the paperwork."

"I don't want you to get in trouble, too."

"It's an easy fix. She kept records on all her patients, so we'll be able to backdate the clinic's computer files. I'll have Sara help, so it can't be traced back. By the sounds of it, it's only about twenty patients, and you're one of them. I'm happy to help."

Before I had closed the door another set of headlights turned into the drive. I waited and watched Marilyn crawl out of her ancient Toyota and walk to the door.

"Welcome, Marilyn. Doc's filling a plate. We have plenty, so help yourself."

"I'm so nervous, I don't think I can eat. I was told trouble was heading my way. Do you know what's going on?"

She stepped inside, and I closed the door before answering. "My mother."

"Ooh, I hate that woman."

"Yeah, me too. I found a file my mother had on you. She has photos and notes of you giving me prescription drugs. Doc's going to help put the records on the clinic's computer, so they look legit. My mother and I are nearing a war, and I don't want you to become collateral damage."

"I knew the risk I was taking, sweetie. Don't you stick your neck out for little ole me."

"You stuck your neck out for lil' ole me when I needed it, remember? Besides, Doc says he has it covered, and I trust him. You can too."

"Well, I trust you, so I'll do as your Doc says and hope for the best. And that food smells divine, so maybe I'll have just a bite or two."

After dinner, Grady and I helped Carl unhook the cameras from the ceilings while Nicholas boxed the equipment, and Tech deleted the electronic files.

Sara was helping Doc and Marilyn enter the false medical records into the clinic's computer server. Sara said something about the IP download needing to be deleted from the main server, but whatever she was talking about, Tech understood and said he'd stop at the clinic the next day and take care of it.

My phone rang, and I saw it was Hattie calling. I walked down the hall to my bedroom to answer the call. "Hey, Hattie. How's Texas?"

"Wonderful, sunshine," she said. I could hear the smile in her voice. "I talked to the kids earlier, and they said you were home. Sara also said trouble was brewing, and it had something to do with your mother. Do you need Pops and me to come back? We can fly out tomorrow."

"No, stay in Texas. I'll let you know if I need you, but we're still gathering intel. I'd rather you both were there to keep an eye on Wildcard and Reggie."

"Why? Are they in trouble? They were over for dinner earlier, but didn't say anything."

"You don't know? They're supposed to be on lockdown. Ernesto Chaves was released and has the names of all the guys who did the sting in southern Texas."

I heard her talking to Pops, but she must've put her hand over the receiver because it was muffled. A minute later, she spoke into the phone again, giggling. "We didn't know, but Pops is calling them now and telling them to get their butts over here. We'll make them stay put until we hear it's safe."

I laughed. "Good. Ground their asses."

"How's everything else going? Are things settling for you at all?"

"Yes and no." I was quiet for a moment, trying to decide how much to tell her. "Hattie, I told the rest of the family some truths today that you and Pops have a right to hear. When I was a kid, I did some things I'm not proud of. It's upsetting, though. I'm not sure how much you want to know."

"I know enough, sunshine. I know that you were fourteen, taking care of yourself and another child. That couldn't have been easy. I don't need to know the rest. You'll always be my sunshine. And to Pops, you'll always be his baby girl."

"You're the best, you know that?"

"I try," she said. "I heard you hired a teacher for the kids. I was scolded for calling during class, but then Sara told her that I was like their grandma, so she let them talk to me."

"Beth's great. You'll like her. She's keeping the kids on a schedule and is including Carl in the mix here and there. I'll let her know that we're okay with you calling whenever you want."

"No worries. I'll call before or after school. I think it's great they have a teacher, and I don't want to mess up her schedule. We're pretty busy here, anyway. I'm overseeing the little ranch you're having built on the property across the road. You're going to love it."

"I didn't know construction had started."

"Grady and Pops worked out the details. Grady was supposed to tell you. Oh gosh, I hope it wasn't a surprise. I'll feel terrible if I ruined it."

"I'm sure with everything else going on, Grady just forgot to tell me."

"Forgot to tell you what?" Grady asked, walking into the bedroom and throwing himself on the bed.

"Construction started in Texas?"

"Damn! Yes, I forgot! I found your designs in the bin and sent them with Pops back to Texas along with a check to cover the costs."

"You used my designs?"

"Of course." Grady grinned, closing his eyes. "It's going to be a sweet little ranch house."

"Grady caught me up. It's all good," I said into the phone.

"I heard. Glad all is well. The boys just pulled into the driveway so I better get off the phone. Pops keeps eyeing his shotgun and muttering things like: *damn foolish offspring* and *wring their scrawny necks*."

"Sounds about right. And, Hattie?"

"Yes, sunshine?"

"I love you. I'm not sure I've ever said that, but I do. You're my rock."

"And you're the sunshine that brightens my days. Love you too."

I set the phone on my desk and walked over to the bed, sitting beside Grady.

"You okay?" Grady asked, rubbing my back.

"She didn't want to know what happened when I was a kid."

"I bet she guessed a long time ago. Pops too. They're wiser than the rest of us fools. We all should've figured it out."

"None of you are fools. I lied. It's that simple. And I'm not proud of it."

"You didn't lie. You just left out a few years of your past. I get it. I shouldn't have gotten mad at you for keeping it a secret. But I want you to know you can count on me to unload that shit. You don't have to hide it from me."

"You were right, though. It was eating at me."

"And now?"

"And now we deal with it," I said, turning to take his hand. "Together."

"Finally," Grady said, pulling me back to lie on top of him.

Chapter Twenty-Eight

I was up by five in the morning, but when I walked into the kitchen Lisa was already there. She handed me a cup of coffee and filled a plate with French toast and sausage for me.

"Would you like syrup or glazed strawberries and whipped cream on your French toast?" she asked.

"Neither. I just want coffee."

"You have to eat," she said, spreading a layer of the strawberry topping on before adding a dollop of whipped cream from a nearby bowl.

I ignored her and took my coffee into the dining room where I leaned over the portable crib to look at Abigail. "Your mother's a nut," I whispered.

"I heard that," Lisa said, walking in and setting the plate of food and a set of silverware next to my coffee. "She's at an impressionable age. You shouldn't talk to her like that."

"How should I talk to her?" I snorted, sitting in my chair and sliding the plate away.

"I've been teaching her the ABCs. You could practice them with her."

"And when she's old enough to focus on a book for more than the three seconds it takes her to drool on it, maybe I will."

Whiskey lumbered down the stairs and walked into the kitchen. He returned a moment later with a cup of coffee, taking the chair next to me. I slid the plate and silverware his way.

He smiled broadly as he looked down at the sugary concoction. "Why's the silverware wrapped all fancy in the napkin?"

"I thought it would be more efficient," Lisa explained before returning to the kitchen.

Since the rooms were designed with an open layout, I watched Lisa as she emptied the coffee pot into a carafe and then scrubbed the pot until it gleamed. Then, and only then, did she proceed to make a new pot of coffee.

"Did you sleep last night, Lisa?"

"I did. I feel great this morning."

Donovan was walking through the front door and heard us. He looked at me and shook his head.

"You're still staying at home today, right?" I asked her. "Just in case I need some help."

"Are you sure you need me? I was hoping to work at the store for a few hours."

"The truth?" I asked.

She looked up from her task of scrubbing the kitchen faucet. "Were you going to lie to me?"

"Sort of. But if you want me to be honest, I think you're losing your mind. I don't have a grasp of what the hell is going on with you, but I don't think everyone else needs to be worried you'll have a mental break in the middle of the store."

"I'm not losing it!" she yelled, throwing the bottle of Lysol into the sink.

I raised an eyebrow and waited. Her right eyelid started twitching before she growled and picked the Lysol bottle back up and washed the outside of the bottle.

Donovan sighed, rubbing a hand across his forehead. "Lisa, I need you to stay with Kelsey today. You've been up since two this morning, and I need to know you're with someone while I work for a few hours at Aces. Please. Just stay here, and I'll try to finish work early."

"You're all being ridiculous! But fine. I need to clean the bathrooms anyway," she said before storming into the main bathroom and slamming the door shut.

Whiskey pointed his fork at the strawberry French toast. "This is really good."

I ignored Whiskey and turned back to Donovan. "What was she doing up at two in the morning?"

"Steam cleaning the basement carpet," he answered, falling into a chair. "If you want, I can ask someone to cover for me at Aces."

"No. We'll be fine," I said before going to the kitchen to retrieve a cup of coffee for Donovan. It was typically a help-yourself household when Hattie was away, but he looked desperate.

When I returned and slid the cup in front of him, he looked up and grinned. "Thank you, sunshine."

I laughed. "You're welcome, Donovan."

"Are you two laughing at me?" Lisa yelled as she walked back out of the bathroom.

"We weren't even talking about you. And stop yelling before you wake the whole house up."

"Too late." Anne yawned, walking down the stairs.

Sara trailed after her, dragging her blanket. Nicholas swayed, only half awake, down the hall, slamming himself into my hip and wrapping his tired arms around me. Abigail started to cry, and Whiskey reached into the crib to pick her up.

"Finally," Lisa said, moving back into the kitchen. "I was getting nervous no one would get up for breakfast. Give me a minute to serve everyone."

Anne looked at the clock before looking at me with a raised eyebrow. I shook my head and sat, pulling Nicholas onto my lap in the process.

~*~*~

Two hours later, Anne, Whiskey, Katie, Tech, Alex, Goat, and Bones left for the Changing Room to work the busy Saturday shift. I convinced them at the last minute to take Nana with them. I was pretty confident that between Carl, Lisa, and the kids, I'd have my hands full. Donovan went to work at Aces, and I sent the kids to their rooms to get dressed and brush their teeth. I went back to the bedroom to check on Grady. It was near seven, and he was usually up by now.

"Hey, sleeping beauty," I said as I opened the door and walked into the room.

Grady was awake and setting his phone on the nightstand. "Hey, beautiful. Please tell me you're coming back to bed."

"Can't. I'm on kid duty today, remember?"

"Yeah," Grady groaned, leaning back and scrubbing his hands down his face. "I remember."

"Don't look so stressed. I signed up for duty, but you're off the hook. You can do whatever you want today."

"Really?" he asked, watching me with an eyebrow cocked.

"Yes, really. You've taken more than your fair share of shifts lately. Take the day off. Lisa will be around if I need help. And your trainees are all working crowd control at the store today."

"Shit. What do men do with free time? It's been so long, I forgot."

"I don't know. Belch and watch sports?"

Grady laughed and climbed out of bed. "Coffee and a long run sounds more my style. You sure you're good?"

"I'm sure." I pulled the blankets off the bed and stripped the sheets and pillow cases.

"What are you doing?"

"Washing the bedding. Why?"

He laughed. "I've never seen you do something so domestic."

"I'll have you know that I change the bedding every week when I'm home. I just normally do it when you're not around."

"That's funny. Because I've been doing it too."

"Weekly?"

Grady nodded. "Ours, Nicholas', and Carl's sheets get washed every Tuesday. We have to work on our communication skills, babe." Grady winked at me as he dragged on a pair of sweatpants before walking out of the bedroom.

I reached across the bed for the last pillow, but knocked Grady's phone off the nightstand in the process. Walking around the bed, I picked up his phone, setting it back on the stand. The backlight flashed, showing the last caller was someone named Sebrina. I didn't know any Sebrina, but there were a lot of employees at Silver Aces I didn't know yet.

I snorted, remembering the time I suggested to Donovan that we host an annual picnic for the employees.

He asked what we would do with the clients if everyone had the day off, and I shrugged and said we should invite them. He didn't think that the high-level CEOs and celebrities would be as agreeable. I suppose he was right, but who doesn't like a good picnic?

"Mom?!" Nicholas called from somewhere on the other side of the house.

"Coming!" I called back as I gathered the sheets to take to the basement.

~*~*~

The morning was busy with dishes, laundry, and getting Drake and Trigger started on the search for my mother's storage unit. By mid-morning, I had finally convinced Lisa to take a nap on the couch, but the kids and Carl were wound up so we went for a walk in the woods. Carl scooped Abigail up like it was the most natural thing in the world and walked ahead of us down the path. The kids and I kept up as they drilled me with random questions. Most of their questions centered on the types of trees and plants we passed. Being I lacked most nature skills, Carl answered for me. Then the questions started to get more personal.

"Are you going to marry Uncle Grady?" Sara asked.

"Not today."

"Someday?" Sara asked.

"Maybe."

"Will that make him my dad?" Nicholas asked.

"I suppose that's up to you," I said, shrugging. "He's sort of doing the job already, without the title."

"Does he want to be my dad?" Nicholas asked.

"I think so. Maybe you should ask him."

"Will you wear a white dress if you get married?" Sara asked.

"I'd look better in a black dress."

"Mom!" Nicholas laughed. "You can't wear black to a wedding."

"Why not? Most tuxes are black."

"But the boys wear the tuxes."

"Maybe I'll wear a black dress, and Grady can wear a white tux."

"Do I get to be your flower girl?" Sara asked.

"What if I don't get married until you're an adult? You might be too old to be a flower girl."

"No fair!" Sara pouted. "That means it will be Abigail's turn."

I snorted and pushed them to hurry along so we didn't lose Carl. When we finished the loop on the west property, I guided them back to the house so I could restart the laundry and get the beds put back together. Lisa had woken from her nap and took Abigail.

I had just finished putting the last of the clean coffee cups away when Lisa came into the kitchen with tears streaming down her cheeks. I reached out to take Abigail from her. "Do you want to talk about whatever is bothering you?"

She shook her head no.

"What do you need? What can I do to help?"

"I don't know, but I don't want the kids to see me like this."

"I'll call Donovan and take care of Abby. Head home and call if you need me."

She nodded and slipped out the garage door. I grabbed my phone and called Donovan. I also sent Alex a text, asking him to check on Lisa if he got a break.

As I was setting my phone on the counter, Abigail made a gurgling noise. I froze, not wanting to look as something warm and smelly ran down the opening of my sweater and into my bra.

"*No...* Abigail!" I groaned. "Please tell me you did not just puke on me!" I looked to see Abigail grinning spit bubbles up at me.

Grady and Whiskey started laughing from the entrance of the kitchen.

"Take her!" I hissed, holding her out to them.

Whiskey took Abby over to the sink to clean her up as I walked past a still laughing Grady. Carl, Sara, and Nicholas giggled as I walked past them and down the hall. I went straight to the bathroom and saw the puke had hit more than my chest. "My hair!"

"It will wash," Grady said, coming in behind me. He walked over and started the shower before he turned to help me with the sweater.

He went to throw the sweater in the hamper but I took it and threw it in the trash. "I own a clothing store. I'm never wearing that sweater again."

Grady laughed as he took the trash out of the bathroom with him.

"He might think it's funny, but he obviously doesn't think I look sexy covered in baby puke. Otherwise he would've stayed to shower with me," I said to myself as I finished undressing.

"You think a little baby spit-up is going to scare me off?" Grady chuckled from the bathroom door as he pulled off his T-shirt. "I just didn't want to hear you bitch about the smell when you got out of the shower."

"You can't be serious?" I laughed, looking at my hair and chest.

He kicked the bathroom door shut. "Whiskey said he'd watch the kids for us while I helped you clean up."

~*~*~

Twenty minutes later, my hair still wet, I carried a stack of files into the dining room. "Okay, everybody," I called to the kids, Carl, Whiskey, and Grady as I dropped the stack of files on the table. "I need to get some work done, and either everyone helps me, or they have to watch TV in the family room."

"I'll grab my laptop," Sara said, running up the stairs.

"Me too," Nicholas said as he ran down the hall.

"Tech took my laptop," Carl whined.

"What did you do this time?" Grady sighed, taking a seat at the dining room table.

"Nothing," Carl said as he shuffled a sock covered foot back forth across the carpet.

Whiskey laughed, handing Abigail to Grady before unlocking the credenza and retrieving both Carl's laptop and the house laptop. "He used Tech's credit card to buy five hundred dollars of lottery tickets online."

"Did you win?" I asked.

Carl grinned. "I won four dollars!"

"And lost four hundred and ninety-six," Whiskey reminded him.

"Carl, you need to pay Tech back," I said.

"I can't. Scott has all my money," Carl said, referring to the group home leader of the home in Florida where Carl used to live.

"Call Scott. Confess your sins, my friend."

"He can't." Whiskey laughed. "Tech took his phone too. I've never seen Tech so pissed."

I pulled my phone and handed it to Carl. He walked into the living room with it. I looked down at Grady who was shaking with laughter. "Admit it," I said to him. "Your life was boring before you moved here."

"Living here is a non-stop adventure." He reached for my hand, lifting it up to his lips. "You and yours are so odd."

"I'm not odd," Sara said as she came down the stairs.

"Shh," I said to Grady, whopping him on the arm. "Don't ruin it for me. They're free labor."

The kids giggled, and Carl returned, handing me the phone. "I think I'm in trouble," Carl pouted. "Scott wants to talk to you."

"Hey, Scott," I answered, walking down the hall to talk in private.

"I scolded him for the lottery tickets, but that's not why I wanted to talk to you."

"If he doesn't have the money to cover the tickets, I'll pay for it and make him earn it back. I was hoping you'd scold him though, so it's all good."

"He has the money. That's why I wanted to talk to you. Carl has sold a lot of inventions over the years. As his power of attorney, I've let the money pile in a savings account. It's grown to an amount, though, that I'm not sure what to do with it. And since Carl's been living there, maybe it's time to move his belongings and transfer the power of attorney."

"Carl may decide he wants to go back to Florida—"

"No! No! Don't send me back!" Carl screeched from behind me.

"Scott, let me call you back," I said before hanging up.

Carl ran down the hall before I could stop him and out the living room sliding door.

"What's wrong?" Grady asked, grabbing my arm to stop me.

"He thinks I want him to go back to Miami."

"Stay with the kids," he said to me as he handed Abigail back to Whiskey. "I'll go chase him down and talk to him."

Grady ran out the sliding door which was still open.

"You don't want to send Carl home, do you, Mom?"

"No, dummy," Sara said. "He's family. Family's forever. He's stuck with us."

"No name calling, Sara. But you're right. Carl's family," I said, leaning over Sara and giving her raspberry kisses on her cheek as she giggled. "We're all stuck with each other."

"Even Abigail?" Nicholas giggled.

"Hey, as long as she doesn't puke on me again, we'll be good."

"I put the sweater in the washer. I know Anne will wear it," Whiskey said. "She's not afraid of a little baby vomit."

I cringed, not wanting to think about the sweater. I hit redial on my phone.

Scott answered on the first ring. "He okay?"

"Grady chased after him. When Carl's upset, he goes to the playground behind the store, which is in the field behind the house."

"It sounds like he's in a much safer environment than when he'd run away from here. Which brings me back to the conversation we were having, is he staying in Michigan?"

"Carl's family. He'll always have a home here, and it sounds like he wants to stay. Feel free to ship his belongings to Michigan and reassign his room at the group home to someone who needs it."

"I'll pack and ship the boxes this week. The power of attorney should be transferred too, though. It doesn't make sense for me to control his money when he doesn't even live here."

"That's fine. Will I need to fly to Florida to transfer the paperwork?"

"Probably. Even though Carl's financially independent, he's officially a ward of the state."

"Let's have Cameron, my attorney, figure it out then."

"Gladly." Scott sighed. "I'm better at the day to day of running the home than I am with all the paperwork."

"I hear ya. What about the five hundred? Should I just cover it and have Carl do chores to pay me back?"

"I wrote the check while I was talking to him," Scott said. "Carl only knew the guy's name as Tech. I assume that's not the guy's legal name, so I wrote the check payable as cash."

"Huh."

"You don't know the guy's legal name either, do you?"

I laughed. "Not a clue. And he lives next door above my garage and eats dinner here every night."

"If we do have to go in front of a judge to get this transfer filed, please don't tell the judge that." Scott was laughing as he disconnected.

I looked over at Whiskey. "What's your real name?"

"William."

"What's Tech's real name?"

Whiskey looked at me, squinting his eyes as he thought about it.

Sara giggled. "Theodore. It was on the credit card that Carl borrowed to buy the tickets."

"Oh, that's good," Grady said, walking back inside with Carl. "I can use that tidbit of information."

"Play nice," I scolded Grady. "Carl, why did you run away?"

"I thought you wanted me to leave, but Grady said I heard wrong. He said I get to stay as long as I want."

"Grady's right. You get to stay as long as you want. Scott's going to pack up your room and ship the rest of your belongings."

"What about my silly putty? I hid it under my pillow."

"I'm sure it's dried up by now. And your pillow and sheets will most likely be thrown away."

"It's special silly putty. I made it myself. It doesn't dry up, but it stains your hands purple. That's why I put it under my pillow, so it wouldn't get on my pajamas."

Carl sat at the table and pulled his laptop over to start it up. I sent a quick text message to Scott to warn him about the silly putty. Then I sent a text to Cameron and asked him to figure out how to transfer Carl's accounts and power of attorney to Michigan.

"Okay everyone," I said, pulling some papers out. "Today we need to root out a man named Ernesto Chaves."

"Who's that?" Whiskey asked.

"A bad man from Texas," Sara answered. "I'll email everyone the file we already have on him. He was arrested last year, but he outsmarted the DA, and they dropped the charges. He's also the one who hired the snipers who shot at Grady and Bones the other day."

"Sara!" I shook my head in frustration. "You need to stop eavesdropping."

"It's the only way to hear the good stuff," she whined. "Besides, I might've found something yesterday when I was trying to find him." She walked over to the printer and handed me the printouts.

"What am I looking at?" The papers looked like they were in a foreign language or accounting reports. The only things I recognized were IP addresses in scattered locations.

"It's his computer's log file."

"Don't you have to be signed into a computer to get the log file?" Grady asked, taking the sheets of paper from me.

"You do, but Carl and I have been working on a program to get around that. We tested it out on Ernesto when we located his computer network."

"What kind of program?" Whiskey asked, putting one hand on his hip, while still holding a sleeping Abigail with the other.

"The kind that slips under a firewall and has a pop-up screen offering a discount that you can click on, but the user is really giving permission for remote access onto their computer."

"And what kind of product intrigued Chaves enough to click the box?" Grady asked.

"We tried girly underwear and cigars," Carl said, "but they didn't work. Then Nicholas suggested first-class airfare, and Chaves clicked the button. We got more than the file logs too. We copied all the documents from his computer before we lost the connection."

"I didn't hear any of that," Maggie said, laughing from the kitchen.

"I did," Genie said. "I want to see this program." She ran over and pulled a chair out next to Sara.

I looked at Grady who was once again looking at the table as he laughed silently.

"How the... *heck*... do I explain this to Anne?" I asked him.

"Just be glad it's her kid and not yours," Grady said, smirking.

"And Carl? Scott is going to transfer Carl's power of attorney to me."

"Not a good idea," Maggie said, joining us at the table.

"Agreed," Kierson said as he held the garage door open for Charlie. They crossed the room and joined us. "If Carl's sued for any of his many shenanigans, as his guardian, you could be sued too."

"What else can I do?"

Grady shrugged. "I could do it. I'm well off, but I can't compete with your bank account."

"Doesn't help," Charlie said. "If Kelsey ever caves and marries you, then you're both exposed. I'd do it, but I officially live in Miami still."

"Anne agreed to do it and so did Alex," Whiskey said, holding up his cellphone. "I texted everybody. Katie said no. Tech said yes. For Carl's sake, it's safer to go with either Anne or Alex."

"Alex then." I said. "Chances are if a lawsuit heads our way, both Sara and Carl will be named in the complaint."

Sara giggled, and Carl stuck his tongue out at me.

"Carl, are you okay with Alex being your new guardian? That means he'll be in charge of your money and all the big decisions."

"Alex is my friend," Carl said. "Maybe he'll give me an allowance so I can buy candy and girly magazines."

"What kind of girly magazines?" Grady asked.

"Cosmopolitan," Carl answered as he focused on his laptop.

I laughed as I texted Cameron with the updated information. He texted back smiley faces and said his assistant Jenny, a girl I used to mentor, was digging into it. He also said he'd be in Michigan early Monday morning to meet with the local attorney on the custody case for Nicholas.

I sighed, handing the phone to Grady to read.

"This afternoon we focus on Chaves. Tonight, we'll work on devising a plan to outsmart your mother."

"I want to help," Nana said, coming in through the open sliding door.

"I thought you were helping at the store today," I said.

"They kicked me out. Turns out I'm not so good at retail. I did find a nice group of ladies my own age and people watched with them for a while, but then I got bored and decided to come back here."

"You shouldn't be going anywhere without a security detail right now," Grady said.

"She didn't," Bones said, walking through the sliding door. "I walked with her to the house before stopping to talk to the guys doing security patrols."

"She's in greater danger being near *you*! Or are you forgetting that you're one of the main targets?"

Bones laughed. "Shit. I did forgot."

I pointed to the floor. Bones laughed again, but dropped to do his pushups.

Chapter Twenty-Nine

We had been sifting through thousands of pages of documents for over two hours. Sara had printed everything from Chaves' computer so we could divide and conquer the completely random overload of useless information. The front door opened and Lisa and Donovan entered. I got up from the table and hugged Lisa.

"Are you okay, Aunt Lisa?" Sara asked.

"I'm just tired, Sara. But I took another nap, and when I woke up, I heard you guys were working a case. We decided to come over and help." Lisa walked over and picked Abigail up from the portable crib. "How was Abigail while I was gone?"

"The little brat puked all over me," I complained.

Grady laughed. "Full load of baby vomit right down the sweater."

Donovan and Lisa both whispered congratulatory baby garble to their offspring.

Lisa sat at the table, bracing Abigail with one arm as she pulled a stack of papers over. "Someone put me to work."

"Are you sure you're okay?" I asked, reaching out and laying my hand over hers.

"Donovan and I talked. I think right now I need a little less Abigail time, and a little more anything else time. Does that sound awful?"

"Not at all," Bones said, reaching over and taking Abigail from her. "All you had to do is say so."

"You guys don't think that makes me a bad mother?"

"Really, Lisa?" I asked. "Do you need me to write down a list of all the not-so-motherly crap I've pulled with Nicholas? Because, hands down, you're an amazing mother compared to me."

"You're a good mother," Lisa said.

"She swears too much," Nicholas said.

"And she drinks too much," Sara said.

"And smokes sometimes," Nicholas continued. "And she's really bad at folding laundry."

"That's why they make hangers," I defended myself. "And unless you two want me to start listing your faults, I'd stop picking on mine."

"You do suck at folding laundry," Grady said, leaning in to kiss my cheek.

"I agree. She's horrible," Lisa said. "But I came over here to work. What am I looking for?" She shuffled through the stack of papers in front of her.

"Anything interesting," Sara answered. "Most of it's boring. If it's nothing important, it gets thrown on the floor. If it's something interesting, highlight the good parts, and pass it down to Aunt Kelsey or Maggie."

The floor currently only had a few pages lying on it, but that was because Whiskey already took a bag out to the recycle bin. We'd gone through a case of paper and replaced the toner cartridge already, and the printer was still printing off stacks. Our process was bad for the environment, but it was making sorting the work and passing it around easier. I would definitely owe the planet a few trees though.

"I need a break," I said, standing and stretching my arms over my head. "Charlie? Want to go for a walk with me?"

Charlie looked up from the page she was reading. "I'd rather go for a run."

I rolled my eyes, but went to the bedroom to change into a T-shirt and cotton shorts, and donned a pair of running shoes.

"You ready yet?" Charlie grinned, walking into the bedroom having already changed. "Man, you're getting slow in your old age."

I leaned to the side and lifted my foot to my butt to stretch one leg before doing the same to the other. "Oh yeah, Kid? Is that a challenge?"

"No!" She laughed. "I've been slacking on my workouts, so go easy on me."

"Good. I've been on the road so much, I haven't done a thorough workout in weeks."

After grabbing the smallest pistols and holsters I owned and handing her a set, I followed her out the atrium door. We both stretched before we started for the woods. We followed the outer trail on the far west property. Two miles in, I was already sweating when I glanced over at Charlie. "You warmed up enough to talk yet?" I asked, referring to the trip to see her biological mother.

Charlie released a heavy breath. "She's a mess right now, but I like her. We agreed to have a maternity test done to prove that I'm her daughter, but there's little doubt in my mind."

"She really thought you died?"

Charlie nodded, continuing to run slightly ahead of me on the path. "When she went into labor, she went to the hospital and the next thing she remembers is waking up two days later to be told her baby died. She was sent home the next day with a caesarian scar and a death certificate. Her brother drove down and took her to live with him."

"Did she explain why she had an affair with a married man?"

"Only that once upon a time she loved your father. And that she regretted ever getting involved with him. Not only because he was married, but because your mother made her life a living hell."

"Now what?"

Charlie slowed her jog until she finally stopped. I stopped beside her. Both of us continued to shift our weight from one side to the other, to keep our legs heated.

"Part of me wants to get to know her, but I can't pretend to be her daughter," Charlie said, looking up at me. "Does that make sense?"

"Sure. You're an adult now. But that doesn't mean you can't have a close relationship with her."

"Why would I, though?"

"Charlie," I said, reaching out to grasp a hand. "In the beginning, it was just the two of us. When we moved to Miami, Aunt Suzanne and Uncle Hank took us under their wing. Then my family continued to grow with Pops and the boys in Texas, and now my Michigan family. We might've started out small, but I've learned there's no such thing as too much family. It's okay to form a bond with your mother and make a place for her in your life."

"But she's not your family," Charlie whispered, looking away as she said it.

"No, but Hattie fills the mom role for me. And Pops still intends to adopt your ass eventually as another 'baby girl'. And, you'll need him. Your biological father is a douche bag."

Charlie laughed, slugging me in the arm. "So, we're sisters. For real this time."

"Sisters... Cousins..." I shrugged. "Doesn't matter what label we slap on us. We're family. Period."

"And what about our douche bag relatives? What did you dig up on them?"

"Well..." I said before turning down the running trail and jogging away. "I found out our father killed someone."

"*Wait*! *What*?" Charlie called out as she scrambled to catch up.

~*~*~

We ran the perimeter of the west property twice while I updated Charlie on everything we knew so far about my mother, our father, and everyone else that had a file in Sadler Creek. Since we were at a lull in conversation, I turned down the trail that ran behind the field toward the east property. When we got to the start of the next trail, I paused to wait for Charlie. We both pulled our guns, holding them out to the side as we jogged slower down the trail.

"I hate this section of woods," I whispered.

"Me too. It's like the trees have eyes."

"If it was only the trees and the squirrels watching us, I wouldn't get so creeped out."

"You're spidey senses telling you anything?"

"Not yet," I answered as I scanned the trees ahead of us.

We jogged another twenty feet before I stopped and raised my free hand into a fist. Charlie's movements stilled behind me. I put both hands on my gun and started forward, walking slowly and silently.

"I texted Grady to close the house up," Charlie whispered.

"Do you smell that?" I asked as I stopped and looked over my shoulder at her.

She moved in front of me to smell the air. "Cigarette smoke. Could be one of the security guards from the store."

I shook my head. "Wind's coming from the northeast. Wrong direction."

Charlie crouched lower as she moved down the path, holding her gun out to the northeast. I followed in the same position as we moved about a quarter mile down the trail.

I made a *kuk-kuk-kuk* noise, similar to a squirrel, and Charlie stopped, stepping to the side. I stepped around her and led us down a deer trail which ran deeper into the woods. If we kept going straight, then we'd likely find ourselves in the crosshairs of whoever was out here.

Thirty feet or so into the woods, I turned off the deer trail to move us parallel with the running trail. We had to slow our movements, careful not to step on any dry twigs or slip on mossy rocks, but the decision paid off when I spotted a man standing on the running path with his back turned to us. I looked at Charlie and she nodded that she saw him. We separated and started to move slowly in his direction.

"Don't move," Charlie said, standing with her gun aimed at his back from his left side.

"I wouldn't try it," I said from his right, seeing his hand twitch. "We're both armed and have been shooting at much farther distances most of our lives."

"I can explain," the man said as he raised his hands slowly into the air.

"And we'll give you the chance, but not out here. Move. Walk toward the field. Don't do anything stupid."

I skirted around him before walking backwards out of the woods into the field. I kept my gun trained on him from the front-right. Charlie kept his escape route cut off. By the time we were fifteen feet into the field Tyler and one of the other security guards had joined us, holding their own weapons on the man.

"Let's see who we caught today, Charlie," I said, lowering my weapon but keeping it gripped tightly in my hand.

She removed his sidearm, setting it in the grass, then pulled his wallet. "He's a cop. What the hell?" She held up the badge.

"Local?" I sighed, holstering my weapon.

"Yeah. What's this all about?" she asked.

"Holster your weapons," I ordered.

"I'm going to need to see some permits from everyone," the cop said as he picked up his gun and took his wallet back from Charlie.

"You're trespassing on private property. You don't get to make any demands. You can walk the field to the road and back to your vehicle. And tell your chief that if he wants information, he should find his balls, drive to my house, and ask me. The Feds happen to be visiting right now, so he should be relatively safe."

I turned toward the house, crossing the field. Charlie and Tyler jogged over to catch up.

"You going to tell me what that was all about?" Charlie asked.

"Our favorite Sadler Creek sheriff called the Kalamazoo chief and told him I was a person of interest in some crimes up his way. A little birdie gave me a warning, but I didn't think the local cops would've been stupid enough to trespass."

Tyler snorted. "I don't think they'll make that mistake again. Shithead was trembling when you gals walked him out at gunpoint."

"Dumbass was smoking." Charlie snorted. "Gave himself away."

Tyler laughed. "I'll remember that. No smoking when doing surveillance in the woods."

"No smoking when you're doing surveillance *at all*," I corrected him, narrowing my eyes at him.

Tyler grinned, looking sideways over at me. "Sure. Except when shit hits the fan at your house and I'm assigned a fourteen-hour shift to patrol."

"He's got a point." Charlie chuckled. "You have more security patrols than most people, though."

"The smoke will always give away your location. When it's dark out, you're also telling a sniper every time you inhale where to aim his rifle. As long as you know that, I'm okay with you using your own judgement about smoke breaks."

"Shit." Tyler sighed, rubbing the top of his head and looking back toward the woods. "Got it."

~*~*~

We walked around the house and rang the doorbell. Grady peered out around the door before opening it, tucking his Glock back into its holster.

"Everything okay?" he asked, leaning in for a quick kiss.

"Just our local police department, breaking the law to get eyes on me," I answered, following him into the dining room.

"That was stupid," Bones said. "He's lucky it was you and not one of us. We would've shot his ass."

I raised an eyebrow at Bones. The kids giggled. Bones groaned, dropping for a quick ten pushups, before stomping into the kitchen and pulling a beer.

"Where's Wayne and Alverez? I expected them here hours ago. And what about Trigger and Drake? Any word from them?"

"Trigger called while you were out," Grady said, trying to hide the smirk that curved his lips. "They found the storage unit. Drake tried bribing the owner for information, and when that didn't work, Trigger dragged him into a back room, closed the door on Drake, and convinced the owner to confess his sins."

"I knew I liked that guy." I laughed. "Tyler, can you locate a dark colored, older model SUV for me tonight?"

"No problem."

"Don't bring it here, though. I don't want the cops to see it. I can pick it up at Headquarters."

"Got it," Tyler said before walking out of the house.

"Did Drake or Trigger take any pictures?" I asked Grady.

He handed me my phone. "I swear Trigger's reading your mind."

I flipped through the pictures and smiled at the close-up of the lock. I tucked the phone into my back pocket and turned back to Grady. "What about Wayne and Alverez?"

Grady, Bones, and Donovan looked in every direction except toward me.

Maggie, Kierson, and Genie looked directly at me, smiling.

"What the hell did those two idiots do?"

"Alverez went after the passcode for the security system, and Wayne followed her," Sara said from her spot at the other end of the table.

"Does Alverez know that Wayne is following her?"

"Not yet," Grady said. "But we trained the rookies on how to spot a tail last week. She'll probably figure it out."

I may have growled as I sat in the chair next to Carl. Carl grinned without looking up from his computer. "Did you get the bug planted on Alverez?"

"Nicholas helped me," Carl said, nodding as he turned his computer toward me. "They're in Arizona."

"Damn it. I wanted to get in the storage unit tonight."

"What's the security like at the storage unit?" Bridget asked as she walked into the dining room.

"I thought you were working at the store?"

"They're closing early. Almost out of inventory. I offered to start something for dinner, but I'd rather do a B&E."

"I didn't hear that," Kierson said from the other side of the table.

"Kierson, you're in charge of dinner. Maggie, you're in charge of drinks. Everyone's drink preferences are on the refrigerator. Grady and Bones, suit up for a mission. Bridget, come with me to my lair so I can fill you in on a few details."

"What about me?" Donovan asked.

"Help the kids and Charlie with the rest of this paperwork. And make sure Lisa stays off baby duty for the rest of the night."

Donovan looked over at Bones and grinned as he took Abby. "Got it."

"I can take her. It's fine," Lisa said, holding out her hands.

"I don't think so," Donovan said, holding Abigail out of her reach. "It's my turn. You just sit there and do non-motherly activities like you were told. Kelsey's orders. Her house—her rules."

"Fine. Then I'm drinking," Lisa said. "There's a week's supply of already pumped breast milk between the two houses. If I'm off momma duty, I'm going to get loaded."

I glanced over at Maggie and she winked at me. She'd make sure to keep an eye on Lisa while we were out. Bridget followed me down the hall as I pulled out my cell phone, calling Nightcrawler.

"Tell me you need me to break someone's bones," Nightcrawler said as a way of answering.

"Not tonight," I said. "But if you need a little action, I have something illegal that needs some attention. And the prize afterward is the perfect excuse to run into your favorite brunette."

"Maggie's in town?"

"She is. She's at my place for the weekend. I'm sending Bridget out on a job, and she could use some muscle. If all goes well, then afterward you can join

Bridget for an impromptu Saturday night gathering at my house where I'm sure Maggie will already have had a few drinks."

"Where and when?"

"Meet Bridget at Headquarters in about a half hour to go over the plan."

"I'll be there."

"And Nightcrawler?"

"Yeah?"

"Wear dark clothes, no biker emblems, and bring a face mask."

"Got it. I've got a club brother who's bored. Mind if he joins? Sounds like his kind of party."

"That'll work. Bridget and another guy on my team will make it a party of four. We've already arranged for transportation."

Nightcrawler laughed as he hung up.

"Bones is not going to like this," Bridget said, giggling. "I'm totally getting laid again later."

I laughed, pulling out the photos of the locks and storage facility. "Trigger reported minimal security cameras, only one at the entrance and one in the office. But verify that and protect your identity."

"Got it. What am I looking for when I get inside the storage unit?"

"I need confirmation that the car is still there, but it's evidence so keep your prints away from it. I have no idea what else is in there, though. Anything filled with papers or looks to be potential blackmail-related material, load in the SUV and bring home."

"In other words, I'm doing damage control so when you take your mother down, she'll be all out of ammo?"

"That's the plan. If you get caught by the cops, call Katie for an attorney. If you run into something worse, head north if you can get away." I pulled two simple black watches from the jewelry case resting on top of my dresser. I handed one to Bridget and put the other on. "These are Carl's special jewelry pieces. They have transmitters so he can track us."

"Won't be necessary, but I'll wear it. Who's on my team?"

"Trigger, Nightcrawler, and one of his biker brothers. Tyler's having an older model SUV dropped at Headquarters. Keys should be above the visor, but check the gas tank. Last time he got me a getaway car it was running on fumes by the time I actually got away. Grady keeps gas cans behind the garage at Headquarters, just for these occasions." I pulled a pair of black, low-heeled boots from the closet and slid a set of switch blades in the hidden sleeves before pulling them on.

"Tyler's good, but he's still green," Bridget said, nodding. "What are you guys walking into?"

Reaching into the bottom drawer of my dresser, I retrieved a dual chest holster, and secured it around me, checking and loading two Glocks, before pulling a leather jacket from the closet to hide the weapons. "No idea. Alverez is naïve to think her brother won't kill her. And Wayne is an idiot trying to protect her alone. There's a possibility they'll both be dead by the time we find them."

"Then let's go," Grady said from the doorway. "There's a jet with our name on it, and our bags are packed."

"You good?" I asked Bridget.

"My job's a cakewalk. Just focus on your own shit." Bridget sashayed out of the bedroom.

"You're right," Grady said as he watched her leave. "She's the perfect sidekick for your side of Silver Aces."

"Until she walks into trouble, and then I can only hope that whoever I have her partnered with will keep her safe. Otherwise, Bones will skin me alive."

"After I cut off your fingers," Bones said from behind Grady.

Grady and I laughed, and I led them out the atrium exit. No point in flaunting to the friendly Feds that we were armed and off to break any number of laws.

Chapter Thirty

"What are we walking into?" Bones asked as the jet prepared for landing.

"I'm clueless. Really. Chaves was never on my radar until I questioned the Hell Hounds about Penny's whereabouts last year. Then I sent the Feds to deal with him and never followed up."

Bones winced at the mention of his criminal, power hungry, and very dead ex-wife.

"What about Maggie? She must've profiled him after he was arrested," he asked.

"Chaves refused all interviews," I answered, shaking my head. "The only thing she could tell me is that he seemed confident, in control, every time they brought him in. But he let his lawyer do all of the talking. She couldn't get a psychological or emotional read on the guy. She couldn't even get him to make eye contact with her."

"Any intel from when he was in prison?" Bones asked.

"Nope. He was kept isolated in a nice cushy federal prison. I've got no connections in the Club Fed prisons, and Maggie said she couldn't find a snitch or guard who ever spoke with him."

"Damn," Grady said. "Since meeting you, I'm not sure we've gone after someone you didn't already have a psychic read on."

"I wish I was psychic. I have no idea what drives Chaves to do the things he does. He could be a power-junky, greedy, or just plain crazy. As I said, I'm clueless."

Bones shrugged. "Doesn't matter. We either extract Alverez and Wayne, or we kill Chaves. Knowing what motivates the freak doesn't change the outcome."

"Hear, hear" Grady said as the jet's tires smacked onto the pavement and screeched when the brakes locked.

~*~*~

After we loaded our rental car, Grady drove as I connected my phone to the car's Bluetooth. I called Carl, putting him on speaker.

"Where to?" I asked Carl.

"I'm inputting the GPS coordinates into your navigation system. Wayne and Alverez are northwest of your location. According to satellite images, they appear to be at a giant house with an octagon-shaped pool in the backyard. I think we should get a pool. Can we?"

"That would be nice," Bones agreed from the backseat. I heard the release and snap of his Glock as he checked his clip. "A heated pool."

"It would have to be enclosed," Grady said. "Too many leaves blowing around near the houses. Maybe instead of behind the main house, it should be in the middle of the field?"

"Or over at Silver Aces," Bones said. "Then we can swim laps anytime we want, and we'd be less concerned about snipers taking shots at us."

"Can we focus for just a few minutes here, boys?" I asked, turning the conversation back to Carl. "What else can you see on the satellite images, Carl?"

"Hey, Kelsey," Maggie said over the phone. "I plugged in with Carl when I heard the conversation drifting. Hope you don't mind."

"As long as you understand this is an off-the-books mission, I'm good."

"Charlie took Kierson over to Silver Aces, and Carl and I are in your old war room in the basement. We're covered. And I'm seeing on the satellite that the house is more of a compound. The front side of the property is gated with a guard shack at the entrance. The building itself has three main sections with long corridors connecting them. The wing to the west appears to be for residential use, with the pool behind it. The center structure might serve as a business or more public space and has additional parking off to the side, and the far east structure is an unknown. Seems a bit plain based on the roof layout and the lack of landscaping around it."

"Odd," I mumbled, tilting my head to the side and thinking. "What do you imagine the price tag on such a building would run?"

"In that neighborhood, at least three million."

"So, why have a third of the estate blasé and the rest decked out to the hilt?"

"No clue."

"Can Carl get a signal on what part of the estate Wayne and Alverez are in?"

"No. He only shows that they are on the property. We can't even tell if they're inside or outside."

"What's behind the eastern section? Can we get access?"

"Drive past the house to the far side of the ridge that runs behind the estate. Hope you have the right gear, because you're going to be hiking across some rocky peaks."

"Crap. Well at least I didn't wear my high heels," I complained, looking down at my smooth and unscratched leather boots. They'd most likely be ruined by the time we left.

Grady grabbed my hand, raising it to kiss my knuckles. "If you get Wayne's ass out of this mess, I'll buy you a new pair of boots."

"That's a lot of work for just one pair of boots."

"I'll pitch in for a pair too," Bones said.

"Two pairs of boots. Everyone good? Because we have a job to do here, people," Maggie said.

We remained quiet, smirking at each other.

Maggie sighed loudly before continuing, "When you get on the other side of the ridge, you'll want to head straight up the center and then as you descend, work your way down toward the east. Take a gradual approach. There should be enough shaggy brush to keep your presence hidden, but we have no way of knowing if there are perimeter guards."

"Got it," I said.

Grady pointed to a set of iron gates to the left side of the road. It was dark out, and the house was set back behind pine trees. I could only see portions of the roof structure illuminated by security lights in the far-off distance.

"We just passed the estate. Not much was visible. Anything else we need to know before we go radio silent?"

"Yes. You still owe me one of your famous pot roasts so don't even think about dying out there."

"Understood," I said, hitting the disconnect button on my phone.

~*~*~

Turns out, I'm not very good at climbing rocky cliff sides. The ascent on the backside of the ridge was only a success because Grady was in front of me, lifting me past the sharper inclines, while Bones climbed behind me, catching me when I slid, several times, down the ridge. By the time we reached the top they both were breathing heavy, and I was missing several sections of skin where I had scraped against the rocks.

"You're taking a climbing class in the near future," Grady grumbled as he leaned over to catch his breath.

"What the hell happened on that last incline to make you throw yourself away from the rocks? I barely caught you," Bones asked, also leaning over as his chest heaved from his breathing.

"Something crawled over my hand. Like a beetle, but a couple inches long. Freaked me out."

Bones and Grady exchanged looks, and each of them grabbed one of my wrists, pulling off my gloves and inspecting both sides and my hands.

"What are we looking for?"

"I think she's good," Grady said to Bones. "She's wearing real leather."

"Yeah, I don't see anything."

Placing my fisted hands on my hips, I gave them both glares as I waited for an explanation. "Tell me."

"We'll explain later, city girl." Grady chuckled, smacking my lips with his for a brief kiss. "Put your gloves back on and leave them on."

I quickly pulled my gloves back on and pulled my leather jacket sleeves down over the cuffs. I wasn't sure what kind of giant beetles were around these parts, but if I met another one, obviously the leather was my armor.

"Let's go," Bones said, taking the lead downward toward the east. "Test the rocks beneath your feet with each step. We should be able to walk down, but the ground could be loose."

"Sounds doable," I said, following Bones.

On my third step, my foot slipped out from under me. Grady pulled me to a stop before I slid over the edge.

"Thanks," I whispered.

Grady nuzzled into me, laughing. "You're so out of your element."

"Dark alleys, crack houses, and angry gators are more my specialty," I agreed.

~*~*~

We stopped every few minutes to wait, watch, and listen as we descended. No perimeter guards or surveillance cameras were spotted. No other creatures in the night scurried out to say hello. The back side of the east wing was in full view and I crouched down to study the structure. Grady and Bones stepped closer, crouching down beside me on both sides.

"What are you thinking?" Grady whispered.

"The setup is strange," I whispered back. "There are very few windows, and all of them are small sized and high up, like—" A cold shiver raced from the back of my neck to my toes.

"Kelsey?" Grady asked, reaching out to place a hand on my shoulder.

Bones reached out and rested a hand on my knee. "Like what?"

"Like the dungeon I was kept in when Nola held me prisoner," I said, barely audible.

"You think he's back in business?" Grady asked.

"I don't know," I said, pulling out my phone.

"What are you doing?" Bones asked.

"Texting Maggie that if we don't make it out alive, she needs to get a warrant and raid this place."

Grady nodded. "You're staying here. Bones and I can handle the rest of the mission."

"Excuse me?"

"I think he meant that as a suggestion, not an order," Bones said, laughing.

"Look," Grady whispered. "Last year, we learned the hard way that bombs trigger my flashbacks. We have no idea whether something in that building will trigger one of yours, though."

"You're right. But I'm still going," I said, nodding toward an attached single-car garage. "The garage appears to be the main entrance into the east wing."

Typically, victims of trafficking weren't walked through the front door. If I was right about the east building being used to hold prisoners, then it would make sense that the garage would serve as an entrance, and if the victims died, the exit.

"You'll never get access into the building through the windows, and you'll need my help to get past the locks and security via the garage. Most likely there will be at least one guard inside; I'll let the two of you deal with the guards. But we'll need to keep it quiet."

"I can do quiet," Bones said as he stood in a crouched position and started leading the way toward the garage.

Grady and I followed, with me slightly behind Grady and his right hand grasping my left. He wasn't being overprotective. He had every reason to be concerned for my mental health if we were walking into what I imagined we were walking into. And with him being left handed, we were still able to grip our Glocks in our dominant hands. I released a slow silent breath as we neared the back corner of the garage. Bones raised a fist, peeked around the corner of the garage and then signaled two fingers, indicating two guards were on the other side. Grady lightly pushed my back against the garage wall, before tapping Bones on the shoulder, the signal that he was ready. I stood motionless as they crept silently around the corner and out of sight.

I counted to twenty-five before I heard Grady's owl hoot that it was safe to follow. Stepping around the garage, Bones and Grady were dragging the guards over to a small clump of brush.

"Wait," I whispered, crouching down to search the guard Grady had. "Got it." I held up a security electronic-swipe badge. "See? You needed me already."

Grady leaned over the body and kissed me before he finished dragging it over and dropping it on top of the guard Bones had dumped. I went to the side door of the garage and swiped the badge through the scanner. The red light turned green and I turned the knob, stepping inside. Bones and Grady slipped in behind me.

As expected, the garage was empty and didn't appear to have any cameras. What I hadn't expected was a handprint scanner mounted next to the door that led into the main building. "Shit."

"When I grabbed the other guard's security badge, I may have borrowed a finger," Bones said, holding a severed finger against the scanner.

My insides rolled, and I swayed into Grady's side as the light on the panel turned green. "For a souvenir or because you thought there might be a scanner?"

Bones' teeth glistened in the semi-darkness as he smiled. "Scanner. Seems all these rich assholes have them these days."

I gagged as Bones slide the finger into his cargo pants pocket. Bones shook his head at me before moving into the hall behind the door.

"The guard was already dead. He didn't feel a thing," Grady whispered, stepping around me and pulling me along behind him.

"But Bones is just carrying it around in his pocket. Gross," I said, shaking off the icky feeling as I followed Grady into the dim building.

"It's not as bad as the time he needed an eyeball."

"What eyeball?"

"You don't want to know." Grady looked back at me and grinned, before releasing my hand and joining Bones at the end of the hallway.

"Where to?" Bones asked. "There are doors along the entire back wall, a set of stairs going to the basement, or the walkway into the main section of the compound."

"Down," I answered. "The windows on the backside of the building were dark, so if anyone's inside those rooms, then they're sleeping. My guess is that if Wayne and Alverez are prisoners, they're being questioned. You'd need lights and privacy for a conversation like that."

"Do you want to wait here?" Grady asked. "You can watch our backs in case someone heads this way."

"Thanks, but I'll feel safer if I stay with you."

"Stay close then. If you start to lose it, tell me."

"I'll do what I can, but I can't make any promises. Don't let me jeopardize the mission."

"I hate this," he said, pulling me by the back of the neck into his embrace. "It's too much for you."

"We didn't know," Bones whispered. "But we're here now, and we'll get her in and out as quick as we can. But we gotta move."

I felt Grady nod before he released me from his embrace and once again grasped my hand as we rounded the corner and started down the stairs. I relied on them to be my eyes, and focused my senses instead on trying to hear any noises ahead while I kept conscious of my breathing, moving purposeful, slow, steady streams of air into my diaphragm. When we reached the bottom of the stairs and stepped into the lower room, all the air whooshed from my lungs as I stared at the furnishings. Mounted to the floor in the center of the room was a large wooden cross, from which Wayne was currently hanging unconscious, strapped by his hands. My knees folded, dropping me to the floor. I watched, unable to move, as Grady dragged me over and leaned me against the stone wall before joining Bones in the center of the room to help free Wayne.

From the left, I heard the familiar sound of muffled screams and turned to stare at the solid wood door with black iron hardware. My pulse thumped against my skull as I gasped for a full breath of the musty air. I set my gun behind me, not trusting my reactions at the moment with a loaded weapon. Pulling off my gloves, I placed my palms flat on the damp, cold cement floor, trying to center myself. I'd come full circle. Destined to be a prisoner of my past.

As memories swamped my brain, I was frozen in terror. As if in slow motion, three armed men moved in and surrounded Grady and Bones, who had holstered their weapons to work their knives against the ropes that held Wayne. It was too late. Wayne, finally freed, dropped face first to the floor as two more guards entered from a back hallway. It was five guards against the two of them now. And the guards had automatic weapons.

I sat helpless, barely able to breathe. Grady glanced at me and nodded his understanding. They slowly raised their hands in surrender, and the guards relieved them of their weapons.

One of the men spotted me and laughed as I cowered, covered in sweat, into the wall. He walked past me toward the solid wood door and banged his fist against it. The door opened a crack, and the guard spoke in a hushed tone to someone on the other side. The door closed, opening a few minutes later to Ernesto Chaves wearing a dark suit and shadowed by another guard. The other guard dragged Alverez's beaten body out of the room, dumping her near where I sat. Her hands were bound behind her back as she rolled toward my legs. She looked to the center of the room, her eyes focusing on Wayne's crumpled form on the floor. She screamed through her gag, causing Ernesto to look at her. He smiled coldly, holding her glare, as he kicked Wayne in the ribs.

"So, he's crazy after all," I mumbled to myself, still dazed by the panic and weighed down by fear. I looked down at Alverez who had dropped her forehead to the cement floor as she cried. She was going to die here. We were all going to die here. I looked at Grady, then Bones. Fury raged through both of them. They wouldn't go down without a fight. I glanced again at Wayne, who was still unconscious and covered in bloody marks. They had tortured him. Just like they would torture us.

Something snapped in my brain and the whooshing of my pulse against my skull dulled. I took another slow breath, tucking my chin to my chest as I tried to force sanity to return. I had to save them. The guards thought I was nothing more than a damsel in distress. I could use that. Even if it was close to the truth.

Faking a sob that felt too close to being real, I shifted forward and leaned over Alverez, clutching her by the shoulders and dragging her back so her head rested on my right thigh, and my left leg was bent so my boot rested against her back, near her hands. "Knife in boot," I whispered in her ear, before I sobbed loud enough for the guards to hear. "*I'm so sorry, Ari*! I thought we could help you. I should've called the police."

Alverez played along, sobbing loudly as she reached into my boot and pulled the knife from the inside sleeve. Since her body covered mine from their view, I reached inside my jacket and pulled my spare Glock from its holster, tucking it just under her hands as one of the guards moved over and threatened to kick her. She saw his movements in time and tightened her grip on the knife as she skootched herself and the Glock behind her, away from me and backed into the wall. The guard sneered before turning back to the center of the room.

Grady's hands and feet were being tied as Bones was being strapped to the center cross. Ernesto pulled a large hunting knife from the sheath at his hip.

Bones glanced briefly at me before turning to Grady. "Everybody was talking earlier about the damage I'd do if Bridget got hurt. Kind of makes you wonder what she'll do when she finds out about this."

Grady chuckled. "She's going to be pissed."

"You think?" Bones laughed as his other hand was tied to the ring bolt. "Man, I want to be there for that. I love it when that woman gets mad. Her nipples practically stand up and every hard muscle in that tight body of hers twitches."

Grady laughed. "Lucky bastard. When my old lady gets pissed, watch out. Heads are going to roll. I can't imagine her letting anyone live who goes after me."

"She does have a hell of a mean streak," Bones said, pulling at his wrists and checking to see if there was any slack. "She's pretty damn slow to contemplate shit, though. Has to always think out every angle. That must drive you crazy."

Grady smirked. "I've learned to be patient."

"You two seem quite comfortable with your situation," Chaves said, glancing between them. "I wonder how long that will last."

Chaves pressed the tip of the knife into Bones' thigh and slowly applied pressure.

I brought my knees to my chest and slid my second switchblade out of my other boot. Alverez had maneuvered herself upright with her back against the wall only a few feet away. I glanced over at her. She was waiting for me. My right hand moved behind me, grasping my Glock. We both had one knife and one gun, against six guards with automatic rifles and one crazy bastard with a hunting knife.

Bones hissed between clenched teeth. "Maybe if it was you up here, strapped to the alter, we wouldn't need to be so patient," he said to Grady.

"You think this is payback? Maybe for all the crap you said in Miami?" Grady asked, seeming relaxed as he chatted with Bones.

"I apologized for that!"

Grady snorted, looking down but turning his eyes toward me. He glanced at his hands before looking to me again. Studying the ropes, I realized that the knot was already loosened, and he'd be able to free his hands in seconds. Then he nodded toward the guard behind him. I knew what he wanted. If I could drop the guard, Grady could unbind his hands and grab the assault rifle. I nodded back.

"Ari?" I whispered. "There's no way in hell I'm waiting to be tortured in another dungeon. Do you understand?"

"What are you two talking about?" the guard asked, coming over to us again and crouching down.

With my left hand, I struck the knife into the side of his neck. Rolling onto my knees, I spun him, forcing his body to turn so his back was pressed against my chest to act as a shield. Two of the guards turned their weapons toward us, startled by the movement. Alverez and I fired our Glocks simultaneously and didn't stop until all the guards were down. Only one of them had fired back, filling the guard I held with lead.

"You could've saved me one guard to kill," Grady complained, setting the assault rifle that he had acquired beside him on the cement so he could untie his legs.

"You took too long," I said, shoving the dead guard to the side so I could get up.

"It's true," Bones agreed from the wooden cross, still holding a leg wrapped around Ernesto's neck. "I saw the whole thing. You're slipping, man."

"Is he dead?" Alverez asked, stepping forward as she held a gun on her brother.

"Nope," Bones answered, releasing his hold on Ernesto and letting him fall to the floor. "Just choked him until he passed out."

My knife was still in the neck of the first guard, so I took the one that Alverez held and passed it to Grady. I turned and held my gun on the other guards, just in case a bullet missed its mark and didn't kill them. I was done with surprises tonight.

"There might be more guards on the property," Grady said to me as he worked to cut Bones down.

"I know. There might be prisoners here, too. We need to call this in."

"Shit," Bones grumbled. "Do you know how much paperwork that will cause? They could keep us here for hours."

Grady looked up at Bones. "You might want to ditch the severed finger. That's at least two hours of questions."

I pulled my phone and called Maggie.

Chapter Thirty-One

It was six in the morning before we dragged our bloody bodies back into the house. Bridget greeted us in the kitchen and scowled when she saw that one of Bones' pant legs was cut open and a bandage was wrapped around his leg.

"Sorry," he said with a wide grin on his face. "Kelsey was taking her sweet time when it came to rescuing me."

"And why the hell did she need to rescue your ass?"

"I was sort of tied to a cross, waiting to be tortured."

"How exactly does a badass like you find himself tied to a cross?" Bridget glared, placing her fisted hands upon her hips.

"Well," Bones said, looking down at Bridget's erect nipples. "Let's go out to the garage, and I'll explain what happened."

Grady and I laughed as we walked past them. I peeked into the living room and nudged Grady when I spotted Maggie on the couch, sleeping with Nightcrawler. He chuckled, but pulled me by the hand down the hall, stopping only a moment to look in on Nicholas who was still sound asleep.

"I don't like it when we're both away from Nick at the same time," Grady said after he closed our bedroom door. "If tonight would've gone sideways, he could've lost us both."

"And if we wouldn't have been together, people would've died tonight. There's no winning these mental debates. I can only hope that whoever's left standing takes care of him if something does happen."

Grady remained quiet, sitting on the end of the bed to take his shoes off. "What's all that?" he asked, nodding toward the atrium.

I turned to see the atrium had been filled with stacks of boxes. Some of the boxes were emptied with piles of folders and paperwork scattered next to them. More folders covered the coffee table, the end tables, and the couches. On the far wall were bags of plastic-sealed objects: knives, pictures, letters, and even a gun. "I told Bridget to grab whatever looked like blackmail-related evidence in my mother's storage unit, but I never expected all this."

"Come on. We need to shower and take a nap before Nicholas wakes."

"I took a nap on the jet," I said, walking over to open a folder.

Grady moved behind me, taking the folder and tossing it on the couch. "Okay. So maybe I meant something else when I said we needed a nap."

He grinned as he turned and lifted me, my legs wrapping around his hips. Carrying me back through the bedroom and into the bathroom, he pressed me against the wall and rubbed my core against his jeans-covered erection.

"I like naps," I said, pulling his black T-shirt over his muscular chest.

~*~*~

Our shower lasted a good forty-five minutes before we moved to the bedroom to "nap". By the time we finally made it out of bed, I felt like a different person. Lighter.

The sound of Nicholas and Sara bickering from the other side of the house didn't surprise me. I pulled clothes from my dresser as the fight escalated into high-pitched screeching. I heard Anne raise her voice, followed by instant silence. Anne seldom raised her voice. Grady and I glanced at each other and smirked as we quickly threw on our clothes.

When we entered the dining room, Nicholas was sitting in one chair, arms crossed over his chest, and glaring at his plate. Sara sat at the other end of the table, glaring at her own plate with her fork held tightly in her clutched hand. Anne was in the kitchen slamming dishes around and Whiskey, Maggie, and Nightcrawler were sitting at the table drinking coffee and grinning.

"Well, isn't this a wonderful way to start the day," I said, walking over and removing the weaponized fork from Sara's grip. "What are we fighting about now?"

"She started—" Nicholas started to screech.

"He won't listen to—" Sara bellowed over him.

"STOP!" Grady yelled.

Both kids went silent, turning their glares back to their plates again.

"Okay, then," I said, moving into the kitchen to get us both a cup of coffee.

"I've got some Bailey's liqueur if you need to top that off," Anne said, stepping aside and leaning her forehead against the kitchen cabinet. "I miss Hattie."

I laughed before returning to the dining room and placing a cup of coffee at the head of the table for Grady and taking the seat next to him.

Grady sat. "Okay, this is how it's going to work. Each of you will get to say two sentences, without insulting the other one, to explain what is going on. You say more than your two sentences or drag it out with conjunctions and other nonsense, you'll get sent to your room. Sara, you go first."

"I was only telling Mom how we found the files on Judge Wynhart for the custody case, and then Nicholas started yelling at me, and—"

"Stop—" I said, holding my hand out in front of me. "That's enough conjunctions."

"Nick, your turn," Grady said.

"She had to open her big mouth and rat us out—"

"Stop—" I said. "Grady said no insults. Besides, we get the picture. Sara was excited to find information on Judge Wynhart, but neither of you were supposed to be going through the boxes. When she told about the files, the jig was up, and you were both in trouble."

Maggie hid her grin by taking a drink her coffee. "You're good. It took a lot more screaming between the two of them for me to figure it out."

Whiskey smirked. "You only missed the part that it was two in the morning when they found the file."

"You're both hereby assigned to the following punishments," I said, turning to face them. "One, you'll do all the dishes today, together, and without fighting or more punishments will be added. Two, you both will write a three-page essay on the health benefits of children getting a full night of sleep. And three, you will each recite a list of ten qualities you like about the other one and share your list at dinner tonight."

"Mom..." Nicholas groaned.

Sara wrinkled her nose and glared at Nicholas.

"Clear your plates and start the dishes," Grady ordered.

Anne returned to the table with her coffee as the kids pouted all the way into the kitchen with their plates.

"I can smell the Bailey's," I said to Anne.

She sipped her coffee, looking away and pretending not to hear me. Whiskey and Nightcrawler laughed, and Maggie looked curiously at Anne's cup before going to the kitchen.

"Heard Bones was injured," Whiskey said, turning to Grady. "He okay?"

"He'll live."

I rolled my eyes. "He thinks I was stalling on purpose. He blames me for getting stabbed."

"Were you? Stalling, I mean," Maggie asked, rejoining us at the table. Nightcrawler's hand moved toward her leg under the table as she settled.

"No. Not really. But I wasn't moving at my normal speed either. My brain was a bit foggy."

"Why?" Anne asked, leaning forward looking concerned.

"We were in a dungeon of sorts," Grady answered for me. "It knocked the wind out of her, but she worked her way through it and saved our asses."

"Barely," I whispered, blowing out a slow breath.

"Hey—" Grady said, grabbing my chin and tugging it toward him. "You did good. I'm not sure how you pulled yourself out of the dark hole you drifted into, but I sure as hell was happy when I saw the lights come back on. We would've been goners without you."

"Or you would've been fine if I hadn't been there to distract you in the first place."

"Well, I say, bravo," Maggie said. "I couldn't have done it. Not yet, at least. When I got your text last night, explaining what you thought you were walking into, I ran into the bathroom and puked."

Nightcrawler grinned, raising his hand to stroke her cheek. "And then you brushed your teeth and called Kierson to get a unit on standby. You girls might react differently than you used to, but you're still in the game. That counts."

"What counts is the lives that were saved." Grady agreed. "Four women get to go home to their families thanks to you gals."

"I need more Bailey's," Anne said to herself before going back to the kitchen.

"She's okay," Whiskey said to me, watching me watch Anne.

"Are you sure? First, Lisa was acting all manic, and now Anne seems almost defeated. What gives?"

Grady shrugged. "They're adjusting."

"To what? What's making them act so off?"

"You left, and then Hattie went back to Texas," Whiskey said. "You two were always the glue that kept everyone sane."

Grady nodded. "Lisa felt like she needed to do all the things Hattie used to do, since she wasn't working at the store. Then Anne became obsessed with the kids, since Hattie used to handle a lot of that."

"The new teacher is helping," Whiskey chuckled, "but it's been a long weekend. And the kids don't need as much attention as Anne thinks. She's just worried about them not having Hattie to talk to."

"But they do have Hattie," I said, setting my cup down. "Hattie calls or video-calls with them several times a day. She has one-on-one conversations with them daily, so she knows they're doing okay."

"Does Anne know that?" Whiskey asked.

I shrugged and yelled toward the kitchen, "Sara, did you talk to Hattie yesterday?"

"Yup. I called her in the morning, but Pops wanted her to go over to the new ranch so we video chatted last night before bed."

Anne turned and looked at Sara then at me.

"And what about you, Nicholas?" I yelled again.

"I talked to Hattie and Pops yesterday afternoon, and Pops is going to call me after he goes fishing this morning and let me know how many fish he catches."

"And you two call them whenever you want, right?" I asked.

"You told us we could," Nicholas said, raising his eyebrow and looking at me oddly.

"Why?" Sara asked.

"I just wanted to make sure you both were staying in touch."

Sara giggled. "Hattie would fly back to Michigan if she couldn't talk to us every day. That's why Pops got her a laptop, so she could video call."

I turned back to Whiskey. "See? Hattie's still taking care of the kids. Maybe Anne will settle down a bit now. As for Lisa—" I turned to Nightcrawler "—I need to hire a housekeeper. Someone to manage repairs, pick up groceries, clean, that type of thing. If you hear of anyone, can you let me know?"

"I actually know someone. She's cleaning empty apartments for a few dollars an hour right now. I'm sure she'd jump at the chance to work normal hours."

"Set it up. We'll still handle some of the day-to-day, but we have too much going on to manage everything. She can set her own schedule, but it would most likely be the three houses and maybe Headquarters, at least until the new houses are built."

Nightcrawler pulled his phone, sending a text. He smirked at the immediate reply. "She'll be here at eight tomorrow to get started. Her name's Eloise."

I turned to Grady. "Text Donovan and tell him to hire a nanny for Abigail. And to finish the nursery at Headquarters. Lisa needs to get back to work."

Grady pulled his phone and sent the text. I turned and watched the clock. It took a full three minutes and forty-two seconds for the front door to be slammed open and Lisa to storm inside.

"Who do you think you are, ordering my husband to hire a nanny?" Lisa yelled, pointing a finger at Grady.

"Lisa, sit down," I said calmly.

"I don't want to sit down!"

"SIT DOWN," I ordered, pointing to a chair.

Lisa threw herself into a chair and glared at me.

Grady's phone rang, and he walked toward the sliding door to answer it.

"I told Grady to send the text," I said to Lisa. "We tried things your way, and you went a little cra-cra on us. Now we try my way, which is that you go back to work, and Abigail gets a nanny. If the nanny sucks, Abigail will be surrounded by forty security guards, including your husband, who will step in. Understood?"

She started to say something but then snapped her mouth closed. She turned to see a grinning Donovan walk into the house, closing the front door behind him and carrying Abigail.

"You're a bully." She pouted at me as she reached out to take Abigail.

"And you sometimes need someone to bulldoze past your stubborn streak." I laughed before drinking my coffee.

"You *are* mighty stubborn," Donovan said, kissing the top of her head before moving in the direction of the coffee.

"Don't worry, Lisa," Charlie said from the garage entrance. "You're not the only one Kelsey bosses around." Kierson followed her inside the house, closing the door behind them.

"I only boss around the people who need it," I said.

"That was Wayne," Grady said to me as he sat. "He's doing okay. He has a few broken ribs and a handful of new scars. Doctors say they'll release him tomorrow if he doesn't have any complications from the concussion."

"How many times has Wayne been knocked unconscious?" Charlie asked.

"A lot," Grady answered, laughing. "That's why the doctors want to keep him another night. They said his head CT looked like a jigsaw puzzle."

"Well, I'm glad he'll be okay. I didn't like leaving him alone in the hospital, but Alverez promised to keep an eye on him."

"Wayne's milking it too. By the time they get back here, she'll either hate him, or she'll be sleeping with him."

"Want to place a wager on that theory?" I asked.

"You don't think it will happen?"

"Alverez is all business. She'll shut down his advances, but she won't get mad. It will drive Wayne insane that he can't charm his way into her life."

"I've never seen a woman Wayne couldn't stir a reaction out of. Fifty bucks," Grady said, reaching out his hand to shake mine.

"A hundred," I offered.

Grady nodded, and I reached out to shake hands on the bet.

"Grady," Charlie said, shaking her head. "You just made a bet with a profiler."

Everyone laughed and teased Grady.

I looked at Kierson, who was relaxed in the chair across from me with his arm wrapped around Charlie's shoulders.

"What?" He grinned.

"I don't know," I said, grinning back. "I saw you and it was like I needed to tell you something, but I can't remember what it was."

"Shit," Grady cursed, pulling his phone out. "We forgot about Agent Forrick."

"That's it! You read my mind," I said, grinning at Grady.

Grady winked as he waited for someone to answer his phone call.

"Do you still have guys tailing him?" Kierson asked, pulling out his own phone.

Grady nodded as he talked on the phone. He wrote down an address and slid it across the table to Kierson.

~*~*~

After breakfast, the kids finished the dishes while everyone else picked up around the house. When everything looked less chaotic, I went to the atrium to start digging into the piles of boxes. I stood at the entrance feeling overwhelmed as I looked at the massive piles.

"This is going to take forever," Grady said, wrapping an arm around me.

"No, it won't," Lisa said, walking around us. "I texted everyone. They're on their way."

Donovan carried the portable crib into the atrium and took a sleeping Abigail from Lisa and settled her with her blanket. Anne, Whiskey, Nicholas, Sara, Charlie, Kierson, Nightcrawler, and Maggie moved around the room, each finding a space on the carpet to sit and grab a box. And that was only the beginning of the labor force. Soon we had my entire family, including Nana, several guards from Aces, a handful of bikers from Devil's Players, Genie, Dave, Steve, and Bridget, all elbow deep in a box and calling out information to Sara, Tech, Carl, or Genie to document or run searches on. Lisa was in charge of organizing the files based on importance after they were reviewed. Nicholas was in charge of keeping Nana out of anything too serious. And Maggie and I reviewed the files that were deemed important, once the others had identified them.

I had just finished reviewing the files on Judge Wynhart when the doorbell rang. I crossed the room to the windows and looked over to the front porch. Three police officers stood on the porch with their hands resting on their weapons.

"Keep Carl, Nana, and the kids inside and away from the windows," I ordered as I handed my Glock to Donovan.

"Who is it?" Grady asked.

"Cops," I answered before opening the side door of the atrium and walking out.

I walked around the exterior of the atrium and called out to the officers on the front porch. One of them pulled his weapon, aiming it at me.

"I have no problem with the police department visiting, but I can't say I'm finding the visit all that reassuring. Have your deputy holster his weapon."

"Are you armed?" the Chief of Police asked.

"Not at the moment," I answered, raising my hands and turning in a slow circle so he could see that I didn't have a gun.

"We still need to frisk you." The chief nodded to one of his deputies. "Protocol."

"It isn't protocol unless you're arresting me, but go ahead."

I allowed the deputy to frisk me, but kept my eyes on the chief. When the deputy was done, he pulled one of my wrists behind my back. I raised an eyebrow at the chief.

Grady, Kierson, Charlie, Maggie, and Katie walked out the front door of the house. Kierson and Maggie flashed their badges.

"Ms. Harrison, we've been asked to take you into custody relating to the death of Thomas Harrison."

"My father's dead? Thomas Harrison?" I asked, stunned by the news.

"Nice try," the chief said. "A gun registered in your name was found at the scene."

I snorted. "Impossible. I know where all of my registered guns are."

"It's the unregistered guns that occasionally go missing," Katie said.

"Not helping, Katie," Kierson grumbled. "Chief, when did this murder take place?"

"I'm not at liberty to discuss the case to the public."

"We're FBI. Were not the public," Maggie said, glaring.

"And yet I'm not sure whose side you're on," the chief said, glaring back.

"Let me rephrase..." Kierson said, throwing a look over his shoulder at Maggie. "Ms. Harrison flew out to Arizona early yesterday evening and didn't return to Michigan until dawn. I can provide a list of witnesses, many of them in law enforcement, who can confirm and testify if needed to her whereabouts."

"Maybe we have the wrong Harrison then," the chief said, glancing over at Charlie. "What's your alibi look like?"

"I was here, along with about forty other people until around one in the morning. Then I went back to the hotel. I was a bit loud when I was skinny dipping in the hotel's pool, so I'm sure a few guests could confirm."

"You know skinny dipping in a hotel pool is illegal, right?" Genie asked Charlie as she giggled.

"I'd rather be charged with indecent exposure than for the murder of that douchebag of a sperm donor."

Kierson released a noise that sounded like a cat hissing before he looked back to the chief. "I can confirm that Charlie Harrison was indeed swimming naked in the hotel pool until I dragged her out and hauled her back to her room."

"And what about between two and three in the morning?" the chief asked, squinting his eyes at Charlie.

Charlie grinned. "I was very much—*not alone*—for the rest of the night."

"I can vouch for her being in her room." Genie giggled, raising her hand. "I made the mistake of getting the room next to Charlie's. She's not quiet when she's, uh... um... having sexual *relations*."

The chief pulled out a notepad from his back pocket and dramatically pulled his pen from his pocket. "I'll need the name of the man you were with."

"What if I was with a woman?" Charlie asked.

"Knock it off," Kierson growled at Charlie, handing his ID over to the chief. "She was with me. We've been in a physical relationship for over a year now."

"Off and on," Charlie added.

Kierson glared at her again, but it only made her grin widen.

"Charlie, behave," I ordered. "Deputy, remove the cuffs, or you'll be hearing from my lawyer."

The chief nodded at the deputy and the cuffs were removed. Grady and Katie moved over to stand beside me.

"What information can you share about my father's murder?"

"It's not my case," the chief said, shaking his head. "I was asked to assist with taking you into custody, that's all."

I couldn't stop the snort. "You were asked to arrest me because the sheriff of Sadler Creek would've found himself six feet under if he'd dared to step on my property," I said as I stepped closer. "Now I need some answers. Are you going to be part of the solution or part of the problem?"

"He's a good chief, Kelsey," Steve said, walking out of the garage with Dave. "Cut him some slack."

"I ordered you two to stay away!" the chief yelled at them. "What are you doing here?"

"We followed your orders while on duty." Dave shrugged. "But Kelsey's a friend. And with all due respect, sir, we trust her with our lives. She's not the bad guy here. You're being manipulated by a dirty cop, bought and paid for by Kelsey's despicable mother."

"And you know this how?" the chief glared.

"Enough—" I ordered. "Kierson, can you get the state police involved? I need them to take over the investigation of my father's death. Have them also impound his car from the storage unit."

"Are you sure? I can call the Feds," Kierson asked.

"We don't need the Feds," I said, turning to Charlie. "Reach out to our contacts in Sadler Creek. Start with Marilyn. See what rumors are circulating regarding our father's death."

"I thought she—" the chief pointed at Charlie, "—was your cousin."

I ignored him and turned to Katie. "Get Cameron on a jet to Michigan. We need him to advise us on a few legal matters."

Katie walked toward the street to make the call.

"Grady, we need to finish the research we started. We're running out of time. Maggie, get with Carl. I need the information on this gun that's supposedly registered to me. Keep Genie away from it, though."

"Got it," she said, heading back inside.

"Chief," I said, turning back to face him. "I've run out of goodwill and must ask that you and your deputies remove yourselves from my property. And if I were you, I'd hold off chewing out Dave and Steve for their actions and instead watch the news over the next few days. Expect to see the sheriff's and my mother's mug shots on your TV by dinnertime tomorrow."

The chief looked around, a stunned expression etched on his face as everyone jumped on the tasks that I'd assigned. "Who are you? A federal agent?"

"No. But you might want to google me before you pay another surprise visit to my doorstep," I said, nudging Dave and Steve to walk inside ahead of me. "You dumbasses," I said low enough for only them to hear. "You should've stayed inside."

"Couldn't. You're our girl," Dave said. "Besides, I heard you were hiring a nanny for Abigail and was hoping that I could drop off Juliette a few days a week."

"Talk to Donovan." I smirked. "I'm sure it'll be fine."

Chapter Thirty-Two

"I'm telling you—*it's not my gun*," I said, throwing my hands into the air in frustration. It was almost noon, and I'd lost all patience hours ago.

"Well, ma'am," the State trooper said while scratching his forehead. "The paperwork says right here, it's registered in your name."

"Let me see that," Maggie said, holding out her hand. "No. This can't be right. Kelsey was working for the Miami police department when this was registered."

"So?" the other trooper said.

"She would've registered it in Florida, not in Michigan," Kierson explained.

The trooper shrugged. "She used her grandmother's residence."

"But why would I? I was a cop. Why would I fly to Michigan to buy and register a gun, when I was a cop in Florida?"

"People do strange things," the first trooper said.

I released a noise that was somewhere between a groan and a growl.

"Chill, Kelsey." Charlie laughed. "Maggie, what are the dates on that registration?"

Maggie handed her the paperwork, and Charlie walked into the living room and called someone. I eyed the bottle of Bailey's that was still sitting on the kitchen counter.

"No!" Maggie said, shaking her head at me.

"You're covered," Charlie said, returning to the dining room. "You were working the Delray robberies during those dates. A dozen police reports have you documented as being in Florida. Uncle Hank is faxing the details to prove it."

"Who faked the registration?" one of the troopers asked, scratching his chin.

"My *mother*." I sighed. "She's behind my father's death too. It's just a matter of proving it. Charlie, check with the team and see if my mother had anything on the guy who filed the purchase and registration for the gun."

"On it," she said as she walked down the hall.

"Is she going to bring that paperwork back?" the first trooper asked.

"She'll be back in a minute," Kierson said, waving toward the chairs for the officers to sit. "What can you tell us about the murder?"

"Mr. Harrison was shot point blank while he was getting out of his car. Probably never saw it coming."

"In the garage?" I asked, leaning back to listen.

Both deputies nodded.

"When?" I asked. "When did the shooting happen?"

"Near two in the morning, according to the neighbor who heard the shots. The medical examiner also confirmed the time of death."

"Did anyone check my mother, aunt, and uncle for gunshot residue?"

"No reason to. Your mother was asleep in the bedroom. Your aunt and uncle weren't there until your mother called them later."

"Doubtful, on all counts. But it's unlikely it would've made a difference, anyway. My mother's too smart to leave evidence."

"Why would she murder him at home?" Maggie asked. "Seems risky. And what was your father doing getting home at two in the morning?"

Charlie heard Maggie as she returned to the dining room. "Maybe he has another mistress?" She handed the gun registration back to one of the troopers and handed me a file.

"Or," Kierson growled, "he was just getting back from visiting an *old* mistress." He slammed his palm on the table. "Damn it. Rose kept saying Thomas wouldn't have tricked her into thinking her baby was dead. That he couldn't possibly have been a part of it."

"You think Rose called him?" Charlie asked. "And then what? He drove up north to see her?"

"Easy enough to prove," Maggie said. "I'll have Genie pull a warrant for the phone records."

"This is a state case, ma'am," the second trooper said, holding up his hand to stop her.

"Yes, but we can get things done faster and then share the information with the state," Maggie said as she sent Genie a text.

Charlie paced at the end of the table. "Or I can just ask Rose." She pulled her phone out and made the call. I opened the file she had handed me. My mother had once again collected dirt on someone and turned it around in her favor. She had copies of several fake gun sale receipts and registration documents. I shook my head.

"Are you boys the lead investigators on this case, or are you reporting to someone?"

"There are a lot of officers working the case," one of the troopers said.

"Tell whoever's in charge to contact me or Agent Kierson. In the meantime, you'll want to get a warrant for a guy named Dodd Jenkins. He works at the local gun shop in Sadler Creek. He's selling guns under false names and registrations."

"We need some type of proof," the same trooper argued.

"You have enough," Kierson said, passing the papers from the fax machine to the troopers. "This fax shows that Kelsey was in Florida when the gun was purchased. That's all you need to investigate the gun shop."

"I suppose that might work."

"Don't go to Judge Wynhart for your warrant."

"Why's that?"

"He's dirty. He's in my mother's pocket, along with the local sheriff."

"Got any proof of that?" the other trooper asked, narrowing his eyes.

"Have your boss call one of us." I smiled broadly as I started to think out a plan. "By tomorrow you boys should have this case and several others wrapped up."

"Is that so?" the other trooper asked.

"Kelsey's not someone you mess with, and her mother went too far," Maggie said, inspecting her manicure as she grinned. "By this time tomorrow, they'll all be sitting in a jail cell."

"Cell phone records," Genie said, walking into the room and handing the papers to Maggie. "Right again. Rose called Thomas Harrison early yesterday."

"Yeah, Rose confirmed it," Charlie said, walking back toward the table with the phone in her hand. "She says good ole daddy dearest didn't know I was their love child, but I call bullshit. He had to have known his own sister-in-law was never pregnant. But regardless, after Rose called him, he drove north to convince her in person. He left the Traverse Bay area about half past ten last night."

"I'll need this Rose person's full name and address," the trooper closest to Charlie said, getting out his notepad.

Charlie glanced to me, and I nodded. The other trooper's eyes narrowed as he studied me.

"Oh, yeah," Maggie said to him. "You read that right. Kelsey's holding all the cards. It's annoying, isn't it?"

"And Marilyn called back," Charlie said to me, turning away from the trooper. "Rumor has it that Audrey visited Cecil and Mark for several hours yesterday afternoon. Then around one in the morning, Cecil left the house and didn't return until sometime after two. Twenty minutes later, both Cecil and Mark left together, making quite a ruckus, banging things around and arguing as they got in their car and drove away."

"But when Aunt Cecil left earlier in the night, Uncle Mark stayed home?" I asked.

Grady snorted. He had been leaning against the wall, observing, since the state troopers had arrived. "Between the broken arm, the broken leg, and his face smashed to hell, I doubt Mark was in any condition to do their dirty work for them."

"I'm not sure Aunt Cecil has it in her to pull the trigger, though," I admitted aloud.

"No, she doesn't." Charlie sneered. Her hand tightened on her cell phone, threatening to crack the plastic. "But Cecil *does* like to watch."

I reached over and pried the phone loose as Kierson stood and wrapped an arm around Charlie's waist. She leaned back into his chest, tilting her head toward the ceiling and closing her eyes.

"Shit..." one of the troopers said. "Are you people serious?"

"If forensics hasn't gone through the inside of the house yet, send them immediately," Kierson said. "They might get lucky and find the clothes Audrey was wearing when she pulled the trigger."

"Maybe," I said before looking back at the troopers. "But tell whoever is in charge, not to arrest her even if they do find something. There's a custody case tomorrow, and I'm hoping she shows her face. Should be interesting. You should come watch."

"Oooh." Genie giggled. "I'll bring the popcorn!"

Kierson turned to the troopers, ignoring Genie. "Bring your boss, someone from the state attorney's office, and a handful more police officers to the courthouse," Kierson ordered. "I've seen Kelsey in action, and it usually requires a lot of handcuffs or body bags. Since she's planning on having the showdown in public, then lucky for us, that means she plans on us arresting the bad guys."

"She could always change her mind," Grady said, smirking.

"You and your plan Bs," Kierson said, shaking his head.

Kierson's cell phone rang, and he stepped into the kitchen to answer it. "Special Agent in Charge Tebbs, how can I help you?"

I looked at Grady and winked.

"Yes, sir. One moment, sir," Kierson said as he walked back and handed me his phone.

"Hey, Jack. How's it hangin'?"

Kierson turned three shades of green.

"I assume you're messing with Agent Kierson?" Jack laughed.

"You assume correctly. What can I do for you?"

"I need you to come to Detroit. Agent Forrick isn't talking. I was hoping you could do your thing that makes perps start blabbering their darkest secrets."

"No can do. I got shit of my own I'm dealing with. But Maggie's in Michigan. She doesn't have a green light to work cases until Monday, but if you make an exception, she can pressure Forrick into a legal confession."

"I'm not sure she's ready to do one-on-one interrogations."

"She is. But if you're worried about it, I can send Nightcrawler to babysit her during the interview."

"Nightcrawler? Is that someone's name?"

"They'll be on the road in twenty minutes," I said before hanging up.

"You hung up on him?" Kierson screeched, reaching to take his phone back.

"We were done talking," I said. "Maggie, your services are needed in Detroit. Jack's worried you aren't emotionally stable enough to handle this, so I offered Nightcrawler to go with you."

"You want me to walk into FBI headquarters?" Nightcrawler asked from the other side of the room. "Are you nuts?"

"Your job is only to watch Maggie do the interview and ensure she doesn't go ape shit on Agent Forrick's ass. Nothing you haven't done before."

"Don't take any weapons inside," Kierson growled.

"Especially, unregistered Glocks. The suits get way uptight about the scratched out serial numbers."

Maggie rolled her eyes and started for the door. "I'll be back before dinner. I've already read this guy's file. He'll be squealing in no time."

I turned back to the troopers who were sitting silently, listening to us. "Why are you guys still here?"

"I'm honestly mesmerized by everything happening around me," one of the troopers admitted.

"Is it always like this?" the other trooper asked.

"Yes," Grady, Kierson, and Charlie answered simultaneously.

I ignored them. "You two can leave. We'll call if we need anything."

"Uh, sure," one trooper said as they both stood and walked toward the door. "I'll keep you informed if we find anything."

"You do that," Grady said, holding the door open for them and closing it after they stepped outside.

I glanced up at the clock. It was still early enough that I could get pot roasts going for dinner. "Katie! Anne! Lisa! Alex!" I called out.

All four of them scrambled down the hall.

"We have to hurry. Lisa? Did you pick up the food?"

"Basement refrigerator," she said, grabbing Grady's arm and dragging him with her down the stairs.

"Alex and Katie, I need all the crockpots. Hattie stored them in the basement storage room. Anne, help me get the pans ready to sear the meat."

Anne and I seasoned and seared the meat as everyone else prepared crockpots, rinsed carrots, or washed and quartered potatoes. I dropped bouillon cubes, added water, and dropped large chunks of onions into the pots as Anne followed behind me with the roasts. Everyone then followed behind Anne, adding the potatoes and carrots. Within fifteen minutes we had seven crockpots ready and cooking.

"That has to be a new record," Anne said.

"My hands smell like onions." I pouted, holding them away from me.

"Rub them on the sink," Lisa said as she washed the countertop.

"What?"

"The sink. It's stainless steel. Rub your hands on the inside of it to remove the onion smell."

I thought she was pranking me, but she nodded to the sink again. I walked over and rubbed my hands against the stainless steel. When I was done, I lifted my hands to smell them. "It worked."

"Of course it did."

Grady reached over and grabbed one of my hands to smell it. "I'll be damned."

"How did you know that?" I asked Lisa.

"How did you *not* know?"

"Motherless teenage years, remember? I learned how to cook from internet videos. I never saw any of them rub their hands on the side of the sink."

"Maybe it's an Italian secret." Anne said. "I didn't know either."

The doorbell rang and Charlie answered it. She opened the door wider and Cameron Brackins, our Miami attorney, walked in.

He smiled, seeing all of us huddled in the kitchen. "What are we doing?"

"Did you know that rubbing your hands against stainless steel removes the smell of onions?"

"Yes."

"Are you Italian?" Anne asked.

Cameron raised an eyebrow. "Yes."

"See!" Anne said, pointing to Lisa.

"As fascinating as this is," Kierson interrupted. "Can we get back to work now? We have a lot of files to get through."

"Fine," I said, leading the way back to my atrium. The atrium had always been my sanctuary, but with the stacks of boxes and papers everywhere, it felt like I was walking into a twenty-year IRS audit. "Next time, we dump all the crap in the living room, not in my atrium."

"Bridget wasn't sure if you wanted it out of sight," Anne said.

"What is all this?" Cameron asked, stepping over to a stack of files and opening one.

"The files we stole from my mother," I answered.

He dropped the file like it scalded him and turned to face me. "Define *stole*."

"I may or may not have had someone borrow the boxes from my mother's storage unit."

"Any chance you or the person who *borrowed* them, will be arrested?"

"Hell no," Bridget answered from the other side of the room. "I'm a professional. We used the drop vehicle for each load and met up with the secondary vehicles to move the contents over before going back and taking another load. The security cameras were disabled, and we wore masks anyway. We also had gloves, cleaned all the shelves down after they were emptied, and I installed a replacement lock before I left. The cops would first have to prove there was anything there to begin with, and then they still won't find anything to trace back to us."

"Unless they get a warrant to search the house," Cameron said, waving his hand around the room.

"Why would they?" I shrugged. "My mother doesn't want the police to know about any of this. It only incriminates her."

"What's in the files?" Cameron asked, scrunching his forehead.

"My mother blackmails people. She uses the information either for money, favors, control, or sometimes just for the fun of it. But she has a file on everyone she knows."

"Including you?" Cameron asked me.

"Sure. But I already confessed to everyone except the kids about my past, so she can't hurt me. And she can't prove anything to have me arrested on the rest of it."

"What do you plan on doing with the information?"

I walked over and picked up the judge's file, handing it to Cameron. "That's where you come in. I need your help to figure out how we can use this information without incriminating ourselves."

"Oh boy," Cameron said when he saw whose file it was.

Chapter Thirty-Three

We spent the rest of the day sorting and organizing the files. Maggie returned in time for dinner, and after three helpings she declared the pot roast the best she'd ever had. The kids' lists of top ten qualities of each other proved entertaining. Nicholas nearly choked as he admitted aloud that he thought Sara was smart. Sara in return, very grudgingly, admitted that Nicholas was a decent companion. Grady's shoulders shook as he laughed in silence during both speeches.

After dinner, Maggie, Grady, Cameron, Katie, and I reviewed the files that were set aside for the court battle. Everyone else loaded the rest of the boxes in various vehicles and drove them over to Headquarters to be stored in the basement.

When we finally had a strategy that Cameron felt confident wouldn't get me arrested, we called it a night. We were scheduled to be at the courthouse at ten the next day, and it was close to midnight by the time we called it quits.

I lay in bed, staring up at the ceiling as Grady slept soundly beside me. It was four in the morning, and I had yet to fall asleep. I wasn't worried about going to jail. I wasn't even worried about the custody case. I was worried that my mother had newer ammunition that could hurt my family. And I was floored by the realization that I didn't care that my father was dead. I had no feelings either way. No grief. No sadness. No anger. What kind of person has no emotional reaction when she discovers her father was murdered?

Frustrated, I rolled out of bed and grabbed my robe from the bathroom before leaving the bedroom. I made it as far as the kitchen before I heard hushed arguing from inside the garage. I turned on the garage light and looked out to see Carl and Tyler standing in front of my SUV.

Opening the door and closing it behind me, I walked over to Tyler and snitched a cigarette from the inside of his leather cut. "Why are you two out here arguing at four in the morning?" I asked as I walked out into the driveway so I wouldn't stink up the garage.

"I came over to walk the security route and caught Carl sneaking down the road in his pajamas," Tyler said, having followed me into the driveway with Carl.

"I wasn't sneaking. I was walking. Nobody said I couldn't walk at nighttime," Carl hissed back at Tyler.

"Tyler, why are you patrolling the properties? Chaves was arrested."

"Habit." He shrugged. "You pay me to keep an eye on things, remember?"

I couldn't argue with his logic. "Carl, where were you going when Tyler stopped you?"

"Nowhere," Carl answered, looking down at his feet.

"You're lying," Tech said as he entered the back door of the garage. "Nice outfit," he said to me as he grinned down at my robe.

"Did we wake you?" I asked, looking at the dark apartment above the garage.

"Sleep is overrated. Besides, this sounded more interesting."

I tried to hide my grin as I turned back to Carl. "Fess up. Where were you going?"

"Okay," he whined. "I was going to Headquarters to test something I've been building."

"Is this thing you're building likely to blow up?" Tyler chuckled.

"No," Carl answered, glaring at Tyler. "It's a fighting machine for Grady and Kelsey."

I glanced back at Tech as I exhaled cigarette smoke. He grabbed my cigarette and took a hit off it before smashing it under his boot. Tyler was already pulling a set of keys out of his pocket to my SUV.

"You want to change first?" Tech asked me.

"I keep clothes at Headquarters," I answered as I slid into the passenger seat. Tech and Carl slid into the back.

By the time I had changed my clothes, Tyler and Tech had turned on the lights to the gym and helped Carl haul out his new experiment. I watched in awe as the fighting dummies moved around their circle track and their appendages alternated swinging fake arms or legs, sometimes with weapons, toward the center where someone was supposed to stand.

"Not it." Tyler chuckled.

"I'm out," Tech said. "I'm a computer geek. This is way out of my wheelhouse."

"It's only for Grady and Kelsey," Carl said, shaking his head. "Maybe Donovan, but he has to be nicer to me if he wants to use it."

"Carl? Is that mannequin swinging a lead pipe?" I asked.

"Yes. You better duck. Franky's mean."

"Do all the mannequins have names?"

"Of course. How would you tell them apart without names?" Carl changed the direction of the spinning mannequins and hit another lever on the remote for one of the mannequins to kick a steel-toe boot toward the empty space in the center. "That's Willy. He's a kicker."

"I see that," I said, raising an eyebrow. "What about the fat one? What does he do?"

"That's Meathead. I haven't tested him yet. We'd better not try him until we know the others work the way they should. I have a lock on the remote so I don't accidentally activate him."

I turned to look at Carl as he turned the remote to the side and showed that the switch was in the off position. I wasn't sure I wanted to know why Meathead was more menacing than a dummy swinging a lead pipe and another that kicked with steel-toe boots.

"What about the other two?" Tyler asked.

Carl introduced us to Jimmy and Kimmy, who both had extra long arms and legs and could swing a gloved fist or shoe-covered fake leg well into the center of the ring.

"Are you ready?" Carl asked, looking down at me.

"Carl, that lead pipe could kill someone," I said, pointing to the dummy named Franky.

"I recommend you duck—*fast*," Carl agreed, nodding.

I heard Grady's laugh as he walked across the gym. "You heard him. If you're too chicken, I'll go first. Looks like fun."

I looked back at the fighting contraption, rotating my neck and rolling my shoulders. "What the hell. It looks like a lot more fun than anything else I had planned today."

Carl shut the machine off so I could walk between the mannequins and stand in the center. "Ready?" he asked.

"Tech?" I called out. "You've been watching Carl on that remote, right?"

He laughed. "Yeah. I can shut it down in a hurry if you're knocked unconscious."

I decided to face Franky first, so I'd have a sense of his location before he started spinning around me. "We both know the others aren't a threat," I said to Franky the mannequin. "But you like to play dirty, don't you? A lead pipe? Really?"

"You about done profiling the practice dummy, babe?" Grady asked.

I took a deep breath, staring at Franky. "Hit it, Carl!"

The machine started up, and I crouched and swerved as Franky swung the lead pipe right at the spot I'd been standing. I blocked a kick from Kimmy, pleased to see that the leg reacted to the impact and retreated. Moving back, I tested Jimmy's punch, which also retreated when I blocked it, before Willy kicked me in the stomach, sending me flying into Franky's chest as he swung the lead pipe down into the space I'd been standing. The contraption stopped moving, and I turned and ducked out of the circle. "*Holy shit.*" I laughed, holding a hand over my bruised stomach. "I'm out."

Grady rubbed his hands together and smiled wickedly. "I was hoping you would say that."

"You're insane." Tyler laughed at Grady. "No way in hell I'd get in there."

"Good," Donovan said, walking up behind us. "Then I'm after Grady, and you can watch Abigail." He handed a sleeping Abigail to Tyler, who cuddled her to his chest.

"Carl built it for Grady and me," I told Donovan. "He said you can't play unless you're nice to him."

Donovan looked at Carl and raised an eyebrow. "How long do I have to be nice to you?"

Carl pondered the question before answering. "Two days. Promising anything more would be a falsehood on your part. You should be able to manage two days, though."

"Fine," Donovan agreed. "As long as you leave my cell phone alone and don't steal the parts from inside it."

Carl looked at the remote, then up at the ceiling as he grinned to himself. "To clarify, you mean from this moment on and through the immediate forty-eight hours, correct?"

"Are you telling me that if I were to use my phone right now, it wouldn't work?" Donovan growled.

"Remember," Grady laughed, walking over and standing in the center of the contraption, "if you want to play with the new toy, you have to be nice."

"Fine. Starting right now, I'll be nice to you, Carl, if you don't mess with my phone again for two whole days."

"Okay." Carl said and started the machine as Grady went into attack mode.

Grady did better than me, lasting a lot longer and several times kicking or hitting the dummies to the point that the circular track lifted and tipped before settling back to a level position. But eventually he turned too late to block Willy's kick. Grady, who had been crouched down, took the kick to the chest. It sent him sailing into Franky's legs and the lead pipe came down stopping only inches away from his family jewels.

"*Uncle!*" Grady yelled.

Tech grabbed the remote and shut it off because Carl was too busy laughing.

Grady crawled around Franky and out of the ring before standing. "Damn. That was fun, but shit that hurt." He rubbed his chest as he tried to even his breathing. His T-shirt was damp with sweat and I reached up and wiped the sweat off his face with my shirt sleeve.

"My turn," Donovan said, slugging Grady in the shoulder on his way past to enter the fighting ring.

Carl took the remote from Tech and as soon as Donovan nodded, he started the machine.

Donovan was doing as well as Grady had, maybe even a little faster. He was a good five minutes in when he blocked a kick from Kimmy and we heard something break. Kimmy's leg dangled limply, now motionless and broken, but the rest of the dummies continued on, and Donovan turned to defend himself against Jimmy's fists.

Sensing Carl's anger at seeing his toy broken, Tech and I both darted toward him and the controller, but we were too slow. Carl flipped the side switch, activating Meathead, and threw a lever down. We watched in horror as Meathead vaulted like a torpedo into Donovan, throwing him over Willy and out of the ring. The entire fighting contraption was flipped over, landing upside down, and Meathead landed on Donovan as he slammed into the planked floor and skidded another ten feet.

"Holy shit," Tyler hissed, frozen in place like the rest of us as we waited to know if Donovan was alive.

"Ge-*hhht*," Donovan wheezed, "get this thing off me!"

We ran over to help, still unable to speak. Tyler passed Abigail to Carl, and it took all four of us to move Meathead enough so Donovan could crawl out. The dummy must have weighed five hundred pounds at least.

Donovan glared at Carl as I inspected the back of his head, and Grady checked his arm.

Beth ran over to Carl. "Give me the baby," she said as she took Abigail from his arms. "Run! Back to the house! Sara and Nicholas will protect you!"

Grady and I laughed as Carl ran toward the doors.

"Not funny," Donovan said before he raised his good arm to his chest and coughed.

"I'll drive him to the ER for x-rays," Tyler said, helping Donovan up. "I'll try to have him back before Lisa finds out."

Grady and I walked over to Beth as Tyler helped Donovan limp out the gym. Grady took Abigail who was now wide awake and gurgling spit-bubble grins. "Yeah, I thought it was funny too," Grady cooed to her, lifting her up before bouncing her in his arms.

"Is Donovan going to be okay?" Beth asked, looking back at the doors.

"He's survived worse," Grady said. "What brings you here so early?"

"Bored," she admitted. "I woke up early, drank a pot of coffee, and reorganized my kitchen cupboards. I decided I might as well come here and rearrange the supplies for the schoolroom."

"You can do that later. Follow us over to the house, and we'll feed you. That way we can protect Carl from Lisa when she hears about Donovan's injuries."

"I'll agree, if you let me help cook. Otherwise, I'll just end up drinking more coffee."

"Deal," Grady said. "Gets me off the hook from helping. I'll meet you guys back at the house. I need to get Donovan's spare keys since he's the only one with a car seat."

I turned to Tech. "You joining us?"

"I'll be over," he said, looking over the remote for the fighting machine. "I want to make sure this thing is powered down so we don't start a fire."

"I'd disconnect from the main power pack," Beth said, nodding over to a box sitting a few feet away. "Looks like he rigged a car battery and part of a generator."

"Shit." Tech laughed. "How much do you want to bet that's Katie's car battery?"

"That's a bet I'll have no part of," I said. "Carl's still mad at her for banning him from the laundry services area at the store."

"I warned him not to mess with that broken washer," Tech said, walking over to the power pack. "But he didn't listen."

I steered Beth toward the exit.

"What happened to the washer?" she asked.

"They're commercial washers. He fixed the washer, then adjusted the settings to turn it into a human washer."

"What's a human washer?"

"A contraption you climb into, hit the switch, and close the lid on."

"Oh, boy." Beth laughed.

"He forgot to factor in that humans need oxygen and can easily drown. Goat heard him yelling and had to break the front door on the washer to get him out. The whole laundry room flooded and was covered in suds, and the washer was sent to the scrap yard."

Beth grinned. "But he was clean, wasn't he?"
"That's exactly what he said!"

Chapter Thirty-Four

"Were you at Headquarters?" Lisa asked from the kitchen when we entered. "Donovan took Abigail this morning, but he's not answering his phone."

"Carl tampered with his phone again," I said. "Abigail's with Grady, who will be here shortly."

I pulled three dozen eggs, crescent rolls, cheese and sausage from the refrigerator. I handed the eggs to Beth and Lisa pulled out a large pan.

"Donovan's not coming back for breakfast?"

"Oh, he'll be here, eventually. But there was a wee bit of an accident. Tyler took him to the ER to have x-rays."

"How wee bit of an accident are we talking?" Lisa asked with a fist propped on top of one hip and narrowed eyes.

"Possibly a concussion and a fractured arm. He's actually lucky. That thing drilled into him and nearly crashed through the floor."

"What thing?"

"Well, see, umm..." I hesitated.

Tech and Grady walked through the garage door. Abigail squealed in Grady's arms.

"Quit stalling." Lisa glared.

"Okay, but you have to promise not to get mad at Carl. He didn't mean for Donovan to get hurt."

Grady chuckled. "You sure about that?"

I smirked. "Well, he didn't mean for him to get seriously hurt."

"Carl built a fighting machine," Beth said, interrupting us. "Donovan wanted to try it, but he broke the machine. Carl got mad and hit the other lever which activated the big fighter to fly at Donovan."

Lisa looked at Beth, then at me, then at Grady. "My idiot husband *willingly* participated in one of Carl's inventions and allowed Carl to run the remote knowing Carl easily gets mad at him?"

"To be fair," I said, holding up a hand to hold her at bay, "Carl usually only gets mad at Donovan when Donovan is yelling at him. This situation was a complete fluke."

Grady barked a laugh. "A fluke that required a manual override and a large lever to be flipped."

"And Carl will be punished," I countered. "But by me, not Donovan. And we all knew the risks of getting into that thing. I mean the swinging lead pipe alone could've killed us."

"*Swinging. Lead. Pipe?*" Lisa glared.

"*Please,*" I said, rolling my eyes. "Can you really see your husband turning down something like that?"

"I recorded it on my phone if you want to see it after you've calmed down," Tech said, taking Abigail from Grady and walking into the dining room with her.

I finished rolling out the crescent rolls and nodded toward the oven. Lisa grunted her angst but turned the oven on before storming outside. Grady grabbed the shredded cheese and coated the inside of the rolls as I followed after with the sausage and rolled them up. Beth already had the eggs cooking, so she moved the rolls to cookie sheets.

"It's safe to come down now," I called out.

Three sets of legs came scurrying down the stairs.

"Did Donovan really catapult across the room?" Sara asked as she climbed on top of a bar stool.

"Is he going to be okay?" Carl asked with tears in his eyes.

"How long before breakfast?" Nicholas asked. "I'm starving."

"Yes, Donovan will be okay," I said to Carl. "But we have to come up with a suitable punishment. You can't just get mad at someone and then throw the launch lever like that."

"And I put Katie's battery back in her car," Tech said, scowling at Carl. "You're lucky she doesn't know you stole it."

"Doesn't matter," Beth said. "Stealing is stealing. Carl, go to your room and pick out things you own to give away. For everything you stole, you have to give something of value in return, whether you were caught or not."

"I only have to give them something I own? I don't have to give back what I stole?" Carl asked.

"Yes—*you do*," Beth said, pointing the spatula at him. "If you still have whatever you stole, that has to be returned too. Now get to it."

Carl stomped out the door to Alex's house.

"Well, that covers the stealing. What about the fact that he could've killed Donovan?" I asked.

Grady shrugged. "Donovan's been meaning to clean the gutters and wash the siding on the house. Make Carl do it."

Beth nodded. "Add cleaning his garage, painting the new nursery at Headquarters, and washing his and Lisa's cars."

"Who's going to babysit him while he does all that?" Sara asked.

"We can all take turns and make sure he doesn't destroy their house or disassemble their cars," I said. "But Carl's the worst painter I've ever seen. Let's leave the nursery to the professionals."

Grady grinned before wrapping his arms around me. "Someone else will need to babysit today. We have court, remember?"

"Can we go?" Nicholas asked.

"No, Nick," Grady answered, reaching an arm out to wrap around Nicholas' shoulder. "Just adults today."

"No, fair." Sara pouted.

"My mother is going to say things about me that I don't want either of you to hear," I told them. "Heck, I don't want anyone to hear it, including myself."

"Did you do something bad?" Sara asked, squinting her eyes and watching me.

"No," Grady answered. "She did what she had to, and when you're both adults, maybe she'll tell you. But it's up to her. Got it?"

Nicholas sighed, but Sara kept watching me. I could see her brain spinning with possible scenarios.

"Sara," Beth said without turning around, "can you help Nicholas set the table please?"

Sara was distracted by her new assignment and gathered the silverware from the drawer while Nicholas ran around the bar to get the plates.

"You okay?" Grady whispered in my ear, snuggling me with his arms.

"Not really," I answered just as quietly. "I feel like crawling into a dark cave and hiding the rest of the day."

Grady leaned in and kissed my cheek. "You're no coward, babe. And I'll be with you the entire time."

I nodded, turning my head to watch the kids race around the table and back to the kitchen for the glasses.

The garage door opened and Nana entered, setting her oversized purse on the end of the counter. "Boy, Lisa is an angry woman," she said. "She's ironing Donovan's dress shirts and cussing a blue streak. She gave a few shirts scorch marks, and I think she did it on purpose."

Grady snorted into my shoulder.

"Why is everyone up so early?" Anne asked as she and Whiskey came down the stairs. "It's only six."

"I haven't been to sleep yet," I answered. "I don't know why everyone else is up."

"Early bird catches the worm," Nana said.

"Carl woke me up," Nicholas said.

"Funny. Carl arguing with Tyler woke me up too," Tech said.

"I woke up when I heard the SUV leave," Grady said.

We turned to Beth who shrugged. "I don't sleep much. And there's not much to do in my little apartment."

The oven timer dinged, indicating the rolls were done. Beth was ready with an oven mitt to pull them out and already had platters ready. She also poured the scrambled eggs into casserole dishes and handed off all the dishes to those of us standing around. We loaded the table and everyone helped themselves.

"You-whooo!" Dallas called out as she entered the house. "Oh, good, you're up."

"Sure am. The question is, why are you up this early?"

"I'm here to style your hair, of course," she answered, looking at me like I was short on brain cells.

"And why do I need my hair styled?"

"It's the day of the showdown with your mother. Alex found an outfit that will be perfect, and Bridget bought shoes to go with it. I know you prefer your boots, but she assured me you'd wear the Louboutins if we bought them. They are simply fabulous."

"I really don't care. I'm not sure why you guys do."

"Because it will piss your mother off. The Armani suit alone will send her into a jealous rage," Dallas said.

I thought about it a moment before agreeing with her. "That works. But you owe ten pushups." I pointed to the sign the kids had made and posted above the credenza which in large letters demanded ten pushups per swear word.

Dallas looked down at her halter top, tight skirt, and high heels. "Damn."

~*~*~

After breakfast, I was shooed off to shower and to prepare for my hairstyling. Nana said she'd make sure the kids got dressed and ready for school. Anne and the others cleared the table and wrapped leftovers on plates for those who slept in and missed the first round.

Wrapped in a towel twenty minutes later, I walked in while Grady was putting on his suit jacket.

"Why are you getting ready so early?"

"I was afraid that once Dallas took over, I wouldn't have a chance to use the bedroom until it was time to leave," he said. "You look nice." He tugged on the towel, but I held it in place.

"Later." I smiled up at him. "When this is all over."

"Deal," he said, leaning down to kiss me. "And I'm going to want to see you naked except for the shoes that Bridget bought you."

"Your addiction to high heels is a little disturbing."

"I like what I like. And as long as it's you I want to see in the shoes, you have no reason to complain." He smirked and walked out.

Knowing Dallas would take forever to put me together, I put on a pair of comfortable sweats and a loose-fitting scoop neck T-shirt. I was putting on socks when Dallas waltzed in without knocking and ordered me to sit in my desk chair.

"Is all this really necessary?" I sighed, sitting in the chair.

"You'll thank me later."

"Don't count on it."

Chapter Thirty-Five

This was it. I stared at the courthouse building looming before me. Armed with a leather briefcase, clad in Armani, and flashing a pair of fabulous Louboutins on my feet, I was conflicted whether I felt empowered or scared shitless. I had to admit, though, that when I looked in the mirror before leaving, I was a little impressed. I looked like an upscale New York attorney. One of those sharks who wins all their cases.

"Kelsey," Cameron greeted me as he descended the courthouse steps. "This is Ted Challice. He's officially your attorney since I'm not able to represent you directly. I've prepped him on the case, and what to expect."

I shook Ted Challice's hand, but I was less than impressed when his eyes scanned my body.

"Not a great start," I said to him, and his eyes sprung back to meet mine. "Do as you were advised and hopefully this will be over quickly. If you steer off course, you'll be fired."

He nodded, having the grace to appear embarrassed, before turning back toward the stairs.

I glanced at Cameron who was smirking. "Can you really blame the guy?" Cameron asked. "You look amazing. Like million-dollars amazing. I wish all my clients dressed up for court. I'm lucky if some of them wear a T-shirt without stains and holes."

"She's a bit bitchy this morning," Grady told Cameron. "She'll be fine when this is over."

"I'm not *bitchy*!"

Grady smirked, grabbed my hand, and placed it in the crook of his arm as he led me up the stairs. Katie and Anne giggled behind us. Behind them was, well, everyone. Only Tyler, Donovan, and Whiskey had stayed behind with Carl, Nana, and the kids. Donovan was on pain killers for his fractured arm. The others would keep Carl and Nana out of the trouble while the kids were in their schoolroom with Beth. Dallas also stayed at the house, having convinced Nana that the showdown would be easier on me if she wasn't there to witness it.

Cameron held the door open, and I found Maggie, Kierson, and Genie waiting in the lobby as we entered.

"Shouldn't you guys be at work?" I asked.

"We called in sick." Genie grinned.

I looked over at Kierson and raised an eyebrow. "All of you?"

"I didn't pretend I was sick, if that's what you're asking," Kierson said. "I did call in that I needed to take a personal day." He held an arm out for Charlie, who slipped her hand through the bend at his elbow. She was trying to appear confident but her fingers clenched his sleeve.

I nodded a chin-up to her as I continued down the hall and around the corner. And then, I saw them. Hattie and Pops, hand in hand, were waiting for me outside the courtroom doors. My eyes started to water, and I waved both hands in front of my face, trying to dry them before I made a mess of my makeup.

"That's right, sunshine. This isn't the time for tears," Hattie said, wrapping her arms around me. "Did you really think we wouldn't be here? Hmm?"

"Hattie, there's going to be things said..."

"We were warned," Hattie said. "And we don't care. In fact, I don't give a gerbil's butt what that woman says. As far as I'm concerned, I'm your mother now. Charlie's too, if she'll have me. You're all my girls, and I'm damn proud of you."

"Ditto for me," Pops grumbled, stepping around Hattie to steal a hug. "Now shoulders back, chin up, and let them see that they messed with the wrong filly."

"End this, babe," Grady whispered from beside me.

"And not for Nicholas—or for me," Charlie said, stepping beside me. "This time, do it for you. Stand up for yourself. No mercy."

Tears still threatened to fall, and my chin quivered. I closed my eyes and took several slow breaths in and out to reclaim my composure. My family circled me, hiding me from my enemies.

When I was ready I nodded, and they parted. I led them into the courtroom with Grady and Charlie flanking my sides. Everyone else entered with heavy, determined footfalls behind me as they filled the left side of the room, leaving half of our group standing along the outside walls.

My mother's eyes pierced me as I stepped behind the defendant's table and emptied the files I would need from my briefcase. Cameron stood to my right between Mr. Challice and me, and Grady stood to my left, always by my side. Hattie, Pops, Lisa, Anne, Alex, and Charlie stood in the row behind me. I looked over at Grady and smiled. With everyone here to support me, I felt strong.

"That's my girl," he said, seeing the fire in my eyes.

"Don't even think about it," Pops growled from behind me.

I turned to see my mother had been about to approach me when Pops stepped in her path.

"I've never hit a woman, but I wouldn't hesitate," he said to my mother.

"You don't have to worry about hitting a woman," Hattie said to Pops as she stepped in front of him. "If she dares to take another step toward my girl, I'll flatten her like a pancake." Hattie shook a fist at my mother.

I laughed when my mother retreated to her own table. "Bravo, Hattie."

"Nobody messes with my sunshine," she muttered, moving back to her bench.

Pops winked at me before he stepped back beside Hattie and wrapped an arm around her shoulders.

I turned to Grady who was looking down at the table and silently laughing. "If you ever dump me, I'm keeping your family."

"They do seem to keep you entertained."

He barked a laugh as the door opened to the judge's chambers.

"All rise," the bailiff called out.

We were all still standing, but remained so until the judge was seated. "You may sit," he mumbled toward the microphone. Everyone behind us who had a seat available, sat. The judge finally looked up and his eyes widened at the silent crowd.

"Maybe we should make this a closed courtroom," the judge said, looking toward my mother who shook her head slightly. "But it's the public's right to witness as long as there are no disruptions," he quickly added.

I turned, smiling at everyone behind me. All of my friends and family wore broad smiles. There were definitely going to be a few disruptions.

"We are here today for the custody case of Nicholas Harrison. Audrey Harrison is seeking visitation rights of said minor via suit to Kelsey Harrison. Is that correct?"

"That is correct, Your Honor. I'm Stephen Haulk for the record, representing the plaintiff, Mrs. Audrey Harrison."

"And who do we have at the defendant's table?" the judge asked.

"Ted Challice, representing Ms. Kelsey Harrison. Beside me is Cameron Brackins, her attorney from Miami. And on her other side is Grady Tanner, her fiancée."

"Very well. Audrey, I heard about Thomas' passing. In light of his death, do you wish to reschedule today's hearing?"

"He would want me to continue, Your Honor. It was his wish that we'd have the opportunity to bond with our grandson."

"What a load of—" I was cut off by Grady placing a hand over my mouth.

"Excuse me?" the judge asked, glaring at me.

"She was saying that her mother must be carrying a load of grief," Cameron said to the judge which caused most of the room to giggle or chuckle.

"Right," the judge said sarcastically, turning back to my mother. "Condolences on your loss, Audrey."

"Thank you, Your Honor," she said before dabbing a tissue at her dry eyes.

Katie snorted loudly behind me, which caused Grady to bark another laugh before turning his head into my shoulder to hide his face.

"Is there a problem?" the judge asked.

"If I may, Your Honor," Mr. Challice said, briefly glaring my way before turning back to the judge. "We have a motion to have the venue of this case changed. My client does not live in this county, so we feel it should be heard in the county where her child resides."

He passed the papers to the bailiff who carried them to the judge.

"Denied," the judge said without reading anything in the folder.

"Very well, Your Honor. Then we'd like to submit a motion for you to recuse yourself from this hearing," Mr. Challice said, handing the bailiff another stack of papers.

The bailiff looked shocked, but took the papers to the judge and handed them over.

"On what grounds?" the judge asked.

"I'd rather not say, Your Honor."

"And I'd rather not be insulted in my own courtroom. State the reasons you feel I should recuse myself."

"Because you're crooked and in my mother's pocket," I said loud and clear. "She's been blackmailing you for over two decades. She has pictures of your affair with the court clerk and has kept records of every case she's had you decide in her favor. You're looking at much bigger issues than recusing yourself, Your Honor. You're looking down the barrel of an expensive divorce from your wife of thirty years, and time in prison on corruption charges."

"How dare you!" the judge said, standing and glaring at me as his face turned beet red.

"How dare I? I'm not the one breaking my marriage vows or the sworn oath taken when you were appointed into office."

"What proof do you have to support these slanderous, outrageous accusations?"

I took the file that Grady placed in my hand and tossed it in front of me to the courtroom floor. Pictures of his sordid affair drifted out of the folder for everyone to see. Hundreds of pages of court documents scattered about.

"Bailiff! Pick up those documents. And young lady, I advise you to sit down and let your lawyer do the talking or I'll have you arrested."

"By the crooked sheriff?" I snorted as I pointed to the sheriff. "The same man who raped me when I was just a child?"

"Lies! She's a liar, Your Honor. Always has been!" the sheriff yelled.

"I can vouch for the sheriff in this matter, Your Honor," my mother said as she stood. "My daughter has made up lies about good people her whole life. I tried to steer her in the right direction, but she rebelled and ran away. For years she prostituted herself in our very own town. The sheriff tried to help me on several occasions to get her to stop selling her body. He's probably the only man in this town she didn't sleep with."

"And yet I have a video of him raping me when I was only fourteen years old," I said, tossing the flash drive to one of the state troopers sitting in the gallery.

The trooper looked down at the drive in his hand and grimaced. "You were fourteen?"

"Arrest him." I nodded. "I'll testify against him."

"Now wait a—" the sheriff started to say.

Two nearby state troopers grabbed him, cuffing him and dragging him out of the courtroom.

"You were saying, *Mother*?"

She looked a bit shocked, staring at the doors.

"Oh, yes, I remember. You were telling everyone that I was a child prostitute. I didn't honestly listen to the rest of your babbling, because it was all BS. But the prostitute part was accurate. I already told everyone though, so I'm not sure what you hoped to gain by telling the court."

"It's a crime!" She glared.

"So is blackmail." I laughed. "And I have evidence of you blackmailing thirty-two people, most of whom you convinced to break the law for you. Should we talk about that? Or should we start with my father? And how you blackmailed him into marrying you? Though, honestly, what was he thinking? I'd rather go to prison for vehicular manslaughter than marry into your craziness. And he ended up serving what? A thirty-six-year sentence? With you as the warden and prison guard? That was, at least, until you murdered him."

"That's outrageous!" my mother screeched. "I loved your father!"

"You have no concept of love," I said, shaking my head. "You manipulate, control, and destroy anyone who comes in contact with you. You kept files on your own children," I said, lifting the files into the air before passing them to Katie.

She carried them over to my brothers who were sitting in the middle row, four rows back from my mother.

"That's a lie!" she said, reaching out into the air as if she could reach the files.

"The notes are in *your* handwriting!"

"You're the reason I got kicked out of college?" one of my brothers asked.

"You blackmailed my high school girlfriend about the abortion?" another brother yelled as he stood.

"You've always been cold," a third brother said. "But this is too much. My wife was right. We need to cut you out of our lives—and our children's."

My other brothers nodded, glaring at our mother.

"Oh, hey. You think that's bad?" I asked my brothers. "She also had a doctor falsify a death certificate and fake a birth certificate. Charlie's our half-sister."

"The old man had an affair?" Jeff asked, running a hand over his chin.

My other brothers' eyes looked ready to pop.

"Yup. Then dear old Mom made sure the woman believed her baby died and gave the child to Uncle Mark and Aunt Cecil to raise."

"It's not true," Aunt Cecil said, turning to face Charlie. "You're my daughter."

"There's no way in hell I'm your daughter," Charlie said, snorting. "I met my mother. And the DNA results came in this morning confirming it. It was pretty easy to figure out after I read the file Audrey kept on you and Mark. Don't think for a minute she didn't keep records on the two of you. She documented all your crimes." Charlie handed three files to a nearby state police officer. "In addition to Mark beating me from the age of two until I was twelve years old, they both willingly kidnapped me," she said to the officer. "And I'll testify against them in court. So will my biological mother."

"You bitch!" Cecil screamed at Audrey. "After everything I've done for you! I even helped you cover up murdering your husband!"

"*And there we have it!*" Grady yelled.

My friends and family cheered as Cecil yelled her involvement over the crowd, incriminating my mother. Officers cuffed her and Mark, dragging them from the room.

"Can we arrest your mother now?" one of the state troopers asked with a grin.

"In a minute." I walked around the table and approached my mother. She trembled with rage. She was well past angry and looked murderous. "I'm not mad at you for killing my father. As horrible as it sounds, I had no feelings for the man who sat back and watched me drown in chaos. I'm not mad at your involvement in having Charlie kidnapped. That's her war to fight. I'm not mad at you for your silly ploy to get visitation rights over my son. You never had a chance." I took a step closer and tilted my head as I studied her face. "But I am angry. I'm angry for all the years you screamed or hit me to be quiet. I'm angry for all the years that you treated me like I was nothing. I'm angry that you found it amusing that I was raped. I'm angry that you had me followed and had pictures taken of me during the years that I was a teenage prostitute. And I'm angry that the same blood that runs through your veins runs through mine. Because you, Mother, are the sickest, coldest bitch I've ever met. And I've been kidnapped and tortured by the best of them."

I stepped away, waving my arm toward my brothers.

"You brought us—your children—into this world, not with the intent to love and raise, but to control and dominate. And when I refused to be owned by you, you made it your mission to go after my family. My *real* family." I pointed to the other side of the room. "The ones in this courtroom who I can tell my deepest darkest secrets to. The ones who walk beside me. Hold me when I cry. Push me toward the door when it's time to fight. And protect my son when I'm not around. They give me their strength, so I can stand up to you today and say..." I turned back to glance around the room, my eyes landing on Grady. He had tears in his eyes, but he nodded for me to finish. I took a deep breath and turned back to my mother. "To say to you—I hope you suffer every day, for the rest of your life, in prison."

A round of cheers erupted again as I walked back to my table, nodding to the officers as I passed. I knew by instinct when my mother charged after me, but I didn't turn to see the officers tackle her to the ground and cuff her. Instead, I walked over to Grady and allowed him to fold his strong arms around me.

I heard Kierson call out to have the judge arrested, and Maggie telling another officer to have the local doctor and two deputies arrested. They had the files to turn over as evidence. Maggie and Kierson would help the state police pull the strings on the weaker cases to get confessions. My opinion was that as fast as the house of cards was falling, the wolves would turn on each other. I'd follow up personally with anyone who was lucky enough to walk free.

I let the noises around me float away as I looked up at Grady. "Take me home, Grady Tanner."

"With pleasure, Kelsey Harrison," he said, leaning down and kissing me like every woman dreamed.

Epilogue

Three days later...

I walked around Anne to get the dinner plates out of the cupboard. "Where is everyone?"

"No clue," she answered, glancing up at the clock. "Whiskey was babysitting Carl today while he cleaned Donovan's garage. Donovan didn't trust Carl not to tear apart his generator again."

"They finished the garage hours ago. I talked to them after my run."

"They're in the basement at Headquarters," Sara said, running down the stairs.

"Why?"

"I don't know why. The door was locked so I couldn't follow them."

"Since when is the basement locked? There's nothing but office supplies down there."

"I don't *know*!" Sara sighed. "*Geesh*."

Nicholas had been sitting at the table quietly listening.

"Do you know something?"

Nicholas raised his shoulder in a half shrug. "Grady said it was a project for men only. They locked the door yesterday and have been hauling packages down there."

I texted Grady that dinner was ready. He texted back that he'd be late and to eat without him. I texted again, asking if they still had eyes on Carl. He answered: *Yes*.

"They want us to eat without them."

Sara giggled. "Whiskey's never late for dinner. And he knows we're having fettuccine chicken alfredo tonight."

The garage door opened and Bridget walked in carrying Abigail. Lisa followed her inside, loaded down with a diaper bag and a case of beer.

"Why did you bring beer?" I laughed, taking it from her and setting it on the counter.

"Donovan asked me to buy it. Said he'd have one of the guys come get it. They're working late on some project."

Bridget handed Abigail to Anne but raised an eyebrow at me. "After dinner, do you want to see the new war room?"

"Yes!" Tech answered, coming in from the back deck. "I want my office back. I can't believe you hid the keys."

"Only until the big reveal," Bridget said.

I looked back at Anne and winked. "Sure. We can go after dinner as long as we can make a detour to the basement to see what the guys are hiding."

"The lock on the door has a magnetic card reader," Sara said.

We all turned to Tech. "Fine. I can get you past the card reader. It's worth it if I get my war room back."

"*Our* war room," I said.

Tech smirked. "That's what I said."

"You handle the card reader, and I'll handle the lock," Bridget said. "I've already checked it out. It's top of the line, but so am I."

"I'm guessing Bones is part of the secret men-only gathering down there?"

"Oh, yeah. He said he'd be working late and not to wait up. So much for taking the time to shave my legs this morning."

Alex jogged up the basement stairs and scooped Abigail from Anne's arms. Katie walked inside through the garage door and slammed it shut.

"What's gotten into you?"

"I tripped in my apartment over Carl's pile of shit. What the hell am I supposed to do with a bean bag, a Led Zeppelin poster, and a bag of soldering tools?"

"He returned a pile of stretched out clothes to me," I said, smiling.

Lisa snorted. "I don't know what you two have to complain about. My living room is currently piled with Carl's bed, his Spiderman pillow, an assortment of pajamas, three boxes of miscellaneous electronics, and a full-size tire. If I didn't agree with Beth and Kelsey that he needed to be taught a lesson, I would've taken it all back to Alex's."

"What other option did he have?" Alex asked.

"What do you mean?"

"Carl's got plenty of money to buy stuff, but he's never had access. He either has to beg for things or steal them. If he asks for the money, he's grilled with a million questions and usually told no."

"If you give Carl access to his money, he's likely to buy plutonium," Tech said.

"Give him a prepaid Visa," Katie suggested. "Throw a couple hundred on there a month and see how it goes."

"I'd still suggest some kind of monitoring," I warned.

"Set the account up to email you the receipts," Katie said. "We'd have plenty of advance notice before liquid nitrogen or rocket launchers were dropped off by FedEx. Maybe sometimes packages accidentally get lost in shipment."

"I don't have access to his money yet, but I'm willing to throw a couple hundred of my own funds on a card to test it out," Alex agreed. "And, luv, can we reconsider some of his belongings being returned?"

"I didn't realize he gave up his bed and Spiderman pillow." I laughed. "Let's keep the odd crap, but give him back the basics. He can earn the rest back if he behaves."

"Lisa, what kind of tire do you have in your living room?" Katie asked.

"I don't know. It's big, round, and black. Donovan said it looked new."

Katie looked at Tech who was grinning. "I'll check after dinner."

I raised an eyebrow at Katie.

"It's likely the damn spare for my SUV," she answered as she pulled the milk and filled three glasses.

I followed her over to the table, setting plates down for the kids as she set their glasses of milk beside them and the third glass in front of Tech.

"Aunt Katie..." Sara said.

"What?"

"You owe thirty pushups," Nicholas said, laughing at her.

"Damn it," Katie swore again. "Cr—" She fisted her hands, pinched her lips together, and jumped up and down, mentally swearing.

"Forty." Sara giggled.

"You have issues," I said to Katie as she got on the floor to start her pushups.

"Where's Nana?" Anne asked, changing the subject.

"She flew home this morning. Charlie left with her."

"Is Charlie coming back?" Katie asked between pushup twenty-one and twenty-two.

"No. She wants to travel for a while. She promised Pops and Hattie she'd stop in Texas at some point this winter."

"Will Aunt Charlie be back for Christmas?" Nicholas asked.

"That's about the only date on the calendar that she knows where she'll be. Blizzards and hurricanes couldn't keep your aunt away from spending Christmas with her two favorite brats."

The kids giggled as they scooped large portions of fettuccine into their mouths.

"Smaller bites, you two," Anne scolded, setting filled plates down for us. "You want anything to drink?" she asked me as she held a hand out to help Katie up.

"Nope. I plan on shoveling down my dinner so I can go snoop on the boys."

"Can I go?" Anne asked.

"Sure. But we need someone to watch the kids."

"I'll keep an eye on them," Alex said.

"Abigail too?" Lisa asked.

"Absolutely," Alex answered as he made funny faces at Abigail. "Uncle Alex found this adorable outfit for you today. We'll have a mini fashion show while the crazies go break into a basement, instead of asking their better halves what they're up to like normal people."

"They'd lie," Bridget said. "Besides, that lock is a 500-Series F18 Prosecure lock. They're a treat to pick."

"It also gives me a chance to show you how to bypass the card readers," Tech told Bridget. "If you're going to be working cases for Kelsey, you'll need to be ready for anything."

I frowned. "I promised Bones I'd keep Bridget out of trouble."

"No, you didn't," Katie said. "You promised him that Trigger would shoot anyone who was a threat to her. You know better than to promise Bridget won't find trouble."

"Are you guys ready?" Bridget asked, clearing her already empty plate. "We've got things to do."

We all scarfed down our food.

~*~*~

"Don't turn on the lights," Tech warned when we entered the gym. "They rigged a sensor to alert them when someone turns them on."

"Those sneaky bastards," I said, leading the way with my flashlight across the gym.

When I reached the basement door, I stepped back and held the light for Bridget and Tech. In less than three minutes they had the door open and nodded to me to lead them down the stairs. Anne and Lisa giggled. I glared over my shoulder at them, and they fell silent.

I turned my flashlight off and stepped down the stairs, one at a time. Everyone else followed just as quietly. In the distance, I could hear Grady and Bones laughing. The basement was divided into three sections. The first section at the bottom of the stairs was cluttered with racks of old files and office supplies. At the other end of the room was a hallway that led to the middle section where I expected to find the men. The last section was a mechanical room in the back.

I crossed the room and signaled for everyone to remain quiet as we entered the hallway to the center section. The door at the end was propped open. I neared the door and crouched down, so the others could see over me. Bridget and Katie crouched down beside me. Lisa, Anne, and Tech leaned over us to look around the corner.

In the center of the room was Carl's fighting contraption. Carl was teaching Bones how to run the controls. In the center of the ring, Donovan, with one arm in a sling, was fighting the mannequins. Meathead appeared to be missing, replaced by a much more fluffy-looking mannequin. Franky's lead pipe had been replaced by a plastic sword. Willy still had the kick of a donkey, though, and caught Donovan from behind, sending him sailing into Franky before he was hit by the plastic sword.

"Uncle!" Donovan yelled, laughing as the machine shut down.

"You got your ass kicked, brother," Grady teased.

"I've only got one arm!" Donovan argued as he crawled out of the circle.

"You still scored higher than me," Whiskey said, offering Donovan a hand to get up from the floor.

"Who's in the lead?" Bones asked.

"Hang on," Grady said as he scribbled on a notepad. "Bones is still two points ahead. I've got second place, and Donovan is ten points behind in third place."

"We should buy a scoreboard. Mount it to the wall," Donovan said.

"One like they use in the Olympics," Whiskey agreed. "Where you can have several competitors listed."

"I can find one online," Carl said.

"You find one and let us know how much it is before you buy it. If it's cheap enough, we'll all pitch in," Grady said. "Who's next?"

"I am!" Lisa said, pushing me into Bridget so she could walk into the room.

"*Shit.*" I giggled. "Why did we bring her?"

"If she actually gets in that ring, it'll be worth getting caught," Anne said, running out to join Lisa.

I looked at Bridget who shrugged, stood, and walked into the room. Tech, Katie, and I followed.

"Lisa..." Donovan sighed. "You can't get in the ring. You could get hurt."

"But you can go in with a fractured arm and a concussion?" Lisa glared. "If it's safe enough for you, it's safe enough for me."

"Watch out for Willy. He has a mean kick," I warned her.

She grinned, stripped off her shoes, and entered the ring.

"*Wait.* Bones, don't you *dare* start that thing!" Donovan ordered, following her inside the circle and dragging her out by the elbow.

"What the hell do you think you're doing?" Lisa asked as she glared at his hold on her arm. "Let me go."

"I said it's not safe," Donovan growled.

"*Let. Her. Go*," Anne ordered.

Donovan sighed and released his hold on Lisa, but turned to block her path into the ring. Donovan would never hurt Lisa, but we all knew Anne saw red whenever anyone was held against their will.

"Get out of my way, Donovan," Lisa hissed.

"What can I do to convince you not to do this?"

"Promise you'll never go in that... *thing*... again."

Donovan looked down at the floor and released a long sigh. "I can't promise that."

She stepped around him and entered the ring, nodding to Bones to start it. Bones looked at me and I shrugged. Bones looked at Grady.

"Slowest speed and dial Willy's kick back to about half power," Grady instructed.

Carl was bouncing up and down with a wide grin on his face.

"Get ready," Bones called out to Lisa as Donovan growled. "Three, two, one... go."

The contraption started spinning, and Lisa was hit and kicked a few times before she started to get the hang of it. Donovan kept his eyes glued to her as he paced back and forth. Whiskey stood nearby to jump in if needed. Willy kicked out, but Lisa leaned out of the way in time. Then she turned and blocked Franky's arm as it came down with the sword. Bones hit the switch for Meathead, and I sucked air between my teeth as the mannequin tilted forward and launched.

The newer fluffy version still sent Lisa sailing, but she landed in a safety net on the back side of the ring and easily beat the pillow-filled mannequin away from her as she crawled out of the net, laughing.

"That was fun," she said, pointing to the machine while she walked over to us. She looked up at Grady. "How many points did I get?"

"Six," Grady answered.

"What's the high score?"

"In a single bout—forty-two."

"I didn't do so good, huh?"

"For not having studied the predefined patterns, you did exceptionally well," Carl said, patting her on the shoulder a bit harder than necessary.

"Thank you, Carl."

"You're welcome," Carl said before he walked over to me. "Am I in trouble?"

"No. Why?"

"Because I was late for dinner. I told them we had to go home for dinner, but they wouldn't listen."

"As long as we know you're safe, it's okay. And the guys let us know you were with them."

"But I wanted to go home and eat."

"I'll drive you," Lisa offered. "I want to get back to check on Abigail." She turned and look back over her shoulder. "Donovan, best you come home too. We need to talk."

Donovan shoulders sagged as he followed Lisa and Carl out of the room.

"So why the secret?" I asked, walking around the machine to see the updates.

"Yeah?" Bridget asked. "What's the big deal?"

"That's Donovan's fault," Whiskey said. "He said that if any of you found out, you'd make him tell Lisa. And he knew with his fractured arm she would blow a fuse."

"Can't say as I blame her," Anne said. "He could easily break that arm if he doesn't take it easy and let it heal first."

"We know," Grady said. "But he was trying to follow everyone's advice and find a project to work on with Carl in hopes that Carl would stop messing with him. They started redesigning the Circle of Hell, and Donovan kept wanting to test out the changes."

"Circle of Hell?" Katie asked.

"Donovan and Carl named it together," Whiskey said. "When it's kicking your ass, the name fits."

"I like the safety net," I said. "And is the track bolted to the floor?"

"Yup," Grady answered. "We didn't want to bolt it to the wood planks upstairs. Besides, down here we can control who uses it."

Bones grinned. "And Mr. Pillow Pants is less dangerous than Meathead. I still can't believe Carl filled Meathead with sacks of sand."

"Let's not forget the launch speed set to forty miles an hour," Grady said, laughing. "It took a lot of convincing to get Carl to lower it to five miles an hour, and even that will send you into the net instantly."

"What you guys did for Carl was sweet," Bridget said. "You helped him rebuild his toy and made him feel like one of the guys."

"Now he wants to have a tournament," Whiskey said.

"Who's invited?" Katie asked, eyeing the Circle of Hell.

"Anyone who wants to participate," Grady said. "We picked a Saturday later in the month. Wildcard is even making the trip. We sent him a video, and he texted back that he booked a flight."

"Donovan told me Ryan was heading back too," Bones said. "A lot of the guys are, actually."

"I'm not expected to feed and house everybody, am I?" I asked.

"No," Grady said, shaking his head. "I put a kibosh on that. We're moving the bunk beds over to the dorms and setting up extra beds there. We'll also buy some grills and cook in the yard between the apartments and headquarters."

"I don't have to worry about anything? I can just show up, fight, and eat?"

"You only have to worry about beating my score, babe," Grady said, leaning down to kiss me.

"Oh, I'll beat your score old-man," I said, turning toward the exit. "Come on, Bridget. It's time to see what you did to the war room."

"Yeah!" she squealed running past me.

~*~*~

Thirty minutes later, Tech and I stood speechless at the doorway as Bridget bounced around the room showing us all the smaller features like the adjustable bins for our case files, the pull-down wipe boards, and the pull-down maps.

My mind was completely blown. Bridget had outdone herself. The center of the room had a long and wide planked table with multiple sections that could be raised for standing workstations. The conference phone was suspended above the table by a heavy chain. The walls had been covered with a fake brick mural, inclusive of 3D images of robbers and monsters jumping into the room. Mounted on the walls were archaic weapons: swords, shields, and spears, along with modern weapons of guns, throwing knives, and brass knuckles—and the floor was covered with a 3D mural, appearing to be a thick slab of concrete with the center section broken out, dropping into the depths of hell below our feet.

I felt like was standing in the middle of a crime fighting video game. "This is badass."

Tech glanced at me, showing off a broad smile. "The guys are going to be so jealous."

THE END… OR A NEW BEGINNING?

WE SHALL SEE.

Diamond's Edge

A life of violence, sex, and evading the law...

Raised on the wrong side of the tracks, I know how to break up a bar fight, mule drugs under the cops' noses, and how to get what I want out of most men. But I'm trying to become a better person—a better role model for my teenage brother and to maintain a healthy distance from a prison cell.

Good intentions don't always work out, though.

Balancing the interest of two devilishly handsome men who want to screw me, staying out of the grips of a crime boss who wants to hurt me, evading an FBI agent who wants to arrest me, and hunting whoever is hiding in the shadows, stalking me... I find I must choose between the life I wanted and the life I was born to live.

The hell with normal. *I intend to survive.*

Diamond's Edge is a standalone novel thick with violence, sex, adult-language, and questionable moral decision making. You're welcome. Available at Amazon.com

Special Thanks

Special thanks to the below individuals for helping me get this book across the finish line and into the hands of readers.

Kathie Z. for your beta reading and mental-coaching services. You help me keep it all in balance.

Judy G. for your detailed notes and proofreading. You've saved me from many word blunders. Much appreciated.

Sheryl Lee with BooksGoSocial Editing Services: Your proofreading service was spot on, and I learned a lot from your notes. Thank you!

Books By Kaylie

Kelsey's Burden Series
Layered Lies
Past Haunts
Friends and Foes
Blood and Tears
Love and Rage
Day and Night

Standalone Novels
Slightly Off-Balance
Diamond's Edge

ABOUT THE AUTHOR

I've seen many sets of eyes glaze over when others talk about their pets, so feel free to skip this section if you are one who has no tolerance, because I'm about to do just that.

Years ago, I randomly decided I wanted a dog. And a few weeks later, after a lot of research on Border Collies, a black and white, five-inch-tall, growling fuzzball attacked my tennis shoe. She was the one. Maggie Ann Houdini, born the 4th of July, 2003.

Over the years, Maggie challenged me on many levels. She embarrassed me at obedience training—dropping a steamy pile of poo on the mats. She learned to set the car alarm off if I left her to wait in the car. And during her younger years, she destroyed everything I owned: all my shoes, every plant, cases of toilet paper, my living room carpet, and even tore off the arm on my couch during one particularly loud thunderstorm. One night, I went to turn on the TV and realized she had chewed the power cord in half. The other half was still plugged into the wall!

Eventually, she learned not to destroy things, but unfortunately, destruction still came naturally to her. While I was hanging drywall in an upstairs bedroom, she snuck past me into the small section between the porch roof and the mudroom below. I noticed her at the same time her body tensed. She looked back at me, her eyes round, as the ceiling below her paws gave out. Maggie, the ceiling panels, and a hell of a lot of insulation dropped to the first floor below. After sufficient screaming on my part, I ran downstairs. She was fine, but oh, what a mess.

But Maggie was more than just destructive. She was super intelligent and loaded with energy. She knew and followed both verbal and hand commands. I told her once to go take a shower (while my then boyfriend was in it), and she ran and jumped in the shower with him. He wasn't happy, but it made me laugh. I was picking up sticks after a big storm and tossed one for her. After she brought it back, I called her out to find another. An hour later, I sat in the lawn chair with my cocktail as she happily brought me more sticks for the overflowing burn pit next to me.

Maggie was patient and passive with kids, even when I discovered my niece, who was a toddler at the time, lying on top of her and poking at her eyes. But she was also very protective of me, baring her teeth and hiking her fur when the creepy neighbor came through the woods while I was in the backyard. I'm not sure what she sensed about him, but I trusted her instincts, and when asked if she would bite, I said yes. He never bothered me again.

Maggie loved to sing and dance with me. Her favorite song during bath time was *Singing In The Rain* and when enjoying a campfire, *Old Man Tucker* always got her howling and prancing about. She loved to chase mice and track ground moles, but unfortunately, she'd release them after playing with them. She loved car rides, especially to Grandma's house, as her tail thumped against my arm when she saw we were only minutes away.

She had a romantic tryst with an English springer who liked to escape the invisible fence and have adventures in the swamps. He, of course, taught her to do the same which meant I was the one who had to clean the black muck from her long thick fur. And after the first accidental litter of pups, her mate being just as crazy as her, chewed a hole through the garage overhead door so he could knock her up again. (I always wondered if she taught him how to accomplish that level of destruction.)

Overall, she had a full life. She outlived her best friend Boots, and her boy-toy Fox. She played hard, ate well, and was always there for me. During the nearly fifteen years we were together, she had become the one constant in my daily routine. Some people talk of their pets like they're their children. And maybe at times, especially when she was younger, that's what our relationship was. But for most of our years together, she was the friend who rode shotgun, literally and figuratively. She was my protector, my comedic relief, and my favorite dance partner.

She was Maggie Ann Houdini, born the 4th of July, 2003, leaving us in April 2018. I think of her daily but know she's somewhere in the Ever-After, playing tug-of-war with her best friend Boots and running the swamps with Fox. And I hope that someday we'll meet again, and we'll dance to *Old Man Tucker* beside a roaring fire as she '*woo-hoos*' the lyrics.

Until then, my friend, know that you are missed.

Best wishes to all,
Kaylie Hunter

For updates on new releases, follow Amazon author page: Kaylie Hunter. You may also find author on Facebook at: Author Kaylie Hunter or on Twitter: @BooksByKaylie

Printed by Amazon Italia Logistica S.r.l.
Torrazza Piemonte (TO), Italy